ENCHANTED
AUTUMN

ENCHANTED AUTUMN

by

Ursula Klein

2022

ENCHANTED AUTUMN

ISBN 13: 978-1-63679-104-3

This Trade Paperback Original Is Published By
Bold Strokes Books, Inc.
P.O. Box 249
Valley Falls, NY 12185

First Edition: February 2022

CREDITS
Editors: Victoria Villaseñor and Cindy Cresap
Production Design: Stacia Seaman
Cover Design by Inkspiral Design

For my parents, who always encouraged me,
and for my wife, who continues to inspire me

CHAPTER ONE

C'mon, Hazel, I *really need it*."

"No. You know I can't hand this stuff out like candy."

"But this time I really need it. Come on, bestie, pleeeeease."

"As your bestie, I'm telling you, I shouldn't let you have any more."

"You sound serious." Roxy's pink lips flattened out into a straight line.

Hazel could tell she was getting frustrated. Until that moment, there had been a lightness to their exchange; suddenly, the mood had changed. Roxy liked to get her way, but Hazel needed to put her foot down. She was her oldest friend, after all, and she wanted nothing but the best for her. She felt guilty, but she was determined to put a stop to what could be an addiction of sorts.

"I'm sorry, Roxy, but this stuff can be dangerous. And I'm worried about you. This won't make you happy—not in the long run."

Roxy groaned. "How do you know? Don't you want me to be happy?"

"*Of course* I want you to be happy. That's not fair. You're my best friend." Hazel rubbed her arm. "And that's exactly why I don't think I should give you any more."

Roxy changed tactics. "Look," she said, leaning forward on the stool across from Hazel. She put her elbows on the countertop and cupped her chin in her hands, her big brown eyes sparkling with trademark Roxy charm. She smiled at Hazel, and Hazel couldn't help smiling back. "This is the last time. I promise. Alicia is the real thing.

She just doesn't want to admit it. All I need is a tiny bit of love potion to move things along, and it's in the bag."

"You're not actually going to put Alicia into a bag, are you?"

"Come on. I'm not that desperate." Roxy chucked a stray paperclip at Hazel, who batted it away, and they both laughed.

"Okay, okay, all right," Hazel said. It wasn't really ethical, but she had a hard time saying no to Roxy.

She went to the back room of the Witch Is In, unlocked a cabinet, and came back to the front counter with a small vial of light pink-colored liquid that shimmered and sparkled in her hand. She placed it in a velvet drawstring bag and handed it to Roxy, who tucked the whole thing into one of the ample pockets on her button-up flannel shirt. She patted the pocket protectively.

"I'll take good care of it," she said and gave her a devilish wink.

"Just remember, you *both* have to agree to use it. You can't just dump it into her drink without telling her. That's a consent issue." Hazel gave her a serious look and for once, Roxy dropped some of the bluster. A look of sadness marred her features momentarily before clearing up again.

"Of course." Roxy cleared her throat. "Thank you. I really appreciate it."

Hazel smiled. Roxy liked to pretend she was all swagger, but beneath that brash exterior was a sensitivity most people had no clue about. Roxy had been through a lot in her twenty-five years, and Hazel knew she was still dealing with issues from her parents' divorce—or rather, divorces.

Hazel hugged Roxy. "I know."

They stepped apart.

"What would I ever do without you?" said Roxy, her tone light and jovial again.

"Luckily, we don't have to find out."

"You know, that's a good point," said Roxy, putting on her buffalo plaid jacket. "Why haven't you ever fallen deeply in love with me? It would solve a lot of problems for both of us."

This was a conversation they'd already had many times. Despite her jolly tone and the playful punch she landed, ever so unromantically, on Hazel's arm, her question was more loaded than usual.

"It's not like you're crazy for me, either, my dear," said Hazel, sitting back down at the counter and absent-mindedly straightening up the area around the cash register. The shop was getting busier and busier since Halloween was just over a month away. Soon it would be nonstop crowds for the Salem Halloween festival.

"It's a shame. Two good-looking ladies like us, who have known each other forever, and we could be happily in love instead of 'just friends.'"

"There's nothing the matter with being 'just friends.' You know I love you like a sister. And I really do want you to be happy. I'm just not sure that Alicia is 'the one.'"

Roxy rolled her eyes. "We've been through this over and over again. What Alicia and I have is magical. Pun intended. When we're together—"

"In bed, I assume?"

"Yes, of course. But not *just* in bed. Even when we hang out—"

"Doing what?"

"What?"

"What are you doing when you're not hanging out in bed?" Hazel asked innocently.

Roxy hesitated. "Oh, you know…whatever. Having breakfast. Or dinner." She stumbled around for the right answer before Hazel burst out laughing. "What's so funny?"

"It sounds like Alicia is just another sleepover friend." Hazel wiggled her eyebrows. "Are you sure you want to waste your last ever love potion on her?"

"That's not fair. You don't know Alicia. She's…she's…" Again, Roxy was lost for words, and Hazel supplied her with some options.

"Good in bed? A great lay? A perfect pillow princess?"

Roxy laughed, but Hazel got the impression that it wasn't sincere laughter. Ever since her mother's second marriage had failed about five years earlier, Roxy had been on a quest to date as many women as possible. Hazel wasn't a shrink, but it didn't take a degree in psychology to figure out that Roxy wanted to succeed where her parents, evidently, hadn't. Hazel had tried to broach the topic with her several times, but each time Roxy shut her down; she wasn't ready to talk about it and Hazel respected that.

Hazel started the business of closing up the shop for the evening. Technically, the shop closed at six, but she usually didn't lock up until a little later in case anyone needed something at the last minute. A good portion of her customers were day trippers who wanted to shop at a store like the Witch Is In as part of the whole "Salem experience." For them, she had postcards, souvenirs, essential oils, numerology guides, short and easily digestible Salem history books, various stones and minerals, as well as a wide assortment of tchotchkes relating to the supernatural world. She had a contingent of local, regular customers who liked to browse her used books section or pop in for sage smudging kits.

Her shop was also patronized by local witches like herself; for them, she had a special section that most customers never knew about. Witches, wizards, and fey customers were the ones who might come in for spell scrolls or potion ingredients like butterfly wings or mandrake roots.

Today was a quiet day, though, and there were no last-minute shoppers. Hazel let her assistant, Rita, go home early. While she locked up, swept the floors, and did some dusting, she let Roxy tell her all about the wonders of Alicia—both in and out of the bedroom.

"I'm sorry you haven't had a chance to really get to know her," Roxy concluded after regaling Hazel with how they had met by chance at a club in Boston and then both realized they lived in Salem. According to Roxy, the honeymoon phase had been a wonderful whirlwind, though Hazel was getting the impression that it hadn't lasted very long. Hence the need for a love potion. "She's so busy these days trying to set up her online business. I keep offering to help, but she wants to do it all herself. I told her you could probably give her some great pointers on running a small business, but I think she felt intimidated."

More like threatened, Hazel thought to herself. She had a feeling that Alicia was, in actuality, using Roxy for sex and then ghosting her the rest of the time. Meeting Roxy's friends would mean having to admit they were in a relationship. Sadly, Roxy had had many "girlfriends" like Alicia—women who weren't looking for anything serious, who just wanted to have some fun.

And Roxy was fun. She was funny and outgoing and terribly adorable, with her mop of dark curls, cropped close to her head, her sparkling brown eyes, and her irrepressible dimples. She was tall, athletic, and full of butch swagger. She was too cute for her own good, apparently—she attracted all the wrong women.

Hazel wished Roxy could meet someone who deserved her, who

actually made her happy for more than a night at a time. Alicia was obviously a loser. Hazel regretted giving Roxy the love potion and wondered if she could take it back. Her potions were carefully crafted so that they only worked to heighten existing feelings between people—sort of like hitting the accelerator in a relationship. They didn't work if there were no real feelings to build on, and Hazel had a pretty good idea that Alicia's feelings for Roxy weren't very strong, in which case, the potion wouldn't do anything at all.

"Earth to Hazel. Come in, Hazel," Roxy was saying, waving her hand in front of Hazel's face. "Are you ever going to finish sweeping?"

"Sorry. I'm done. I just need to feed the cat."

Hazel's familiar, a large black cat with golden eyes named Beezle, was currently out chasing squirrels or whatever he got up to during the day, but she liked to leave him a little bowl of crunchy food at night.

Sometimes he showed up at the shop; other times he showed up at the house; either way, Hazel always left him a treat. As a familiar, Beezle was a magical animal whose rights to roam couldn't be curbed. He was always around, though, when Hazel needed him.

"So, I'm seeing Alicia later tonight, actually, and I can give her the potion right away," Roxy said as they left the shop and walked down the street to the coffee shop, the Magic Bean. It was a chilly evening in late September, and the wind blew down sharply, making Hazel shiver in her cardigan. It was time to pull out her autumn cape.

"I think you mean, you can *both* take it tonight. And shush! Don't talk about it so loudly." Only a few of her closest friends and some trusted, regular customers knew about her side business of brewing up distinctly non-FDA-approved love potions. She didn't need to get investigated because of Roxy's indiscretion.

"Sorry. Sheesh, don't be so paranoid."

"Remember that you have to be the first person she sees after taking it. And you need to take some, too."

"That's silly. I'm already crazy about her."

"It's how the potion works—and it ensures that there isn't any consent issue."

"What's that supposed to mean?"

"I've told you this before. It only enhances existing feelings—it can't force someone to fall in love with you."

The love potions that Hazel brewed were meant to help existing couples get through a rough patch. The idea was that even healthy relationships had problems sometimes and partners could grow distant. The potion would take the rough edges out of arguments and restore some peace of mind while reminding partners what they loved about each other. Ideally, *both* partners should take some for it to work correctly.

Currently, the person or people in question still needed to see the object of their affection in order for the potion to work. There was a slight chance that the potion wouldn't work otherwise. Hazel was working to improve the potion to eliminate that requirement, but the new batch needed some crucial ingredients that she wouldn't be able to collect until the next new moon.

"You know, if she doesn't have any feelings for you to begin with, then the potion won't work. I can't just magic something that isn't there."

"I'm not asking you to," Roxy assured her. "Alicia is just scared to admit her feelings. The potion will allow her to relax into them, that's all."

"You could just wait. Keep dating. It could happen organically. Why force things?"

Roxy heaved a sigh; it seemed she was actually putting some thought into her answer.

"I don't know…I know we're only twenty-five, but I just…I feel like a failure. I've never had a relationship. You know that. At least you had Camille, even if it didn't work out. Sometimes I just wonder if it'll ever happen."

Roxy's voice was small, almost shy sounding, by the time she finished the last words, and Hazel's heart squeezed.

"Of course it's going to happen! I just know it. You're a catch, and don't you forget it." Hazel hugged her around the shoulders, and Roxy flashed her a grateful smile.

They reached the café and walked in. The warm air of the café engulfed them pleasantly after the evening chill of the street. It was agreeably cheerful inside, with lots of squashy vintage furniture and mismatched chairs and tables. The café was about half full, and Hazel and Roxy stood in line to order at the counter.

"Are you telling me you can see the future now too?" said Roxy, attempting some humor.

"I think I can already see it. It's called hot chocolate and I'm buying."

"I won't say no to that as long as I can have a chai! I'm feeling spicy tonight."

"Oh, I think we can manage that."

They both grinned as they approached the counter, and Hazel saw that Roxy's good mood was restored.

"You two are in a good mood," said Joanna. She was the proprietor of the café and spoke with a thick accent. Joanna was originally from Poland, but she'd been running the café for the last ten years, and it had become a standby along Salem's main drag. She was in her late fifties, but looked good for her age, and she and Hazel were both on the board of the Chamber of Commerce for Salem. Sometimes Hazel wondered if Joanna had some magical abilities, as she always seemed to know what was going on in everyone's lives. But that could just as easily be explained by the fact that the café was a popular hangout spot for locals, and anyone could learn a lot by listening to people's conversations.

"Just talking about Roxy's love life."

"Oh, must be interesting," said Joanna. She took their order. "What about *your* love life, Hazel?"

"I'm married to the sea, don't you know?" said Hazel, affecting the mannerisms of a hoary old sea captain. She took an imaginary pipe out from between her lips. "Aye, she's a rough mistress."

The three of them laughed and made more small talk as Joanna prepared a chai latte for Roxy and poured a hot chocolate for Hazel. Hazel's love of all things chocolate was legendary among their friends.

"Thanks, Jo," said Roxy, offering to carry Hazel's drink and her own to a nearby table. Their "usual" table was far enough away from the door to stay warm in the colder months, but close enough to the air conditioning units in the summer to stay cool. It also had a perfect view of the front door, as they shared an incorrigible love of gossip.

The shop doorbells jingled, and Hazel and Roxy turned to see who was entering the café. A woman there was struggling with a large suitcase. Before anyone else moved, Roxy jumped up to help her. Together they lifted the heavy, over-packed suitcase into the shop interior, and the newcomer huffed in relief.

"Thank you so much." Her voice rang out sweetly, clear and

cool in the dry autumn air, with a hint of an English accent. When she lifted her head, Hazel grew dizzy. The woman was the most beautiful, enchanting woman she'd ever seen. And by the look on Roxy's face, she thought so too. There was no question in Hazel's mind things were about to become complicated.

CHAPTER TWO

Hazel's heart skipped a beat. The tall blond woman talking to Roxy at the door of the café was stunning and elegant. Her long overcoat was a frosty blue that perfectly matched her striking blue eyes and contrasted well with her light blond hair. Her hair was chin length, stylishly cut, and as she unbuttoned her coat, Hazel saw she was tastefully dressed in a cream-colored turtleneck and perfectly tailored gray slacks.

Damn, thought Hazel. She could tell Roxy was similarly entranced by the newcomer, whoever she was, and Hazel had a feeling that Alicia would be soon forgotten. It was a shame, though, because Hazel's attraction to the woman was instant and intense.

She watched Roxy gesturing over to their table, obviously inviting the newcomer to join them, and she waved and smiled. The woman smiled gingerly at her, looking a little overwhelmed by Roxy's friendliness. Roxy was like that—an extrovert to the extreme. She could overpower quieter folks with her exuberance. Sometimes she could come off as a bit of a bully, but Hazel knew it was Roxy's excitement for meeting other people and wanting to make them feel welcome. Kind of like a really friendly Great Dane.

A moment later, Roxy was heading over to Hazel, the coat and suitcase of the new person in tow. Meanwhile, the stranger headed to the counter to place her order.

"Oh my God, isn't she *gorgeous*?" said Roxy in a not-so-subtle stage whisper. She laid the beautiful icy blue overcoat on a nearby chair and situated the suitcase there as well. She was obviously hoping the new person would sit on the couch with her. "*Wow.*"

"Shhh, she'll hear you. And yes, I noticed. She's beautiful. Who is she?"

"Dr. Elizabeth Cowrie," said Roxy, putting on an awful British accent. "She's here to do research in some archives. From England," she added unnecessarily.

Hazel's eyebrows shot up in surprise. This was intriguing indeed.

"Think she's single?" said Hazel, shooting a look at Roxy.

"Oh, believe me, I've already asked," said Roxy, laughing. "Single indeed. But don't get any ideas. I call dibs."

"How can you call dibs when you have a love potion in your pocket right now for Alicia?"

"Oh, please. Dibs is non-situational. Plus, you said yourself Alicia probably isn't interested. And I got the distinct impression that this woman is very interested. In me, I mean."

Hazel felt a sudden, sharp pang of disappointment tinged with something uglier—jealousy, perhaps? For a second, she even felt some anger. Just once, she wished Roxy wasn't so ready to jump ahead.

"She looks even better from behind."

"Don't be crass, Roxy," said Hazel, forcing a laugh.

Roxy surreptitiously pulled out the velvet bag with the potion in it from her shirt pocket and pressed it into Hazel's hand as Dr. Cowrie approached them, carrying a large cup of tea.

"Take it," hissed Roxy, and Hazel quickly slid the packet into her purse. "I don't need it any more. I have a good feeling about Elizabeth."

"Hello." The tall, blond, beautiful Elizabeth put her steaming cup of Earl Grey on the table before sitting down, ever so elegantly, next to Roxy on the squat, orange upholstered settee across from Hazel. She put her hand out. "I'm Elizabeth."

Hazel grasped her warm, shapely hand and gave it a squeeze; she felt her heart speed up at the touch. She was dizzy at the closeness of Elizabeth.

"Hi, I'm Hazel. Nice to meet you."

Elizabeth smiled and Hazel almost melted. She had a large, warm smile that made her initial blonde iciness disappear instantly. She looked like a movie star—a young Jodie Foster or Linda Hamilton, perhaps.

"Thank you for helping me with my bags. It was really lovely of you. I don't know what I was thinking when I packed for this trip."

"What exactly's in there?" asked Roxy, gesturing to the large suitcase.

Elizabeth blushed. "I hate to admit it, but it's full of books and papers. In other words, loads of rubbish I don't need for an archival trip. It's as though I packed like I wasn't going home at some point." She chuckled ruefully at herself.

Roxy was obviously enchanted with her accent, and Hazel could see her mouthing some of the words Elizabeth had said.

"How long are you here for?" asked Hazel after a beat, since Roxy was far too entranced to keep the conversation going.

"It all depends, I suppose, on how well my research goes. I'm hoping to stay until December and then go home for Christmas, and then possibly come back to Boston and New Haven for additional research."

"Sounds fun," said Hazel. "What are you researching?"

"Witch trials, I'm afraid."

Roxy and Hazel burst out laughing.

"Of course you are. We get lots of people around here researching that time period," said Hazel. "There's plenty here to read about and experience. Did Roxy already tell you that she does some ghost tours around town for tourists? She's an excellent tour guide."

"Really?" said Elizabeth. "Do you know, I've never been on a ghost tour? I suppose this is the place to do it, isn't it?"

Roxy nodded enthusiastically. "I would be happy to give you a *private* tour sometime."

Elizabeth smiled at Roxy, and Hazel had to admit that Elizabeth appeared pretty taken with her. But was Elizabeth a lesbian? It wasn't like she was wearing a badge or anything. Maybe she was a really nice, genuine person. Time to test a theory.

"Roxy, haven't you been working on a LGBTQ tour of Salem, too?" Hazel prompted her.

"Really? That sounds absolutely wonderful," said Elizabeth. "I have always found the connection between witches and lesbianism a fascinating one."

That's a good sign, thought Hazel, smiling to herself, although the second statement sounded more like the thoughts of a researcher.

"And Salem has some great lesbian and gay bars too, if you're into that kind of thing," added Roxy, taking the hint. "There's a nice quiet bar where a bunch of us gay ladies hang out around the corner—the Scarlet Letter." Roxy gestured theatrically to herself and Hazel as if wanting to make sure there were no misunderstandings to be had.

Hazel had to admire Roxy's brashness. She was all in for trying to pin down Elizabeth.

"I'm not much of a partyer or bar-goer, I'm afraid," said Elizabeth, "but if it's as quiet as you say it is, I suppose it might be fun to check it out. With you, of course," she added, and Hazel could see Roxy's eyes light up. "I've never been one to go to pubs by myself, but I went a fair amount with my ex-girlfriend."

Now they knew for sure. Hazel and Roxy shared a knowing glance.

"Great. We should definitely plan that," said Roxy, nodding enthusiastically. "Now, tell me all about your research. Is there anything we can help you with? We are local experts, after all. I'm a tour guide, and Hazel owns the shop just down the street, the Witch Is In. She's got lots of stuff in there for the tourists, but it's also a bookshop with some great local history."

Elizabeth smiled at Roxy's enthusiasm, and although Roxy had included Hazel in her "pitch" to help Elizabeth, Hazel could tell it was time to give Roxy some space for her wooing. Plus, she really should take the vial of love potion back to the shop and lock it up. Love potions were the kind of thing that could cause a lot of trouble if they were left out for anyone to find.

Hazel finished the last sip of her hot chocolate and made her excuses. Roxy shot her a grateful smile as Hazel waved good-bye to them. She left them deep in conversation, and despite her initial attraction to Elizabeth, Hazel could see that Elizabeth was attracted to Roxy almost as much as Roxy was attracted to her.

Just my luck, thought Hazel, as she stepped out into the brisk night air, Roxy has two romantic prospects and, as usual, I have zero.

❖

By the time Hazel reached the front entrance of the Witch Is In, her light autumn jacket wasn't enough to keep her warm. The weather had turned much cooler, and her hands were numb as she fumbled for the keys to the shop.

The shop was Hazel's baby—a dream holding on to reality by the barest of ties. Even with all her magic to help her, there was no way to predict whether a small business would sink or swim. There were many shops like Hazel's in Salem. It was, after all, witch-hunting central in the seventeenth century, and the town had, in more recent decades, embraced its haunted history with kitschy abandon.

There were "museums" dedicated to the witch trials featuring dramatic voiceover narration through loudspeakers as well as Puritan wax dummies placed in tableaux from the town's ghoulish past. Beyond that, there were many shops dedicated to all things witchy and "magical": magic crystals, tarot cards, charms against the evil eye, numerology guides, and palm reading.

The Witch Is In offered all of those things and more.

Hazel prided herself on the fact that her shop had a wide selection of books and movies in addition to all the usual tacky souvenirs and paranormal gimcracks. She also offered palm readings and tarot card readings by appointment, as did many of the other shops and salons on the main drag. Still, she liked to think that hers was likely the most authentic of them all.

And then there was the secret menu at the shop, for an exclusive clientele only. They were mostly locals or, at the very least, repeat customers who lived in the area and frequented the shop. The special offerings were available via word of mouth, and Hazel made sure that only trusted souls would be informed of her select services, like the love potions.

Aside from those, Hazel occasionally made other kinds of potions in addition to doing the purification of homes, herb garden consultations, and the occasional dis-enchantment. A few antique dealers in the area had approached her to help chase away unhappy spirits who were haunting otherwise quite saleable antique clocks and cupboards, and Hazel had enjoyed quite a bit of luck in that line of work.

The shop was her home away from home, her refuge, her dream come true. Normally, her small charms and enchantments ensured that the shop always felt like a safe place in which to relax and be comforted.

Stepping into the store tonight, Hazel didn't feel the usual sensation of warmth and relaxation that she often did there, and alarm bells went off in her head.

As she walked toward the back of the shop, her neck began prickling with a sensation that was familiar though not instantly identifiable. Instinctively, she braced herself as she walked to the back of the shop, through the room where she did palm and tarot readings, and past the back storage rooms and office. At the very end of the hallway, she could see a shadow looming in outline behind the frosted glass of the back door entrance to the shop.

Hazel threw the door open, her heart racing.

"Well, hello there," said a familiar voice.

"Oh," said Hazel, feeling silly and annoyed at the same time, peering out into the night at the visitor. "It's you."

"Who'd you think?" Camille turned in profile, and the distant glow of a streetlamp lit up her pale features.

She was shorter than Hazel, though not by much, and instantly imposing, with long, curling black hair, perfectly arched black eyebrows, and large, almond shaped eyes that Hazel knew were violet, even if she couldn't quite see their color in the dim light of evening. Her ruby red lips were curled into a mischievous grin that didn't reveal the sharp, shining white teeth Hazel knew were beneath. She was wearing a dark cloak over a black dress, and even on a cold autumn evening, it had a plunging neckline that made Hazel shiver—from cold, she told herself, not excitement.

Camille hadn't changed a bit, thought Hazel, trying to collect her thoughts. It wasn't every day that her vampire ex-girlfriend showed up on her doorstep.

"Sorry, it was dark and creepy in the shop, and I didn't know who was out here."

Camille pouted. "Aren't you going to invite me in?"

"And here I thought you had the run of the place," said Hazel, momentarily surprised.

"I guess you were angrier with me than you remembered," said Camille, her expression unreadable, though there was a hint of derision in her otherwise sultry voice.

"Sorry," said Hazel, trying to be amenable, and immediately cursing herself for apologizing. After all, it was Camille who had ended things, badly. Still, Hazel found it impossible not to be gracious to people; Roxy sometimes told her she was a doormat, which was pretty rich coming from her as she'd benefited many times over from Hazel's generosity.

In any case, she and Camille were history; their relationship had ended over a year ago, and she was over it. It had taken a while, but Hazel *had* gotten over it. She wasn't angry anymore, only curious. And a little worried. Why was Camille here? Now?

"Please, come in."

Quick as a flash, Camille was inside, and the funny, prickly feeling was now explained: it was Hazel's self-installed Camille alarm spell. She had installed it right after the breakup and had, apparently, forgotten all about it.

"Ouch. That's a bit harsh," said Camille, rubbing at her arms as though she felt the spell physically.

Hazel snapped her fingers, muttered an incantation, and broke the spell.

"Better?"

"Much," said Camille, still rubbing her arms. Now it was her turn to snap her fingers, and suddenly the lights were on, and it was much cozier in the shop. "You see? I do still have some tricks of my own." She winked at Hazel the way she had a thousand times when they were dating.

Hazel studied Camille a moment; it was hard not to look at her. Vampires had that quality; as a witch, Hazel couldn't be hypnotized or glamoured like a mere mortal, but she wasn't totally immune to Camille's glittering, dangerous beauty either.

By the warm light of the shop, Camille didn't look any less undead than before, and her skin glowed with an ethereal, moon-like quality that Hazel had once found exceedingly attractive. Her violet eyes flashed beneath her long lashes, and Hazel couldn't help but recall their last happy memory.

They had gone for a moonlit hike up to an overlook with a view of the water. The lights of the dinghies and boats had flickered in the night, and the summer air had enveloped them in its soft, dewy embrace. Camille had kissed Hazel that night as she had a thousand times before, skimming her preternaturally soft lips over Hazel's lips and neck, nibbling there but never biting, holding her tight in her arms. Hazel remembered her desire, warm and pulsing through her blood, lighting her skin on fire. They had spread a blanket down on the ground and lain there, together, and—

Hazel made herself stop reliving the moment and come back to the present. She was grateful that Camille couldn't read her thoughts, another perk of being a witch.

She forced herself to remember the very next day, when Camille had broken up with her. She had cheated on her with another vampire and left with her to Oregon. It had all happened quite out of the blue, and aside from one random postcard from Camille, Hazel hadn't heard from her since then. This visit was quite unexpected.

"So? Why are you here?" She tried to make herself sound casual, though she had a feeling that Camille could see right through her paltry attempts at studied indifference.

"That's not a very nice way of greeting an old friend, is it?" Camille walked through the main aisle of the store, running her hands familiarly across the counter and shelves full of knickknacks and souvenirs. "Not much has changed here."

"I know you're not here to discuss my third quarter earnings."

Hazel tried to keep her tone light, but it was hard. Her mind was working overtime trying to figure out what Camille was up to. A sudden, suspicious feeling had taken hold of her that she couldn't quite explain. Was Camille moving back to Salem? Did she get dumped herself? Was she playing mind games again?

Camille laughed, and her laughter sounded like the tinkling of a wind chime. It had been one of Hazel's favorite sounds when they'd been dating. After Camille broke her heart, she'd thrown out all her wind chimes and refused to sell any at the shop. Yes, there *had* been some dramatic moments after that breakup.

"No, no," said Camille, sauntering back toward Hazel, who was standing with her back against a bookshelf full of magic-themed children's books. "Really, I just came here to see you, Hazel my dear."

She stood dangerously close, so close that Hazel could smell her usual, intoxicating scents: vanilla and lavender and something a little spicy that, no matter how hard she tried, she couldn't identify. Roxy had joked that it was *eau de vampire*.

Hazel tried to pinpoint any hint that Camille was being facetious, but Camille didn't look like she was joking; in fact, Hazel could swear that Camille was one hundred percent in earnest.

"I missed you," said Camille, her voice low and soft. "But I guess you haven't missed me, have you? Maybe you even have someone new."

"No." The word escaped Hazel's lips a little too quickly. Why couldn't she ever lie in a situation like this? "Not as yet." She paused, trying to find something dignified to say. "I like being single."

Camille would never buy it.

"Ah," said Camille. "I see. Nothing but work, work, work for my little Hazel, is it?"

Camille leered seductively and reached out to touch her arm, but Hazel instinctively moved away and flinched. Those small movements registered with Camille and put her off. She moved away and began to pace the room, looking at random things on shelves and talking to Hazel with her back to her.

"Seriously, Hazel, I thought you'd at least respond to my postcard."

"Why would I do that?"

"I thought we were friends."

"You didn't *really* think so, did you? Not after what you did," said Hazel, trying not to let her voice shake. She wanted to say "after what you did *to me*," but her voice caught in her throat and she paused, letting the unsaid words hang in the air between them.

Camille's demeanor suddenly changed and became businesslike.

"I'm sorry for thinking we could reminisce a bit," said Camille, walking back over to Hazel, this time with her large, black patent leather purse shining between them and her tall patent leather heels click-clacking across the floor. "I thought we could include some pleasure with our business."

"Business?"

"Yes, I have a business proposition for you, my dear."

Hazel pushed against the counter, holding it tightly. A proposition from your vampire ex-girlfriend could never be a good thing.

CHAPTER THREE

Elizabeth watched with some disappointment as Hazel put on her cloak and left the café with a friendly wave. She had enjoyed the easy conversation between the three of them; now, alone with Roxy, things felt a bit more intimate. Not that Elizabeth necessarily minded; Roxy was cute and flirty and clearly working *very* hard to entertain her. Elizabeth had forgotten how nice it could be to flirt with an attractive woman.

Roxy offered to buy them both another drink—something a little harder than tea and hot chocolate. Elizabeth knew she'd be up early the next day due to jet lag, but at the same time, a glass of wine sounded like just the thing after a long international flight.

From her perch, she could observe Roxy walking toward the counter. Her figure was tall and striking, and Elizabeth enjoyed the view.

Roxy brought back their drinks and sat down comfortably next to Elizabeth, handing her a glass of California Merlot before taking a long swig of her beer.

"Not bad," Elizabeth said appreciatively.

"Glad you like our American wines," said Roxy, and they clinked drinks in a little toast. "To new friends." Roxy winked.

"Yes, that sounds nice," Elizabeth said. "You're quite the welcoming committee, Roxy. Do you do that for all the lesbians who come to Salem?"

"Sure do," said Roxy, with a laugh. "Though none of them are nearly as pretty—or interesting—as you."

Elizabeth blushed and tried to turn the conversation back to safer topics. After all, it wouldn't do to shag the first lesbian she met in America.

"No, but, seriously, you must know simply everything there is to know about Salem," said Elizabeth, trying to regain her composure and taking another sip of wine. "I appreciate being able to meet such a wonderful guide on my first night here."

Roxy's grin got even bigger, if that was possible. Elizabeth was starting to worry that her face might crack.

"I *love* Salem. You know, I grew up around here. I know every nook and cranny of this town and all its secrets."

"Are there lots of secrets, then?" Elizabeth was genuinely interested. She had read so much about Salem from an academic point of view, but she was dying to know more about it from a local's angle.

"Oh yeah," said Roxy. She paused, and her eyes got a fuzzy, far-off look in them.

The pause lengthened to a good minute—or at least it felt like that to Elizabeth. "Roxy, are you okay?"

Roxy blushed.

"Oh yeah, sorry. I was thinking about all the places I want to show you around town. What are you doing tomorrow night?"

"Goodness, I hardly know. I've got a feeling I'll be still recovering from jet lag." Just as she finished the last word, she felt a yawn coming on; her face was stiff and tired from being awake for nearly twenty-four hours.

"Of course," said Roxy. "What was I thinking? Silly me. How about the day after?" Her voice was boisterous and eager, and her energy reminded Elizabeth all the more of the massive amount of work she had ahead of her at the archives.

"I'm so sorry, but I'm going to be stuck in the archives for the rest of the week. I've been having difficulty accessing some of the catalogs online, so it's all going to take much longer than I would like."

"But a girl's gotta eat, though, right?"

Elizabeth tried to smile as warmly as she could, while also keeping her tone of voice light and friendly. Roxy was cute, but Elizabeth wasn't in Salem for romance. She was there to do research and finish the book that would help her climb up the ladder of academia back in England or perhaps even here in the United States—and hopefully prove to her family that a life in the ivory tower was something they could be proud of.

"I just got here. I need to settle in. I hope you don't take offense to that. But why don't we do something on Saturday? That'll give me plenty of time to start my research and make myself at home."

Elizabeth could see that her proposition wasn't exactly what Roxy had in mind; she was pouting a bit but managed to smile, nonetheless.

They made small talk about what Roxy wanted to show Elizabeth in town, and before they knew it, it was after ten.

"Oh dear." Elizabeth yawned. "It's so late. Dreadfully late."

"Aw, it's only ten fifteen."

"Yes, but I'm exhausted and jet-lagged. You won't mind if I pop off now, do you?" Elizabeth rubbed at her eyes.

"Of course not, as long as you let me walk you home."

Elizabeth couldn't help smiling at Roxy's determination. And since she had zero sense of direction, it really was an excellent proposition. She didn't like the idea of trying to get into her rental by herself in the dark in a new place.

They left the café together, Roxy gallantly offering to take Elizabeth's suitcase off her hands, and, laden down with her luggage, the two of them made their way to the house Elizabeth was renting for the next few months.

As they walked, Roxy asked question after question until Elizabeth felt like she was giving an interview. What kind of things did she do for fun? What was her favorite kind of cuisine? Could they exchange phone numbers in case she changed her mind about dinner during the week?

Despite feeling slightly overwhelmed by Roxy's enthusiasm, Elizabeth was flattered by the attention—and she certainly couldn't deny that having someone carry her luggage for her was nice. Of course, she could have taken a cab to her rental, but the evening air was refreshing after hours and hours on a plane and train.

Still, Elizabeth knew it would take a whole day just to set up her home office and get organized, and her work schedule wouldn't permit her to hang out before Saturday. There were simply too many things to take care of, errands to run, plus other complications that she explained to Roxy as they walked: revisions on an article, writing a conference paper, giving her graduate students back in England feedback on their essays.

Elizabeth could see Roxy's enthusiasm diminishing somewhat as she detailed all the items on her to do list.

"Gosh, I had no idea that being a researcher was so much work," said Roxy, her enthusiasm somewhat dampened. "Are you going to have any time for fun in Salem? It really is a fun town."

"I'm afraid it's much more work than most films would have you think," said Elizabeth before double-checking the address of the rental on her phone. It was indeed the same as the small bungalow in front of her, which, thanks to a particularly well-placed streetlamp, was quite easy to make out.

"This is it," said Elizabeth, using the check-in information on her phone to input the correct code on a lockbox and pull out a key. "Thanks so much for walking with me and dragging my suitcase. Do you need the loo before you go?"

Roxy looked at her blankly.

"Loo. Toilet?" Elizabeth wrinkled her brow in concentration "What on earth *do* you all call it here? Oh, bathroom."

Roxy laughed. "No, I'm good. But thanks for asking. 'Loo.' That's cute."

Elizabeth grinned at her. "Glad you think so. Well, good night then. It's terribly late, and I simply must get to bed."

"Of course. It was so nice to meet you." She helped pull the luggage up the stairs onto the porch and they exchanged phone numbers. "I'll definitely give you a ring on the weekend if I don't see you before then. But it's a small town, so I probably will."

"I hope so. And maybe you can invite Hazel as well. I'd like to get to know her, too. Good night."

And with that, Elizabeth entered the house and closed the door behind her. Yes, she had a lot of work ahead of her, but having something fun planned for the weekend with Roxy and Hazel would be excellent motivation to stay on task. She really hoped she could get to know Hazel more. She seemed quieter and a bit easier to talk to than Roxy. She was pretty, too, in a different way than Roxy: softer, curvier. Yes, she really was attractive—though her leaving so early on suggested maybe she wasn't as interested in getting to know Elizabeth as her friend.

Elizabeth shrugged and heaved another yawn. She would see them both that weekend, most likely, and in the meantime, she needed to get some rest and get to the archives. She unpacked, showered, brushed her teeth, and fell asleep almost as soon as her head hit the pillow.

❖

After Elizabeth closed the door, Roxy stood there, dumbfounded. Up until that moment, she'd thought Elizabeth was bluffing—that she was actually going to relent and invite Roxy in. If only she'd gotten over the threshold. Maybe they could have at least kissed. Sure, it would have been a bit quick since they'd literally just met, but so what?

As Roxy walked into the cold night air by herself, she couldn't help but think about Elizabeth's request to have Hazel join them. What if she wasn't interested in something romantic? Roxy's deeply rooted beliefs in fate and love at first sight wouldn't allow for that possibility. She'd felt a spark with Elizabeth, there was no doubt about it.

On the street corner, Roxy paused. She was so close to Hazel's house. Maybe she'd take a look and see if Hazel was home.

She walked the streets that, even in the darkness, were familiar. She had grown up in this neighborhood, living there with her parents and brothers until the age of twelve. Then her parents had divorced, and they'd each moved to different neighborhoods. It'd been heartbreaking because Hazel lived two streets over and they were always tight. Still, they remained close friends, and now that Hazel had inherited her family home, Roxy always had a reason to revisit her old haunts.

As she walked the streets of her childhood, Roxy's thoughts turned, as they often did in this neighborhood, to her parents' divorce. The yelling, the arguments, the doors slamming. Hazel's house, with its smell of baking cookies and the happy sounds of Hazel's parents talking to one another, laughing, acting like normal parents: it had been a refuge for Roxy. And Hazel had always been there for her. When times were toughest, Roxy knew she could always go over to Hazel's for a sleepover. They'd watch silly scary movies like the old *Dawn of the Dead* or *Rosemary's Baby*, make freshly popped popcorn, and look up at the stars through the family telescope. Hazel's family didn't mind that Roxy was "over the top" or "loud"—things her teachers often wrote on report cards. They accepted her as she was—and she accepted them and their magic without question. She and Hazel had bonded over being different, not fitting in at school, and not *wanting* to fit in. They were their own perfect club of two.

Of course, things had changed when Hazel went off to a liberal arts college on scholarship and Roxy went on an athletic scholarship to State—a scholarship she couldn't keep when her grades dipped too low. She'd been forced to come home in shame: a shame her father didn't care about because he thought college was for losers, and a shame her mother liked to remind her about every time they talked. Hazel wasn't a snob, and she only cared that Roxy did what she loved. She was supportive and kind, and they always had each other's back. Hazel was there for Roxy when her mother divorced again and when Roxy had to drop out of college, and Roxy was there for Hazel when her father died and when Camille broke Hazel's heart.

They were tough broads, and they could always count on each other. Roxy knew how lucky she was to have Hazel as her bestie.

She made her way to Hazel's front porch but was surprised to find the house dark. The porch light wasn't on, and Beezle was sitting outside, giving Roxy a knowing look. Roxy knew Beezle had special powers, and his glowering stare at her convinced her something was up.

It was unlike Hazel to be out so late. When she'd left the café, Roxy had assumed it was to give her space with Elizabeth, but now she wondered if everything was okay. She had a funny feeling, and soon she was speed-walking back to the Witch Is In.

CHAPTER FOUR

It was nearing eleven by the time Hazel and Camille had discussed Camille's business proposition, and Hazel still wasn't sure she was making the right decision. Luckily, just as her brain was getting fried, there was a knock at the back door.

"Are you expecting anyone?" said Camille suspiciously.

"No. I'll just go see who it is."

Hazel was glad of the distraction. She was getting more and more tired by the minute, and she couldn't help wondering if there were subtexts to Camille's offer that she wasn't seeing.

Camille had never been very good at the honesty thing. To a certain extent, it came with being a vampire. You couldn't be immortal and live off blood and have the power to hypnotize your prey without harboring some secrets. And Hazel had her own secrets, of course, what with being a real witch in Salem. But the secrets had simply gone too far in Camille's case. Beyond that, she'd always gotten the sense that Camille enjoyed being secretive, something Hazel couldn't deal with.

Hazel could sense Roxy's presence before she opened the door. Roxy's aura was strong and bright and always had a healing quality.

"Hey."

"Hey. I was worried about you when I went to the house and saw it all dark."

"Aww, that's so sweet of you." Hazel pulled Roxy into a big hug. She was thankful that now she had an excuse to go home. Roxy and Camille got along like oil and vinegar.

"That's what friends are for, right?" Roxy grinned. "So why are you still at the shop? I thought inventory wasn't due for another couple months."

"You are absolutely correct. I got held up here when I came back to lock up that love potion." They walked through the back rooms and into the main part of the shop—but it was now deserted. "She was just here." Hazel looked around in surprise, but there was no sign of Camille at all—except the books and the product samples she had left behind.

"Who?"

"Camille."

"Camille?"

"Yes, she showed up out of the blue."

Roxy made a face. "I bet she did. She always did like to make an entrance."

"True."

"You're not still into her, are you?" A note of real concern entered Roxy's voice. "I mean, it's been over a year."

"A year and three months to be exact."

"Exactly. And I thought you were finished with her."

Hazel shrugged. "I am. But she showed up here with a 'business proposition'—her words, not mine." She gestured to the stuff Camille had left behind, and Roxy inspected it.

"Hmm. *The True Confessions of a Vampire*? Sounds awful."

"The book is apparently a true memoir by one of Camille's vampire friends. She promised to try to find some stores to sell it. Of course, it'll be read as fiction. I told her I'd read a couple of chapters to see if it's worth putting out. Camille suggested that her friend could even do a reading here."

Roxy's eyes widened as she tapped the author's name on the book cover. "Grizelda Suarez? She's not the girl she cheated on you with, is she?"

"No, thank goodness."

Roxy breathed a sigh of relief. "At least she's not that scummy. But what about this other stuff in the packets?"

Hazel pointed to each and listed what was in it. "Belladonna, dried mandrake root, dehydrated vampire blood…basically all sorts of dangerous, magical stuff that she knew I'd be interested in."

Roxy shuddered. "Gross. And is it safe to keep this stuff around?"

"It's definitely not for mass market sales. In fact, I don't think I'd sell any of this to any regular person. A lot of it would come in handy for my own potions, or for other witches in the area. I do occasionally get customers like that. Used correctly, belladonna and dried mandrake root have medicinal properties."

"And the vampire blood?"

"I'm less sure about that." Hazel paused. "Roxy, don't freak out, but Camille wants the shop to start selling products to vampires. She says there's vampires around here who would pay good money for some of these products."

"*What?* Hazel, you can't be seriously considering this. It sounds like a massacre in the making."

Hazel sighed. Roxy knew quite a bit about the magical world from Hazel—far more than most people. But her ideas about vampires were taken straight from a film. Of course vampires were dangerous, but they were few and far between, and in the twenty-first century, most who lived in civilization managed their unusual diet through a hookup at a local blood bank. Still, she didn't like the idea of going into business with Camille. The old Hazel would have said yes right away to the proposition just to be nice; the older, wiser Hazel told Camille she would think about it as a way to buy some time. She had promised herself after the breakup to stop being such a pushover. "I agree. It's messy." Hazel heaved a sigh and then immediately yawned. "I think I might be too tired for this conversation. I don't suppose you want to walk me home? You can tell me all about Elizabeth, and we can have a little nightcap?"

Roxy's eyes lit up at the mention of Elizabeth. "Yes. That sounds great."

Within a half hour, they were ensconced in the back parlor of Hazel's familial mansion. The house was a beautiful Victorian that had been in Hazel's family for generations without much upkeep. Her parents had lovingly restored it using a combination of elbow grease and their magical abilities; when Hazel's father died of a heart attack some years ago, her mother made Hazel the sole owner before moving up to Maine to be closer to the rest of her extended family.

The untimely death of her beloved father had been a huge blow for

Hazel, but she loved living in the house that he'd put so much work into. It helped her keep his memory alive and reminded her of all the good times they'd had in that house together, cooking meals in the kitchen, dancing down the massive staircase, brewing potions together in the converted attic…Both of her parents had contributed to her magical education, but it was her father who'd recognized her talents in potion-brewing and had encouraged her to experiment.

Hazel also had a much older sister who'd left Salem many years ago and moved to Canada after marrying a Canadian wizard. Hazel loved her family but rarely saw them. Running a business was like having two full-time jobs. Still, she loved the Witch Is In, just like she loved living in Salem and inhabiting her childhood home.

The house was a true "painted lady," complete with wraparound porch, turrets, vaulted ceilings, built-in bookshelves, and even a twisty, twirly staircase that led from the library up to the upper floors and the widow's walk. There were two parlors, of course: a front parlor and a back parlor, just like in Hazel's favorite Jane Austen novels.

And then there was Colin, the convivial and rather harmless, if annoying, spirit who haunted the house. He had been the previous owner in the early nineteenth century, but his haunting of the house had led it to be unsaleable—except to a family of witches and wizards like Hazel's. In spite of his occasional shenanigans, he was a friendly spirit and unlikely to bother anyone, unless they happened to bring up fox hunting in casual conversation, which rarely happened anymore.

Generally, Colin and Hazel had an agreement that he wouldn't make any appearances in front of anyone but her and occasionally Roxy, though it scared the bejeezus out of her.

Hazel flopped on her favorite chair, right next to the fireplace where she magically whipped up a fire in the grate, for which they were both grateful. Roxy folded her long legs under her on the couch and sipped at her hot chocolate.

She looked around warily. "Your resident ghost isn't about to make an appearance, is he?"

"Colin? No, I don't think so. He's usually out in the backyard this time of night. Says the night breezes refresh him."

Roxy rolled her eyes. "How can a ghost be refreshed? Isn't being dusty and creaky part of the job description?"

"I couldn't say. When I'm a ghost, I'll come back and tell you."

"Don't you dare." Roxy tried to point at Hazel but ended up spilling drops of hot cocoa on her lap instead. "Ouch."

"Serves you right for pointing fingers. There's a bad history of that here in Salem." Hazel grinned.

"Don't I know it?" Roxy's own family, like Hazel's, had ancestors who had been living in Salem during the infamous witch trials.

"So, tell me all about Elizabeth. It was so cold outside, I feel like all I could concentrate on was getting home."

"She's delicious," said Roxy, finally. "Sweeter than this cocoa, and smart, too. I hope she's not too smart for me." Suddenly, Roxy looked like she was actually upset by the thought.

Roxy had never been much for book smarts; Hazel had helped her with a lot of homework in their school days. But, as Hazel often reminded her, Roxy had other kinds of smarts. She was a skilled boatwoman, avid kayaker and canoeist, and an excellent skier. She gave ski and snowboard lessons in the winter and led river tours inland the rest of the year in addition to the witch tours and history tours she led in town. She was an avid history nut, if self-taught. Hazel, who had done a joint BA/MA in college, never found her conversation with Roxy lacking.

"Hey. Don't insult my best friend that way."

"No, really, Hazel. What if she finds out that I didn't finish college, or 'uni' as she calls it, and she decides I'm not...I dunno...interesting enough for her? Or well-read enough?"

"That's not the only thing that matters, and you know it." Hazel tried to be reassuring, even as she had to quash the disappointment in her heart. "You read history books all the time. And you're fun to be around. Anyone would be lucky to have your beauty, brains, and brawn."

"Awww, thanks, Hazel. I sure hope she thinks the same thing." Roxy paused and her eyebrows furrowed a bit. "At the café it seemed like she was really into me. It felt like we had an instant connection. But I can't shake the feeling that at the end of the night she blew me off."

Hazel's heart sped up a bit when Roxy mentioned Elizabeth blowing her off. Maybe Roxy and Elizabeth wasn't a foregone conclusion?

"What do you mean?"

Roxy gave Hazel a play-by-play of their conversation at the café, Elizabeth's insistence that she wouldn't be free until the weekend due to work, and then the lack of follow-through at the door.

"…and just like that, I was alone on the porch," said Roxy.

"You just met. What exactly did you think would happen tonight?"

"Oh…I don't know." Roxy sighed. "I guess I thought we might have one of those long conversations into the night. Really get to know each other. You know I hate waiting. I wish we could skip all the wondering and mooning about and get right to the good stuff."

"You're forgetting that the beginning is part of the good stuff. Besides, wouldn't it be good to slow down for once?" said Hazel. It was like Roxy to want to rush through everything. "Work on getting to know her without getting into her pants."

Roxy laughed. "I don't want to get into her pants! I mean…not yet. I'm just worried. How can I get to know her if she's working all the time?"

"She's a human being, not a robot. I'm sure there will be plenty of opportunities to see her. Didn't you just tell me she wants to hang out this weekend?"

"I guess." Roxy sounded despondent again.

"What on earth are you doing back here?" A tenor voice floated into the room, soon followed by the pale gray floating vision of Colin.

Colin had been in his late thirties, still handsome but no longer in the best of physical fitness, when he had died in his study, choking on his own cigar stub as he dozed in a chair by the fire. As a result, he spent his days dressed as he was at his death: in a Victorian three-piece suit, complete with iridescent pocket watch, and ghastly plumes of smoke that continued to emanate from his mouth whenever he spoke. Luckily, the effect was more comical than frightening.

"Get out of here, Colin, before Roxy throws another pillow at you."

"Sticks and stones, my dear, tut, tut," said the ghost, grinning at the two of them as he floated through the room and right through a wall.

Roxy shivered. "He creeps me out."

"Honestly, sometimes I think he does it because he *knows* it creeps you out. He never does that kind of thing when it's just me. Usually, we have a laugh together."

"Gee, so sorry I'm not better friends with your ghost," said Roxy, and they both dissolved into giggles.

There was a moment of silence between them. Roxy fiddled with her now-empty mug before setting it aside and sitting up straighter.

"I think there's potential, Haze. We were having such a great conversation, and I thought we were building up to setting up a date. But then she remembered about all her work and stuff, and it went from possibility to, like, maybe I'll see you around."

"Maybe she was tired. Didn't she just get here from England? That's a long flight. Plus, don't forget, she had to get from Boston all the way up here. I'm sure she was exhausted."

"True." She sighed. "I don't want to miss my chance. You know how hopeless I am when it comes to real feelings and love. I mess things up."

"It's not like I'm some guru. I've been single since Camille and I broke up, and that wasn't exactly the healthiest relationship."

"Now you're the one being hard on yourself, Hazy," said Roxy, using her pet name for Hazel from childhood. "Camille was the one who ruined that relationship, not you."

Hazel smiled. Roxy was the only person she'd allow to use that name. "Thanks."

They shared another few moments in companionable silence, and Hazel reflected on how, despite her bluster and bull-in-a-china-shop instincts, Roxy really was a great friend. She bit her lip as she weighed whether she should bring up the fact that she too was attracted to Elizabeth. And she felt ready to move on. Seeing Camille that night, despite how much it upset her, also reminded her that it really was time to move on. It was more than that, though—she had felt an instant attraction and interest in Elizabeth. It was unusual that she and Roxy were interested in the same woman, but maybe it could be kind of fun to have a shared crush?

Just as Hazel opened her mouth to tell Roxy how she felt about Elizabeth, Roxy spoke first. "At least you've had relationships, Haze... I've just been sitting here, thinking about how I'll be twenty-six in January, and I've never had a girlfriend I'd bring home to Thanksgiving dinner."

Hazel resisted the urge to remind Roxy that given her family's dysfunctionality, that was not necessarily a bad thing. She saw that

Roxy was serious, though. Maybe she would finally realize that she couldn't hurry love, and she couldn't force it.

"You're going to meet someone great someday. You will find love. You're a great friend to me, and someday you're going to make some lady very lucky."

"But why can't it be Elizabeth? I mean…what if I'm meeting the right people all the time, and I just keep screwing it up?"

"Sure. It could be Elizabeth. Or someone else. You can't rush these things, you know?"

Roxy paused, as if considering Hazel's words, and for a moment, Hazel was hopeful that Roxy would simply let things develop organically.

Finally, she looked up at Hazel with a gleam of an idea in her eyes. "We have to figure out a way to get her on a date with me."

Hazel realized that Roxy hadn't been listening to her at all. Roxy was back to her usual tunnel vision, and she couldn't help responding with some friendly sarcasm. "So not only do I have to supply you with love potions for unsuitable lovers, but now I have to court unavailable women on your part, too?"

"Aw, come on. You love that kind of thing. Your favorite book is *Emma*."

"Yes, but you forget that in *Emma*, the main character is terrible at setting up her friends in love."

"Oh yeah, I forgot. Mostly I remember Gwyneth Paltrow looking hot."

"You're a veritable Austen scholar."

"Okay, okay, so literary allusions aren't my strong suit. But give me credit for trying."

Hazel sighed in mock chagrin. "Fine. C plus." She glanced at her watch. "Let's discuss it more tomorrow. It's after one, and I have to be at the shop by nine."

After Roxy left, Hazel locked up and went back into the kitchen to wash their dirty mugs. As she washed and tidied up, she found her thoughts returning to her conversation with Roxy. She wished Roxy wouldn't be so oblivious sometimes. She should have told her about her own interest in Elizabeth. Or maybe not? Sure, she found Elizabeth attractive, but Elizabeth *was* attractive; that wasn't news to anyone.

As she got ready for bed, though, her thoughts kept returning to Elizabeth: her smile in the café, her athletic figure, her delightful accent. She found herself wondering about her research and what she was looking for in Salem. Most people came there looking for witches, and Hazel could certainly help with that.

Still, if Roxy was right and she and Elizabeth had good chemistry already, then maybe there was no point to thinking about this any further. Maybe Roxy was right; after all, the quickest way to find out if she and Elizabeth had a connection would be to set them up on a date. The sooner the better.

Hazel found Beezle waiting for her in bed, curled up on the pillow next to hers. "What do you think, Beezle? Should we get to know Elizabeth better?"

Beezle blinked slowly at Hazel and purred.

CHAPTER FIVE

The following Saturday, the shop was humming with activity. All morning, Hazel felt like she was being pulled in a million different directions as she ran from task to task.

One moment she was helping a customer choose a tarot deck, the next minute she was coming to Rita's rescue at the cash register, helping her void a mistake, and right after that she had to package up some fragile stained glass ornaments a customer had purchased. She never thought she'd see the day they were short-staffed, but that morning they really were.

She was absolutely relieved, therefore, when Camille showed up unexpectedly after lunch, offering to help with the shop. She'd worked the odd shift when they dated and knew the run of the place, and of course her vampiric intuition, though dampened somewhat during the daytime, was still keener than that of most humans. She was the ideal salesperson.

For example, that very afternoon, she convinced some out-of-towners to buy the most expensive thing in the shop: a garden statue of Samantha from *Bewitched*—a copy of the one that stood a couple of blocks away in downtown Salem. Hazel could hardly believe it; she'd purchased it sort of as a joke, thinking it would end up a part of the store's decor. But no, Camille really had sold it, somehow upselling the customers in the process.

Try as she might, Hazel couldn't be annoyed with Camille, not today. It was madness; it seemed that Salem's popularity as a fun day trip during the spooky season had spread far and wide; the purchasers of the Samantha statue were all the way from Buffalo, NY.

The glut of customers didn't slow until the dinner hour neared. Around five thirty they all had a chance to breathe and, for the first time, the shop was relatively quiet.

"That's my cue," said Camille, pulling her large leather purse from behind the counter and ceding her spot at the cash register to the shop's assistant, Rita. Rita simpered at Camille; she obviously had a huge crush on the beautiful vampire.

Rita belonged to the thriving subculture of Goths in Salem, from her steel-toed black lace-up boots to her ripped black jeans, black band T-shirt, black dyed hair, and many, many facial piercings. She was about nineteen, which Hazel deemed important—she needed someone around to keep her in the know about what was still fashionable with Salem teens. And she knew that Rita's usually sullen demeanor was partly a facade that went along with her Gothness. She was the edgy darkness to Hazel's own good witch vibes. Of course, none of that protected Rita from the charms of a beautiful real-life Gothic vampire like Camille. Not that Rita could have ever guessed that Camille was a *real* vampire.

Camille winked at Rita playfully, and Hazel had to stop herself from rolling her eyes. Camille was happiest when everyone was at her feet, worshipping her.

"Can you manage up front here on your own for a few, Rita?" asked Hazel. "I want to talk to Camille for a few minutes."

Rita assented, though somewhat wistfully, shooting an envious gaze at Camille's naturally black hair and pale skin.

Hazel and Camille walked to the back room, and Hazel tried not to notice how beautiful and alluring she was, even half hidden in shadows.

Camille was wearing a scarlet velvet dress with, as usual, a plunging neckline, and long silk sleeves; her hair flowed over her shoulders and her lips were a brilliant carmine that appeared to shimmer in the light. Her violet eyes were a deep purple during the day—almost brown. Camille loved the fashion of the time she'd been born in, and in a town like Salem, she fit right in.

"Thanks for helping out today," said Hazel, trying to balance gratitude with disinterest. "You really couldn't have shown up at a better time."

Camille shrugged with affected nonchalance. "I've always had good timing. Glad to help. I was also wondering if you've given my proposal any thought. About the other products. And about selling to vampires."

Hazel sighed. She had given it a lot of thought, and if it weren't for the arrival of a certain Dr. Elizabeth Cowrie, she probably wouldn't have thought about anything else that week.

"Yes, of course, I've given it a lot of thought, and I'm going to have to pass on selling to vampires. At least for now."

Camille looked genuinely dismayed. "I thought you'd at least give it a trial basis. The vampire community deserves to have some services available to them in a place like Salem."

"I guess I don't see it that way. I don't think encouraging vampires to be more visible, much less giving them a place to purchase illicit substances, is a good idea for me or for Salem. Plus, I would have to run extra hours at night, and I don't have the coverage for it."

"This is the way of the future, Hazel. Don't you see? Witches and vampires ought to be on the same side. I thought we always saw eye to eye."

All of Hazel's gratitude for Camille's help was melting away with every sentence out of her mouth. "I thought we did, too. And then you broke my heart. You left me for another vampire—and you said it was 'the way of things,' if I remember right. Like goes with like, or something like that."

"I see that I misjudged the situation." Camille brushed something away from one of her eyes.

Was she crying? Hazel couldn't be sure, as Camille had turned away to study the pictures hanging on the wall in the back room: the photo of the shop when it first opened, Hazel standing at the counter making her first sale, Hazel and Roxy arm in arm on the top of Mount Katahdin after Hazel's college graduation. There was no photo of Hazel and Camille—how could there be? Camille couldn't be photographed. But she'd given Hazel a miniature, painted by a famous artist of nineteenth-century Paris, that had a place beneath the photos. The miniature wasn't there anymore. Camille looked over at her, the question clear in her eyes.

Hazel went over to her special cupboard and unlocked it. There, in the middle compartment, at the back of a drawer, was the precious miniature locked in the original velvet box. She took it out and handed it to Camille.

"I still have it. I took it down, but I didn't throw it away."

Camille studied Hazel, her expression blank. She didn't reach for the box, however. "Oh. Are you sure you don't want to keep it?"

"Please take it. We're history. Ancient history. And I don't want any of your products either." It felt good to say it so plainly, and to make a decision that was good for her, not just because someone else wanted something from her.

A look of pain passed over Camille's face before she rearranged her features again into a look of complacency. "Of course, Hazel." She took the box from Hazel's hands and placed it safely in her purse.

Hazel suddenly felt like a jerk. Camille had, after all, helped out so much that afternoon. "I'm sorry. I didn't mean to come off quite so cold. I guess I'm still hurt from what happened with us. And it's weird having you back here and then trying to make a business deal without so much as an apology for what you put me through."

"I hoped we could at least be friends."

So much for the hope of an apology. Vampires weren't terribly humble creatures, though. "I suppose we can try."

There was a long pause, as neither of them seemed to know what to do to start that process.

"Do you want me to give you back those samples?" Hazel finally asked.

"No, not at all, my dear." Camille's voice was back to its usual velvety tones. "Keep them. A small repayment for the pain I've caused." She smiled at Hazel. "What did you think of the book? My friend's memoir?"

"Oh, yes, I nearly forgot. I can sell it. But no readings. I'm not allowing vampires any more contact with the public than necessary. I'm sorry, but if you want a shop that caters to vampires, you'll have to find a vampire to open one, as far as I'm concerned."

"Of course. I'll pass on the good news to my friend in any case."

Somewhat awkwardly, Hazel worked out the details of selling the vampire book at the store with Camille, and finally Camille was on her way out as the main shop door opened and the bells there rang out, announcing a new visitor.

"Hello, Hazel."

Hazel looked over and suddenly felt light-headed. Elizabeth stood in the doorway of her shop, looking simply gorgeous. The cool, brisk autumn air had put a bloom in her cheeks, and her smile lit up her face as though they were old friends. Hazel felt a thrill of anticipation as she wondered what had brought Elizabeth to the shop, but then just as quickly winced at the thought of Camille watching what was about to unfold.

❖

Elizabeth had spent the week somewhat fruitlessly trying to get access to the local archives and libraries she was hoping to use during her time in Salem, in addition to all her other professorial duties. It was astounding how different the procedures were for each archive and library. Some places practically let anyone in to peruse old manuscripts unsupervised, while others acted as though they had the Declaration of Independence drafted in Thomas Jefferson's own hand under lock and key. She had jumped through several hoops that week and was now officially registered as a reader at the local historical society and in the city archives.

Running around town getting everything set up for her research meant that other tasks had gone neglected, so she'd used Saturday to catch up on student emails, feedback, and article copyedits. By late afternoon, she was hungry, and her eyes were tired from staring at the computer. She picked up a late lunch at a local deli and decided to peruse the bookshops in town. She was a bit of a book hoarder and couldn't resist the opportunity to buy some books for work—and pleasure.

She'd saved the Witch Is In for last. To be honest, although Hazel had attracted her interest for her friendliness and beauty, Elizabeth was hesitant to go to her shop. She wasn't a fan of the kitschy side of Salem, and she was even less tolerant of New Age mumbo jumbo. Many people assumed she was interested in that type of thing due to her research interests, but it couldn't be further from the truth. As a researcher and historian, she prided herself on being logical and focusing only on what could be supported with hard evidence.

So many of the other shopkeepers and even a few of the librarians she met had spoken highly of the book selection at the Witch Is In, though, that she finally felt compelled to visit it.

The outside of the shop was neat and tidy with elegant signage that was encouraging. Inside, the shop was well lit, with displays clearly labeled, signs hanging from the ceiling directing patrons to different parts of the shop, and nothing felt cluttered or kitschy. As soon as she entered, Elizabeth felt a sense of warmth and welcoming that had been absent in her life the past week, and she realized she'd barely spoken a word that week to anyone that wasn't related to a purchase in a shop or materials in an archive. Roxy had texted her several times asking about lunch or coffee, but she'd politely refused. She simply didn't have time for socializing during the week; focus was what would keep her on the ladder to making her dreams come true.

It was with relief that she saw Hazel: a friendly face amidst all the strangers in Salem. She was thankful she'd allowed Roxy to talk her into dinner with the two of them that evening. She'd bumped into Roxy at the coffee shop while picking up her morning Americano; her rental had a French press, but she preferred espresso drinks.

"Hello, Hazel." Elizabeth smiled warmly as she approached Hazel. Another woman was standing next to Hazel, dressed in what appeared to be an honest to goodness velvet dress and cloak. Elizabeth wondered if the over-makeuped stranger was a tour guide like Roxy— perhaps one who took her vocation a bit too seriously?

Hazel, on the other hand, looked very put together in a green wool dress with a tasteful boatneck and a large chunky amber necklace. Her light brown waves surrounded her heart-shaped face. Elizabeth couldn't help noticing the big brown eyes framed with long dark lashes and alluring pink lips that appeared, at that moment, to be struggling between a smile and a grimace. Elizabeth hoped she wasn't interrupting an important conversation. Although how you could have an important conversation with someone dressed like that was questionable.

"Oh. Hello, Elizabeth." She paused and glanced at the dark-haired woman next to her who was, at that moment, staring somewhat intensely at Elizabeth. "Elizabeth, this is my…friend Camille. Camille, this is Dr. Elizabeth Cowrie, a researcher from England."

Camille put out her hand. "*Enchanté.*"

"Nice to meet you as well." Elizabeth had to work hard not to wince at the coldness of the hand proffered her.

"Please, do come in. You don't have to stand in the doorway." Hazel ushered her into the main part of the shop before turning to Camille. "You were on your way out just now, weren't you?"

"Yes, of course." Camille took her leave, shooting a final, appraising glance over at Elizabeth.

Elizabeth wasn't sure if she'd offended Camille or whether she was always that curt, but in any case, she was glad to have Hazel's undivided attention.

The shop was quiet, except for the low hum of a few other customer voices from another part of the shop. A shop assistant was puttering in one of the displays, rearranging things, as there wasn't anyone in line at the counter.

"What a lovely shop you have here." Elizabeth was standing next to a display of jewelry and crystals, and she looked them over before meeting Hazel's gaze again.

"Thank you. It's been a labor of love."

"I can see that." Elizabeth's voice was full of genuine awe. "My grandparents ran a knickknackery shop back home for ages, and I loved visiting it as a child. It seemed nearly as magical as this one."

"We do what we can to please our customers. Obviously, most people who visit Salem want a little bit of that 'local flavor.' But I do also try to stock a lot more than just knickknacks. I've got quite a few nonfiction books, maps, and historical information, too."

"So I've heard! Everyone keeps telling me what a wonderful bookshop you've got here. In fact, at the town archive, they told me that your shop had one of the best selections of authoritative histories of Salem and witchcraft in the Northeastern United States. High praise indeed."

Hazel colored a bit, and her eyes shone with pride. Elizabeth couldn't help smiling. It was clear that Hazel put all her energy into making the shop a success, and Elizabeth always admired people with passion. While others sometimes called Elizabeth a workaholic, she preferred to think of herself as dedicated and ambitious, and she couldn't understand people who didn't have that same kind of drive.

"I hope they didn't oversell it," said Hazel, still blushing with pleasure. "There are lots of historic homes and museums in town whose gift shops carry academic works and histories, too."

"Now, don't be modest, Hazel. The archivist was very encouraging."

"Scott? He's a friend and therefore a little biased, but still, that's nice to hear. I'll walk you over to the history section and you can judge for yourself."

Hazel led her through the shop, and Elizabeth took note that they passed several shelves of books on ridiculous topics like numerology, palmistry, astrology, and other pseudosciences that Elizabeth found absurd. She had a sinking feeling that this was a waste of time.

They rounded a corner and Elizabeth found herself facing an enclave with floor-to-ceiling shelves and a sign reading "History." She was stunned to realize that the first book that caught her eye was one that she'd used for her doctoral exams. All around it were other books with familiar titles and authors—and then many more she hadn't heard of. Nearly all of them were with university presses or independent presses and there wasn't a vanity press in sight.

Immediately she pulled three books off the shelves with promising titles.

"These look excellent." She felt like a kid in a candy shop as her eyes gobbled up the tables of contents before returning to the shelves and scanning for more.

Hazel laughed. "I'm glad there's something interesting for you here. Here, let me take some of those for you."

Elizabeth passed the growing stack of books to Hazel, who placed them on a small table next to a squashy leather armchair that would be perfect for sitting in as she decided which books to buy. It was already clear that it would be a monumental task to decide which ones to purchase. There were so many excellent choices. She was pleasantly surprised.

She pulled a few more books for the stack, before pausing and sighing with pleasure. She loved a good bookstore, and Hazel's unassuming shop was, apparently, a gold mine of books on Salem. The archivist wasn't kidding. Evidently, the books on magical mumbo jumbo were a misdirect.

"Looks like I'll be here the rest of the evening," said Elizabeth with a smile.

"You're welcome to stay and look as long as you need to. That's why the chair is here. I've always felt it's impossible to buy books without first sitting down and reading a little bit of them."

"I'm the same," said Elizabeth, her smile broadening. "Do you enjoy reading Salem history? Or is it all old hat by now?"

"I'm fond of the occasional history book, but I tend to read fiction for pleasure," said Hazel. "But I think it's important to stock the shop with books about Salem since obviously people who come here are interested in it."

"Of course. And I noticed a lot of shops have books about Salem, too, but none with collections this extensive."

"I enjoy ordering books for the shop almost as much as reading them." Hazel looked sheepish. "It's kind of a problem. Roxy jokes that I opened a shop just so I have an excuse to keep ordering more books."

"I have a book buying habit, and I don't have that excuse," said Elizabeth with a laugh.

A small ding from the main room of the shop let Hazel know that a customer was ready to check out. Elizabeth felt a small pang of disappointment when Hazel left; she'd been enjoying their conversation.

Soon enough she was engrossed in flipping through the books in her stack, deciding which ones to buy and, inevitably, starting to make notes for her research. She finally gave up on trying to whittle down the stack and decided to buy the lot. She made her way to the counter with five books and several pamphlets for good measure.

"Good haul?" Hazel had just finished ringing up a customer, and she smiled as Elizabeth approached with her stack of goodies.

"Yes. I haven't seen these titles elsewhere around town, and it feels like I've been just about everywhere this week."

"That sounds like a lot of running around." Hazel started to ring her up. "You've made a lot of great choices. All of these are ones that I ordered because they sounded interesting, informative, and well-researched. I wasn't sure they would sell, actually." She put the books carefully into a brown paper bag.

"Oh? Why is that?"

Hazel shrugged. "I wasn't sure there would be a market for academic histories, but Salem is just funky enough that there's a market for a lot of different kinds of books. I guess that's kind of what I like about this town."

"Well, I'm grateful for the extent of your offerings. They're going to make my life a lot easier." Elizabeth reached into her bag for her wallet, and as she did, she couldn't help but look at some of the earrings in a display that she'd noticed earlier.

"I'm glad my little shop could be of service," said Hazel. "Is there anything else? I saw you admiring those blue tourmaline earrings earlier. I think they'd really bring out your eyes."

"Oh! Was it that obvious?" Elizabeth picked up the blue stone earrings and held them up to her face. "What do you think?"

"Oh, uh, yes…Definitely. They really bring out your eyes." Hazel hemmed and hawed a bit before answering. "Sorry, I just said that." She blushed again.

"No worries. They really are lovely," said Elizabeth. "I think I'll take them."

Hazel rang them up. "Would you like to wear them out?"

"That sounds like a lovely idea. They'll be perfect for our dinner." Elizabeth's stomach was rumbling again, and she wished she was meeting Hazel and Roxy sooner at the restaurant, though she supposed Hazel had to lock up the shop first.

"Oh, you mean tonight at Luigi's?"

"Yes! That's right. My goodness, I wish we were meeting sooner. I'm starved."

A look of confusion passed over Hazel's face for a brief moment, and Elizabeth wondered if Roxy had remembered to invite her. But no, that was silly. She was certain Roxy had mentioned Hazel coming as well when she'd invited her to dinner.

"You're going to love Luigi's. It's Roxy's favorite," said Hazel finally.

"Wonderful." Elizabeth paid for everything and buttoned up her coat tight. The sun had set, and it was looking quite chilly beyond the door of the shop. "These books will be so helpful. I can't wait to dive into them."

"I'm going to throw a little sample in here of some lavender mist," said Hazel, putting the sample into the bag with everything else. "Spray a little on your pillow, and you'll have lovely sweet dreams." She smiled. "It helps with getting a good night's rest, too, which I'm sure you'll be needing with all your research."

"Cheers. That's lovely." Elizabeth was genuinely touched; she already felt more at home in Salem after her jaunt to the Witch Is In. "I'd better head off. I still have a couple more errands to run before dinner. See you soon!"

"Of course," said Hazel. "Have fun."

Elizabeth left the shop feeling warm and content. She'd found so much more at the shop than she'd expected—and not just in terms of books. Hazel was easy to talk to and just as much of a bookworm as she was. She was suddenly very glad indeed that she'd let Roxy talk her into dinner that night with the two of them.

❖

Elizabeth arrived at Luigi's just after seven, as they'd agreed. Roxy was already waiting by the bar with several wine glasses in front of her.

"Oh, it that a wine tasting?" said Elizabeth. "You must have read my mind."

"I thought we could do a tasting while we wait. I couldn't get a reservation until seven fifteen."

Given that Hazel hadn't arrived yet either, this was an excellent idea in Elizabeth's opinion. She hung her coat over the back of the barstool, set her bag of books on the floor, and sat down next to Roxy.

"I don't know much about wine, but I figured this might be a fun way to learn more," said Roxy.

"My family and I have been traveling to France for wine tastings for years, so I can play expert tonight," said Elizabeth, perusing the wine list and reading up on the wines they were tasting. Soon she found herself enjoying schooling Roxy in tannins and steel cask fermentation styles, and she found Roxy an apt and enthusiastic pupil.

Promptly at seven fifteen, they were ushered to their table, and Elizabeth had the opportunity to take in the restaurant's ambiance and décor. The place had a warm, inviting atmosphere. Roxy had already mentioned it was one of her favorite restaurants in town and that she liked to save it for a special occasion.

It was an Italian restaurant in the classic New York style: red-and-white checked tablecloths on small round tables, exposed red brick walls, accordion music on the speakers, and low lighting accented with actual candles in old bottles of Chianti on each table. The proprietor, Sal, immediately came over to their table to say hello to Roxy and introduce himself to Elizabeth. He explained he was the grandson of the original Luigi, an immigrant from Naples, and Elizabeth felt sure Sal was full of the same Old World charm she imagined his grandfather had brought with him from Italy.

Sal had reserved Roxy's favorite table for her and Elizabeth—in the corner by the front window. This table was a little isolated from the other tables, close enough to the speaker to enjoy the music but not so close that they couldn't talk comfortably.

When their server came by, Elizabeth ordered a wine for the table—a warm, deep pinot noir with notes of cherry and dark chocolate that she had particularly enjoyed at the tasting.

"And how many glasses?" asked the server, making a note of their order.

"Two," said Roxy.

"Three," said Elizabeth at the same time.

The server gave them a quizzical look.

"Two," repeated Roxy.

The server went to get the wine and some breadsticks for them. Once she was out of earshot, Elizabeth couldn't help asking after Hazel. "Is Hazel not coming after all? I just saw her at the shop, and she didn't say anything about changing plans."

Now it was Roxy's expression that turned quizzical momentarily. "Oh, uh, yeah…she texted me. Said she couldn't make it."

"That's a shame. I was really looking forward to getting to know the both of you tonight."

Before Roxy could reply, their server returned with the wine, wine glasses, and a basket of warm breadsticks. Elizabeth tasted the wine and nodded to the server to pour them both a glass. The restaurant had a surprisingly good wine list for a small-town Italian place, and the breadsticks were baked fresh from scratch. It was disappointing that Hazel couldn't join them, but perhaps next time.

The server told them the specials, and without much ado, they put in their order. The special was pasta puttanesca, Elizabeth's favorite, so there was really nothing else to do but order that and hope the restaurant's food was as good as its wine.

"You say you and your folks go to France a lot to taste wine? That sounds kind of ritzy," said Roxy, taking a big bite of breadstick and following it with a gulp of wine. "My folks are more of the 'drink a Budweiser on a lazy river' kind of vacation people."

Elizabeth winced a little as Roxy spoke with a mouth full of breadstick.

"It does sound a bit posh, doesn't it? Funny that, since my parents didn't grow up posh either. I think they would quite enjoy a lager and a lazy river."

"Oh really?"

"Definitely. My mum's parents owned a shop; my dad's dad was a car mechanic and my dad's mum was a nurse. They didn't grow up poor or anything, but they always saw themselves as working class. I think that's why money and financial success is so important to them."

"What'd they think of you becoming a professor?"

Elizabeth made a face.

"That bad?"

"Let's just say that 'history professor' was not what my dad had in mind for his only daughter. He went into business for himself and was, is, quite successful. He wanted me to go into the family business."

"Which is?"

"Car parts. He started off as a purchaser for the auto shop where my grandad was the mechanic. Eventually, he started his own company. Amazingly lucrative, apparently."

"Fascinating stuff," said Roxy with a grin.

Elizabeth grinned back. "Especially to a bookworm daughter whose idea of a good time is reading biographies of Oliver Cromwell."

"Really?"

Elizabeth nodded with a rueful smile. "It's really no surprise that I finished school with hardly any friends. I'm afraid I was a terrible bore. Anything that happened after the invention of the automobile wasn't of interest to me."

Roxy laughed. "I totally relate. My one and only friend in school was Hazel. I was the kid who couldn't stay in her seat, who cut her hair off with classroom scissors, and who routinely brought weird bugs to school. Having a pocket full of worms didn't exactly win me lots of friends."

Elizabeth had to smile at the mental image of kid Roxy, the tomboy, playing with crickets and beetles. She was enjoying the conversation immensely. Roxy was so different from the academics she spent much of her time with; she was forthright and personable and very funny—it was refreshing.

"In any case, once Dad's business was doing well, he and Mum decided they wanted to upgrade everything—their house, their cars, their vacations. I'm not even certain they liked wine, but if the Smith-Joneses are going on a wine tour of France, well, the Cowries can't be worse, can they?"

"Wow, sounds like they care a lot what people think of them."

Elizabeth rolled her eyes. "It's all they care about. At least, that's what it feels like. And having a daughter who wants to study history definitely was not on the list of things that sound impressive."

"But isn't being a professor kind of impressive?"

"You'd think. But not to their set. Professors don't make enough money to be impressive."

"I'm sorry." Roxy paused. "More wine?" She winked at Elizabeth.

"Absolutely!"

Roxy poured them each another glass.

"It's fine," continued Elizabeth. "I've gotten used to it. And they're proud of my successes so far. They won't read my book when it's published, but I'm sure they'll brag about it to their friends."

Just then their entrees arrived, and their conversation turned to the food. The pasta was delicious, and Elizabeth enjoyed every bite.

"It's really a shame Hazel couldn't join us," she said, after cleaning her plate.

"Er, yeah," said Roxy, absently playing with her earlobe. "But this is nice, isn't it? Just the two of us? Having a heart-to-heart over some great pasta?"

"Of course. It's not every day I have a tour guide all to myself."

"Very true. You're very lucky in that regard. I have to admit, though, it's easy being a tour guide in Salem. The place is full of fantastic history. It's the best job in the world being a tour guide here." Roxy's enthusiasm for her hometown was palpable.

"You really love it here, don't you? I hope I can learn to love it, too."

"I hope so. Salem is such a unique historical site, even if that history isn't all good. But I love being a part of it. I've read just about every history book there is about the witch trials and basically any other weird thing that's ever happened here. Ever since I was a kid, I wanted to lead ghost tours, so I've been literally living the dream since I got my tour license."

Elizabeth bristled inwardly at Roxy's mention of her historical knowledge; she had a feeling Roxy didn't have many academic histories on her reading list. But it wouldn't do to sound like a snob.

"What kind of people do you get on ghost tours? I've seen tours like that advertised all over places like London and York in the UK, but I've never been on one."

Their dessert arrived as Elizabeth finished her sentence, and the conversation paused as they both took a big bite of tiramisu.

"Oh, all sorts of people come on the tours," Roxy was saying, her mouth still full of lady fingers and mascarpone cheese. "Mostly it's tourists—families, groups of friends, dates. Occasionally people from a conference. My favorite, though, is when Believers show up."

"Believers?" Elizabeth was savoring the last bite of tiramisu and enjoying Roxy's storytelling; she could see how Roxy would be the perfect guide for a corny, kitschy "ghost" tour.

"Yeah, you know, people who believe in ghosts. Witches. Magic. All of it. People like me," she added with a smile.

"Do you get a lot of those?" Elizabeth was suddenly pulled out of her tiramisu-induced reverie, a note of surprise and disbelief entering her voice as she chuckled incredulously.

"Of course. Magic and ghosts and witches *are* real. At least, I've always thought so. I mean, what we see in this world can't be all there is." Roxy's voice was full of lightness and conviction; she obviously had no clue that Elizabeth found the topic ridiculous.

"Oh, I get it," she said, after a pause. "That's what you tell people on the tour. Part of your act. That's a good idea—get more tips that way, I'm sure."

"You're joking, right?" said Roxy, her tone suddenly much cooler.

"What?" Elizabeth was confused. Weren't they joking about believing in witches and magic? Roxy's expression had lost all its joking demeanor.

"I'm a Believer. I've seen ghosts and I—" She faltered for a moment before continuing, her voice growing louder. "Ghosts are real. And maybe those witch trials were fake, but there are people who can do magic."

Roxy's face flushed with indignation, and Elizabeth felt all her enjoyment of the evening ebbing away. She didn't want to get into an argument, but Roxy was nearly yelling at her at this point.

"Do you mean, like, New Age stuff? Crystals and tarot cards?"

Elizabeth was having a hard time stopping the condescension from creeping into her voice. She was hoping to be friends with Roxy, but Roxy wasn't acting very friendly.

"No, I do not mean crystals and tarot," said Roxy, her voice loud enough that patrons at nearby tables glanced over at them. "Though tarot is real, too. Don't you know Hazel does tarot readings?"

"All the shops at Salem seem to do them," said Elizabeth gently. Roxy's expression was cloudy and her eyes were flashing with a dangerous kind of glitter. "It's like your tours. You talk about ghosts and haunted houses because it sells—not because it's real."

"Sure, I give tours, but all the information on my tour is true. I've researched it all."

"That's not how research works," sputtered Elizabeth, suddenly finding herself on home turf. "Just because someone said they saw a ghost doesn't mean ghosts are real. Surely you don't—"

"I do. I believe in the supernatural. I thought because you researched it and you were writing a whole book on it, that you believe in it, too." Roxy's tone mingled disappointment and barely concealed outrage.

"Why are you getting so angry? I thought we were having a friendly conversation," said Elizabeth quietly, desperately trying not to cause a scene in the restaurant. Already she felt like everyone in the restaurant was staring at them.

"I'm not angry!" said Roxy, practically shouting. She was flushed, and she ran an agitated hand through her hair. "I'm not angry. I just don't understand why you're making such a big deal of this."

"*I'm* making a big deal of it? I think you are. And to return to your earlier statement, I am not writing a book about the supernatural. I'm writing a book on a historical topic. If you'd asked me about my book, I would have told you that it's actually about—"

Roxy interrupted. "People have believed in ghosts and magic since the dawn of time. I know people personally who have seen ghosts. I've seen them, too." She leaned back in her chair and crossed her arms, as if daring Elizabeth to contradict her.

"I think we'd better call it a night," said Elizabeth. She didn't know why Roxy was so upset, and honestly, she hardly wanted to know why. They'd been having such a nice time over dinner, and now Roxy was acting like a madwoman. This was why she didn't have any friends—everyone else was mad, apparently. Elizabeth sighed, suddenly exhausted.

"What? Wait," said Roxy, but Elizabeth was already pulling on her coat and taking out her wallet. She pulled a couple of twenties out of it and put them on the table.

"I think I'll go home now, if that's all right."

Roxy stood up as well. "No, it's not all right. We were having a perfectly reasonable conversation, and now you're running out on our date."

"Date? I thought we were having dinner as friends. With Hazel." Suddenly, understanding dawned on Elizabeth. Roxy thought they were on a date. That's why Hazel wasn't there. And that was why Hazel had been confused earlier. "Oh my God. You think we're on a date. Well, this is some way to treat a woman you're interested in."

She hadn't meant her tone of voice to come across as so cool and harsh, but now that the words were out in the air, she couldn't take them back. Roxy's face crumpled and her chin began to wobble.

"I've upset you. I'm so sorry."

She'd tried to sound as genuine as possible in her apology, but it was hard to muster sympathy after being yelled at in a restaurant. There was nothing left for Elizabeth to do but leave. As she stepped into the cold night air, she felt how hot her face had gotten during the conversation. They'd been having such a nice time. Why did Roxy have to ruin it?

Elizabeth walked quickly in the direction of her house, her frustration and irritation propelling her faster and faster. It had taken a lot of work to step outside her comfort zone and try to make friends in a new place. Normally on a research trip she'd just focus on work, but three months seemed like too long to be a hermit, so she'd gone out on a limb. Gone to dinner. A nice friendly dinner. That's all she'd wanted.

She groaned in frustration, scaring away a black cat who suddenly showed up out of an alley. *Great, now a black cat has crossed my path.* The ridiculousness of the situation pulled her out of her cloudy thoughts, and she laughed at herself and slowed down.

Maybe she'd been a bit harsh with Roxy. She hadn't meant to sound so condescending. She reminded herself that a lot of people believed in the supernatural—after all, wasn't that why the witch trials happened in the first place? People wanted to believe in something beyond the everyday. Elizabeth knew she had a tendency to be snobby and a bit rigid, and those were qualities she was trying to change about herself.

She would have to find a way to make up with Roxy, though she'd also make it clear she was doing so platonically. It hadn't crossed her mind for a second that it was meant to be a date, despite their earlier flirtation.

It had really been a shame that Hazel hadn't joined them. She was sure things wouldn't have gone so wonky so quickly if it'd been the three of them. Plus, she wanted to get to know her better after seeing the shop and her excellent book selection. Elizabeth made a mental plan to find her the next day and ask her out to coffee.

CHAPTER SIX

Hazel closed up shop around seven on Saturdays and usually did some tarot readings right after. That evening there had only been one tarot reading. She'd let Rita go home a little earlier, as traffic had slowed down considerably from the earlier part of the day. Still, it was almost eight thirty by the time she locked up and headed down to Luigi's to see how Roxy and Elizabeth's date was going.

She'd promised Roxy she would magically "check in" and lend a helping hand if anything was going askew. Honestly. How Roxy convinced her to go against her own interests was a question Hazel never had the answer to. She was so convincing.

She'd sent Beezle on ahead of her to keep an eye on things, and he had obliged her, but not before giving her a withering look, as though to say, *this* is the kind of errand you have for me, your familiar? Spying on a date?

"Don't give me that look," said Hazel, trying to appear dignified.

After he'd left, Hazel locked up and set off after him, but not before popping one of her favorite milk chocolate truffles in her mouth to soothe her nerves. She'd texted Roxy earlier that Elizabeth apparently had no idea this was a date, but Roxy was notoriously terrible at checking her phone. Hazel had a sneaking suspicion that Roxy had actually left her phone at home that evening.

As she walked to the café, she felt a buzzy, butterfly sensation with each step. She had to admit, she was excited to see Elizabeth again, even from afar. It'd been a pleasant surprise having her in the shop that evening, and their conversation had flowed so easily that it was hard not to hope she might still have a chance with the beautiful professor.

She arrived during the entrees. She popped another chocolate truffle and plopped on the bench outside the restaurant window, using her magic to make herself invisible and whispering an incantation that would allow her to eavesdrop.

Things were going so well that eventually Hazel was only half-listening. She was watching Elizabeth talking animatedly between bites of pasta. She was wearing a beautiful bright blue sweater and a matching blue-stone necklace that made her eyes, even through the windows of the restaurant, burn with blue fire. She was elegant and classy, and her eyes shone with pleasure, giving her an added luster. Hazel felt her heart speed up as she watched Elizabeth spoon dainty bits of tiramisu into her pretty pink mouth.

Suddenly, the conversation turned stormy and before Hazel even had a chance to whisper a quick incantation to make everyone feel more relaxed, she saw it was too late. When Roxy got on her high horse, there was little anyone could do to stop her. Moments later, Elizabeth was putting on her coat, and it was all over.

Beezle stepped out of the shadows, gave Hazel a disapproving look, and, tail in the air, walked off into the night.

"Don't even think about abandoning me," said Hazel to the cat. "You follow Elizabeth, make sure she gets home okay."

She could swear the cat rolled its eyes at her. She let go of the spell so that Roxy could see her waiting outside, and she didn't miss the tears Roxy was dashing away with the back of her hand.

After Roxy calmed down and paid the bill, the two of them walked over to their favorite watering hole. The evening was a chilly one; September was almost over, and October was only days away. The daytime temperatures were perfect, but as soon as the sun set, it became quite chilly. Luckily, the Scarlet Letter wasn't too far away, down a couple of blocks and around the corner from Luigi's. It was a speakeasy-style lesbian bar, and it walked a fine line in its décor between faded glamour and straight up dive bar. Despite the perpetually sticky floors and lack of functioning locks on the bathroom stalls, it was a favorite of Hazel's and Roxy's.

The bar was run was by Adele, a giant of a woman who dressed like a butch right out of the 1950s, with pompadour hair, button-down shirts, and dark wash jeans cuffed at the bottom over black work boots, and who happily claimed the title of "bull dyke."

Hazel had to admire her commitment to the look, even if she'd intimidated Hazel for a long time with her swagger and brashness. Next to her, Hazel had, as a young lesbian, felt like a fake. Now, older and wiser, she was able to admire women like Adele, and the other butches who hung out at the bar. After going to college, traveling, and making her way in the world a little, Hazel finally understood that it took a lot to be comfortable in your own skin, and these women found a way to do that all their own.

Hazel, by contrast, preferred to be more feminine and had accepted that about herself as well. And the Scarlet Letter attracted all types. The more she went there, the more variety she saw; as Salem expanded, so did the clientele of the bar. It was a wonderful space accepting of everyone, even if the floors weren't washed very often.

Hazel and Roxy slid into their favorite booth; despite it being a Saturday night, the locale was fairly empty except for some regulars at the bar and at the pool table. It would likely get busier later in the evening. Hazel was glad of the relative quiet. She wanted to distract Roxy, but she also wanted them to be able to talk without having to shout over other people's conversations.

Roxy bought the first round, and when they were finally sitting together at the table, Roxy with her Sam Adams Octoberfest and Hazel with an amaretto sour, they rehashed the whole dinner.

"I don't understand how it could have gone south so fast," Roxy finished, taking another big slug of her beer. She was still a little tipsy from the wine at dinner, and her speech was beginning to slur.

Hazel made a mental note not to let Roxy go up for more drinks if at all possible. Sad, drunk Roxy was no fun. "You did get a tad huffy in there."

"I know, I know. Why do I do that kind of thing? I'm always stepping in it."

Hazel nodded. "Agree."

"Hey, you're supposed to take my part in this." Roxy grinned to show she was kidding.

Old Hazel would have tried to help Roxy figure out how to win Elizabeth over, but tonight, Hazel was going to try something new.

"Actually, I think I kind of am. I'm your best friend, and I'm here to say: what if you and Elizabeth aren't compatible?"

"What do you mean?" Roxy looked genuinely confused. "You

should have heard us at the wine tasting. We were having a great time. You missed that part, so you don't know. We were really hitting it off."

"But she didn't think it was a date. And from what I heard, she wasn't interested in making it a date."

"Ouch. That's harsh."

"I'm just trying to save you some heartache, Roxy. Why try to hook up with yet another woman who isn't interested? There's plenty of fish in the sea."

She watched Roxy carefully; she didn't react well when she heard stuff that didn't square with her opinion. She was flushed from the beer and wine, but otherwise the pained, disappointed expression from earlier was still visible in her features. Her dimples were MIA, a sure sign she was really unhappy. Roxy ran a hand through her already tousled hair, making her look like a disgruntled schnauzer.

"I mean…In a way, I guess you're right. I don't know if I could date someone so anti-magic. You know?"

"Yeah. I know." Hazel sighed. It meant she didn't stand a chance with Elizabeth, either. If she didn't believe in Roxy's version of things, she certainly wouldn't believe in Hazel's being a witch. But still, now was as good a time as any to tell Roxy the truth about how she felt about Elizabeth.

"It's disappointing," said Roxy, staring somewhat absently into space.

"I'll say," said Hazel, taking the plunge. "Especially since I kind of like her, too." She felt her heart speed up, and a tremor of excitement passed through her just saying the words out loud. She was grateful that in the noisy bar, not even Roxy would notice.

"What?" Roxy was coming out of her reverie.

"I didn't want to say anything earlier because you were so interested in her. And I guess I thought she was really into you, too."

"Wow. I never thought it would happen, but I guess it finally did."

Hazel couldn't quite read Roxy's tone of voice. "What?"

"We're into the same girl! Ha!" Roxy's face broke into a true smile that lit up her face; it was the happiest she'd looked all evening. Hazel breathed a sigh of relief.

"Oh good, I thought you'd be mad."

"Mad? Why? I think this is hilarious. I always thought we had such different taste in women, but I guess it took a hot professor to change that."

Hazel smiled. "You're crazy. I guess that's why I love you."

"I love you, too, kid," said Roxy. She raised her nearly empty beer bottle as if to toast. "A toast! To falling for the same lady."

Hazel clinked with her glass and laughed. "It was bound to happen. We both have such good taste."

"Absolutely," said Roxy. "Great minds think a light!"

"Don't you mean 'alike'?"

"No. It's 'light.' Like…we both have the same lightbulb going off."

Hazel laughed. It was just like Roxy to remember sayings incorrectly and then have a rationale for it, too.

"Oh, crap."

"What?"

"Crap on a stick. Alicia just walked into the bar." Roxy raised her hand to her forehead, shading her face. "God, don't let her see me. She's the last person—"

Too late. Alicia was there, standing next to the table with none other than Camille. Hazel's blood pressure spiked.

Camille looked like she'd walked off the cover of a tawdry historical romance. She wore a crushed velvet and black lace dress that exposed a lot of cleavage, with a blood red cloak, and her eyes, rather than her usual violet, were much more indigo, with a dangerous, ultraviolet glow. Hazel couldn't help rolling her eyes; it was like Camille *wanted* everyone to know she was a vampire.

"Fancy meeting the two of you here," she murmured, studying Hazel with those seductive eyes.

Hazel bit back a nasty reply. What on earth was Camille doing here with Roxy's ex-something or other. Ex-fuck buddy? Whatever.

"We could say the same of you," she said after a beat, realizing that Roxy was absolutely dumbfounded. It was apparently too much in one night to deal with: a terrible non-date and a run-in with a woman she'd ghosted.

"Roxy. I can't believe you're here. I thought you'd fallen off the edge of the planet." Alicia looked genuinely concerned, and Hazel wondered if she'd misjudged her interest in Roxy.

She was Roxy's usual type: dramatic eye makeup, pouty lips, fake nails, lots of cleavage, ripped-up jeans, and self-esteem issues she wore like a neon sign. Still, maybe Hazel was too quick to judge.

"Just been busy," said Roxy, who was clearly trying to gather her thoughts. She gave Alicia a sad smile. "I've moved on to greener pastures. And I see you have, too." Despite her bravado, the last sentence came out sadder than Roxy had probably intended it. Seeing Alicia on Camille's arm was unpleasant. Like a lamb off to the slaughter. And the worst thing was that Roxy and Hazel couldn't even warn Alicia—she would think they were just making fun of her if they told her Camille was an honest-to-goodness vampire.

"Just off to have some fun. Camille is taking me barhopping tonight." Her voice wavered a little, and Hazel got the distinct impression that Alicia wished she was barhopping with Roxy, not Camille.

Camille laughed. Several other women checked her out; she always knew how to make herself an object of admiration.

"Come on, Alicia. You're boring them." Camille pulled Alicia away and sat them down at a booth on the other side of the bar where they couldn't be seen by Roxy and Hazel.

"That was annoying," said Hazel, finishing her drink and wishing very much she'd insisted on a double.

"For real." Roxy groaned again. "Did I make a mistake? Should I have stuck with Alicia and just given her the love potion?"

"Don't be silly. Didn't you say yourself that she wasn't serious about you? Anyone who knows how wonderful you are wouldn't be ghosting you all the time."

"Thanks, Hazel." Roxy paused, lost in thought momentarily. She was thinking so hard, Hazel could see the gears turning in her head. After a moment, she perked up. "Okay. I think we need a plan."

"A plan?"

"Yes. Of course. I know what we have to do." Roxy had recovered from her encounter with Alicia—even as Hazel was still wondering what Camille was up to. It wasn't like her to date mere mortals. She found them boring and predictable: her words, not Hazel's. Was this just another way of trying to stick it to her? But why? It didn't make sense. Was Camille really so upset that Hazel didn't want to be friends?

"What was that?"

"Are you even paying attention?"

"Sorry. Camille distracted me."

"Forget her. Let's focus on the now." Roxy paused for drama. "We have to convince Elizabeth that magic is real." She looked triumphantly at Hazel with a gleam of mischief in her eye.

"Um, what exactly did you have in mind?" said Hazel cautiously.

Roxy was her best friend and partner in crime, but Hazel was well aware that she was also infamous for many a harebrained scheme. Roxy had been the kid at school who sold other kids sticks of gum in an early get-rich-quick scheme; as a teen, Roxy had dabbled in shoplifting and joyriding in her dad's old Chevy while he was away on business trips; and she'd gotten Hazel in trouble for skipping school by convincing her that it was okay to skip as long as they did something educational. But of course they never made it to the Museum of Science in Boston, as the truck blew a tire on the highway, and they had to call their parents from a nearby police station to pick them up. Of course, now they could laugh about that kind of thing—high school hijinks made great memories—but adult Hazel knew that messing with people's sense of reality was a step too far.

She had her first real dose of that when she'd tried to help a roommate in college find love. She had already begun dabbling in love potions, and when her roommate's boyfriend dumped her, she secretly added some of the love potion to his favorite energy drink.

He became obsessed with the roommate, refusing to leave her alone even for a moment, until finally she had to get a restraining order. Hazel confessed it all to her mother, who whipped up an antidote—but not before giving her the longest, most serious lecture of her life, as if it hadn't been bad enough to see the torment her roommate had gone through.

Of course, since then she'd honed her arts, and she'd promised her mother—and herself—that she would never use a potion on someone without their knowledge. She'd also improved the recipe to make the effects milder and only truly noticeable when there was already an existing bond.

She had found, too, that while many people *wished* for magic to be real, they didn't actually *want* it to be so. Her potions clientele was small and select, and even among those, Hazel felt certain that very few of them were interested in knowing how far her magic could go. If they knew she really could read the future with her tarot cards or listen in on conversations when she wasn't in the room, she was convinced they would be scared of her.

She had a strong feeling that *forcing* Elizabeth to confront the supernatural was not a good idea.

"Come on, Hazel." Roxy interrupted her thoughts, setting down another drink in front of her. She'd zoned out and hadn't noticed that Roxy had gone back to the bar. "Think. What would convince Elizabeth that magic is real?"

"If she doesn't like the idea of magic being real, then that's not the right approach."

"Of course it is." Roxy went blithely on, the beer doing most of the talking at this point. "Think about it. She thinks I was being unreasonable because she doesn't think magic or the supernatural are real. But this stuff *is* real. She has to respect that. Plus, wouldn't it be the biggest scoop for her book?"

"I don't think that's the kind of thing that gets you tenure."

"Okay, forget that angle. But don't forget that if either of us is going to have a chance with her, a *real* chance, she has to accept that magic *is* real."

Roxy's voice was getting louder and louder as she went along, and Hazel saw some of the bar patrons nearby staring at them, evidently annoyed. If anyone could make a spectacle of herself twice in one night, it was Roxy. "Shhh, don't say that so loudly!"

"Oh yeah, sorry."

"But you have a point. Except that trying to convince someone that magic is real is…dangerous. It could go wrong in so many ways."

"Come on, Hazel. Lighten up." Roxy paused and stroked her chin as if deep in thought. "How about a séance? You could channel a friendly ghost."

"Really, Roxy. That would be too much. She'd either go insane from the blow to her sense of reality or she'd accuse me of being a total fraud."

"Point taken." Roxy took another swig of her beer and wiped her mouth with the back of her hand. It was about time to take Roxy home and put her to bed before she did anything stupid.

As if the bartender had read her mind, the music suddenly got a lot louder and the lights became even dimmer as the DJ took the booth, replacing the 90s grunge rock with more upbeat electronica.

"Let's go," shouted Hazel over the music, and the two of them grabbed their coats and made their way to the exit. Hazel couldn't resist a glance in the direction of Camille and Alicia's table, but her view of them was blocked by women on their way to the bar's makeshift dance floor.

The night air felt pleasant on Hazel's face; the air was cool, but not cold. The humidity had risen, and they were probably due for some rain. But not for several hours, as the sky was still a deep, dark violet color, smudged with gray clouds and dotted faintly with stars.

As they walked in the direction of their homes, Roxy again brought up how to show Elizabeth that magic was real.

She suggested all sorts of possibilities, all of which Hazel negated, citing their impracticability, illegality, or cruelty: showing Colin off to Elizabeth, having Beezle talk to Elizabeth with a human voice, turning Elizabeth's pen into a snake and back, having them fly on a broom together, and on and on. Walking side by side, Roxy couldn't see Hazel rolling her eyes, and that was a good thing.

They got to Roxy's apartment first, and suddenly Hazel remembered she still had Elizabeth's purchases in her bag. She'd forgotten they were in there because her bag was enchanted and could fit much more stuff than it appeared to. Elizabeth had left the books when she huffed out of the restaurant.

"Roxy, this is perfect," she said, pulling the books out of her purse. "You have an excuse to go find her tomorrow. You can give these back to her and apologize."

Roxy had sobered up on the walk home, and her expression now was rather dubious. She ran her pale hands through her curls, an expression of doubt painted across her elfish features.

"I don't know…I'm probably the last person she wants to see. Why don't you do it? I mean, you sold them to her. She probably admires your taste in books if she bought so many."

"True," said Hazel. "Are you sure? We could do it together if you like."

Roxy looked sheepish. "I don't deserve a friend like you. You're too good for me." She gave Hazel a quick hug.

"What was that for?"

"Because you're my oldest and wisest friend. And you deserve a shot with Elizabeth. I had my shot tonight, and I blew it. Clearly. So now you should have your shot."

"Are you sure?"

"Absolutely. And this is the perfect way for you to smooth things over with Elizabeth. You've got an excuse to go see her. I will definitely apologize to her at some point, too. But she should get her books back sooner than that."

"Okay. I'll try to catch her at the café tomorrow morning. It opens at half past eight on Sundays, so maybe I have a chance of bumping into her before the Halloween festival board meeting."

"Thanks, Haze. You're the best." Roxy gave Hazel a friendly punch on the shoulder. "And don't give them back before the beautiful professor agrees to a date!"

With that, they parted ways. Hazel shook her head with mild disbelief as she headed home. After all this time, Roxy was still capable of surprising her.

The night was beautiful, with the moon glowing brightly behind a few clouds. Hazel walked the familiar sidewalks to her home and enjoyed the night air. Beezle joined her as she turned the final corner to the house, and his contented demeanor suggested that all was well with Elizabeth. Hazel was grateful for that. She was also glad to have an excuse to see Elizabeth the next day. Only another nine hours or so until she could catch her on the way to the coffee shop for her ritual Americano.

Hazel felt a flutter in her stomach just thinking about seeing her again, and soon her brain was going into overdrive. What should she wear tomorrow? What kind of date should she suggest? Would Elizabeth even be interested? She hoped so. Ever since she'd seen her in the coffee shop on the night of her arrival, Hazel had felt a strong attraction, and she hoped she'd have the opportunity to get to know Elizabeth better. With Elizabeth's stay in Salem being tied to her research, Hazel knew that time was ticking.

CHAPTER SEVEN

The next morning, Elizabeth felt exceedingly silly for having walked out on dinner with Roxy. Well, maybe "walked out" was too strong a term, but regardless, it had been quite rude of her, and she couldn't abide rudeness.

On top of everything else, she'd left her bag of books at the restaurant. She'd called Luigi's when she got home, but the manager told her that the bag wasn't at the table any longer. She hoped that meant that Roxy had taken it with her.

She texted her the next morning, but by the time she was leaving the house at a quarter to nine, she still hadn't heard back. She supposed Roxy was probably sleeping; most people liked a lie-in on a Sunday morning.

She, however, wasn't most people.

As she strode with purpose toward the café, she made a mental list of all the things she needed to do that day. She preferred to work in public places like cafés or libraries, as she always found working at home too distracting, so she was looking forward to a day of work at the café.

She needed to make a plan for her archival work that week, now that she had the catalog lists and her reader registrations. But she also had to read an MA thesis chapter for a student who needed feedback. And out of the blue two other students had asked her for letters of recommendation that needed to be done ASAP. She groaned inwardly; she enjoyed writing such letters for deserving students, but she found it incredibly frustrating when these requests were made less than two weeks before the deadline.

It was a lot to try to get done in one day, but if she started work at nine in the morning, then there was hope she'd be done by four. That way she'd have time to go for a jog while it was still somewhat light out. It didn't solve the question of what she'd be having for dinner, but she could always order some takeout.

As she entered the café, it was with pleasure that she recognized Hazel making chitchat at the counter with the proprietor.

There was something different about Hazel that morning that caught Elizabeth's eye. She was wearing a very pretty ankle-length red skirt with a black turtleneck and a denim jacket. The effect was very chic—especially with her hair swept up away from her face. That was it—until then she'd only seen her with her hair down. Today's hairstyle brought out her beautiful hazel-colored eyes. Elizabeth wondered how she hadn't noticed them before, they were so striking.

"Hello. It's so nice to see you," she said, with genuine pleasure. "I was really sorry you couldn't make it last night."

"Oh, yes. Yes. I was sorry, too." Hazel's expression was guarded, so Elizabeth decided to put her at ease.

"Has Roxy already told you that things ended a bit abruptly?"

Hazel nodded. "Yes, she, uh, called me right away. And then debriefed me at the Scarlet Letter."

"Oh dear. I must have come off quite badly in the retelling of the evening."

Elizabeth noticed the proprietor, Joanna, giving them a curious look as if listening in on their conversation, so she suggested that they sit down and chat more at a table. Elizabeth ordered her giant Americano with extra espresso shots and a splash of steamed almond milk and then followed Hazel to a table in the far corner of the café.

"Hey, so, uh, you left your books yesterday," said Hazel, pulling the tote out of her purse and handing it to Elizabeth.

"Cheers. I called the restaurant yesterday, but they said the bag was gone. I was hoping Roxy picked it up."

"I want you to know—"

"I don't know what Roxy's told you, but—"

They paused, and Hazel giggled a little. Elizabeth couldn't help smiling, too. They were as awkward as teenagers.

They sat there waiting for each of them to start, until finally Hazel gestured that Elizabeth should speak.

"I'm sorry. I feel so awful. I left in a huff. I was rude. I can't believe I overreacted like that."

"No, it's okay. Roxy can be very intense sometimes, especially when it comes to Salem and all things witchy." She paused. "At the bar last night she admitted she'd let herself get wound up. She was really sorry and asked me to pass on her apologies."

"I texted her this morning about the books and apologized as well. I felt like she was being so unreasonable yesterday when I left the restaurant. Then I got halfway home, and I realized what an arse I'd been."

Hazel smiled. "Don't beat yourself up. I'm sure it was a misunderstanding. You should have seen how upset Roxy was about it. She blamed herself."

One of the waitstaff came over to the table just then and set down the coffee in front of Elizabeth.

"Mmmm, the coffee here really is wonderful," said Elizabeth. "I could almost believe in magic when I drink it."

"I'm glad you like it. This is one of my favorite places in Salem."

"We have so many chain coffee shops in England now that I rarely go anywhere that's independently owned. This is somehow nicer, though. I like the idea of supporting a small business."

"That is music to my ears," said Hazel, sipping on her mocha. She checked her watch. "Oh shoot. I have to get over to the Halloween festival meeting in just a few minutes."

"Oh, that's a shame. Here I thought you'd help me procrastinate a bit longer." Elizabeth smiled at Hazel. In just the few minutes they'd been chatting, she'd completely forgotten about her long to-do list. What was happening to her?

"And I would've loved that," said Hazel, gathering up her things. She looked just as disappointed as Elizabeth felt. "What are you doing this afternoon? I was going to say we could get coffee, but it looks like you might not need more. We could go for a short hike near here if you prefer. I need to do some foraging, and I could do with the company. My assistant will be closing up tonight, so I'm done at four. Would you like to join me?" She smiled encouragingly at Elizabeth, who, after a moment, smiled back as well.

"Yes, that would be lovely. And now I have some motivation to get work done by then so I can join you." Instead of going on a run, she could just as easily do a hike with Hazel, after all.

"Great. It's a date. Stop by the shop at four, and we'll leave from there."

Hazel left for her meeting, and Elizabeth turned, somewhat reluctantly now, to her work. She suddenly had no desire to sit in front of the computer all day, but she comforted herself with the knowledge that the sooner she got in the zone, the faster time would pass, and the sooner it would be time to meet up with Hazel.

❖

Promptly at four, Elizabeth showed up at the Witch Is In dressed in a new outfit—one more appropriate to traipsing around the woods than what she'd been wearing at the café. She'd traded in her work clothes for dark navy hiking pants, a button-down sky blue shirt with an SPF filter, and a light, water-resistant jacket in the same navy color as the pants. She even put on hiking boots, just in case it was muddy.

She loved walking the hills of the South Downs when visiting her family in Sussex and, in general, she enjoyed hiking in her limited spare time. Her current job was close to the Peak District, but she never seemed to have time during the academic year for hiking there. She was delighted, therefore, that barely a week into her stay in the US, she had the opportunity to wear her hiking clothes.

Hazel had changed from a skirt to jeans, but otherwise, she was dressed the same as earlier.

"I'm afraid I may have oversold where we're going," she said as they walked to her car. "The trail there is very well-maintained and there won't be any strenuous hiking."

"That's all right. I like to be prepared."

She unlocked the passenger side door, and the two of them hopped into Hazel's well-loved little compact car, which she jokingly called "Cara Mia," in honor of the Italian classes she'd taken in college.

"That's adorable," said Elizabeth, enjoying seeing the jokier side of Hazel.

They drove out of town, and ten minutes later, Hazel pulled into a small parking lot next to the trailhead. Daylight savings was still in effect, so they had a fair bit of light, and they walked together down the broad trail into a hardwood forest with Hazel stopping every so often to pick some necessary herbs, roots, and flowers.

The discussion in the car had been light, following Hazel's reveal of her car's nickname, and they focused on study abroad, travel, and student days. Elizabeth was delighted to realize how easy it was to talk to Hazel.

Now on the trail, though, their conversation turned back to Roxy and the disastrous dinner.

"I feel like such a massive arsehole. I've never walked out on someone like that. How pedestrian."

"Roxy doesn't make it easy sometimes. She can let her emotions get away from her." Hazel stepped off the trail for a moment to collect some plants. She placed them carefully into a small bag and laid it gingerly in her basket before returning to Elizabeth. "Is there a reason why the conversation bothered you so much? I mean, aside from Roxy's overreacting?"

Elizabeth considered the question. Why *did* she react the way she had?

"I suppose it has to do with my research," she said slowly. "When I was doing my doctoral degree, I got a lot of shit for the topic. From male graduate students. From male professors. History is still a boys' club."

"That sucks. I'm sorry."

"Some of my fellow graduate students thought it would be funny to try to scare me. They started leaving little notes and twigs and things around the building—just like horror movies. You know the drill: twigs tied up with twine to look like hanged men and things? I knew it was just them being awful, but it still got to me." She shuddered visibly with the memory.

Hazel was familiar with that kind of bullying. She'd had her own share growing up. "How awful. Those little shits. And let me guess—no one ever got punished?"

Elizabeth laughed ruefully. "Of course not. When I complained to my supervisor, he said it was 'good fun,' and I was taking things too seriously. I believe his actual words were 'don't be so uptight.'"

Hazel's jaw dropped. "He didn't. What a dick. Sorry. I mean—"

"Don't be. He *is* a dick. He also happens to be one of the most important historians of North American history. Or he was until he retired last year." She sighed and shrugged. "It's fine. It's all in the past. I shouldn't let it get to me, but I guess it still does."

"What got you interested in the witch trials?"

"The women, really. The role of women in them, both as victims and as accusers. I took a fantastic course on women and witchcraft at uni, and the ways that magic and the supernatural have often been associated with women were fascinating to me. It made me so angry that it had been used against women, as a way of controlling them, silencing them. I wanted to learn more about it."

"It is a fascinating history, but a painful one. There are a lot of witch hunts in history, though. Why Salem?"

Elizabeth cleared her throat before answering. "It's a bit embarrassing really. My father, in his obsessive desire to be better than everyone, took up genealogy some years ago. He was convinced there was a lapsed earldom in our past. Turns out, there are no earls, but there were some witch hunters."

Hazel stopped in her tracks. "Really? As in, from the Salem witch trials?" She looked questioningly at Elizabeth, who nodded. "Wow. I guess we have that in common, then." Hazel smiled at Elizabeth.

"What?"

"Just about any of us who had ancestors living here at that time are related to people who accused others of being witches. Or they were complicit in the trials. Or they were accused. Or all three."

Elizabeth sighed. "I suppose that does make me feel a bit better. I have to admit, I think a part of me wanted to write a book on the topic in some desperate attempt to exonerate my family's role in the whole thing."

Hazel nodded. "That makes sense."

"It's another reason why the whole magic question is distasteful to me. I have to stay rational about the whole thing given how my family is all mixed up in it."

"That's interesting. I'd have thought the opposite—that having ancestors who were there might make you more of a believer."

"Oh no," said Elizabeth forcefully. "If it ever got out to my colleagues, I'd never hear the end of it."

"I suppose that makes sense."

"I had an aunt who was into crystals and all that New Age stuff. She'd always be on about chakras and auras, and no one took her seriously. She was always 'loony Aunt Laura.' I wouldn't want to be 'Dr. Loony.'"

They both chuckled at that before falling into a thoughtful silence for several minutes. Elizabeth admired the beautiful trees and shrubs whose leaves were still sporting shades of yellow and orange that brightened up the otherwise gloomy woods while Hazel gathered some more herbs. Soon her basket was full of little bundles and baggies, and she declared they could turn back.

"How's your research going?" she asked, breaking the silence.

Elizabeth heaved a sigh. "Slow. I haven't found anything very useful so far. I know I've only just gotten here, and I've barely had time to sit in the archives, but I'm having a difficult time locating anything that might really help my book project."

"Archival work sounds frustrating."

"It's the nature of the thing," said Elizabeth with a shrug as they arrived back in the parking lot, and Hazel stowed her goodies in the trunk of Cara Mia.

"Should we get some dinner? Roxy might be home from work by now, and I can invite her over. I've got everything at home for a perfect pasta dinner. What do you say?"

Elizabeth hesitated for a moment. She'd enjoyed their chat in the woods, and a part of her really didn't want their twosome to become a threesome.

"You're not going to go home and work more today, are you?"

"I could easily spend the rest of the night working. I'm so dreadfully behind on everything." Oh God, I sound like such a bore, thought Elizabeth.

"All the more reason not to work at all." Hazel grinned conspiratorially. "Come on. It'll be fun. And I know Roxy will be relieved to know you're not angry."

Elizabeth relented, and Hazel texted the good news to Roxy.

"Looks like she's just gotten home from her river tour," said Hazel, checking her phone once they were in the car. "She's going to wash up and head over as soon as she's ready."

The conversation on the drive back to the house was cheerful and upbeat. They discussed favorite Italian dishes and the intricacies of making one's own pasta and sauces, and they were excited to find that they were both foodies.

For a moment on the drive home, Elizabeth imagined that she and Hazel were going to have dinner alone together. They would eat Hazel's delicious, homemade vodka sauce with gnocchi, sip some of her favorite Pinot Grigio, and continue their conversation about witch trials, Salem history, her research project. They had so much to talk about, and it all came so easily. She was flattered that Hazel had taken the time to ask her about her research; not many people did.

But there was no point in thinking "what if," since Roxy was already invited over. Elizabeth tried to remind herself that it would be good to have the opportunity to apologize to Roxy in person, and to get to know both of her new friends better.

By the time they got back to Hazel's house, the lights were on, and it was evident that Roxy had beaten them to the house. A large black cat was sitting on the porch, his tail flailing wildly, and Elizabeth briefly wondered if this was the same cat that'd crossed her path the night before.

"Wow. Your house is beautiful. It's right out of a fairy story." Elizabeth was struck by the beautiful Victorian mansion, painted tastefully in sage green, with cream and maroon detailing. There was even a turret, and she was curious what it looked like from the inside. She hoped very much Hazel would give her a tour of what was obviously a very well-maintained historical home.

"Thank you. It's been in my family since the nineteenth century, but it'd fallen into disrepair. My grandparents weren't very handy, so it was falling apart by the time my parents married and moved in. They updated it, restored it, and then my mother signed it over to me when my father died."

"Oh, I'm so sorry."

"Don't be. It's been several years now. I'm glad to have the house. It's full of wonderful memories."

They entered through the main door so Elizabeth could get the full sense of the house, and the cat followed them in, winding his warm little body around Hazel's ankles before plopping lazily on the entryway rug.

Elizabeth wasn't usually a cat person, but this cat seemed to like her. He let her rub his belly and purred loudly.

"Awww, Beezle likes you," said Hazel, crouching down next to Elizabeth and petting the cat as well. She was close enough to Elizabeth that she could smell her perfume: something warm with notes of vanilla and cinnamon. It reminded Elizabeth of a bakery in her hometown and the Chelsea buns she would buy there with her allowance. Her stomach growled at the thought.

"Guess you're hungry, huh?" said Hazel, standing up. "Follow me to the kitchen."

As they walked through the house, Hazel gave Elizabeth the tour. The entryway was all aged walnut her father had worked diligently to restore. Off the entryway to the left was the front parlor, Hazel's mother's favorite parlor, which she'd decorated the way she imagined a parlor would have looked like in Jane Austen's time. Light blue and cream predominated, with many leather-bound books on custom, built-in bookshelves, a window seat, and many vintage pieces of furniture that her parents had upholstered together in peach, dainty yellow, and pastel green colors.

There was a functioning fireplace there as well, though Hazel explained that she never used it for fear of trampling ash into the perfect blue and white Louis XIV style rug. It was a room that was more of a set piece, but Hazel did occasionally use it for charity events and tea parties she would host for the chamber of commerce and the society of women small business owners. Elizabeth was impressed with the attention to detail, the beauty of the renovations, their historical accuracy, and especially with the nod to Jane Austen—one of her own favorite authors.

She found herself wishing she could meet Hazel's parents. They sounded like extraordinary people.

To the right was the formal dining room, done in a turn-of-the-twentieth-century style and inspired by the Tiffany glass that was Hazel's father's favorite. There were Tiffany lamps above a geometric dining table and an area rug in a geometric pattern as well. The large windows in that room also had stained glass in them that painted the cream-colored walls with a kaleidoscope of diffused colors. The effect at sunset was especially marvelous.

"I'm in awe, Hazel. Really, I am. Your parents have lovely taste; everything is beautiful."

"Yoo-hoo!" came a voice from the back of the house. "Is that you?"

They walked through the dining room and a butler's pantry and into a beautiful, modern kitchen—the only part of the house Hazel had changed when she moved in. Her parents had waited to renovate the kitchen, but never got around to it. Hazel loved to cook and had used part of her inheritance when her grandmother died to put in a real chef's kitchen. It was light and bright, with white tile and yellow paint, butcher block countertops, and a large island in the center with copper pots and pans hanging over it. At the large, six-burner gas stove, Roxy already had a pot of water set for the pasta.

"Hey, I can boil water," she said. "Just don't trust me with anything else. Unless it can be microwaved."

Elizabeth could tell that Roxy had done her best to clean up. She was wearing fitted dark jeans, Docs, and a crisp black button-down shirt with the sleeves rolled up—an outfit similar to the one from the night before. Her curls were shiny and glossy from a recent shower, and she was flushed with excitement.

Hazel excused herself to go put her herbs and mushrooms away in the pantry. Elizabeth sensed that now was the moment to clear the air with Roxy.

"I'm so sorry about last night. I shouldn't have walked out like that. And I shouldn't have judged you for your beliefs. That was rude of me."

Roxy smiled, her dimples huge. "Gee, when you put it that way, it sounds pretty bad."

Elizabeth grinned in return. "I mean it. I overreacted. I'm so sorry."

"I'm sorry, too. I don't know what made me get so defensive. I guess I do that a lot, according to Hazel." It was Roxy's turn to sound a bit sheepish.

"I left in such a rush yesterday—"

"That you forgot your books."

"I was going to say, I left in such a rush, that I didn't even get around to asking you if you'd ever done research at the Historical Society or the local archives for your tours. I could really use a friend with some local knowledge." Elizabeth tried, ever so slightly, to emphasize the word *friend*. A look of understanding crossed Roxy's face.

"Oh yeah, I gotcha. Yeah, I'm happy to be a friendly helper but you're barking up the wrong tree. I've never done any research in those places—though I guess maybe I should, huh? But you know, Hazel and

I were just talking about maybe helping you out. We could help you look through materials, right?"

"We could help do what now?" Hazel had returned from the pantry with arms full of ingredients for their meal.

"I was just suggesting that we could help Elizabeth with her research. You never know. Three sets of eyes have got to be better than one," said Roxy enthusiastically. "Plus, I've never been in an archive. This will be neat."

Elizabeth was warming to the idea. It would take some preparation, but in the long run, it might be the best way to get through the stacks and stacks of materials she needed to look at if she had a shot at finding anything new or interesting for her book.

"It'll be nice to have some company, that's for certain," she said. She turned to Hazel. "It can get a little lonely in smaller regional archives like these where there aren't lots of other researchers around."

"We'd love to help," said Hazel, and Elizabeth found herself excited all over again to get back to her research—and not just because she was a huge archive nerd.

The water was boiling, and all three of them set to putting together the meal. They enjoyed a delicious dinner together, and Elizabeth soaked up the easy banter between the two friends. She felt relaxed in their company, though she found herself looking more often at Hazel than Roxy. There was something about her that commanded her attention. Was it the cute curl that had escaped her hair clip? Was it her delicious vodka sauce, the equal of which Elizabeth had never had? Or was it something else, something less tangible, something Elizabeth couldn't quite identify?

It was with a jolt of disappointment that Elizabeth looked at her watch and realized it was after nine. She hadn't finished the two letters of recommendation, and she had a full week of work planned, so there really was no way she could put off going home.

Roxy volunteered to walk her home. Before they left, however, they made plans to go apple picking the following weekend—a required autumn activity, according to Roxy. They also discussed possibly helping her with some of her research the following week. They were eager to start right away, but Elizabeth explained that she would need another week to really know what exactly she needed help with.

Now that they'd established the parameters of their friendship, Elizabeth enjoyed the walk home with Roxy. In fact, she was somewhat relieved she didn't have to figure out how to get from Hazel's house to her own in the dark. A brisk wind had picked up, sending showers of leaves down from the trees and careening across the streets. The moon was covered in clouds, making everything darker and more ominous. Their conversation, though, in which Roxy regaled her with some funny incidents from the kayaking tour she'd given that afternoon, kept her entertained until they said good-bye on the sidewalk in front of her rental.

Inside, Elizabeth started her nightly routine to get everything ready for the next day's work, but she found herself distracted with thoughts of Hazel. They'd had such a lovely time in the woods, and then back at the house. She found herself wondering if maybe the two of them could grab dinner together that week. Maybe even the next day? She wanted to know more about Hazel's upbringing in that gorgeous house, what made her vodka sauce so perfect, and how on earth she'd had the time to remodel her kitchen while running her own business. More than anything else, though, she kept returning to the image of Hazel in her mind, sitting at the kitchen table, holding a glass of wine, and smiling over the table at her with a twinkle in her eye as Roxy held forth on something or other. Elizabeth hadn't been paying attention to Roxy at that moment; she'd had eyes only for Hazel.

Chapter Eight

The shop wasn't usually open on Mondays or Tuesdays, but Roxy knew that Hazel used Monday mornings to check the accounts, go to the bank, and take care of other business, working in the office at the back of the shop. Roxy used Mondays to clean her boats and gear, but by lunchtime she was at the shop, rapping on the front door and holding bags full of bagels and schmear, as well as a coffee carrier with two large coffees.

"Ooooh, perfect timing," said Hazel.

Roxy spread everything out on the table as Hazel saved and minimized the spreadsheets she was working on and heaved a big sigh. Roxy wondered why she couldn't enchant the spreadsheets to balance themselves. That would make things a whole lot easier.

The two of them sat down at the table and dug in. Roxy had worked up quite the appetite herself, so she polished off an entire bagel and half her coffee before launching into her pitch. She'd been thinking about things a lot in the last twenty-four hours, and she felt sure she had a great idea.

"We have to get Elizabeth to believe in magic. It's the elephant in the tomb."

Hazel looked at her. "What did you say?"

"I said we can't avoid the topic. Of magic."

"No, I meant after that. Did you say, 'the elephant in the tomb'? As in *tomb*—like a burial place?"

Roxy was confused. "Yeah. So? Don't you know that saying? It's when there's a topic everyone knows about, but no one wants to acknowledge it."

Hazel laughed. "Cripes, Roxy. I know the saying, but you aren't saying it right. It's not 'the elephant in the tomb.' It's *room*—the elephant in the *room*." She was nearly shaking with laugher by the time she got to the end of the sentence.

Roxy looked at her in disbelief, even as a smile curled around her lips. "No. That's crazy. 'Elephant in the *room*'?" She began to laugh along with Hazel, and her laughter encouraged Hazel, until finally they were both laughing so hard they were crying. "Crap. I've been saying it wrong for years."

Hazel laughed so hard she wasn't even making any sound. "Oh my goodness. I needed that. Thank you, Roxy."

"Anytime," said Roxy, wiping tears away. She was glad she could make Hazel laugh; it was important for Hazel to be in a good mood so she would go along with Roxy's plan. "Anyway, I think I've figured out a great way to help Elizabeth with her research *and* show her some magic without completely freaking her out."

"I don't know, Roxy." Hazel's expression betrayed suspicion as she crossed her arms over her chest. Roxy loved her, but sometimes she was such a rule follower. Roxy always felt that rules were there to be broken—or at least bent a little.

"C'mon. Let me tell you, and then *you* can decide whether to help me or hurt me. It'll be your 'Sophie's choice.'"

"I don't think that means what you think it means."

"Whatever. Look: if you're going to have a shot with Elizabeth, like, for realsies, then you've got to make her into a believer. It'll be a lot easier for her to fall in love with a witch if she's open to magic and the supernatural."

"Wait, wait, wait. Whoa. Who said anything about love?" Hazel's eyes narrowed and she stared at her intently. "There's something you're not telling me."

"What do you mean?" Roxy felt her face get warm. She'd hoped Hazel wouldn't ask too many questions, but as usual, Hazel knew when she was trying to hide something. She rolled her eyes when Hazel continued to look at her pointedly.

"Well…" Roxy couldn't meet her gaze just then. She looked at the floor instead. She sighed. It was better to admit the truth. She could never hide anything from Hazel anyway. "Here's the thing. And don't judge me. Saturday night, I went back to the Scarlet Letter. And I kind of maybe sort of hooked up with Alicia."

"What? I thought you were done with her. I'm so confused."

Roxy wrinkled up her nose and shrugged. "You know me…I hate rejection. I felt so awful after that dinner with Elizabeth, and then you said *you* liked her, and I figured you'd probably have a lot more in common, so then it just seemed like the best thing to do would be to get Alicia out of Camille's clutches—"

"And into your bed?"

"Guilty as charged."

"Oh, Roxy," said Hazel, shaking her head in disbelief. "You're incorrigible. Was it worth it?"

"Oh, absolutely." Roxy wiggled her eyebrows. Her mind flashed back to the R-rated part of Saturday night, when she brought Alicia back to her apartment after wrestling her away from Camille. Well, the wrestling at the club was only figurative; Camille hadn't tried very hard to keep Alicia interested.

"Don't be lewd."

"Speaking of lewd…" Roxy gave Hazel a knowing look.

"What?"

"Based on last night, I'm pretty sure a certain professor is interested in you, too."

"Really? You think?"

"Are you kidding? Only a corpse wouldn't laugh at my pigeon-on-the-ghost-tour story, but Elizabeth completely missed the punchline. Because she was staring all googly-eyed at you." Roxy enjoyed being the center of attention, so when both her crush and her best friend barely spoke a word that wasn't to each other, she knew that something was going on. And it didn't include her.

Was she disappointed? Of course. The sexy professor was, well, sexy. She was nearly as tall as Roxy, which didn't happen too often, with a killer figure and hot accent. On the other hand, she wasn't into magic or ghost tours, and she spent most of her time inside dusty libraries. Maybe it was true you had to have stuff in common in order to be soul mates. But for Hazel? This was just the ticket to get her out of her dating funk. It was natural to mourn a relationship, but in Roxy's opinion, it was time to get back out there. And what better way than to have a short-term fling with a hot blonde?

Plus, she got the benefit of feeling like she was taking the high road and stepping out of the way of her romance. It helped that the late-night rendezvous with Alicia had been super hot, and they were texting now more than ever before.

"Are you sure?"

"Absolutely. The two of you were making eyes at one another while I was basically keeping the conversation going all on my own." She paused. "You're welcome."

Hazel rolled her eyes, but Roxy could tell she was pleased.

"Thank you." Hazel wrapped up the garbage on the table and tossed it into the trash can before sitting back down and taking a long sip of her coffee. Suddenly, she heaved a deep sigh, and her expression was thoughtful. "It's a nice idea. But is there even a point to dating Elizabeth? She doesn't seem like the type to have a fling. And she's only in Salem through December."

"Oh come on! Where's the romantic in you? If you feel something, act on it!"

"That's more like you than me. I've never been one to rush in. And what if this is just a crush? Last night we had so much fun, all three of us. And if no one takes it any further, then no one gets hurt when she leaves."

"You mean, no one gets crushed?"

"I walked right into that one."

"Look, nothing ventured, nothing gained, right?" Roxy was tired of seeing Hazel give up on opportunities before even giving them a try. She put all her energy into the shop since the breakup with Camille, and it was a distraction—not just from the breakup, but from everything in the last few years: her father's death and her mother's move to Maine. "Live in the moment. Give it a shot. Carpet diem!"

Hazel laughed, clearly won over, and Roxy was happy to see her smiling again.

"Okay. So what's the grand plan of yours?"

"Listen up, bucko. I've got it all figured out."

Roxy sketched out her plan, and soon enough, even Hazel was sounding half-convinced that maybe, just maybe, they could help Elizabeth with her research with some of her magical abilities. And Roxy was sure that once they helped her find something really juicy, Elizabeth would be so grateful she wouldn't care what means they'd used to locate it.

Just as they finalized their plans, Hazel's phone beeped with a new message. "It's from Elizabeth."

"What's it say?" said Roxy. She loved being right, and just then, she was sure that Elizabeth was making a move on Hazel.

"She wants to meet up tonight after dinner. She's invited me over for tea and biscuits."

"Biscuits at night?"

"That's what English people call cookies."

"Well then, why don't they just call them cookies? Jeez." Roxy affected annoyance. "So? Write her back. Say yes to the biscuits."

"Okay. Yes, to the biscuits," said Hazel, typing up her response to Elizabeth.

"See? I knew she was into you," said Roxy, happy in the knowledge that she'd been right—and that Hazel had a shot with the sexy professor. One of them should, at least. It only seemed fair.

❖

Promptly at eight, Hazel found herself on Elizabeth's doorstep, her stomach full of butterflies, and her hands clutching at a bottle of Chianti. She was so nervous, she didn't trust herself not to drop the bottle.

She took two long, slow breaths to steady herself. Why was she nervous? She still wasn't sure there was anything going on aside from two new friends hanging out.

But if Roxy was right, and Elizabeth had been staring at her at dinner last night, then maybe she was, indeed, interested in Hazel. There was only one way to find out.

She rapped on the door, and moments later it swung open to reveal Elizabeth.

"Come in!"

The first few raindrops were starting to fall as Hazel entered the charming little bungalow. Inside, it was warm and welcoming. The bungalow dated from the 1950s and was located just a ten-minute walk from her house.

She followed Elizabeth into the small kitchen, which looked like it hadn't been updated since the house had been built.

"This place is so cute," said Hazel, noting the rounded doorways, hardwood floors, and black and white tile in the kitchen. "I've passed by this row of bungalows my whole life, and I've always wondered what they looked like inside."

Elizabeth took the bottle of wine from Hazel and set about opening it.

"Yes, I was very lucky to get this place for the semester. It was a sabbatical swap, if you know what I mean."

"Oh?"

Elizabeth pulled out the cork and poured them each a generous glass of Chianti. "The woman who lives here is staying in my flat in England while I stay here. She's a professor at Boston College."

"Neat," said Hazel, taking a sip of the Chianti. It was as good as she remembered. Elizabeth appeared to be enjoying it as well.

"I'll give you the tour," said Elizabeth with a big smile, and Hazel was happy to follow her.

Elizabeth was dressed more casually than Hazel had ever seen her before, in jeans and a teal long-sleeve tee, and yet she still looked more elegant than Hazel ever felt she could possibly be. Hazel had opted for something that was comfortable but still looked nice. She didn't really own any "lounge" clothes; her favorite casual outfit was soft black leggings and a long tunic of sweatshirt material in a deep red that was cut to be cozy while still accentuating her best features. She hoped it struck the perfect balance of looking nice without trying too hard.

Elizabeth gave her a quick tour of the small cottage, and before she knew it, they were ensconced on the cushiony couches in front of a small gas fireplace that Elizabeth turned on for them. There were, indeed, "biscuits"—Elizabeth had picked up some cookies from Hazel's favorite bakery in town: surely a good omen.

"You know, if I didn't already have a house, I think I would want a cottage like this one," said Hazel. "It's so cozy, and a lot smaller and easier to maintain. It's just so charming."

"No," protested Elizabeth earnestly. "Your house is amazing. So historical and, I'm sure, full of fond family memories."

"Absolutely," said Hazel. It was true; every room in her home reminded her of good times with her family. "I know I've been lucky to have such a happy family life growing up. Especially compared to Roxy's family."

"Her parents are divorced, is that right?"

"Yes. And it was never a great marriage to begin with. Roxy would often spend the night at my place growing up, if you know what I mean."

The concern on Elizabeth's face was genuine. "I'm sorry to hear that. Does she have a good relationship with her parents now? We didn't quite get that far in our conversation at Luigi's."

"No, I'm afraid not," said Hazel. "Both of her parents remarried and had second families when Roxy was a teenager. It was the typical situation where the child of the first relationship falls through the cracks. But then her mother divorced again a couple of years ago, and apparently that guy was a real jerk. He skipped town, doesn't pay his alimony, and her mom is always pumping Roxy for cash."

Elizabeth looked shocked.

"That's awful."

"Yeah. She had a grandfather she was close to as a kid, but he's in a nursing home now."

"I'm sorry. I guess I've been lucky in that respect. My parents and I don't see eye to eye on what's important in life, but at least their relationship with each other has always been solid."

"It's unusual, these days. When my sister got married, it was a huge to-do to figure out how to seat everyone who was divorced so they wouldn't be at the same table as an ex."

"Is your sister happily married, then?"

"Oh yes. I found out recently I'm going to be an auntie."

"Congratulations," said Elizabeth with a warm smile that lit up her face. At first Hazel had been disappointed that they weren't sitting on the same couch, but now she appreciated the fact that she could look at Elizabeth while they chatted without craning her neck.

"Thank you. What about you? Any siblings?"

"Afraid not. It's just me. Growing up I really wished I had a brother or sister, though, to take some of the pressure off me. Honestly, even now it would be nice. My father still hopes I'll leave academia and go to work for him, take over the family business someday."

"But you love your research," guessed Hazel.

Elizabeth nodded vigorously. "Yes. I really do. And working all day in an office doesn't appeal at all. I know to some it might appear that on the surface, sitting at a desk, whether in a car parts company or in a library, is the same thing, but it couldn't be further from the truth.

When I'm doing research, I feel like I'm on a quest to discover new knowledge."

"That makes sense. I get that. I enjoyed doing research for papers in college. To be honest, the research part was a lot easier than writing the actual paper."

Elizabeth laughed. "I couldn't have said it better myself." She paused for a moment to sip her wine and top off both their glasses. "At the moment, though, I'm not enjoying myself very much. I've done archival work before, so I know it's not a simple process, but I'm feeling quite stymied here in Salem. I'm glad to have some company next week."

"Great. I'm looking forward to it, too. I feel a little sheepish admitting I haven't been there in years and years. What exactly will we be looking for?"

"As I mentioned before, my book is about the women in Salem at the time of the trials—but not the ones who were accused of witchcraft. I'm hoping to find some evidence of what the other women in the area thought of the trials. Something like a diary or letter would be worth its weight in gold."

"Any chance you might be looking for traces of your ancestor as well?"

Elizabeth looked a bit embarrassed. "Yes. I hate admitting that, as it seems silly, but I would love to find evidence of what she thought at the time. Her husband was one of the citizens who pointed a lot of fingers." Elizabeth paused, a thoughtful expression etching itself on her face. "This project means so much to me, both personally and professionally. I have a feeling that there must be some piece of evidence *somewhere* that would clinch my arguments."

Hazel felt like she, too, had a stake in this project now. Elizabeth's enthusiasm and ardor were catching. Maybe Roxy was right. If she could help Elizabeth uncover some new evidence, then wouldn't that serve a double goal of helping her with her book, but also expanding everyone's understanding of women's roles in the trials—or their criticism of them? It was an exciting proposition, as Hazel herself loathed the idea that witchcraft and magic were an easy way of getting rid of "difficult" women throughout history, especially women who loved other women.

"Do you discuss the connection between lesbianism and witches in your book, too?" said Hazel, giving voice to what she'd been thinking about.

"I've been thinking a lot about that," said Elizabeth, practically bursting out of her seat with enthusiasm. It was undoubtedly the most animated Hazel had ever seen her. "I really want to discuss that—if I can find a convincing way to work it into my current project. But of course, it's yet another element of my work that I have to be careful with." She gave Hazel a knowing look. "The boys' club doesn't look kindly on works dealing with sexuality."

Hazel groaned. "That's irritating."

"Incredibly," said Elizabeth. She shrugged, as if trying to physically shimmy out of the very idea. "I'm so glad you know what I mean. At uni, I had so many wonderful female professors of history, and somehow, for my doctorate, I ended up in one of the most masculine-centered programs in the country. My current department isn't much better. It's quite nice, actually, to be away for a year. And in such good company, too."

Elizabeth's last words were uttered so warmly, and with such an enticing smile, that Hazel was starting to think Roxy was right: maybe Elizabeth reciprocated some of her feelings.

The conversation turned to the Halloween festival in town, and Hazel filled Elizabeth in on Salem's big day. Soon, though, the hour turned late, and Hazel saw Elizabeth stifling a yawn. She gathered up her things, and Elizabeth walked her to the door.

"I had a lovely evening," said Elizabeth, opening the door for Hazel. The rain outside had stopped, luckily, and Hazel had no need of her umbrella—or any magical dryness incantation for that matter.

"Me, too. Thank you for inviting me. I loved hearing about your project." On impulse, Hazel gave Elizabeth a quick hug. "Bye!"

"Bye!"

Hazel turned to leave, but not before taking note of Elizabeth's broad smile. The whole way home, she couldn't stop thinking about the hug; even though it had been just a quick moment, there'd been a spark of warmth between them. Even more importantly, Elizabeth had hugged her back. Good omens all around.

Back at the house, Hazel set to work perfecting some spells for the archives. Beezle and Colin observed her, though neither of them was very helpful.

"Using magic in front of a mortal?" said the ghost, blowing plumes of ghostly smoke into Hazel's face as she practiced an incantation. "Tut tut, my dear. Going to get you into trouble."

Beezle, who usually detested Colin, appeared to agree with him for once. He gave Hazel a stern look that she meticulously ignored.

"I'm just going to help it along a bit. That's all," said Hazel, more to herself than to Beezle. "I don't need my cat's permission to help someone."

She quashed any remaining concerns about helping Elizabeth and instead focused on what she'd told her about the project. How important it was to her. How much it meant to her. Roxy was right for once—they *had* to help Elizabeth.

CHAPTER NINE

Elizabeth never expected archival work to be easy, but somehow the rest of the week in the archives was possibly one of the most frustrating of her career thus far. It seemed she was coming up empty at every turn; by Friday night, she was ready for a break. Although she already had plans to see Roxy and Hazel the next day for apple picking, she decided to go ahead and text Hazel to see if she was free that night.

As luck would have it, Hazel texted back right away that she would be free at seven and in need of food. Elizabeth felt the thrum of anticipation as she walked home from the archive and, on impulse, bought some delicious cheeses and charcuterie at a local gourmet food shop, along with olives, a baguette, and some grapes. This was one of her favorite dinners: easy and satisfying, while still feeling indulgent.

Hazel arrived just after seven, and before long, they were enjoying the spread Elizabeth had prepared along with a Sauvignon Blanc that paired beautifully with the Manchego cheese she'd bought.

"This is delicious," said Hazel, sitting back in the chair with a sigh of contentment. "I don't know why I never think to just have a cheese board for dinner. It's a great idea."

"I'm glad you like it," said Elizabeth, helping herself to another small round of baguette slathered in double cream brie with a dollop of raspberry jam on top. "It does feel a bit like cheating at making dinner, though. I promise I'll cook for you sometime."

"I'd love that. Maybe you could make me something British?"

"You aren't afraid of our legendarily bad cuisine?"

"Actually, I'm kind of a fan of bangers and mash. I mean, what's not to like? Sausage, potatoes, gravy." Hazel flashed a smile and Elizabeth felt her heartbeat speed up.

"A woman after my own heart," she said, hoping the words didn't come out sounding too loaded. "I don't know that I can find true British bangers here, though. But maybe an Indian curry? I practically lived on them at uni. Not exactly British, but very nearly our national cuisine these days."

"Mmm, that sounds delicious, too," said Hazel. Her warm brown eyes rested on Elizabeth's face, and she wondered if she was imagining an attraction on Hazel's side or if it really was there. She could stare into those liquid amber eyes for days, it felt like.

"I completely forgot about pudding," said Elizabeth, realizing her cupboards were empty of anything sweet she could offer after their meal.

"Pudding?" Hazel looked a bit confused. "Oh, you mean dessert." She smiled again. "No worries on that end! I always have chocolate with me." She grabbed her bag and pulled out several individually wrapped fancy chocolates from her large bag and set them on the table between them.

"You're full of surprises," said Elizabeth with a smile. She'd forgotten Americans called pudding "dessert." She examined one of the chocolates, delighted to see it was a very fine brand of dark chocolate. "Dark chocolate is my favorite."

"I had a feeling that might be the case," said Hazel with a flirtatious smile. "I can read people's chocolate preferences from a mile away."

"Oh really?" said Elizabeth, popping the chocolate into her mouth and tasting its rich flavors along with something else. "Is that sea salt in there as well? And toffee?"

Hazel nodded. "You like?"

"So much," said Elizabeth. "Clearly, you have a gift."

"Why thank you." Hazel popped a chocolate as well. "I very nearly started a chocolate shop in town, but I was advised not to."

"Why not?"

"Just not as secure a venture," she said with a shrug. "Everyone who advised me suggested to go along with the themes of Salem."

"Your business appears quite successful," said Elizabeth with true admiration. "You've managed to take a very silly concept and make it something extraordinary."

A look passed over Hazel's features that dimmed her pleasant demeanor, and Elizabeth realized that her words might have come off as rather flippant. It was difficult for her not to think of the kitschy side of Salem as nothing more than a tourist trap—and shops similar to Hazel's, full of "magical" flimflam, were the worst kind of scam in Elizabeth's opinion. But it wouldn't do to insult Hazel's hometown, or her profession.

"I'm sorry. I didn't mean to sound so judgmental. I was trying to pay a compliment, but apparently very badly."

Hazel smiled. "It's all right. I know there's a lot of silly stuff in Salem. But I hope that in time, you'll come to enjoy some of the silliness. I try to think of it as camp. That makes it a bit more artsy, right?"

Elizabeth smiled. "Sure, I'll give it a try."

It was still early yet as they cleared up the remains of dinner, and Elizabeth suggested watching a film together.

"That sounds nice," said Hazel. "What're you in the mood for?"

"I was actually going to ask you the same question," said Elizabeth, unsure what Hazel's tastes ran toward. The television was set up with various streaming services, and the owner had assured her that she could also rent films through the services at no additional charge, as long as it wasn't more than two or three a month.

Hazel plopped into the same squashy couch she'd sat in the previous Monday, and appeared to ponder the question. Elizabeth, meanwhile, situated herself catty-corner to her on the other couch and observed how lovely Hazel looked in her lounge. She could get used to that view.

"Since we were just talking about campy silly stuff, how about something campy and silly to get us in the mood for Halloween? It is October now, after all."

"Sure."

"Let's watch *The Witches of Eastwick*."

The title didn't inspire Elizabeth with confidence, but once the film started, she found herself pleasantly surprised. Starring Michelle Pfeiffer, Cher, Susan Sarandon, and Jack Nicholson, the film told the story of three magically gifted women who are seduced by the Devil—only to have to turn the tables when they got tired of him. It was light and funny and extremely silly, and Elizabeth found herself unexpectedly enjoying the film. It helped, of course, that Hazel was enjoying it as well, and her laughter at certain moments of the movie was music to Elizabeth's ears. It was quite possibly the cutest laugh she'd ever heard.

"Well, did you like it?" Hazel looked at her anxiously once the movie ended.

"Absolutely," said Elizabeth without hesitation. She smiled broadly. "I really hadn't expected to enjoy it, but it was delightfully wicked."

"I'm so glad," said Hazel with a look of relief. "All October long I like to watch Halloween-appropriate movies. I hadn't watched this one in a few years, though. It's my mom's favorite."

"That's a fun tradition. Sort of like watching Christmas movies in December?" Elizabeth had never been the type of person to watch very many movies, preferring to spend her evenings reading articles or academic books to get ahead in her research. Occasionally, she liked to watch a film, but it had to be an award-winner or an independent film to catch her interest. She'd forgotten how fun it was to watch a good comedy.

"Absolutely. My dad always liked to take those traditions to the extreme. Eventually, there was a movie theme for every month of the year. We'd watch Irish films in March for St. Patrick's Day, and Fourth of July themed movies in July—"

"Wait, what? What's a Fourth of July movie?"

"You know…movies that take place on Independence Day."

"Are there a lot of those?" Elizabeth was genuinely intrigued.

"*Independence Day, Jaws, The Sandlot*…"

"Okay, okay, you've convinced me," said Elizabeth with a laugh. "Was your father really so patriotic?"

"Oh, gosh no," said Hazel. "He just liked the idea of themes and parties. He was a huge extrovert, and he loved costumes, dressing up, any excuse to have a party, and the party had to have a theme. It was just a logical extension of those interests to have themed movie months." Elizabeth could tell from the warmth in Hazel's voice just how much her father had meant to her.

"Sounds like you were very close."

"Yes," said Hazel quietly.

She looked pensive suddenly, and Elizabeth hoped she hadn't, yet again, said the wrong thing. She didn't know why she kept saying the wrong thing; it was like being around Hazel was making her jumpy, or nervous or...something. She wasn't quite sure what she was feeling, but it was hard to think straight when her heart was beating so hard. "I'm sorry. I don't mean to bring up a sad topic."

Hazel looked up at her and smiled.

"Not at all. I love talking about my dad. Makes him feel more alive to me. He loved *The Witches of Eastwick*, too." She smiled a bit more broadly now, and Elizabeth felt she'd never seen Hazel more beautiful. "In fact, it was their first date, seeing that movie together."

"Really?" said Elizabeth. The import of those words sunk into her slowly. Was this Hazel's way of saying she was interested in Elizabeth? Her breath caught a little in her throat as she tried to weigh the meaning of it all.

Hazel nodded. "Uh-huh. Isn't that cute?"

"Absolutely."

Soon after, Hazel gathered her things to go, and they hugged good-bye again. There was a moment when Elizabeth thought about giving her a peck on the cheek as well, but she chickened out. She wished Hazel didn't have to leave yet, but it was going on midnight by that point. She consoled herself that the very next day, they'd be apple picking together with Roxy, and she'd be able to enjoy more of Hazel's company.

❖

Bright and early the following Tuesday, Elizabeth met Roxy on the steps of the Salem Museum archives. The memories of the weekend were still with Elizabeth as she hailed Roxy outside the archives entrance. Apple picking had been a huge success, and she'd been amazed that an activity that sounded like work could actually be so enjoyable. The weather had been ideal, and it all felt very American. They'd walked through a corn maze, drank apple cider, and bought several pumpkins to decorate the outside of the shop with. It felt like she was living in an American sitcom version of autumn, and she was really enjoying it. Roxy had been funny and full of stories as usual, and fortunately there remained no awkwardness between them. More importantly, though, she felt she was getting to know Hazel better and better, and for some reason she wasn't ready to think about just yet, that was very important to her.

Now it was time to get back to work. She spent Monday organizing everything for their joint foray into the archives, and today was the day. The shop was closed, Roxy had the day off work, and they were both supposed to help her comb through stacks of archival materials. Elizabeth was feeling confident that with some help, something new and interesting might come to light to help her research project.

She felt a small jab of disappointment when she saw Roxy was alone.

"Is Hazel already inside?" said Roxy, as she followed Elizabeth in.

"I thought she'd be coming with you."

"That's weird. Maybe she got held up. Anyway, you can count on her. She'll be here soon, I'm sure."

The museum archives were probably Elizabeth's best bet for finding something for her book, as the historical society holdings were actually rather small. Many of the most important and well-known papers had already been digitized through the University of Virginia, but her historian's instinct told her that there was more to be found. She would be spending time in the city archives as well, but she liked to be methodical: one thing at a time.

She rather enjoyed the museum archives anyway. They were quiet and almost picturesque, located in a beautiful old building not too far from the city center. The head archivist, Scott, was friendly and efficient, unlike the people at the city archives whose slow pace and suspicious attitude had been another reason why Elizabeth had decided to focus on the museum archives.

Elizabeth smiled and waved to Scott, who was visibly surprised when he saw Roxy with her.

"I see you have a helper with you today?"

"Yup." Roxy nodded enthusiastically. "We're going to find historical gold in them stacks."

Scott rolled his eyes.

"Do you know each other?" asked Elizabeth.

"Oh yeah," said Roxy. "High school. We had algebra together. Something else, too, probably."

Scott's lip curled disdainfully, and Elizabeth got the sense that Roxy wasn't Scott's favorite person, so she set about getting her a reader card as quickly as possible. She'd already dropped off the list of materials she wanted to look at the previous afternoon.

"It's all ready for you," said Scott, gesturing to the reading room. "You'll need to leave everything in the locker room before going in, though." He gave Roxy a stern look.

Elizabeth led them to a doorway on the left, and they found a small locker room where they hung up their coats and left their bags. Inside the archives, they weren't allowed to have anything with them except for themselves, paper, and pencils.

"Wow, they're pretty serious about everything here," said Roxy, hanging up her coat and hat.

"A lot of archives are like that. They're the custodians of the materials, and it's their responsibility to make sure everything survives for future generations." She hadn't meant for it to sound like a lecture.

When they were both ready, Elizabeth led the way back to the lobby and across the hall into the archives reading room. There were four large tables, two of which were already covered in papers, some tied together with strings, some sewn together like books, and other folded into quartos and octavos.

Roxy looked around. "Wow. This is amazing." She reached out to touch one of the packets of papers before quickly retracting her arm.

"Shoot, do we need white gloves or something before we touch these?" She looked questioningly at her.

"Oh, no," said Elizabeth, gesturing for her to join her across the table. "Paper made prior to the nineteenth century was made of repurposed rags, so it's quite durable. It's nineteenth-century paper that crumbles at the touch. This earlier stuff—here, feel it—is entirely different. It's made to last."

Roxy looked around the room. They were the only ones there, and their voices the only sound. "It's so quiet in here, it's like a ghost set up all these papers."

Just then a door slammed behind them. Elizabeth nearly jumped out of her skin.

"You okay?"

Elizabeth's heart was racing, and she clutched a hand to her chest. "Sorry! These smaller archives make me a little jittery."

"I thought you'd don't believe in ghosts." Roxy smiled.

Elizabeth sighed. It was ridiculous to still have this fear even years after the practical joke that had started it, but there it was. "I don't. But when I was doing my doctorate, some other students tried to prank me by locking me into one of the study rooms at the library. I'd been working on transcribing some archival letters in the rare books and documents sections, and I was so wrapped up in my work I never noticed until they were turning the lights off in the library."

"What? That's awful." Roxy's voice filled up the quiet reading room and echoed off the walls.

"Shhhhhh," said Elizabeth out of habit. "I appreciate your indignation. At the time, it was terrifying. I'd had to check my phone in at the door, so I couldn't call anyone. Luckily, I had my computer, and I was able to email a friend, but still…it took several hours for someone with a key to show up and let me out. By that time, I was starving and angry—"

"And I bet you had to pee like a mother racehorse," added Roxy, looking incredulous.

Elizabeth laughed. "That's one way to put it. In any case, whenever I'm in one of these smaller, less popular archives or libraries, especially if I'm all alone, I get a bit paranoid about everything. I know it's silly—"

"It's absolutely not silly," said Roxy, still looking and sounding outraged. "That's terrible what they did to you."

Just then, Hazel showed up out of breath. "I'm *so* sorry I'm late," she said, plopping into a chair next to Elizabeth and across from Roxy. "Really, I'm never late like this, but I had the craziest morning."

"What happened?" Elizabeth was both curious and a little concerned. Hazel sounded upset.

"Beezle, you know, my cat? He tore up a bunch of the couch cushions this morning. The filling was everywhere, and he was trying to eat it. I had to clean it all up, and while I was doing that, he kept getting in my way. At one point we were in a tug of war over the stuff. I don't know what got into him. He's never like that. And then the milk in the fridge had spoiled, and I was out of eggs and bread, so I couldn't make myself breakfast. And I was starving, so I had to stop by the café, but it was closed due to an electrical issue, and by then I was so late that I came straight here, but I got lost on the way. I don't even know how it's possible. I know Salem like the back of my hand."

She looked so upset and worried that Elizabeth couldn't help but smile reassuringly and pat her on the arm. "It's all right, really. I'm sorry you had such a shit morning."

"Thanks." Hazel caught her breath and looked around the table. "So, what are we doing?"

Elizabeth was about to launch into that day's work, when she noticed Roxy making strange signs with her hands, including pulling a finger across her throat in an unmistakable "kill it" sign.

"Roxy, is everything okay?"

"Oh? What? No. Not at all. Sorry. I had an itch." Roxy scratched her throat theatrically.

"Em, okay. Where was I?"

"You were just telling us what we were going to work on today," Hazel prompted her.

Elizabeth gave them each a list of key words to look for, as well as specific names of historical persons she was hoping to learn more about. She explained some of her project, and she was happy to note that both Roxy and Hazel looked interested.

"Anyway, anything you see, note it down on a legal pad," concluded Elizabeth, handing them each one along with a sharpened Number 2 pencil. "Write down the document information and any relevant notes, and then set the document over here." She gestured to a spot next to her where there were two thin documents in a small stack. "I'm not very hopeful, but who knows. Maybe with some research assistants, I can find something faster." She smiled encouragingly and began her own work.

She had barely begun skimming through the first few pages of the stack in front of her when Roxy cleared her throat.

"Uh, Hazel? Could you come around over here and help me with this knot?" She picked up a stack of papers held together with some string. "I just can't get it."

Elizabeth tried to stay on task while Hazel got up and went over to Roxy's side of the table, but soon their whispers were distracting her. She looked up at them.

"Everything all right?"

"Yes, definitely," said Hazel with a smile before shooting a look at Roxy so clear that even across the table, Elizabeth noticed it. What was going on? Were they fighting?

Hazel came back over to Elizabeth's side of the table. "Sorry about that. Roxy's all thumbs today, apparently."

Elizabeth nodded and got back to work.

Soon a pleasant silence fell over them all, and Elizabeth became absorbed in her work. She was methodical and quick, making notes on things that sounded mildly interesting, but mostly just setting aside everything that was useless—which was the majority of what she was looking through.

About a half hour in, just as Elizabeth was hitting her stride, she felt a sharp kick in the shin.

"Ow!"

"Sorry!" Roxy said, looking awkward. "I was trying to get Hazel's attention."

"Hmmm?" Hazel looked up from her own work.

"I could use the bathroom. Do you know where it is?" She winked at Hazel.

"I don't know where it is. But I'm sure Elizabeth does."

Elizabeth tried not to let her frustration show; there was so much work to do, and she hated to break her concentration. But having just talked about the importance of needing a bathroom in an archive, it seemed petty to show Roxy her chagrin.

She walked Roxy out of the reading room, through the lobby, and past the locker room to the toilets.

"Find your own way back?"

"Oh sure," said Roxy, sounding oddly strained.

Elizabeth returned to the reading room only to find it empty. She felt a shiver of nerves again. The stupid stunt in the study room was over three years ago. Why couldn't she get over it?

And yet, there it was, still with her. Moments like this, her mind flashed back to that feeling of desperation and fear. Of course, she would have survived until the next morning. She wasn't going to starve spending one night in a study room, but the humiliation of it was what stuck with her. Because she would have had to pee somewhere. And there weren't many options in the small study room.

Moments later, Hazel rejoined her in the reading room.

"Where'd you go?"

"I put in an order with Scott. I, uh, I studied the catalog before coming, and I had a brainwave about where we might look for more materials."

"Oh?" Elizabeth didn't want to squash Hazel's optimism, but she'd already made a comprehensive list of everything worth looking at, and she very much doubted there was anything she'd overlooked.

"Oh, hey," said Roxy, joining them as well. "What'd I miss?"

"I just ordered some more stuff," said Hazel. She sounded so enthusiastic, Elizabeth didn't have the heart to tell her that she'd be much more helpful if she just stuck to looking through what she'd already ordered.

"Oh, really?"

Elizabeth sat back down in her seat and had just picked up a new document to peruse when she heard more whispers. This was exactly why she hadn't wanted any "help" with her research. Other people, especially people with no archival experience, were simply not helpful—even if they were lovely in other ways.

"Hazel!" The name came out of Roxy's mouth in a weird, strangled way, and Elizabeth had to try very hard not to sigh out loud in frustration. She lifted her head and saw Hazel going to the door where Scott was trying to open the door with a very large stack of boxes filled with documents.

What had Hazel done? To Elizabeth's practiced eye, she had ordered more documents than she could look at properly in a week, much less one day. She sighed and tried to concentrate on her own work.

Eventually everything settled down again, and Elizabeth got in the zone. When that happened, it was like everything else around her was on mute. She worked through several more useless documents before landing on a last will and testament that was very interesting indeed. It was a woman's will—and it listed a woman as the sole inheritor. It was dated 1692, the year of the Salem witch trials, and the name on it—Mary Amelia Waters—was somehow familiar to her, though she couldn't say right away how.

"I think I've just found something really fabulous," said Elizabeth, turning to Roxy and Hazel, eager to share what she'd found.

"Me, too," said Hazel, her voice practically quivering with

excitement. Elizabeth couldn't help smiling—she doubted very much that in that short time, Hazel had found anything of note, but her enthusiasm for the project was endearing.

"What is it?"

"Yeah, Hazy, whatcha got?"

Gingerly, Hazel held out her hands which held a small, very old-looking book in a cracked leather cover. Elizabeth's breath caught in her throat.

"Is that…?" Her voice trailed off.

"I think it's a diary," said Hazel quietly, a little bit of question in her voice.

Carefully, Elizabeth picked up the book and opened it. The handwriting was difficult to decipher, but Elizabeth had taken many paleography courses, and she was able to make out a name and a date: E. Cowley, 1714. She leafed carefully through the first few pages.

"This is incredible, Hazel. You're right. It's a diary." Her heart was racing, and she could hardly believe what she was looking at. The name of the author of the diary was the same as the woman named in Mary Amelia Waters's will. With barely disguised excitement, she shared that information with Roxy and Hazel, both of whom looked appropriately amazed.

"Where did you find this?" Elizabeth knew the catalog inside out after staring at it for the better part of a week. She knew there was no entry for a diary.

"Last night, while I was walking home, I thought about when we came here on a school trip. I remembered the archivist back then telling us that stuff was mislabeled all the time. And they also told us about how stuff used to be categorized in a kind of sexist way. So like, 'important' 'masculine' stuff having to do with business was better organized than 'women's' stuff—like recipes, cookbooks, conduct manuals and stuff like that." Hazel used her fingers to make air quotes.

"That is genius," said Elizabeth in admiration. "So where did you find the diary?"

"In this box full of nineteenth-century family recipes. Some of the recipe cards have the same last name as the woman in the diary. It was probably part of a family donation that no one ever really labeled thoroughly. At least, that's my guess," she added, looking a little uncertain.

Elizabeth gazed with appreciation at Hazel. She was full of surprises. She was about to say something to that effect when she felt the table vibrate beneath her hands.

"Did you feel that?" she said. It was the oddest sensation. After a moment, it stopped.

"Feel what?" said Hazel, suddenly looking quite concerned.

The table vibrated again, and this time, Elizabeth felt the floor beneath her feet vibrating as well. After a moment, it stopped.

"Wow, that was weird," said Roxy, her voice sounding strained. "Hazel, I have to talk to you. In the hallway. *Now.*" She practically dragged Hazel out the door behind her, leaving Elizabeth alone in the room, wondering what was going on.

The lights started flickering, and she felt a shiver down her spine. Hazel had mentioned an electrical issue at the café that morning—was there something going on in other parts of Salem, too? The logical, rational side of Elizabeth was telling her that's all it was. Probably some work on the electrical grid. That would explain some weird vibrations, too, if the work was underground.

The temperature suddenly dropped in the room and the lights went out. Immediately, Elizabeth broke out in a cold sweat as her heart was hammering in her chest.

This was harder to rationalize. Even if the heat had turned off that moment, it wouldn't become cold immediately. Not like this. Elizabeth could see her breath.

It just figured she'd be alone when something weird was happening in the archive. She had to do something. This wasn't normal. A feeling of dread was clawing up from her stomach; she felt nauseous. She was about to speed-walk to the door to try to find Roxy and Hazel when, before she could move, a piece of paper suddenly fell onto the table in front of her.

"What the—" Before she could finish the sentence, the room was filled with papers flying through the air. Soon books were whisking their way through the room, flying into walls, and flapping into her face, like errant birds. She batted them away from her, a strangled scream working its way out of her throat.

Where were Roxy and Hazel? Why weren't they checking on her? The noise in the reading room was deafening. Where was Scott? Why was she all alone?

The final straw was when she heard manic laughter as though from far above one of the bookshelves.

She ran to the doors of the reading room and nearly pulled her arm out of her socket trying to open the door. *It was locked.*

Elizabeth felt her throat closing. She was panicking, and her vision was tunneling. Everything became blurry, and she felt herself slipping to the floor...

CHAPTER TEN

"What? What? What is it?" Hazel rubbed her arm where Roxy had squeezed it, half-pulling, half-dragging her out of the reading room.

Roxy looked nearly as frustrated as Hazel felt. She ran her hand nervously through her unkempt hair.

"I've been trying to tell you since you got here *not* to go through with the magic." Roxy heaved a frustrated groan. "Don't you know what *this* means?" She pulled her finger across her throat.

"I thought you were trying to tell me to stop yapping so we could get to work," said Hazel. "It would never occur to me that after all your persuading, you didn't want to go through with the plan."

"Yeah, well, let's hope it's not too late."

"What do you mean? Why is it a good idea yesterday and a bad idea today?"

"Because today she told me about a terrible prank that some assholes played on her in her PhD program, and it made me think maybe this wasn't a great idea." Roxy was pale and guilty looking.

"You mean the whole thing where they hung up little Blair Witch figures in her office?"

"*What?* No. My God. She must have gone to the worst school in England. She told *me* about some other terrible thing—they locked her in a study room when the library was closing. It took her hours to be freed. The poor thing was shaking just telling me about it. You should have seen her jump out of her seat when the door slammed earlier."

"Oh my God," said Hazel, feeling a headache coming on. She

rubbed her temples. "Hopefully, my little search and retrieve spell won't cause any permanent damage. And we *did* find something really awesome."

"Let's hope it was worth it," said Roxy just as they both noticed the same vibration as earlier and several muffled thuds on the other side of the doors. "What the—?"

Hazel's eyes widened. She remembered right then why she didn't come to the museum archives, why she avoided them at all costs: there was a very annoying spirit who lived there and didn't appreciate visitors—especially magical ones like Hazel.

Crap. It's a poltergeist.

The commotion on the other side was getting louder, and when Hazel touched the door handle to enter the reading room again, she found it freezing to the touch—and stuck closed.

"Help me, quick. We have to pull it open and get her out of there." Hazel was desperate to get to Elizabeth.

Roxy joined her and started pulling. "What's in there?" She was terrified.

"Poltergeist," said Hazel under her breath just as the head archivist showed up.

"What on earth?" He looked suspiciously at Roxy and Hazel. "Let me through."

"We can't get it open," said Hazel, just as someone on the other side grasped the door from the inside and shook it violently, followed by a loud thumping sound and silence.

Scott pushed Hazel and Roxy out of his way, grasped the door handle, and easily opened the door toward them. As the door swung open, Hazel was shocked to see Elizabeth's unconscious form on the ground just inside the reading room.

"Oh my Lord," said Scott. "Call 911."

Hazel barely heard him, though; she was already on the ground next to Elizabeth. She touched her wrist and felt a pulse. She massaged the slender wrist and used her magic to send a tiny jolt of energy to Elizabeth. A moment later, Elizabeth's eyelids fluttered open, and her cornflower blue eyes were looking back at Hazel in confusion. She heaved a sigh of relief.

"She's okay," she said, turning to Roxy and Scott.

"I am most certainly *not* okay," said Elizabeth hotly as she stood up and dusted herself off.

"Are you sure you should be standing up so quickly, Dr. Cowrie?" Scott already had his phone in his hand. "I think I should call an ambulance to make sure you're okay." His gaze swung out beyond Elizabeth and his jaw dropped open. "What in the hell have the three of you been doing in here?" He rounded on Roxy. "I knew you were trouble as soon as you showed up."

"What? No. It wasn't me. How could you even think that?"

"The glue in the locker prank? The hilarious science fair project in the pool prank? You have a history of destroying things, Roxy." Scott's eyes flashed with anger and his voice dripped with sarcasm.

"Roxy, is that true? Did you really throw Scott's project into a pool?" Elizabeth looked at Roxy with nearly as much outrage as Scott. Hazel was trying hard to think of a way to defuse the situation, but she was far too distracted by the possibility that the poltergeist might wreak even more havoc on the archives.

"That's *not* the whole story," said Roxy.

Scott wasn't listening anymore, though; he'd run over to the table where the three of them had been working. It was covered in ripped paper the size of confetti. He looked positively ill at the sight of the mess.

Hazel glanced from him to Elizabeth, who still looked a bit green around the gills, and she felt like a supreme idiot. Why hadn't she consulted her diaries? Surely, she'd noted down *somewhere* that there was a poltergeist hiding out at the Salem archives.

"Is all this some sort of stupid joke to you people?" Elizabeth's tone was frigid, and when Hazel met her gaze, she saw that Elizabeth had ice in her eyes, and she was pale with anger and outrage.

"What?" Her mind was working overtime to try to come up with a plausible explanation for what'd just happened, but her mind was a blank.

"You and Roxy left me in here alone, and suddenly there's funny sounds and papers flying through the air? The same week that I confided in both of you about how I've been pranked before? And hated it?" Her tone was somewhere between anger and hurt as she took a big breath to steady her quivering voice. It was clear that she was on the verge of tears. "I don't know how you made it cold in here or where the laughter was coming from, but it all sounds just like some stupid horror movie. You think that because I don't believe in the supernatural you would test me to see if it's true?"

"Elizabeth, please, you can't possibly think that either of us would have done anything so low, can you? How could we?" Hazel tried to be as gentle as possible.

"No way, never," said Roxy, putting her arm protectively around Hazel. "Hazel is the sweetest person in the world. She never plays pranks." She paused as Elizabeth turned her suspicious gaze toward her. "And I don't either. Scott gave you the wrong impression. I never put glue in his locker. I swear. And the science project was a misunderstanding. I was helping Scott carry it to the gym, and a bunch of jocks grabbed me and threw me in the pool while I was still holding the display. I was always getting shit for being out in high school."

Roxy's explanation had drawn Scott away from the table full of papers, and Hazel used the opportunity to sneak away and inspect the damage. She breathed a sigh of relief when she saw that what looked initially like torn up documents was actually just blank paper ripped to shreds. She risked a tiny bit of magic to get most of it off Elizabeth's stacks of documents and onto the floor where it could more easily be swept up.

She returned to the small group by the doors.

"It looks like all your documents, including the diary, are still in order on the table. I'm guessing the electrical work that closed down the café must have affected us here just for a moment, turning off the lights and the heat." Hazel hoped the explanation sounded plausible.

"That's what I thought, too," said Elizabeth defensively, "until the papers started flying through the air and the door was locked. A book nearly hit me in the face."

"Stuck," Scott corrected her. His voice was apologetic. "I opened it no problem. You know, the old wood can expand and contract depending on the time of year. It was probably stuck. And we do have cold spots occasionally. Drafts can get in and rustle up papers, make it feel colder. I'm surprised you've never had that experience at another archive."

He gave Hazel a knowing look and then walked back to his post at the main desk. He must have felt bad for harboring a grudge against

Roxy for all those years, thought Hazel. Or maybe he decided to come up with an explanation for the sake of his own sanity. Either way, she was thankful.

Elizabeth, however, wasn't buying it.

"You're all against me now," she said. "You have no idea how frightening the last five minutes were. It felt just like those pranks when I was a grad student." She paused and breathed deeply. Hazel wished there were something, anything, she could say to make her feel better, but she had a feeling it was best not to say anything at all just then.

Elizabeth sat at the table where she'd been working and stared at the diary in front of her. Roxy moved as though to follow her, but Hazel put her hand out to stop her. There was something about Elizabeth's posture that suggested she was still processing what had happened.

She turned to the two of them after a moment.

"Please don't take this the wrong way, but I'd like to work alone now."

"Are you sure? You just said you didn't want us to leave you here by yourself," said Roxy, confused.

Hazel, however, understood. Elizabeth was embarrassed, and she needed to be alone.

"I'm very behind in my work now, and I think it'd be best if you both left. You've done enough damage as it is."

The words stung Hazel to the quick. It wasn't *her* fault the poltergeist had chosen that moment to act up. "Come on, Roxy. Let's go."

"Fine. I can see when I'm not wanted."

The two of them filed out of the reading room and gathered their stuff from the locker room in embarrassed silence.

Back out on the sidewalk in front of the museum, Hazel hardly knew what to say. They'd made a mistake, sure, but Elizabeth's final words to them had been harsh. Part of her wanted to be sympathetic; she obviously had some residual trauma from how she'd been treated in the past, and that made her experience with the poltergeist that much worse. On the other hand, her final words to the two of them bordered on rude, and the mere suggestion that they would have pranked her like the jackasses in her doctoral program made Hazel bristle with the injustice of the comparison.

"Hey, are you okay?" Roxy's big puppy dog eyes were full of concern.

It made Hazel smile, and just then, it felt really good to smile. "Yeah. I'm fine. I think." She shrugged. "That was…not great."

"Boy, you can say that again." Roxy let out a low whistle.

Hazel laughed. "Exactly."

Roxy groaned. "Ugh. It's your ex."

Hazel whirled around and found herself face-to-face with Camille.

"Can we talk? Alone?"

Hazel hesitated before turning to Roxy.

"I can stay if you want me to," offered Roxy.

"No, it's okay. I can handle myself. Let's meet in half an hour at that Polish deli for lunch."

Roxy set off to the deli to grab them a table, and Hazel turned back to Camille.

"Fancy meeting you here," said Camille. "Hmm, you don't look so good. Archives got you down?"

Camille's ruby red lips lifted into a smile and, despite being out in the daylight—not the ideal time for vampires—she was attractive as hell. Distraught as she was, Hazel had to admit she could still occasionally fall under Camille's spell.

Hazel shook her head as if to shake off that thought. Camille only spelled trouble. "I was helping a friend with some research."

"Done so soon?" The curiosity in Camille's voice was evident, and Hazel wondered what was up with her. Why was she so curious?

"Yes. She found what she wanted, and now she has to take notes. She didn't need me and Roxy after that." Hazel didn't know why she was offering Camille so much information. How could she still distract her even after all this time?

"Roxy? You got Roxy to go to a library? I'm impressed." Camille's attempt at banter came off sounding condescending. It was one of the many, many reasons why Roxy didn't like Camille and never had.

"What are you driving at, Camille?"

A strange expression came over Camille's face, and she looked over Hazel's shoulder toward the archives building. She shuddered.

"Were you doing *magic* here?" she said incredulously. Her violet eyes were a deep eggplant color today, and her lips shimmered with glittery lipstick like candy.

Hazel sighed. She had forgotten that as a vampire, Camille was much more sensitive than mere mortals to the presence of magic. And magic always left a trace for those who were attuned to it.

"Yes," she admitted with a sigh. "I was just trying to help…"

"In a public place?" Camille looked around as if she was concerned that there were people nearby who might hear them, but it was eleven on a Tuesday; it was fairly quiet. They were the only ones on the street. Camille lowered her voice to a hoarse whisper. "That's not a good idea. I'm a little worried about your judgment." She reached out and placed her cool hands on Hazel's warm ones, but Hazel pulled away.

"Oh, please. Don't be so patronizing. I'm pretty certain you were using some kind of glamour on that woman Alicia the other night."

Camille was offended. "Please, my dear. I don't have to stoop to such low tricks to get a beautiful young woman interested in me. I have many fine attributes." She winked flirtatiously.

Hazel felt herself getting annoyed. "But I guess Alicia's back with Roxy now. Couldn't hold on to that one after all."

Camille was unmoved. "Alicia was a plaything. I'm after more exciting bait."

"I hope it's nothing to do with Elizabeth. Dr. Cowrie, I mean."

Camille gave her a withering look. "Dr. Cowrie? A workaholic professor and a skeptic of magic? Not my type." She paused. "I hope *you're* not falling for her." She gave Hazel a penetrating stare. "I thought, when I first saw the good doctor at the shop, that maybe you were interested in her."

Hazel felt herself involuntarily blush, and she sincerely hoped that Camille would attribute that reaction to the strong wind that was kicking up the leaves. She knew that was a false hope, however, as very little got past Camille. "That's none of your business." The old Hazel would have spilled her guts then and there, but the new Hazel held her tongue.

"I see."

Oddly enough, Hazel felt fairly certain she detected a fleeting expression of sadness, or perhaps disappointment, pass over Camille's beautiful features before she returned to her usual ironic expression.

"Same old Hazel. Always the martyr."

"I really have to go, Camille, unless you have something else you need to tell me." Hazel was getting tired of this kind of banter. She didn't need her ex-girlfriend telling her she was making mistakes in her love life.

"Wait, Hazel. Hold on a minute. I didn't mean to sound so blasé. We *did* have a relationship once upon a time. Maybe I could help? We could go to a nice café and have an early lunch. You could eat, and I could watch. We could chat." Camille sounded sincere, but Hazel wasn't fooled. She didn't know why Camille was still in town, and clearly, she had some ulterior motives for showing up. She'd turned down her business proposal, so there was no reason for her to stick around.

For a moment, Hazel considered going with Camille somewhere for lunch—*not* the Magic Bean, with Joanna's penetrating stare—but maybe somewhere a little quieter. Hazel was tempted; she wanted to know what Camille was up to. Was Salem in for a vampire emigration? She shuddered just thinking about it. Or maybe Camille needed some love advice herself. Now that was an interesting proposition.

But no—the situation with Elizabeth was more immediately pressing. And knowing Camille, she could just as easily be in town to torment Hazel. Or because she was bored. Who knew?

"As tempting as that sounds, I've got work to do," said Hazel finally, avoiding Camille's searching gaze. She looked down the windblown street and realized with a jolt that she was freezing. She had momentarily forgotten while arguing with Camille, but now she hugged herself tightly.

Camille shrugged her beautiful ivory shoulders, as if to say, "your loss." She pulled her cloak up over her head and, somewhat surprisingly, leaned over to give Hazel a gentle, if quite chilly, kiss on the cheek.

"As you wish, my dear. But try not to awaken any more poltergeists." She squeezed Hazel's hands reassuringly and sauntered off in the opposite direction. For a moment, Hazel watched her walk away, wondering what on earth was going on in that beautiful head of hers.

As she turned away to meet Roxy, though, the full impact of everything that'd happened in the archives hit Hazel all over again, and she felt tears welling up in her eyes. Had she lost any chance she'd had with Elizabeth?

❖

"Oh, Roxy, what've I done?"

Hazel felt tears threatening to overtake her yet again as she sat at an outside table with her plateful of pierogi, suddenly not very hungry after all. Roxy put her tray down opposite Hazel and sat down.

"Hey, hey, don't be too down on yourself. We're going to make this right." Roxy dug into her potato dumplings with gusto. "Besides, it was all my fault."

"It's sweet of you to say, but it's really my fault. I should have remembered about the poltergeist."

"How could you possibly expect a poltergeist?" said Roxy reasonably. "Nobody expects a poltergeist—" She giggled. "Except the Spanish Inquisition. I bet they *would* expect one."

Hazel chuckled, too, and felt a little better. It was often like that with the two of them; even in a crisis they could make each other laugh over something silly, like a Monty Python reference.

"Whew. Glad to see I can still make you laugh," said Roxy through another mouthful of dumpling. "God, what was I thinking? Showing Elizabeth that magic is real? I mean, I'm crazy, right?"

Hazel considered the question seriously. "Maybe not exactly crazy, but it wasn't one of our best ideas."

"True. How're we going to fix it?"

"I have no idea. And I think the archive fried my brain." Hazel's mind had been reliving the last hour over and over in her head, wishing she'd never gone to the archive that day in the first place. In fact, now that she thought about it some more, she realized that Beezle—and nearly all of Salem—had been trying to tell her just that. She should have listened to the universe when it sent her so many clear signs.

She picked at her food, but she just couldn't bring herself to eat, which was a shame, because this deli had the best pierogi.

"Let's talk about something else," said Roxy, looking concerned again. "We can't do anything right now, but we do still have to make a plan for our costumes for Halloween."

"Very true," said Hazel with a small smile.

With Salem's reputation as a tourist destination for all things creepy, Halloween was the high season. All the shops decorated for Halloween, and the Chamber of Commerce even gave an award to the best decorated storefront. There was also increased customer traffic at the stores, higher demand for the ghost tours, and lots of meetings with the various groups that participated in the festival.

All month long there were events on weeknights and weekends, and it all culminated with a carnival on Halloween itself—the Halloween festival. Every business in town had a booth to promote itself, and there was a parade as well, so Hazel would have her hands full all month. If Black Friday was the most important day for most businesses in America, then Salem was the exception, because Halloween was the defining business day there.

"What about something classic?" asked Roxy, pushing her empty plate away and taking a big swig of iced tea. The day had turned unexpectedly warm.

"What do you have in mind?"

"I dunno," continued Roxy. "How about a werewolf and a mummy?"

"Didn't we do a *Mummy* themed costume two years ago?"

"Oh, yeah." Roxy's smile widened. "That was a great costume idea!" *The Mummy* was one of Roxy's favorite movies, and two years earlier, they'd dressed up as the Rachel Weisz and Brendan Fraser characters from the film.

"Let's do another themed pair."

"I like how you think."

"What about a werewolf and Little Red Riding Hood? We could do a whole bunch of revised fairy tales as part of the decorations."

"Ooh, I like that," Roxy said, getting excited. "The fairy godmother and Cinderella or the evil fairy and Sleeping Beauty."

"The witch in 'Beauty and the Beast.'"

"Hansel and Gretel and the witch."

"These fairy tales all have angry witches or fairies who get revenge on others. It's a little sexist," said Hazel.

"True. We need more dude villains. I like the idea of a werewolf and Little Red Riding Hood. But you know, we could make Red a badass. She could have a giant sword hidden in her red cloak."

"Hmmm, not bad," said Hazel, considering it. "That could be fun. Which of us is the wolf and which is Red?"

"I mean, I figured I'd be the wolf. I'd make an excellent wolf, if I do say so myself."

"Isn't that what everyone expects? Wouldn't it be more interesting if *I* were the wolf and *you* were the badass Red Riding Hood?"

Now it was Roxy's turn to consider the proposition.

"And we could interpret the costume however we wanted?" Roxy now had a gleam in her eye. "It wouldn't have to be traditional, right?"

"I don't see why not. The contest judges usually prefer something original anyway."

"Okay, I think I have an idea."

Roxy told Hazel her idea, and Hazel agreed enthusiastically. Since they had the rest of the day free, they decided to fill the time with getting materials for the costumes and decorations for the store.

As they walked over to her car, Hazel felt grateful for the distraction. If not for their errands, she knew she'd spend the rest of the day obsessing over what'd happened at the archive and how to fix things with Elizabeth.

By the end of the day, Hazel felt a thousand times better. In fact, after giving it some more thought, she realized that although she'd made a mistake, Elizabeth wasn't innocent in how things had worked out either. She'd jumped to conclusions and made some really insulting assumptions. Maybe it was best if both of them took a break and focused on other things.

Chapter Eleven

Several days passed, and Elizabeth still felt too embarrassed to text either Hazel or Roxy, even though each of them had, separately, tried to contact her. In fact, Elizabeth hadn't the energy or willpower to do much in the way of anything at all since the strange day in the archive. She felt off her game for several days, and after asking Scott for permission to photograph several pages of the diary, she'd practically run home to continue her work from the safety of her little bungalow.

Now it was Friday, a whole three days later, and she was finally starting to feel a bit more like herself, which meant, also, that she was feeling really very sheepish about the whole thing.

She'd always prided herself on how logical she was, how cool-headed, and here she was, hiding herself away from the world because she'd fainted in an archive. She wasn't sure what was more embarrassing—the fainting, or the fact that she'd acted like a jerk to the only two people she was on friendly terms with in Salem.

She forced herself to get up bright and early on Friday and go for a long run to clear her head. She'd been skimping on her workouts, rationalizing that she needed to rest up after her fainting spell, but really it was an excuse. She hadn't wanted to run into anyone she recognized. Now, though, it was high time to get back out into the world and enjoy the good weather.

She was also getting behind on her research agenda. The photographs of the diary were useful, and she'd been able to do a lot with just that. She'd caught up on all her letters of recommendation, her editorial work, as well as the final page proofs of an article. But now, there really wasn't much else she could do from the house.

As she jogged, she thought about the events of Tuesday morning. In her memory, now, she couldn't really understand why she'd gotten so upset. She supposed it was some kind of residual trauma from what'd happened to her as a doctoral student. She hadn't mentioned to either Hazel or Roxy that she'd actually gotten in trouble over the whole study room stunt—she'd been blamed for her own imprisonment, as the head librarian had reminded her that it was the students' responsibility to check out of the study rooms in a timely fashion. The whole episode had stung and left a foul taste in her mouth. Apparently, she hadn't quite dealt with the pain from that incident. Although…she couldn't explain the way the books had flung themselves through the air. A breeze could shift paper, certainly, but the books… It still made her feel queasy. It was best not to think about it until a more rational explanation presented itself.

It was time to put that behind her and move forward. What was Hazel thinking of her at this point? Did she think about her at all? For some reason she wasn't quite ready to admit to herself, Elizabeth felt that Hazel's opinion of her mattered. Especially since she'd been the one to have the brilliant brainwave that led to finding the diary. She'd helped her enormously, and how had Elizabeth treated her? Like a jerk, that's how.

By the time she was back home and showering, Elizabeth was determined to get over her sense of embarrassment and apologize to Hazel and Roxy. She could hardly believe she'd wasted the last three days without apologizing sooner. She'd be lucky if they forgave her.

Overnight, it seemed to Elizabeth, Salem had become Halloween central. The streetlights were festooned with black and orange garlands, and the streetlights on the main drag each had a scarecrow tied to it. Most of the shops had Halloween-specific decorations, and Elizabeth was impressed that the already very witchy town managed to find a way to become even spookier. They certainly embraced their history with open arms, and for once, it made her smile a bit. This was a way of healing from past traumas, and she could stand to learn from them.

She arrived at the shop at around lunchtime. It looked to be quite busy, but she hoped not too busy, as she entered the Witch Is In. It looked quite the same as before, though she did notice the pumpkins they'd purchased the weekend before in the window displays, as well as some orange and black garland festooned above the cash register and Halloween-themed paper cutouts on the walls. She could hardly believe it was less than a week since they'd been apple picking. She smiled to herself. What a week it'd been.

She approached the counter, where the teenage cashier was just finishing ringing someone up. As the customer stepped away, she caught the young woman's attention. Her name tag said "Rita."

"Hello. I was looking for Hazel?"

The young woman appeared to be sizing her up for a moment before finally answering. "She's helping a customer, I think. If you want, I can go get her."

"Oh no, it's all right. I'll just browse until she's free."

Another customer stepped up to the register, and Rita turned away to help them. Elizabeth made herself busy studying one of the table displays in the center of the shop: it was an entire display devoted to books about Halloween: its history, monster mythologies, Halloween-themed kids' books, Halloween-themed cookbooks and the like. Elizabeth was somewhat taken aback at all the books relating to the holiday. Back home in the UK, it was barely a blip on the calendar, and trick-or-treating was only just catching on thanks to the American influence. It was nothing like what they had here.

She was about to pick up one of the cookbooks when she heard Hazel's warm tones getting closer.

"I'm sure your niece will love that deck. And the book is very good for beginners."

Elizabeth watched as Hazel escorted a woman in her sixties to the counter to be rung up. She looked lovely and was dressed appropriately to the season. Elizabeth supposed it was expected by tourists that the owner of a shop like this one, and one who did tarot card readings to boot, would wear long flowy black dresses in crushed velvet, but somehow, the look was very natural to Hazel. Rather than looking like a hippie witch, the whole outfit was very put together. Even the black velvet choker, which could look very silly and nineties, only served to accentuate Hazel's beautiful neck. Her brown curls were pulled back away from her face again, and Elizabeth couldn't help admiring how attractive she looked at that moment, especially with the flush of energy and passion in her countenance. It was obvious that she loved running her own business and working with people.

"Hello," she said, stepping around the book display toward Hazel.

She waved a bit shyly as Hazel turned to look at her. Her expression brightened at the sight of Elizabeth.

"Hello! I'm so glad to see you." As if on impulse, she took hold of Elizabeth's hands with her own and gave them a squeeze. "I was getting worried." When she let go of her hands again, Elizabeth felt a prickle of disappointment. That squeeze was nice.

"I'm *so* sorry. To be honest, I haven't been answering your calls or texts because I've been embarrassed." She looked down at the floor, unable to meet Hazel's eyes.

"Embarrassed? Really?"

"Yes," said Elizabeth, finally returning her gaze again. Hazel looked concerned. "I can't believe I fainted like that. And then I blamed you and Roxy when you were just trying to help. I don't know what possessed me."

Hazel shook her head. "There's no need to be embarrassed. Please don't be. Roxy and I felt awful about what happened. Even if it was a weird set of coincidences, it must've been really terrifying to be alone in there."

Elizabeth shivered at the memory. "It was. But I've always prided myself on being cool-headed and logical. Must work on that, mustn't I?" She gave Hazel a self-deprecating smile.

Before Hazel could answer, several customers approached the register at once. One of them needed help locating some books on local history.

"I've got to go. Duty calls," said Hazel.

"Before you go, please, I'd love to make up for my rude behavior."

"Really, it's nothing," said Hazel.

"No, please, I want to." Elizabeth had a stroke of inspiration. "Could I help you here at the shop tomorrow? I insist. I have quite a bit of experience with tills."

"Oh my gosh, that would be amazing," said Hazel. "Seriously. I can't say no to help like that."

"Wonderful," said Elizabeth. "It'd be my pleasure."

The next morning, Elizabeth showed up at the Witch Is In fifteen minutes before opening. Hazel had been so busy the rest of the afternoon that Elizabeth had merely taken note of the opening time and texted her later. Poor Hazel. The shop's popularity was both a blessing and a curse.

It was another spectacular fall day, and Elizabeth was a little disappointed they couldn't spend the day on a hike, but she was planning to ask Hazel to join her on her next day off—even if it meant cutting into her own research schedule. She had ordered several boxes of documents that were held offsite, and they wouldn't be available for her to look at until Tuesday at the earliest anyway. That gave her Monday to hike with Hazel—provided Hazel was interested. And she really hoped she was.

The shop was shut still, so she made her way to the back entrance and rapped on the door.

"Come on in," said Hazel. "I'll give you the grand tour."

Before she knew it, Elizabeth was holding her own at the register along with Rita. For the Halloween season, Hazel had set up a second register with a tablet that would only process credit cards and other forms of electronic payment. She'd explained to Elizabeth that she hoped this would speed up checkout on the busy weekends leading up to Salem's big holiday.

Elizabeth was pleasantly surprised at how easily all her customer service skills were coming back to her. Though it'd been years since she'd worked the till at her grandparents' shop in Brighton, all that knowledge had stuck with her—and working the tablet register was extremely easy compared to cash and the ancient till her grandfather had insisted on keeping in the shop well past its usefulness.

In the early afternoon, Roxy arrived to help Hazel string up more twinkle lights outside the shop. Elizabeth found herself wishing she was the one outside in the sunshine helping Hazel string up the lights, but she consoled herself that she was doing Hazel a massive favor by working the till. And she was enjoying it. She was endlessly fascinated by the various items that customers bought at the shop—things she'd never think to buy or never even heard of: sage smudging kits, salt lamps, aromatherapy diffusers, and much, much more. Her favorite were the customers buying books, and there were plenty of those as well. Books on the witch trials, books on Salem's history, books about Halloween and fall in New England.

Around two, there was a bit of a lull, and Hazel and Roxy came back inside, their voices loud and boisterous, laughing about something one of them had said a moment before.

Roxy smiled broadly at her and approached the counter.

"Hazel's corralled you into working for her, too?" she said without preamble. She smiled and winked.

"It was my idea. She helped me so much finding that diary, and all I did was be extremely rude to her. To both of you. I'm really sorry about how I behaved on Tuesday."

Roxy waved her hand. "Oh please. It was nothing. Wake me up before nine a.m., and I'm way ruder than that."

"Regardless, I'd love to buy you both a drink. How about tonight?"

Hazel and Roxy readily agreed. The shop was open until six that day, so they planned to meet up at eight at a new martini bar that'd just opened across the street from the Scarlet Letter.

Elizabeth wasn't needed at the shop after four when traffic slowed down. She found herself leaving rather reluctantly, though. It'd been fun to do something so different from what she usually spent her days doing. She was glad she could apologize to both of her new friends—and she was especially glad she could help Hazel. It was the least she could do after the help Hazel had given her in the archive.

The diary had been a real find. It was difficult to decipher the faded handwriting, but she was making some headway and she was sure that once she had deciphered all of it, she would find something there that, together with the will, would be an amazing addition to her book's arguments.

She walked home slowly, enjoying the last rays of sunshine and taking in all the beautiful fall colors in her neighborhood. The air was pungent with all the smells of fall: the earthy smell of falling leaves, the sharp scent of wood-burning stoves, and subtle notes of cinnamon coming off a neighbor's decorative broom. She took a roundabout way home so she could walk by Hazel's beautiful villa. She took note of the big black cat—Beezle, was it?—sitting on the porch.

He recognized her and trotted over to where she was standing on the sidewalk before flopping down next to her feet, evidently waiting for her to bend over and scratch his belly, which she did. He purred loudly.

"You're a friendly one, aren't you?" said Elizabeth, scratching him under the chin. "I just hope your mistress likes me as much as you do."

CHAPTER TWELVE

The forecast for Monday called for rain in the afternoon, so Hazel and Elizabeth hit the road just as soon as the worst of rush hour was over. It was a chilly, overcast morning, and Hazel was pleasantly surprised when Elizabeth pulled a thermos out of her backpack when they arrived at the trailhead.

She'd picked a trail about a half hour's drive from Salem, somewhat inland, in a state park with a beautiful forest and several ponds that, this time of year, reflected the blazing fall colors still left on the trees. They'd driven mostly in silence, each enjoying the company of the other without recourse to conversation.

The night out on Saturday had been a big success; the three of them had bar-hopped in Salem while also enjoying light conversation and a large late-night slice of pizza to cap off the evening. Although the evening had been far from intimate, Hazel had gotten the feeling that she and Elizabeth were closer now. Working together in the shop and then spending the evening together, even with Roxy there, and even with the noise at the bars, had made Elizabeth more of a real person to Hazel rather than just a crush object. She handled herself expertly at the register and had shown a relaxed, more casual side of herself in the evening. They'd even done some dancing together at the Scarlet Letter, and it'd really gotten Hazel's heart racing to see Elizabeth letting loose on the dance floor. When Elizabeth had quietly suggested a hike on Monday, making it clear the offer was for Hazel alone, she'd readily accepted.

She enjoyed the piping hot Earl Grey from Elizabeth's thermos at a picnic table next to the trailhead. It was a nice contrast to the chilly breeze on her neck. She found herself wishing she'd packed a light scarf for the hike, even though she knew she'd warm up soon enough on the trail.

"Do you like it?" said Elizabeth. She was sitting across from Hazel at the picnic table with a second cup of tea. "I know most Americans don't take their tea with milk."

"True," said Hazel, "but I enjoy tea in just about all forms. It's one of my favorite drinks."

"I'm glad you're enjoying it."

"Thanks for bringing it. What a good idea. I didn't think it would be quite this cold today," she added, shivering a little now that the cup was empty and she was cold again.

"Would you like a scarf?" said Elizabeth, untying the one she was wearing.

"Oh no, it's fine."

"Please, I insist. You're cold, and I'm not. I'm feeling a little hot actually. I may have overdressed."

Elizabeth stood up and walked around the other side of the picnic table and wrapped the scarf around Hazel's neck. Hazel wondered if she felt the same spark she did when her warm hands touched her skin.

They started down the trail, and while the views were gorgeous all around them, Hazel found herself distracted by Elizabeth's scent on the scarf around her neck. It was something very delicate and feminine, but fresh. Citrus maybe? Underneath it was something spicier, muskier. It was intoxicating. Between that and the knowledge she was wearing something that had moments ago been next to Elizabeth's skin, she was hardly paying attention to where she was walking.

So, when Elizabeth stopped short ahead of her, Hazel didn't notice and walked right into her, hard enough that they both pitched forward.

"What's happening?"

"Stop! There's a snake," said Elizabeth, regaining her footing and pointing ahead on the trail at what looked like a moving stick.

The two of them stood stock-still as the snake slithered into the leaves on the other side of the trail and disappeared. Hazel's heart raced, though she doubted it had anything to do with the snake, as it was a common garter snake. It had much more to do with the fact that she was standing so very close to Elizabeth.

"Oh, it looks harmless," said Hazel. "Sorry about running into you. My head was in the clouds."

"No worries," said Elizabeth with a smile. "Are you all right?" She put her hands gently on Hazel's shoulders and inspected Hazel's face with concern.

Hazel rubbed her nose which was throbbing just the tiniest bit. "Yes, I'm fine. I guess I need to pay more attention." Just then, some movement farther in the woods caught her eye. "Look. Deer."

Elizabeth turned and followed Hazel's finger. They watched as one, then two, then several more deer picked their way through the forest before being startled by something they couldn't hear and running off into the distance. It was a magical moment offered them by Mother Nature.

"That's a much nicer wildlife sighting," said Elizabeth.

"Agree."

They started walking again, and soon enough they reached one of the ponds. In spite of the overcast sky, the reflections were still quite stunning in the mirror-like water, and they sat down on a small blanket Hazel had brought with her.

"This is quite the lovely spot," said Elizabeth, and Hazel beamed with satisfaction. This was, in fact, one of her favorite places to go when she needed an infusion of nature. So many of the other green spaces near Salem were packed with people all the time; this park had been one of her family's favorites. She was about to share that with Elizabeth, when a large cold drop of rain landed on her forehead. And then another landed on her shoulder, and another on her hand. Big, fat drops that splattered into smaller drops.

The pond in front of them was no longer a flat mirror; instead, it was covered in ripples of raindrops.

They scrambled to their feet, even as the rain intensified, and Hazel felt her hair and face getting wet. She grabbed the blanket and looked around, squinting through the rain, until she spied a clump of pine trees with branches high enough that they could shelter underneath.

"There!" She pointed and started half-walking, half-running toward the dry spot. They made it under the trees just as the clouds burst and the rain turned into a true downpour.

They caught their breath and watched as all around them,

everything became wet and the pond turned into a gray mist of bubbling water.

"We got here just in time," said Elizabeth, laughing. "We'd be soaked!"

"I'm halfway there, I think."

The air felt much colder now, and Hazel shivered. She'd made the mistake of wearing a thick fleece rather than her rain jacket, and she could feel water soaking through parts of her sleeve.

"Rain like this won't last long," said Elizabeth reassuringly.

"Let's hope so."

Hazel watched as the rain continued to pound into the ground, creating rivers and streams all around them. They were lucky that the grove where they'd taken shelter was relatively dry. The rain let up slightly, but it was still a downpour.

Hazel shook out the blanket and laid it down next to their feet. "Might as well be comfortable," she said, sitting down.

Elizabeth joined her. There wasn't much room under the tree that was dry, so they sat flush next to each other. Hazel wondered if Elizabeth could feel her heart pounding in her chest.

"I know this isn't ideal, but it's kind of nice anyway," said Elizabeth. "I feel like we're in a bubble here, held hostage by the elements."

"True. We'll just have to wait it out."

"Not the worst thing in the world. Of course, in England we're constantly getting caught in the rain. I don't know why I didn't think to bring an umbrella."

"Do you go hiking a lot back home?"

"Not as much as I'd like. I've been so worried about making a good impression at my job and doing lots of research that I find myself spending more and more time at my desk."

"That's understandable," said Hazel, appreciating the warmth of Elizabeth's body next to hers. "The shop keeps me busy, and sometimes I resent it. It'd be nice to have a job where I can take a personal day and just go to the woods if the weather is nice."

"Can your assistant run the place on her own if you needed to go somewhere in an emergency?"

"Good question. Not really. She's working more during the

Halloween season, but normally she's very part-time. I'd probably have to close the shop in case of an emergency."

"That's hard," said Elizabeth, her voice tinged slightly with sadness. After a thoughtful moment, she continued, "That makes me think about when you have to fill out medical forms and they ask you who to contact in an emergency. I still list my parents, even though they live hours and hours from where I work."

"I know what you mean. It's hard being on your own like that." Hazel took a breath to steady herself and decided to plunge in with her next question. "You've never had someone to list as your emergency contact, aside from your parents?"

Elizabeth chuckled. "That's a very clever way to ask me about my romantic history." She gave Hazel a sidelong glance. "No, I haven't. I had a girlfriend at uni, but it was never very serious. Before that, I was far too shy and nerdy to date anyone. You?"

Hazel blushed a little. "I had a girlfriend in college, too, but she was a year ahead of me and when she graduated, she went home to California, and we didn't want to do the whole long-distance thing. And then there was Camille."

"Camille?" Elizabeth's face was blank. She clearly didn't remember their earlier introduction.

"The woman I introduced you to at the shop last week? The one who looks like a character from an Anne Rice novel?"

Elizabeth laughed at the description. "How apt. Yes, I remember now. Does she always dress like that?"

"Oh, yes. A Goth teenager all grown up. And of course in Salem, she fits right in. She used to do vampire tours and ghost tours."

"Was she a rival of Roxy's?"

"Only for a short while. She gave it up. Got bored of it. When we were dating, she'd help out a lot at the shop."

"What happened? If you don't mind my asking."

"Not at all. It's ancient history." Hazel made her voice as decisive as possible. "She cheated on me and left me for—" Hazel stopped herself. She'd nearly said, "for another vampire." She was getting a little too cozy with Elizabeth. She was going to have to be more careful.

Elizabeth didn't seem to notice the unfinished sentence. "That's awful. What a terrible person," she said, her voice filled with disgust.

"It's all in the past. Really, it's okay. I've made my peace with it."

"I'm so sorry you had to go through that, though. Really, who on earth could cheat on someone as wonderful as you?"

Elizabeth's voice had turned softer, more tender than Hazel had ever heard it before. Her eyes met Hazel's and somehow, before she knew how it happened, Hazel felt Elizabeth's soft lips on hers.

It was the work of a moment, and yet it was perfect. There, beneath the sheltering branches of a large pine, in the middle of a downpour, they kissed, and Hazel felt the kiss from the ends of her curls to the tips of her toes, even soaked as they were with rain inside her evidently *not* waterproof boots.

Elizabeth pulled away and smiled. Just then, the rain began tapering off and sunshine burst from behind the clouds.

"Did you plan that?" said Hazel with a shy smile.

"I wish I had that much power over Mother Nature."

They looked out from under the branches as the clouds moved off, revealing a perfect cerulean sky dotted with fluffy white clouds. The clean smell of rain lingered in the air along with the warm, earthy scents of pine needles and wet leaves. The sun sparkled off the pond, and Hazel felt as though the universe were conspiring to create the perfect memory of a first kiss just as she saw something that truly felt like a good omen.

"Look. A rainbow." Hazel got up and offered Elizabeth a hand. Together they stepped out from the grove of trees and took in the beautiful half rainbow glimmering in the sky.

"How lovely," said Elizabeth, putting her arm around Hazel.

At that moment, everything felt perfect. Hazel didn't want it to end.

"Oh no."

Hazel followed Elizabeth's gaze across the sky to where more dark clouds were massing on the horizon. This was only a pause in the day's rain.

Quickly, they put away the blanket and found the trail again. They speed-walked to the car, concentrating too closely on the trail to talk. The last five minutes of their hike back was done in drizzle, and the entire car ride home was dogged by torrential rain. There was no opportunity to talk as Hazel had to concentrate on the road the whole time. It was disappointing, but at the same time, Hazel was a tiny bit grateful. She found herself utterly tongue-tied after their perfect first kiss.

Back in Salem, Hazel dropped off Elizabeth at her place.

"I had a wonderful time," said Elizabeth. "Rain and all." She smiled warmly at Hazel.

"Me too," said Hazel, reaching out a hand and squeezing one of Elizabeth's. "Text me later and we can do dinner."

"Sounds like a plan."

Elated, Hazel drove the few blocks through a steady rain, her mind full of their hike, Elizabeth, her lips, and plans for the rest of the week. It wasn't until she was home, showered, and eating a late lunch, that she finally checked her phone. There was no reception out in the woods, so it'd been hours and hours since she checked her messages.

She was surprised to see several missed calls from Roxy, a text message to call her as soon as she saw it, and an equally mysterious text from Camille. Her email inbox was also full of unread messages: there was an emergency meeting that night of the Chamber of Commerce. There'd been an act of vandalism downtown, and everyone participating in the Halloween festival was gathering to discuss what should be done. Hazel had a sinking feeling. Her first thought was for her shop. Had it been vandalized?

Her second thought was for Elizabeth. How could they make any plans when Hazel would have her hands busy with everything else going on?

❖

Roxy checked her phone again. Still no message from Hazel. She knew that reception was pretty spotty in the woods, and she was probably fine, but still. There'd been a tornado warning that morning, and Roxy was worried. When the rain hit Salem, just as she was hauling a bunch of kayaking gear into storage, her first thought had been for Hazel and Elizabeth. What a day to be outside. She'd finished up at the outdoor adventure shop where she worked part-time and managed to make it home between downpours.

Stuck in her apartment while it rained, she was bored. She knew she should be working on the new tour she was developing for the

Christmas season, but she was distracted. She'd seen Alicia the night before and things had gotten a bit complicated.

Her mind replayed the night in her head. She'd met up with Alicia at the Scarlet Letter, as they'd agreed, though the plan was to stay there just for a quick drink before grabbing dinner at a new Mediterranean place before going to Alicia's for some adult fun. At the bar, though, they ran into a group of Alicia's friends and Roxy'd had the novel experience of being introduced to her date's friend group. As a "girlfriend" no less. She liked the sound of it. Maybe Alicia wasn't "the one," but she was a lot of fun, had a great sense of humor, and they were definitely compatible in other ways. They'd been compatible all over Roxy's sheets the previous Friday. She smiled at that memory.

Last night, though, when she went to the bar to get a second round of drinks, she'd bumped into none other than Camille. Instantly, she'd felt a shock of white-hot rage upon seeing Hazel's ex.

She had a lot of nerve coming to human bars, thought Roxy, especially knowing that it was one of her and Hazel's favorite watering holes in Salem. Just as she was about to tap Camille on the shoulder and tell her exactly what she thought of her, Camille turned to face her.

"Roxy, I'm so glad to see you," she said with a big smile.

The sentiment was genuine and in the absence of her usual dripping sarcasm, Roxy had no idea how to react.

"Uh...yeah." She couldn't muster the energy to say, "nice to see you, too." It was never nice to see Camille.

"Can I buy you a drink?"

"Okay." Roxy had Camille pay for both the drinks she'd been about to buy. She'd never say no to free drinks.

As they waited for the drinks, Camille tapped her credit card on the bar. It made Roxy wonder how on earth she could have a credit card. Did vampires have credit? Would they have to forge new documents every eighty years or so? Not that she knew exactly how old Camille was. She'd rather not know.

"Are you here with Hazel?" Camille looked around the bar in a not so subtle fashion.

"Nope. I'm here with Alicia," Roxy emphasized the last word, hoping to rub it in Camille's face a bit.

"You're done with the professor, then?" Camille handed the drinks to Roxy and signed the receipt.

"The professor prefers Hazel," said Roxy, feeling like she'd just put the cherry on Camille's turd sundae. That would teach her to take someone as amazing as Hazel for granted.

Camille, however, didn't look sad or disappointed or angry or jealous or any of the other negative emotions Roxy was trying to stir up, and she immediately wondered if she'd made a mistake revealing all her cards.

"Oh? Are you sure? She seemed very interested in you last night at Shaken Not Stirred," said Camille, referring to the martini bar the three of them had gone to together the night before.

"I didn't see you there last night."

"Looked to me like you and Elizabeth were having quite the tête-à-tête. Maybe you were so engrossed in her that you missed little old me at the bar." Camille gave her an innocent look.

"You've got it all backward," said Roxy, a little less forcefully. "She's into Hazel. Not that I don't find her attractive."

"Of course. Who wouldn't?"

"Only a corpse," said Roxy, using her standard line, forgetting that Camille was, in fact, undead.

She gave her a knowing look. "Even us corpses find the professor attractive." She paused and looked Roxy up and down in a manner that gave Roxy the willies. "You're not so bad looking yourself."

Did Camille think she was cute as a person or as a potential meal? With vampires, it was a tossup.

"Personally, I think you'd be a much better fit for the professor. Like goes with like, if you know what I mean."

"I have no idea what you mean." Roxy tried to shake away the foggy feeling of sudden emotional turmoil in her head.

"Oh, I think you do."

After that, Roxy had booked it back to her table and headlong into flirting with Alicia the rest of the night. But the damage had been done. Her sleepover at Alicia's had been...routine. She was distracted all night thinking about Elizabeth.

Was Camille right? Had she seen something Hazel and Roxy hadn't? No, that was impossible. Besides, her best friend was into Elizabeth, and from what Roxy could tell, the feeling was mutual. Camille was just trying to get into her head. It was all mind games with her.

Still, she could feel her attraction for Alicia ebbing, which was so unfair, because since they'd reconnected, she'd felt like Alicia was into her, like, for real.

Roxy checked her phone again. Finally, there was a message from Hazel.

Saw your missed calls. Just got back from the hike. Is the shop ok? What's going on?

The shop? Roxy had no clue what she meant. She texted back she was fine but that she needed a favor and suggested meeting up as soon as possible.

Sorry, I can't. Vandalism downtown. Have to go to an emergency festival meeting. Stop by tomorrow?

Roxy texted back that was fine, but she was concerned. Vandalism? In Salem? During Halloween season? That sounded bad. She hoped Hazel was okay. She texted back.

Yikes! That's terrible. Let me know how it goes at the meeting. I'll stop by the shop tomorrow with lunch.

She needed to butter up Hazel a little if she was going to get what she needed from her. If all went according to plan, though, things would work out for both of them. Between the news about the vandalism and her own preoccupation with Alicia and Camille, she forgot to ask Hazel how her date had gone in the woods. Instead, she spent the afternoon concocting the perfect plan to get more love potion from Hazel.

CHAPTER THIRTEEN

Most of the year, the shop was closed on Mondays and Tuesdays, but for the month of October, Hazel had extended hours on Tuesdays. It was a busy time of year, and she wanted to make sure she cashed in on the opportunity. It would help her get through the doldrums of January and February, when nobody wanted to visit frigid, icy Salem, and even her special regular clients kept their spell casting indoors.

Still, she missed her quiet Tuesdays catching up on spreadsheets and putting in product orders. Not that the shop was nearly as busy as it'd been on the weekend. Just a small but steady stream of customers. Rita was at the register, always happy to make some extra cash, and Hazel was in the back room, tidying up and taking the opportunity start a new pot of coffee.

She'd just pressed the start button when she heard Roxy in the shop. Evidently, Rita had directed her to the back, and she nearly ran into the room.

"Hey, how's it going?" She threw herself into a chair with her usual energy and dropped a bag of takeout sandwiches on the table for lunch. "I had a yen for lobster rolls. I hope that's all right."

"They're only my favorite," said Hazel with a grin. This was just what she needed to keep her going. "Mmm, I don't think I can wait until noon to eat this. I'll be right back." She walked back into the shop and let Rita know she'd be taking a fifteen-minute lunch in the back, and then they'd switch.

Back in the break room, Roxy was patiently waiting to start on the lobster roll. Another nice surprise, thought Hazel, as Roxy rarely waited to eat, especially when lobster rolls were involved.

They dug in. The lobster rolls were excellent. Hazel moaned with pleasure. "These are heaven," she said after swallowing the last bite. They'd hardly said a word since Roxy'd gotten there.

"Oh man, that was good," said Roxy. "I always say it's important to think with your stomach." She winked at Hazel, who laughed.

"Want some coffee? Fresh pot."

"Sure."

Hazel prepared Roxy's coffee exactly how she liked it: lots of cream and sugar, and then poured herself a cup with just cream.

They sipped their coffee, and Hazel recounted the details of the emergency meeting. It had been a relief to find out that the Witch Is In had *not* been targeted. Bizarrely enough, it was the *Bewitched* statue of Elizabeth Montgomery in town that had been vandalized. Someone had graffitied it with spray paint, and everyone was up in arms.

"I'm glad it wasn't any of the shops," said Roxy. "So, will you fix the statue?"

"You know I can't just use my magic all the time."

"But wouldn't this be using your magic for good?"

"True. But I don't like to set a precedent like that. I can't swoop in and fix everyone's problems."

"How about just my problems?" Roxy grinned at her.

"What do you mean?"

"I think Alicia actually likes me."

"That's great. But how is that a problem?"

Roxy looked embarrassed. "At first I was excited about it, but all of a sudden I'm, I dunno, less attracted to her?"

"Oh, Roxy, you can't be serious." It was just like Roxy to stay in a relationship for the wrong reasons, and then break up with someone for the wrong ones too.

Roxy chuckled awkwardly. "What can I say? Ladies find me irresistible."

Hazel laughed. "Okay. What do you need help with, in that case?"

"I was thinking…maybe I could take some of that love potion? The one that 'enhances existing feelings.' Alicia is hot, we're great in bed together, and I like hanging out with her, but ever since, uh, ever since Sunday I've just been having second thoughts…Which sucks, because now she's into me. I just need a little push. And it wouldn't be a consent issue because I'd be making the decision for myself."

"Hmm, I'm not sure you need a love potion to solve your problems. It's not a panacea."

"A panna-what-a?"

"It's not a cure-all. It sounds to me like you're letting yourself get in your head." Hazel paused and thought about what Roxy'd just told her. "What happened on Sunday?"

"What do you mean?"

"You said that up until Sunday, you were into her. Now you're suddenly not?"

Roxy reddened. "Nothing. I mean…uh…just that seeing you and Elizabeth together on Saturday night made me rethink what I've got with Alicia."

While Roxy's explanation made sense on the surface, Hazel wasn't buying it. "But that was on Saturday. You mentioned something about Sunday. What happened on Sunday?"

Roxy sighed. "I saw Camille at the Scarlet Letter that night. She told me she saw us at the martini bar on Saturday, and she thought Elizabeth looked like she was into me. Not you." Roxy looked away from Hazel. She was clearly embarrassed by it all.

"So? She's full of it." Hazel studied her, realization dawning on her. "And now you can't get the idea out of your head."

Roxy nodded, cheeks blazing red with embarrassment. "I just thought, if you still had some of that old love potion—the one where you have to look at the person—then maybe I could make myself fall in love with Alicia and forget about Elizabeth."

Hazel smiled. "While I do still have that one last vial of the old potion, it won't work in this case. If you have even a shred of a crush on Elizabeth, then it's useless. Old potion, new potion, either way, it's not going to work because your feelings are being stretched between two people." She reached out and touched Roxy's hand. "I'm sorry you still have feelings for Elizabeth."

"Are you sure Camille isn't right?" said Roxy, her voice very quiet.

She couldn't meet Hazel's gaze, and Hazel felt extra sorry, given the news she had to share. "I'm one hundred percent sure Camille is dead wrong." She couldn't keep the excitement from entering her voice now. "Elizabeth kissed me on our hike."

"Really?" Roxy's look of surprise quickly morphed into one of genuine happiness. "Spill. Tell me everything."

Before Hazel could speak, though, they both heard a commotion at the door, followed by the unmistakable hiss and growl of a cat.

"What the…" said Roxy as Hazel leaped to her feet and ran to the back door. She flung it open to find Beezle hissing and growling next to someone lying on the asphalt next to the backdoor steps to the Witch Is In.

"Camille?" Hazel was utterly confused. Why was Camille lying on the ground? Why was Beezle hissing at her?

The cat gave Hazel a murderous glare.

"Don't give me that look," said Hazel. Between this scene and the week before where he'd ripped into her couch cushions, Hazel was starting to wonder if her cat had an antipathy to Tuesdays. But the ripped cushions had been an attempt to stop her from going to the archives…was Beezle trying to tell her something about Camille? She didn't have time in that moment to consider it fully, and she filed that thought away to consider later.

Meanwhile, Beezle scampered into the shop and was soon out of sight. Camille looked pretty pathetic on the ground, her clothes rumpled, hair disheveled. Hazel decided to take pity on her.

"Are you okay?"

Hazel offered Camille a hand to help her back on her feet and was genuinely surprised to see kitty claw scratches on her face. She put her pale hand up to her cheek and winced. Hazel came a bit closer and saw that the scratches were quite deep.

"Ouch." She hissed again in pain. "It really burns."

Hazel's feelings of anger at Camille and her ridiculous attempts to derail her romance were replaced with a sense of concern. And embarrassment. Beezle never attacked anyone. As a familiar, Beezle was semi-sentient and in theory should be less likely to attack people— even if he was trying to communicate something important to her.

"Why don't you come in and I'll give you some salve I have. It should do the trick."

"Thanks, Hazel."

Camille followed Hazel to the office across the hall from the break room. Roxy was nowhere to be found, which wasn't surprising given her most recent run-in with Camille.

Hazel took the key from around her neck and opened up the medicine cabinet where she kept all her potions and salves. It took a minute of looking, as the cabinet was a little disorganized. She'd recently decanted the new love potion into single-use vials, but the shop had been so busy, she hadn't had a chance to label everything. The healing salves had gotten pushed to the back. She took out several vials of different potions and placed them on the counter to get to what she needed.

"Ah, here it is." She turned to Camille and gently dabbed some on her cold cheek with a Q-tip from her magical first aid kit.

Just then, Hazel heard Rita's voice calling her name, and Roxy popped her head in. She gave Camille a disapproving look before reporting to Hazel she was needed in the shop.

"School group," said Roxy, giving her a pained look. "It's nuts out there."

There was a loud crash and the breaking of glass.

"Oh my God," said Hazel, setting down the salve and Q-tip and running back into the shop, Roxy at her side. She took in the scene before her. At least twenty young people around the age of twelve and thirteen were in the shop, all wearing large backpacks, picking up various products, laughing loudly, and, in some cases, roughhousing very close to the window displays. Rita looked frazzled at the register, trying to handle all the purchases. Next to the counter on the floor, Hazel's favorite blue vase lay shattered, the flowers in a disarray, trampled by the youthful customers who hadn't even stopped long enough to pick anything up.

Hazel felt overwhelmed for a moment before springing into action. She told Roxy to go get a broom for the glass, and she went in search of one of the chaperones. She broke up the boys roughhousing by the window display and managed to locate a chaperone and force her to stand by the register and keep the line in order.

Camille reappeared at her side, a small Band-Aid on her face to cover up the scratches. "Can I help?"

"Can you do paper receipts with the other register?" All the young customers were paying with cash, and it was slowing things down on their one cash-ready register. Camille, having worked in the shop in the past, knew how to write up the sales in the carbon copy receipt book. Although the tablet only processed credit cards, she could still use it to calculate totals and tax and then use the paper receipt book for the cash transactions. This freed up Hazel to clean up some of the displays that'd been knocked over. Just as she thought she had everything under control, she saw a group of students wandering toward the back of the shop.

"Oh my God," she muttered again under her breath. "*The potion cabinet.*"

She sent the kids back toward the front of the shop before she ran to the back office. She'd left everything out on the counter with the cabinet door wide open. She tried to concentrate long enough to count up all the vials of potions, but she kept losing count. Then she heard another loud crash from the front of the shop and gave up. She shoved the vials back in the cabinet and vowed to do a proper inventory that evening. She locked up and ran back to the front of the shop as soon as she could.

The school group wreaked chaos on the shop for over an hour. She'd been lucky that Camille and Roxy were both on hand to help. Finally, the last student and chaperone were out the door, and all three of them, plus Rita, breathed a loud sigh of relief.

"Wow. That was ridiculous," said Roxy.

"You can say that again." Hazel was exhausted. "Who takes a bunch of junior high kids to a store on a field trip anyway?"

"Desperate people, that's who," said Roxy, and they all laughed.

If being around that group for an hour was exhausting, what would an entire day be like? Too much, thought Hazel.

Camille came around the counter. "If you don't mind, I'd better be going. Could we talk later, though?"

It was time to clear the air, once and for good. Hazel had thought that keeping Camille out of her life was the best solution, but evidently, direct action was needed. She needed to know why Camille was sticking her nose in Hazel's business all the time and making trouble.

She walked Camille out of the Witch Is In and, out of earshot of the others, agreed to meet her down at an old haunt of theirs after work for a glass of wine and an honest chat.

Just as she turned to walk back into the shop, she spied Beezle sitting up on the nearby brick wall, tail flicking wildly, giving her a judging look.

"Oh please," said Hazel, tired of his antics. "You don't have a leg to stand on."

❖

As usual, Faye's was dim and dark. Hazel found Camille sitting at one of the booths, sipping on something dark and red that Hazel sincerely hoped was wine, though, knowing this particular bar, it could just as easily be blood.

Faye's was the only spot for miles that catered exclusively to magical folks—without discrimination. The name of the bar was, of course, an in-joke, playing on the word "fae" or fairies. Walking into the bar, Hazel wondered why she'd stayed away so long. The place immediately felt comfortable and homey.

Like the Scarlet Letter, Faye's interior was also dimly lit—but there the similarities ended. The darkness of Faye's wasn't seedy or clubby; it was warm and intimate. Everything was clean and neat, and the chairs were of a dark, polished wood with blue and green upholstery that looked vaguely vintage even as it appeared perfectly new. Fairy magic, Hazel knew. The room smelled faintly of all things fresh and comforting without being overwhelming: vanilla, lavender, and lemon. At times, it felt more like a Victorian tea house than a bar, but it served drinks more potent than tea at all times of day or night.

She slipped into the elegant booth across from Camille, and moments later, Andrea, the bartender and owner, came over with one of Hazel's favorite drinks: a pink gin with elderflower tonic, served in a beautiful crystal goblet. The fairies weren't ones for casual drinking. Everything they did or served was beautiful, and this drink was no exception.

"Thanks, Andrea."

"It's been a while," said the beautiful fairy, smiling down at her. Her skin was a deep bronze that shimmered in the dim light, and her deep brown eyes twinkled at Hazel with amusement. She was quite tall and absolutely stunning.

"Yes, I know. I'm sorry. The place is beautiful, as always."

Andrea winked at Hazel in response before sauntering back to the bar. It was hard not to watch her stride away in her body-hugging green silk dress. The fae were all preternaturally beautiful and charming and, from what Hazel knew, open to liaisons with men, women, and anyone else who came across their path and struck their fancy. In another world, on another day, maybe she would have made a move on Andrea. She couldn't deny that dating another Otherwordly made things a lot easier. *Otherworldly* was the term preferred by many in the magic community to differentiate themselves from humans. The fact that Elizabeth didn't believe in magic and, in fact, found the idea of the supernatural both frightening and ridiculous was never far from her thoughts.

But that kiss…the chemistry between them was undeniable. There was a spark of potential there that she wanted to explore further. Somehow, she'd figure out a way to reconcile their differences; she just knew it. If only she didn't have to sit here with her ex to hash things out again. It was the second night in a row that she had to reschedule dinner with Elizabeth, and it was making her impatient. She checked her watch: half past seven. If she hurried things up with Camille, maybe she could still stop by Elizabeth's place for a nightcap.

Camille interrupted her musings. "I feel like you're barely here."

Hazel studied Camille. She was beautiful, as always, with a glittering iciness that attracted the gaze of all who saw her. Still, at that moment, she looked strangely drawn, almost tired. She seemed *old*, somehow, even if it wasn't possible for her to actually appear old. She could only ever be ageless.

"Is everything okay?" said Hazel.

A new thought occurred to her. Maybe Camille had come back to say good-bye? Perhaps she was dying of some kind of rare vampire disease? Hazel had never heard of such a thing, but she supposed it was possible. There could be a death warrant out for Camille if she had upset some other, more powerful and older vampire—though it hardly seemed possible. Camille, despite thinking of herself as a daredevil, was quite self-centered and would never do anything to put her life or livelihood at risk—would she?

Hazel's thoughts swirled yet again, and she found herself ripping up a napkin into confetti out of sheer nerves. She was too wound up to take a sip of her beautiful G&T.

"I'm fine," said Camille finally, looking at Hazel searchingly. "It's you I'm worried about."

"Me?" Hazel was stunned. Why would Camille be worried about *her*?

"Yes, you. You seem…different, somehow."

Hazel felt a sting of annoyance. "Who I am is no longer your concern."

"I've been observing you." Camille continued as though Hazel hadn't spoken. "I thought, maybe, you'd be happy to see me. That you'd missed me. And instead you've been so…distant. It's not like you."

"You mean I'm not a doormat anymore? I have you to thank for that. Yes, I am different. I'm standing up for myself and my needs. I don't know how you could have thought that after over a year, I'd still be pining for you," said Hazel, trying to keep the ire out of her voice. "You left me for someone else."

If Camille had shown up six months ago, Hazel would've had a much harder time not falling back into her arms. But now? She'd accepted the breakup and realized how good it was *not* being with her. For all her charms, Camille wasn't the right person for Hazel. She knew that now.

Aside from the fact that Hazel was now pining for someone else.

"I didn't think you'd be 'pining' for me, not exactly. I thought maybe there were still some warm feelings left between us."

"Why would you think that?" Hazel was honestly curious.

Camille played with the stem of her wineglass, twisting it idly back and forth before answering. "I thought that maybe you felt that way about me because…I still have feelings for you."

Hazel nearly choked on her drink. She had no idea what to think. Was this the real reason why Camille had returned to Salem? To seek her out? To get back together? "Oh."

There was a long pause where Hazel studiously avoided catching Camille's gaze and focused instead on her drink and the tiny pink bubbles of tonic bouncing around the ice cubes of her goblet.

"Am I too late?" Camille's voice was small and suddenly self-conscious.

Hazel decided to change her tone of voice. Obviously, Camille was extremely awkward about the whole situation. She'd bared her heart to her, and she didn't think she'd ever done that before, possibly with anyone.

"I'm…I'm sorry, Camille. I don't feel that way anymore. I've moved on."

"Have you, though?" Camille caught her eye again, and this time, there was a bit of a challenge in her expression.

"What do you mean?" Hazel could feel herself getting warm and a little flustered. An image of Elizabeth painted itself in her mind—blond hair windblown, ice blue eyes framed by long lashes, sculpted cheekbones, and warm, pink lips etched in a smile—and she blushed.

"I've been watching you, Hazel. I know you're not happy with Elizabeth."

Hazel hesitated. That wasn't entirely untrue. She was wildly happy that she and Elizabeth were connecting. That she'd kissed her. But underneath that was the constant concern she had about being a witch dating someone so magic-averse. They'd only started dating, it was true, but how awful was it to be essentially lying right from the start?

It only took a split second, but Camille was suddenly on her side of the table and, before Hazel could speak or move, she felt Camille's arms around her and her lips on hers. There was a seductive familiarity to the moment, and before she could stop herself, Hazel could feel her lips melting into Camille's. She closed her eyes and enjoyed the sensation of being held and kissed in a way that was both new and familiar all at once.

A wolf whistle from the next table over jarred her back to reality. What was she doing? This was crazy. She pulled away from Camille, violently.

"Stop it," she whispered fiercely.

"Why? It seemed like you were enjoying it." Camille's voice was halfway between hurt and seductive.

Hazel was filled with guilt over her response to the kiss. What had she done? She wanted to date Elizabeth, not Camille. She hoped Elizabeth would never learn about this kiss. "I was just falling into an old habit. A bad habit." Hazel refused to catch Camille's gaze and played with the swirly stick in her drink. "That was all in the past, Camille. We can't go back in time."

"Elizabeth doesn't believe in magic. She's a mortal. How is it ever going to work out with her? With us, it was always easy."

"Look, Camille," said Hazel hotly, but still trying to keep her voice down and not attract the attention of other patrons. "You were gone from my heart a long time ago. You cheated on me and broke up with me. You left me with a broken heart, but believe me, I was over you long before Elizabeth ever showed up on the scene, and no kiss can fix what you did to me."

Despite Hazel's outburst, Camille didn't appear overly upset. She shrugged her shoulders in a louche manner and sipped her drink before responding. In the meantime, Hazel tried to calm herself a bit. Camille knew exactly how to press her buttons.

"That was a mistake," said Camille quietly but with intensity, her voice, again, unusually sincere, almost pleading. She reached out to touch Hazel's hand, even as Hazel instinctively moved it away. "I'm so sorry for what I did, Hazel. I truly am. I was an idiot. I didn't know what I was throwing away."

Her eyes were damp, and for a split second, Hazel also felt the weight of all that they had lost.

"It could have been good," said Hazel, reluctantly agreeing. "But I think maybe it's better this way."

"Why?" Camille's voice was petulant, and her brows furrowed. "We can still be together. Elizabeth is from the UK, and she'll leave eventually. You have to get over her. What we have, though, is a history. A past with lots of good moments. And, more importantly, we're both Otherworldly."

Hazel felt herself getting frustrated again. The hurt, sad, regretful Camille was a ruse; she always wanted to be right, and she wanted to be in control. But she'd ceded those rights with Hazel when she'd thrown their relationship out the window. She pushed away her untouched drink and started to gather her things together.

"Are you leaving?" Camille stared at her with surprise.

"Yes. I'm not staying to hear any more of this. You're my past, Camille. And who knows? Maybe Elizabeth is my future. You're not a seer, you don't know everything."

"I think I know more than you do."

Hazel paused, hand in coat sleeve, and took a long look at Camille. She was up to something after all.

"Are you being general or specific?"

Camille smiled a nasty sort of smile, and Hazel had a very bad feeling.

"Oh, very specific." She sipped the deep red liquid in her glass, stretching out the pause. She checked the time on her small, filigreed wristwatch. "Right now, your best friend and your date are falling in love. With each other."

"What do you mean?" Hazel was literally seeing red. She had to sit back down in the booth because her legs felt like they were buckling beneath her.

"I may have helped Roxy get some of that love potion you've been hoarding."

"What?" This time Hazel couldn't control her voice and several patrons at other tables turned to stare at her. Hazel hardly noticed; her mind was spinning from what Camille had just told her. "Hold on. That makes no sense. Roxy wanted the potion to fall back in love with Alicia."

"Silly Hazel. Do you really think I'd leave anything to chance when it comes to securing my future? Our future," she said, tilting her head and smiling slightly.

Hazel's mind was in a jumble. She was trying to piece together exactly what transpired that day.

"You were listening at the door today. That's why Beezle attacked you. Oh, Beezle. How I've wronged you." Hazel felt awful. Beezle *was* trying to warn that Camille was up to something.

"I'm eternally grateful to that cat of yours. I had a whole story planned for how I needed a potion for something or other, and he gave me the perfect excuse to get to your special cabinet."

"But how could you have known that school group would show up right as you…" Hazel's voice trailed off. She sat back down in the booth as the extent of Camille's transgressions hit her. "You glamoured them to show up at a certain time, didn't you?"

Camille bristled. "I did no such thing. Really, Hazel, you think I have to glamour someone to get them to do what I want?"

Hazel sighed with relief. At least Camille hadn't crossed *that* line. "So, you didn't glamour anyone today?"

"I didn't say that. Roxy proved to be quite loyal to you. She didn't want to use the potion on Elizabeth. Kept insisting on using it on herself to fall in love with Alicia. She just needed a little push—her words, not mine."

"You glamoured my best friend to fall in love with the woman

I'm interested in?" Hazel couldn't believe this was really happening. "Don't you see how this behavior is *not* attractive? How could you think I'd fall in love with you when you do things like this?"

"I see it was a bad idea," said Camille, looking contrite. "Won't you stay and talk? Finish our drinks? You haven't even touched yours."

It was true. Every time she reached to pick up the glass and take a sip, she'd been distracted or nervous. Now, she felt a little prick of intuition.

"Did you put something in my drink, Camille? Answer truthfully."

"Ouch. How could you possibly think that?" Camille looked hurt, but there was the tiniest flicker in her eyes that gave her away.

Hazel reached out her hand over the glass and started muttering an incantation that would reveal the contents of the drink. Camille knocked her hand away.

"*Fine*. Yes, I put a little of that potion into your glass. You told me once it was strong enough to even enchant a witch."

"You're impossible, Camille. You think you can have whatever you want, whenever you want, without regard for anyone else's feelings. You're worse than when we were together—the old Camille never would have pulled a stunt so dangerous or illegal. Now tell me: what did you glamour Roxy to do?"

Camille looked paler than before, if that was possible. She trembled before Hazel's angry gaze.

"I'm sorry. It was stupid. I shouldn't have done it. But doesn't it prove just how much I want to get back together? All you need is a little push and you'll see how much you still want me."

Hazel pulled out her phone, hoping to find a text there from Roxy or Elizabeth that would clue her in to where they were, only to remember that there was no cellular coverage at Faye's—human technology was disabled in and around the bar.

"It's too late for that. Tell me. Where are Roxy and Elizabeth? *Now*."

Camille stared at her hard, her ruby lips pursed, and then she relented. "They're at the Magic Bean. But it's too late—"

Before she could say another word, Hazel was off. She had to get to the Magic Bean ASAP. Her heart pounded and the blood rushed in her ears; she hoped she wasn't too late to prevent a mix-up of epic proportions and ruin her chances with Elizabeth in the process.

Chapter Fourteen

Roxy wasn't quite sure how she got to the Magic Bean café that night. The afternoon was a bit fuzzy. She felt hungover, to be honest, which for her wasn't that unusual. She liked to think of herself as a party animal. Still, it was weird to be hungover in the afternoon. That *was* rather unusual.

She felt certain she was meeting Elizabeth at the café. They'd made plans over texts. Again, she knew that, but she didn't remember texting Elizabeth or reading any replies. It was like she had brain fog.

She entered the café, ordered a rather enormous Diet Coke—her to-go drink when she was feeling under the weather—and found a cozy set of armchairs for herself and Elizabeth. Elizabeth wasn't at the café yet, and Roxy basked in the sense that at least she was early, even if she wasn't quite sure what she'd spent all afternoon doing.

She tried recalling everything that'd happened that day. She remembered sleeping in, getting lobster rolls, eating them with Hazel. Then there was the weird thing with Camille. Roxy'd booked it to the front of the shop as soon as she saw that Hazel was going to invite Camille inside, but then they'd had to interact with each other while the school group was running amuck.

Right then was when it all got a bit fuzzy in her head. She rubbed her forehead and took a giant gulp of soda. What happened next?

It was useless. No matter how hard she strained to remember, she couldn't. Instead, she had the overwhelming urge to put her hand into the left pocket of her jeans.

Inside the pocket, her hand grasped something small and smooth, oblong in shape with one curved end and the other end flat. She pulled it out.

It was a small test tube filled with shimmering liquid. It looked like one of Hazel's potions.

That was weird. She felt certain Hazel told her she couldn't use the love potion. That it wouldn't work the way she wanted it to. But what had she wanted it for? That part was foggy, too. Still, if Roxy had the potion, then surely that meant Hazel had given it to her to use. Which meant it was okay to use.

It was all very confusing. Who was she meant to use the potion on?

She sipped more soda and tried to remember.

Elizabeth arrived at the café, and Roxy waved to her. She watched Elizabeth go to the counter to place her order. Even from across the café, Roxy had to admire her. She was always dressed so nicely, so put together. She was gorgeous, but she didn't act like it. She seemed a little stuck up at first, but when you got to know her, it was clear she was a warm, nice person. They'd had a great time on Saturday. A really great time. That part was very clear in her mind.

Roxy put two and two together. Obviously, she was supposed to give herself and Elizabeth the potion. That's what it was for. Because if not, then what on earth could it be for? She remembered Hazel always said *both* people had to take the potion for it to work correctly.

"Hello," said Elizabeth, setting her drink at the table and sitting in the armchair next to Roxy's. "I take it things were a bit of a madhouse down at the shop?"

Roxy nodded enthusiastically. "Oh yeah. It was a trip. I'm glad Camille and I were there to help out."

"Camille was there, too? Isn't that Hazel's ex?"

"Oh yeah. But I wouldn't be surprised if they got back together." Why had she said that? It wasn't true at all. Roxy tried to fight her way out of the brain fog.

"Really?" Elizabeth sounded genuinely surprised.

Roxy tried to tell her she hadn't meant it, but instead what came out was, "Oh yeah. She's always saying how she wished she could have a second chance with her."

It was as though her mind and her tongue belonged to two different people. Why had she just said that? She didn't mean it. Or maybe she did mean it? After all, Camille and Hazel *had* been together in the back room alone that day.

"How odd," said Elizabeth. "She said the very opposite to me."

Roxy thought it best not to open her mouth just then. Who knew what would come out?

"Are you all right, Roxy?"

"Actually no. Would you mind getting me another cola? It's the only thing that gets rid of headaches for me."

Elizabeth looked at her with concern. "Of course."

Now was the moment, thought Roxy. The fogginess in her brain appeared to extend to her hands, though. She felt so slow. By the time she'd loosened the cap on the potion, Elizabeth was walking back with not one but two large cups: one was the soda for Roxy, and the other was a second coffee.

"I thought I'd better get a second cup of coffee for myself, too. For later."

"Are you working tonight? I thought maybe we could grab dinner."

"That's sweet of you, but I've just gotten a student's thesis to read before their defense and the turnaround time is very tight. I bought a coffee for right now and a coffee for a few hours from now, when I'm at home."

"Oh." Two coffees complicated things for Roxy and the potion, and with the fogginess in her head, she didn't quite know what to make of it all.

"Where's Hazel?"

"Hazel?"

"In your texts you said Hazel was coming, too."

Roxy definitely did not remember writing that. "Oh, uh..." She stumbled a bit before looking at her watch and realizing Hazel would be just now closing up before heading out on her mysterious errand. "The shop's just closing now, and she said she had an errand to run. I guess it's just you and me."

"An errand? At night?" said Elizabeth with a frown. "Is everything okay?"

Roxy smiled reassuringly. "Oh yeah. Just some festival business probably having to do with the vandalism."

"So awful about that," said Elizabeth, and Roxy mm-hmmed in agreement. She took a sip of the first cup of coffee. "You know, I think I might add some cinnamon to this coffee. That sounds lovely."

She pulled off the lids of both carryout cups and got up to go get some cinnamon.

This was it. The moment Roxy had been waiting for. As quickly as she could manage, Roxy pulled out the vial, which she had already unsealed, and poured half into the cup Elizabeth had been drinking from and the other half into her own soda.

That should do it, thought Roxy, feeling very pleased with herself and ignoring the tiny niggling feeling in the back of her head that was trying to remind her of something. As she saw Elizabeth approaching again, she finished off the soda with the potion in it. Immediately, she felt a warming effect in her whole body, and her heart sped up. For just a second, the effect was almost too strong: she felt nauseous.

Elizabeth sat down with the cinnamon shaker, tapped a little into each cup, and then returned the cinnamon shaker to the counter. Once she returned to their table, she put the lid back on the cup with the potion and patted it, saying, "This will be lovely when I need some extra fuel tonight." She took a big sip of the un-doctored java in the other cup and sighed with contentment. "You know, cinnamon has a lot of health benefits. And it tastes gorgeous in coffee. I learned that from Hazel."

Roxy couldn't believe it. Elizabeth was saving the coffee with the potion for later. Well, this put a wrench in things. She tried to think of a new plan, but the potion was having an effect on her already, and she was momentarily distracted by Elizabeth's accent and Britishisms. They were even cuter than she'd remembered: "biscuit" instead of "cookie," "jumper" instead of "sweater," and saying that food was "gorgeous" instead of "tasty" or "delicious."

"You talk gorgeous."

"What?" Elizabeth gave her a confused look.

"What? I mean…" What had she meant? She didn't mean to say that. Not until Elizabeth drank the other coffee. She didn't want to give anything away. One thing was for sure: she couldn't tell Elizabeth about the potion. She scrambled for something else to say.

"Uh, I meant to say you talk so much about coffee but…uh…oh.

I don't know how you can drink so much and not have shaky hands."
That was a dumb thing to say.

"Coffee is my jet fuel. I could probably drink it all day and all night."

Elizabeth smiled over the coffee and Roxy smiled back. So what if Elizabeth didn't drink the enchanted coffee right away? They could just hang out together until she did. She managed to get Elizabeth to sit with her for a whole half hour and even convinced her to get some pizza for dinner before heading home to work. For a little while, it almost seemed as though the brain fog had lifted.

"I'll just text Hazel we're going for pizza. Hopefully she can meet us there," said Elizabeth as they got up to leave the Magic Bean. She sounded disappointed, and Roxy felt a momentary sense of confusion as to why she was trying to get with Elizabeth if Elizabeth was so interested in Hazel. Her brain fog was evidently still in place, making it difficult to keep everything straight.

They enjoyed a friendly conversation at dinner, and everything was going well—except that Elizabeth still hadn't touched her second cup of coffee. She really was saving it for later. Roxy cursed herself again for not splitting up the vial, but she tried not to let her annoyance show. Instead, she enjoyed Elizabeth's company—even if it felt, oddly, more like they were just friends than lovers.

The earlier warmth Roxy felt from drinking the potion herself was gone, and she wondered if it was because Elizabeth hadn't yet taken the potion. It didn't help that the fuzzy feeling from earlier was still with her.

Elizabeth allowed Roxy to escort her home, at which point she told her that she *had* to get this work done, she had a *deadline*, and that was that.

With a reluctant sigh, Roxy complied and pretended to walk back home before circling back to observe the house. When the lights at the front of the house went off and the light in her home office came on, Roxy stealthily approached the porch.

She *had* to be there, in person, once Elizabeth drank the potion. Something inside her was compelling her to stick around and wait for that moment. She couldn't explain it, but she knew she had to do it. After all, Hazel always reminded her that the potion would work best if the lovers saw each other directly during or after drinking the potion. It might work even without that, but the surest way for the enchantment to work to was to have a visual confirmation.

Roxy sincerely hoped Elizabeth wouldn't fall in love with her own reflection, or with a doily or a squirrel, just because she didn't see a human being right away after ingesting the potion-laced coffee.

She lay down on the porch swing and allowed her eyes to close. Just for a moment. She was so tired. She just needed five minutes of shut-eye.

When she next opened her eyes and checked her watch, she was stunned to realize it was after nine, and she was freezing. She'd literally been asleep on Elizabeth's porch swing for nearly two hours.

She got up and stretched, rubbing some warmth back into her arms. She yawned and shook her head, but the fuzzy feeling was still there. She sighed. She was tired of feeling fuzzy-headed and uncertain why she was doing what she was doing. She was exhausted and headachy and cold, and now there was little chance of Elizabeth's leaving the house again before morning.

Roxy decided to give it a rest. She went home, set her alarm for four thirty, and cuddled up in her own bed to get some sleep. She would crawl back on the porch early the next morning so as not to miss Elizabeth first thing. Roxy knew Elizabeth often went for an early morning jog; though it was unlikely she would go jogging in the dark, Roxy wasn't taking *any* chances.

Chapter Fifteen

Hazel left Faye's just after eight. The Magic Bean was up the street from the bar, so she speed-walked there as fast as she could while still putting on her scarf and buttoning up her wool coat. She had a terrible feeling that she was far too late to catch Elizabeth before Roxy doctored her drink while under the power of Camille's glamour.

There was no line at the counter, and Hazel found Joanna cleaning out the espresso machine.

"Hello! Nice to see you, Hazel," said the older woman, spotting her right away. She smiled and waved. Hazel waved back but ignored the pleasantries.

"Did Elizabeth and Roxy come here today? Did they say where they were going?"

"Yes, they did. You just missed them. They were here about an hour ago."

"Yes, but where did they go? Did they leave together?"

Joanna paused as if to consider the question. "I'm not sure. I had some customers to serve as they were leaving, but I think…yes, I think they went out to get something to eat. I heard them talking about pizza. Oh! Yes, I almost forgot, Elizabeth bought Roxy a Coke, and a nice cup of decaf for herself to take home for her evening work." She tsked and shook her head. "An incorrigible workaholic, she is."

Hazel ignored the editorializing and inwardly thanked Joanna's business-minded brain for remembering all her customers' orders.

"This might sound a little weird, but were they kissing here? Hugging? Holding hands?"

Joanna gave her a look. "I don't think so. I'm certain I would have noticed *that*."

"Thanks!"

Joanna was clearly hoping for more of a scoop, but Hazel didn't have time. She left the café and turned into the alley a few storefronts away.

Outside, Hazel decided this was an emergency situation. First, she reached out with her mind to locate Roxy. Location spells worked best with people she knew well, so she focused on Roxy. The feeling she got from her was somewhere outdoors, quite cool—not a pizza parlor.

Her mind was piecing together what had happened. Under the power of the glamour, Roxy had added the potion to their drinks—but maybe Elizabeth hadn't imbibed any yet? She was taking a coffee to go, so there was still hope. She tried not to let her anger at Camille cloud her thoughts so she could focus on an action plan. She would deal with Camille later.

She reached into her enchanted leather bag, which was much more capacious on the inside than it appeared to be, and, after digging around in it, she finally pulled out her broomstick in the alleyway. It was a bit dusty, as she couldn't use it too often for fear of attracting attention, but tonight it was necessary.

She also stuffed some chocolate truffles in her mouth for extra strength and courage.

Fortunately, it was a moonless night and the streets were deserted; Hazel muttered some charms—one to get her afloat and another to make it appear, if mortals saw her, that she was nothing more than a bird of prey in the sky. The charm wouldn't last long, but she didn't need it to. She needed to get to Elizabeth's house and make sure she hadn't drunk any of that tampered coffee.

She circled around the house, landing in one of the dark shadows cast by the streetlamp. She set her broomstick at the side of the house, and quickly took a peep at the surroundings. It was a quiet night, and the only lights on at Elizabeth's were in the back rooms.

She spotted Roxy on the porch, asleep in the swing. What was she doing there?

It was only then that Hazel remembered to look at her phone, reaching for it instinctively to look for clues as to why Roxy was on the porch, alone. She'd been in such a rush to get to Elizabeth, she hadn't even thought about the phone since leaving Faye's. She was dismayed to see several messages from Elizabeth asking where she was and if she was okay, and oddly enough, nothing from Roxy.

There was no time to lose. In her stressed-out state, Hazel decided the fastest way to get to Elizabeth and prevent her from drinking the potion would be to bypass the front door and go straight to where the lights were on. She didn't want to risk getting waylaid by Roxy. Her mind in a disarray, worried for Elizabeth and hopeful she could put a stop to Camille's meddling, she walked with purpose to the windows with the lights on.

❖

Elizabeth was disappointed Hazel hadn't been able to meet them at the café. Or for pizza. She wasn't answering messages either. It could be that she was so busy, as she'd claimed, or maybe that kiss in the woods was a fluke. Maybe Hazel wasn't interested at all. Maybe Roxy was right, and Hazel had decided to get back together with her ex.

She tried not to obsess about it; after all, between the vandalism downtown and the school group at the shop, it was entirely possible that Hazel was simply overwhelmed. She was sure she'd message her as soon as she was able. They'd agreed to meet up for lunch the following day, but still…she found herself getting worried when Hazel didn't answer her most recent messages.

Elizabeth decided to keep busy with her work. She got into her pajamas and started working on reading the thesis she'd been sent. She was the third member of the committee, which meant that really, the topic had no connection to the work she did, and her opinion would be the least important compared to that of the chair, but she liked to be thorough in all she did. And if her name was going to be on someone's thesis as a committee member, then it was her reputation on the line. She wasn't going to pass someone who'd written something subpar.

As always, she found her work engaging, and the work had the bonus of distracting her from the lack of messages from Hazel. She'd put her phone in the bedroom to charge so she wouldn't be tempted to keep checking for messages while she worked in the home office. It really was perfect to exchange houses with a fellow academic.

After a while, she could feel her head nodding, and she reheated the extra coffee she'd purchased at the café. It was delicious—better than she remembered. It had a kind of hazelnut flavor she wasn't expecting. And hazelnuts made her think of Hazel.

She found herself completely distracted from her work now. The coffee wasn't making her focus any better. Instead, she found herself daydreaming about Hazel: how pretty and kind she was, how soft and warm her lips had been when she'd leaned in to kiss them in the woods, how much she'd like to see her again and do other, naughtier things together.

Elizabeth realized with a start that all of a sudden she felt very turned on just thinking about Hazel, which made her reflect that it had been a long time since she'd had sex. Too long. It was all work and no play for her ever since she'd started the job after grad school, and she'd been so focused on her promotion to senior lecturer that she'd neglected her personal life.

And Hazel...Hazel was just so lovely. So easy to talk so. So interested in her research. So forgiving when Elizabeth bit off her head in the archives. And so wildly attractive. Elizabeth loved the turn of her neck, her wild curls, and her adorable femme sense of fashion. It was never over-the-top, always tasteful, and accentuated all her curves perfectly. Hmmm, Hazel's curves. Those deserved much more attention than she could muster while staring at a screen.

She hit save on the computer and went to the bedroom, but not before taking another big gulp of the delicious coffee. Perhaps the effects would kick in after a while. In the meantime, she'd just curl up in the cozy armchair in the bedroom...or maybe...maybe she'd lie down on the bed and just think a little more about Hazel...

She was so lost in thought that she nearly jumped out of her skin when she heard a quiet rapping on the window of her bedroom. Although initially startled, she had the sense rather quickly that it was a friendly rapping at her window. She didn't know how she knew it, but she just did.

She pulled aside the heavy curtains and threw up the sash. A gust of cool autumn air hit her face, and she saw Hazel on the other side of the window. She felt her heartbeat speed up. What luck to have Hazel show up just as she was missing her.

"Hazel. Hello. Where have you been?"

"Shhhh," said Hazel, climbing awkwardly through the open

window. Elizabeth grabbed her hand and helped her all the way through. "Roxy's out there—"

"Oh. How strange."

Hazel turned back to the window and closed it, letting the blinds drop down.

"Did you—"

"I'm so glad you're finally *here*," interrupted Elizabeth, drawing Hazel into a big bear hug. She felt a little stiff in her arms, but after a moment, she put her arms around Elizabeth too. *I could get used to this*. She closed her eyes and enjoyed the moment. Hazel was so cold from being outside; she rubbed her back to try to rub some warmth into her and, on impulse, let her hand drop down to her butt and gave it a squeeze.

"Yikes," said Hazel, moving away from Elizabeth.

"You have *such* a cute butt," said Elizabeth with a wink. It was true. She didn't know how she hadn't thought of it before, but as the words came out of her mouth, she realized it was one hundred percent true. Hazel *did* have an adorable butt. She should have told her that in the woods; she'd certainly been thinking it.

"What?"

Elizabeth wagged her finger at Hazel in mock annoyance. "Don't play innocent with me, young lady. Your butt is so cute, it's probably illegal."

This was fun. Here was Hazel, in her bedroom, and Elizabeth in her pajamas—and all hot and bothered thinking about her right before she showed up. Elizabeth moved in to kiss her. She closed the gap between them, stepping up to Hazel, pulling her into her arms, and planting her lips on Hazel's.

It was a kiss both sweet and passionate, and Elizabeth felt her knees buckling beneath her. Fireworks went off in her brain and her whole body was further inflamed with passion and desire. Evidently Hazel felt the same way, as she felt her moving her hands over Elizabeth's back. It was a delicious sensation.

"Wait. Stop."

Hazel was pulling away. Why? She clearly felt the same way as Elizabeth. She was confused. And a bit hurt, too. "What is it? I thought you liked me? You kissed me back in the woods just a few days ago." She felt tears welling up in her eyes unexpectedly.

"No, please. Don't be upset, Elizabeth. There's been a misunderstanding. Hold on—hold on. Don't cry. I just need to go to the bathroom. I'll be right back." Hazel ran down the hallway to the next door and stepped into the guest bath. Elizabeth heard her lock the door, and she was more confused than ever.

Everything had been going fine. Why had Hazel come to the house if she was just going to lock herself in Elizabeth's bathroom?

She took a deep breath and sat on the bed. She tried to think logically, but everything in her head felt foggy. The only thing that was clear was that she had feelings for Hazel, and she couldn't bear the idea that Hazel didn't feel the same way. But she *did* feel the same way, didn't she? Hadn't she reciprocated her kiss in the woods? And what about her hands on Elizabeth's back just now? That was far from a just-friends kind of hug.

Elizabeth felt her heart squeeze and tears threatened to overflow onto her cheeks. Just the thought that maybe Hazel didn't feel the same way about her was unbearable. *Get ahold of yourself, woman.*

She stood up and tried to ignore the feeling of dread, walking instead over to the locked bathroom door and knocking gently.

"Hazel, are you okay? Can I get you something? Some tea or coffee? A glass of water? I'm worried about you."

Elizabeth managed to keep the wobble out of her voice, trying to be solicitous and kind. Maybe if she was extra nice to Hazel, she'd realize that they should be together, and she'd stop fighting their attraction.

That was a weird thing to think. For a moment, Elizabeth felt foggy again. Wasn't it a bit fast to be thinking in terms of relationships when they'd only just started getting to know one another? She'd never thought of herself as one of those lesbians who move in after the first date…they even had a term for them in the US, but she couldn't think of it just then.

"No, it's okay. I'm fine. I'll be out in a sec."

"Oh, good. I'll be waiting for you in bed," Elizabeth replied through the door. Why had she said that? It sounded very naughty. But that made her smile a bit. So what if it was a bit naughty? What better way to get to know one another through some cuddling on the bed…or something more? She smiled to herself as she walked back to the bedroom and flopped on the bed. She hoped very much that Hazel wouldn't be much longer in the bathroom.

❖

Hazel sat on the toilet seat lid and tried to think logically about everything that had happened.

Camille had stolen some love potion and glamoured Roxy to give it to Elizabeth, and possibly had also taken some herself, but because Hazel hadn't even sipped her drink, Camille's plan on that front had failed. And Elizabeth obviously hadn't drunk hers while she was *with* Roxy, otherwise Roxy would be inside the bungalow instead of out on the porch. So, Elizabeth had drunk the coffee alone, and when Hazel showed up...she fell for Hazel?

Suddenly, it came to her. Of course. Camille must have grabbed a vial of potion from the back of the drawer, accidentally picking up the wrong one. She must have picked up the last vial of the previous batch—the one that required the lovers to look at the person they were supposed to fall in love with, the one that was stronger and a little less stable than the new stuff. That would explain Elizabeth's strong reaction to Hazel.

She'd held on to the last vial so as to have a comparison to the new batch. She'd stored it on the same shelf of her locked cabinet in the office; at first glance, the only difference was a variation in color. The old potion was light pink; the new one was lavender. When Camille came looking for something, she swiped the one that she was familiar with, the old one that she'd developed when they were dating...

Hazel cursed inwardly. The old batch of antidote was out of date, and she'd had to toss it. It was irresponsible, she knew, to have the potion on hand and no antidote, but most customers had no need of it. Why would they? The potion was only supposed to be used by couples who wanted a little boost to their relationship, and why would they want to reverse that?

In order to brew more antidote, though, she would need a full moon, and that wasn't for another two weeks. In fact, it was the day before Halloween. The implications of this were...problematic.

On the other hand, there was a chance that in the confusion, Camille had grabbed a vial of the new batch after all, in which case Elizabeth's reaction to Hazel was a product of the fact that she'd already developed strong feelings for her in just the few weeks they'd been hanging out.

Was it possible that Elizabeth had been crushing on her just as much as she'd been on Elizabeth? She did make the first move to kiss in the woods…

Either way, she didn't have an antidote, and she wouldn't know which potion it was until she went to the shop and did a proper inventory—something she hadn't had time to do yet.

Just as she'd reached that conclusion, she remembered Elizabeth's words. Waiting for her in bed?

She felt her heart race when she thought of Elizabeth waiting for her in bed. But of course it was the potion talking. She'd sensed that day in the woods that Elizabeth was interested in her—a kiss didn't lie. She'd felt a chemistry between them from day one, even as Roxy'd swooped in to claim Elizabeth for herself. But she didn't want Elizabeth like this. She was acting lovesick, and it wasn't real. This wasn't what Hazel wanted.

She heaved a sigh.

"Uh, coming…my dear," she said, remembering that for someone under the spell of a love potion, any kind of reluctance—to say nothing of rejection—on the part of the object of their affection felt like physical pain. This was one of the major reasons why it wasn't a good idea to give just anyone a potion, aside from issues of consent, which were already quite murky in this area. Best to use it as a type of couple's therapy agreed upon by all persons in the relationship.

"Sounds good," came Elizabeth's perky reply.

What am I going to do? Hazel rubbed her face as if trying to rub a solution out of her skin. She would have to figure out a way to avoid doing anything intimate with Elizabeth—that would be unethical.

She left the bathroom, only to find Elizabeth was waiting for her in the doorway of the master bedroom with a giant grin on her face. She'd exchanged her sensible pajamas for a slinky white satin nightgown and a matching satin robe. Elizabeth's beautiful, flawless skin glowed in the dim light of the hallway, and she was nothing less than angelic. She smiled warmly at Hazel.

"You should come in here and get more comfortable."

"About that…" said Hazel, trailing behind Elizabeth.

She entered the bedroom and noticed that there were candles lit all over the room. The soft glow made the room picture perfect for romance. The bed was warm and inviting on this cold October night, with the quilt pulled back to reveal cream-colored flannel sheets. There was even a soft, fluffy robe waiting there for Hazel.

"I thought maybe you'd like to take a shower with me," said Elizabeth, almost shyly, resting her warm hands gently on Hazel's shoulders. "It's so chilly tonight, and you obviously walked here. You must be cold, my love." She moved to embrace Hazel again, but Hazel lifted up her hands in warning.

"I was trying to tell you earlier, Elizabeth, but I think I'm actually coming down with something. I haven't been feeling myself all day. I have a headache, and my throat is really sore."

None of this was true, but it was the best Hazel could come up with on short notice.

"Oh no," said Elizabeth, her face etched with real concern. "That's terrible. But we could still take a shower together? That might help your throat. And I have some shower caps to keep your beautiful hair nice and dry."

"Thank you, but I think I need to rest. Sleep. Maybe I should even sleep on the couch if I start coughing." Hazel managed to produce a small, dry, rather unconvincing cough, but Elizabeth appeared truly worried.

"Oh, no, poor dear." She pulled Hazel in close before she could protest, and she could smell Elizabeth's skin—an intoxicating scent of skin cream and citrus and something else completely indefinable.

"It's okay. Let's get you into something more comfortable and put you to bed. I'll go boil some water for tea. I've got plenty of herbal teas."

With newfound purpose, Elizabeth strode out of the room to put on the kettle, and Hazel pondered whether she should leave through the window again and give Camille a thrashing. Before she could decide, though, Elizabeth was back, carrying a set of flannel pajamas.

"I know I'm taller than you, but I think these will fit. Luckily for you, I just did the laundry. Go on, you silly goose. Put on your pajamas."

Elizabeth looked at Hazel expectantly, still holding the warm clothes.

Hazel's hands shook as she took them, wondering how on earth she was going to get out of changing in front of Elizabeth. Again—not because she didn't want to, but because this was so obviously *wrong*.

"Um, can I borrow a toothbrush? My teeth feel really gross," said Hazel, buying time—and an excuse to change in the bathroom.

"Of course, darling. I think there's a spare in the things the owner provided." Elizabeth went to the hallway and soon returned with a brand new toothbrush still in the packaging. "Really lovely owner. They've thought of everything. Well, except for an espresso machine." Hazel couldn't help laughing at that; even enchanted, Elizabeth couldn't get coffee off the brain.

There was a small ding in the kitchen.

"Ah. That must be the water for your tea. I'll get it steeped for you."

Seeing no easy way to get out of the situation, and, to be honest, feeling really quite exhausted, Hazel went to the bathroom, brushed her teeth, washed her face, and slipped into the fluffy gray flannel pajamas that smelled like Elizabeth.

It was hard not to buy into the fantasy that they were in a relationship rather than two people who'd barely gone on a date together. Elizabeth's entire demeanor was that of established lovers, still in the honeymoon phase, but past the initial dating stage. If only it were that easy.

Hazel took a moment to check herself in the mirror before leaving the bathroom. Her thick chestnut-colored waves framed her face quite nicely despite the October breezes and the ride on the broomstick. Her olive toned skin and the light dusting of blush she used every day made her look glowing and happy, and really, she wasn't looking bad. Of course her hourglass figure was somewhat disguised by the loose pajamas, but the pajamas couldn't hide all her curves. Maybe when this was all over, and she managed to disenchant Elizabeth, she could have a real shot with her?

There was no sense in trying to find Camille that night to tell her off, as Hazel imagined she was probably hiding somewhere she'd never find her, knowing just how angry she was. But perhaps she could undo the glamour on Roxy before bed. When she did another location spell, however, she sensed Roxy was at home, safely asleep. With any luck, the glamour would fade overnight—after all, Camille had gotten what she wanted and there was no point in extending the enchantment.

Hazel decided the best thing to do would be to stay with Elizabeth and observe the effects of the potion on her. This would also be less painful to the enchanted professor. Plus, to be honest, she was bone tired from the emotional roller coaster that day. She went downstairs to where Elizabeth and a steaming cup of tea were waiting for her.

Chapter Sixteen

Roxy's alarm went off promptly at half past four, and she immediately hit snooze. The next time it went off, she turned it off again. She was groggy and exhausted and couldn't even remember why she'd set the alarm.

When she woke up around seven, she felt slightly better, but the feeling of having a terrible hangover lingered. She stumbled out of bed and went to the bathroom; she splashed cold water on her face and drank some straight from the faucet before brushing her teeth and toweling dry.

She couldn't shake the feeling that she was forgetting something. Her head was throbbing, though, and she couldn't think about anything other than popping some painkillers and hopping into the hottest shower she could stand.

As the water coursed over her, bits and pieces of the day before flashed in her memory. She concentrated as hard as she could, and suddenly, she remembered: she was supposed to be at Elizabeth's early that morning. Of course. She had to see Elizabeth—the beautiful, talented, super smart woman who'd captured Roxy's heart.

She couldn't quite remember why, but suddenly a sense of urgency overtook her. She turned off the water, dried off, and hopped into some clothes as quickly as she could before running out of the house.

She jogged the entire way to Elizabeth's, which was a fifteen-minute walk. She made it in ten.

By the time she got there, it was nearly eight, and Roxy had a sinking feeling there was absolutely no way she was going to catch

Elizabeth. She couldn't remember why, but it was crucial that she saw Elizabeth before she left the house, and normally, by eight any given day, Elizabeth was usually on her way to the coffee shop or already there, waiting for Joanna to unlock the doors.

As she approached the front door, though, Roxy smelled the delicious scent of pancakes and coffee. Perhaps Elizabeth was home after all.

She knocked on the door. Moments later, Elizabeth opened it looking mildly surprised.

"Roxy? What can I do for you?"

Roxy stood there, staring at Elizabeth, who was wearing a shimmery satin bathrobe and sporting the sexiest bedhead Roxy'd seen in a while. Roxy stepped forward and hugged her—but Elizabeth didn't hug back.

"Hey, you. You're looking gorgeous as always. I was stopping by to see if you wanted to go get coffee. You're usually the first one at the café."

"That's so nice of you, but actually I've just made coffee with the French press. I thought I'd try something new. I'll see you later." And with that, Elizabeth made to close the door. Roxy was stunned. What was happening? She couldn't understand it. How could Elizabeth not want Roxy the way Roxy wanted her?

"Wait. Why don't I keep you company?"

"I'm sorry, Roxy, but Hazel and I are just getting up and having a lazy morning. I hope you understand. You're keeping us from our breakfast." She smiled apologetically before stepping back from the door and making a grand gesture to Hazel, who was standing there like a rabbit frozen in place, holding a mug of coffee, and wearing overly large pajamas. It was painfully obvious she had just gotten out of bed.

"Hi," she croaked out with a small smile, as if this were the most normal thing in the world.

"Hazel?" Roxy took in the whole scene and her brain couldn't comprehend it. What the hell was going on? "Um, Hazel, can we talk? *Right. Now?*"

"Roxy, please, we're having breakfast," said Elizabeth.

Roxy felt her heart squeeze painfully.

"It's okay, Elizabeth," said Hazel, setting down the mug. "I'll go talk to Roxy on the porch, and I'll be right back."

"Like hell you will," spat Roxy, feeling an unexpected rush of rage.

It was clear Hazel had spent the night with Elizabeth—and Elizabeth had enjoyed it. But hadn't Roxy told Hazel how she felt about Elizabeth? That she was in love with her?

No, that wasn't quite right. She wished this damn hangover would go away, as she couldn't think straight at all.

Tears sprang to her eyes and her throat grew tight. What was happening to her? She was like a stranger to herself. She was infatuated with Elizabeth, but Elizabeth didn't want her. She was missing several hours of memories, and she couldn't understand how that was possible unless she'd blacked out somehow. Her thoughts were a disorganized mess, but she couldn't concentrate on the night before because of the pain that Elizabeth's rejection was causing. She was cold all over, and she was starting to shake.

"Hazel, what's happening to me?" Her voice came out wobbly, and her knees were weak—but not in the good way. Hazel jumped to her side and helped her sit down on the porch swing.

Hazel didn't respond; instead, she grabbed Roxy's hands with her own, closed her eyes, and muttered a long sequence of words Roxy couldn't understand. She wanted to pull her hands away, but after a moment, it was as though the curtains in her head had cleared away.

She was flooded with memories from the day before: talking to Camille at the shop, Camille giving her a small vial of liquid to put in her pocket, putting the liquid into her Coke and Elizabeth's coffee, then going out for pizza. All of it flooded back to her, though it took several moments for her to comprehend it. Why on earth would Camille give her one of Hazel's potions?

"Is that better?" Hazel's calm voice interrupted her thoughts.

"I feel...weird. Like I wanna puke. But also somehow better." Roxy looked at Hazel, still utterly confused. "I can remember everything from yesterday now, but it still doesn't make sense." She paused and searched her thoughts. Elizabeth was in them, everywhere, and the pain of Elizabeth's recent rejection stung all over again.

"Camille glamoured you so you would give Elizabeth the love potion. I don't think she counted on the fact that you would give it to yourself, too."

"What?"

"You're more strong-willed than she counted on, Rox," said Hazel with a wink.

"Just goes to show how little she knows me," said Roxy, still feeling faintly sick even if she was oddly proud of herself. "You always say how important it is for both people to take the potion. I guess it stuck with me, finally."

"True. Unfortunately, it looks like the potion magnified your crush on Elizabeth."

For a moment, Roxy was flooded again with the combined sense of hurt and urgency when thinking about Elizabeth—hurt at her rejection and a deep urgency to see her and be with her. It was awful.

Still, there was something here that still didn't add up for Roxy. "When did you figure it all out?"

"Camille as good as gloated about it to me last night. I met up with her after I closed up the shop for the night. That was my errand. Closing up took longer than usual because I was trying to clean up the mess from the school group."

"And what did she tell you?" Roxy couldn't help the hostility that entered her voice just then. She slowly pieced together the previous day. She'd told Hazel she had feelings again for Elizabeth. Then Hazel went out with Camille, and Camille told her she'd set up Roxy with Elizabeth. Roxy couldn't figure out why Camille would want to set her up with Elizabeth, but regardless, the fact remained that Hazel went in search of Elizabeth *first*...not Roxy.

"Just that she'd glamoured you to give Elizabeth the potion. She wanted me to have zero chance with Elizabeth, so that I'd somehow see that it was Camille I should be with."

"Sounds to me like you wanted *me* to have zero chance with Elizabeth." There was a hard edge to Roxy's voice now. She stood up from the porch swing. She had to get away from Hazel. "You came here, knowing Elizabeth would drink the potion, and you wanted it to be *you* that Elizabeth saw first."

"Roxy, I've told you a million times that visual confirmation is only one part of the love potion's power."

"Whatever. You knew I'd been glamoured, and you didn't come and find me. You didn't un-glamour me. All you wanted was to be with Elizabeth. Some friend you are." Roxy was fit to spit nails. She couldn't believe it. It was bad enough finding out you'd been zombie-fied by your best friend's vampire ex-girlfriend, but now Hazel expected her to understand that she was no longer Hazel's number one priority? That getting together with some British chick who'd be gone by Christmas was more important than breaking some awful spell? It was damning. "Do you even know what it feels like to be glamoured? It feels like shit."

Hazel didn't say a word. If there was ever confirmation through what *wasn't* said, this was it. She saw Hazel's eyes glisten with tears, and she was glad of it. She shouldn't be the only one who felt the pain of the situation.

"I'm *so* sorry, Roxy. I can't begin to imagine how awful that must feel."

"Yeah, it was awful. I thought I was losing my mind." She paused, waiting for Hazel to say something, anything, to explain her actions, to tell her how she was going to make it right, but she just sat there. "So, you'll lift the spell now, right? You have an antidote."

"I don't have any."

"What? Why not?"

"There wasn't much left, and it was old. It went bad, and I had to toss it. The ingredients for the antidote take time to mature, so I can't make it right away. It's going to take time."

"When will it be ready?"

"Halloween."

"Gee, that's convenient." Roxy couldn't believe it. Her best friend who was always so careful, such a planner, so methodical, had messed up. Or was she lying? Roxy couldn't tell if her suspicions were so strong because she was under the spell of the love potion or because they were justified. They'd never been in such a situation before where they were both interested in the same woman; it was impossible to tell what was normal.

"So I'm stuck like this for...two weeks?" Roxy felt something between outrage and despair. She'd always enjoyed crushes and infatuations—the roller coaster of emotions was something she thrived on. It made her feel alive, but this...this was unbearable. She felt constantly nauseous, like riding a manic merry-go-round.

"I'm sorry, Roxy, I don't know exactly why you're feeling the effects of the potion in such a terrible way. When I find Camille—"

"Send her to me. I'll wring her throat." Just the thought of that evil vamp made Roxy's blood pressure skyrocket.

"I'll deal with Camille. And I'll make the antidote. But you're going to need to be patient, and try to remember that what you're feeling for Elizabeth is potion-induced, okay?"

"Fine, you do everything." Roxy felt like crying, but she also felt like punching something. She knew then and there she needed to get away from Hazel and Elizabeth. She needed to be far away from other people or else she'd end up saying something she'd regret. "Make that antidote, and don't come looking for me until it's done."

Without another word, she stomped off the porch and down the street, barely aware of what direction she was walking. The cool autumn air felt good on her hot face, and when it started to rain, she didn't care. The raindrops were a perfect camouflage for the tears that were now freely running down her face.

CHAPTER SEVENTEEN

I s everything okay? It sounded like you two were arguing."

Elizabeth was waiting for Hazel in the kitchen feeling inexplicably worried. It was as though when she wasn't with Hazel, she felt empty inside. It was silly. She'd only just kissed Hazel a couple of days ago, and while she'd had an intuitive good feeling about Hazel from the very first time she laid eyes on her, this was something different.

As Hazel came back inside the house, Elizabeth saw her face was blotchy and her eyes were wet. Just the sight of Hazel upset made her upset as well. She walked over to her and put her hands on Hazel's hips.

"You should have seen how upset she was," said Hazel in between sobs. "And she's right. I came here last night because I was more worried about you than about her."

Elizabeth didn't really understand why Hazel was worried about either of them, but she rubbed Hazel's back in a soothing motion and shushed her.

"She knows you care about her. Whatever it is, I know you'll patch it up."

Hazel sniffled a little. "It's just, we've never, ever had a fight like that. And we've been friends since forever...since we were girls playing pretend in the schoolyard."

"Why don't you sit down and have some more coffee?" said Elizabeth. "A glass of water might not go amiss either." She poured Hazel a glass and handed it to her. "Important to stay hydrated whilst crying."

Hazel smiled and took a big gulp of water, and Elizabeth was pleased she could be of help.

Hazel heaved a sigh that ended in a groan. "I just got up and already I feel so tired. Everything is a mess." She went back to her cup of coffee and sat down on the stool.

"Do you want to talk about it?"

Hazel was silent for a moment, and Elizabeth felt a pang of concern that Hazel wasn't ready immediately to share what she and Roxy were talking about on the porch.

"It was a misunderstanding," said Hazel finally. "Roxy is a little jealous…of us."

Elizabeth blushed slightly. "That's silly. She must know nothing would ever have happened between us." She tilted her head slightly. "You know, it's the strangest thing. I feel like I can't get enough of you. Like I'll stop breathing if you're gone too long. How odd."

Before Hazel could pick up her mug, Elizabeth scooped it up and put it in the microwave.

"Can't have you drinking cold coffee. Especially not when you're getting over a cold." While the mug nuked, Elizabeth came over and kissed Hazel on the nose. "There's my sweet Hazel."

The microwaved dinged and a moment later, Elizabeth placed the piping hot mug in front of her and pulled out the pancakes from the oven, serving Hazel only the biggest, fluffiest ones. It'd been so long since she'd made anything from scratch, it was shocking. She'd taken a cooking class at uni and loved it, but once she was in grad school, she couldn't be bothered to cook anything that took longer than five minutes. She'd been working so much in the last five years; it couldn't be healthy. Something about spending time with Hazel made her reevaluate how she was spending her time.

"That was delicious. Thank you, Elizabeth."

"The least I could do. I'm so sorry you quarreled with Roxy. I hate to think I was the cause of it."

Elizabeth sat on a barstool next to Hazel and put her arm around her shoulders. Even sitting down, Elizabeth was taller than Hazel, and her arm was perfectly positioned to drape around Hazel's shoulders.

"Mmmm, that feels nice."

"Do you have to go to work today?" said Elizabeth. "I was thinking

I could take the day off and we could do something fun together. Maybe go for another hike? That was so nice when we did that."

She barely knew where the words were coming from. It was so unlike herself to take a day off when there was so much work to be done…but on the other hand, there would always be time for work.

Just then came the patter of rain on the windowpanes.

"That's a shame," said Elizabeth, checking her phone's weather app. "Oh dear. Rain all day."

"That's okay. With the Halloween festival less than two weeks away, there's a ton of work at the shop to be done. I'm not sure I'll have time to go for another hike until after Halloween."

Elizabeth pouted for a moment before smiling and rubbing Hazel's arm lovingly.

"Oh, all right. I guess there's always more of that diary for me to decipher. And that sounds like a good goal—get as much work done before Halloween so we can enjoy the festival and the fruits of your labors."

"Thanks. That sounds nice."

"It's high time we hopped into the shower, in that case. I don't want you late to work."

Hazel glanced at her phone. "Oh no. It's so late. I'm sorry, Elizabeth. None of my clothes are here. And I have some festival stuff at home that I need to bring to the shop. And we're due to open in a half an hour."

Hazel ran to the bedroom.

Elizabeth followed her. "Are you sure? I can go with you to your house. Think how nice it would be to go downtown together."

All too soon Hazel was dressed and ready to go.

"I'm sorry. I've got to dash. I'll see you later, okay? I'll text you. I promise." She breezed past Elizabeth and practically ran out of the house.

"Wait!" Elizabeth grabbed an umbrella from the hallway rack provided by her hostess. "At least take an umbrella. You'll get soaked."

Hazel doubled back and grabbed the proffered umbrella before setting off at a fast clip.

Elizabeth sighed. She stood on the porch, watching Hazel's figure receding into the distance. Once Hazel rounded the corner, Elizabeth shivered in the wet October breeze and went back inside, deep in thought.

She marveled at how strongly she was feeling about Hazel now. A week ago, she'd only had the faintest sense that she and Hazel were connecting, but now it seemed so obvious, so clear, that they were meant for each other. She wanted to spend every moment with Hazel, though she acknowledged that of course she still needed time for her research... She smiled. Hazel had even helped her with her research. She would always have Hazel to thank for that. Some of her feelings of urgency around the research project were allayed now that she'd found some truly new and exciting primary sources for her book project.

It was disappointing not to get to spend the whole day with her darling Hazel, but Elizabeth knew better than anyone the pressing demands of a deadline. She would have to catch Hazel later in the day. They could have dinner out—or, better yet, Elizabeth could cook some spaghetti Bolognese and they could dip into the hot tub at the bungalow before finally sleeping together.

Mmmm, that sounded nice, thought Elizabeth. She would surprise Hazel at the shop later. But for now, it was time to get to work.

❖

Elizabeth knew that beginning this week, the shop had extended hours until seven every day until Halloween. She showed up promptly at six fifty to find the shop still besieged with customers.

She'd spent the day at the archive, working as diligently as she could to decipher as much of the diary as possible. She was making notes and photographing sections that seemed particularly useful, but there were many sections that she couldn't yet make out. It was especially frustrating because halfway through, there was a break, and the diary picked up several years later. Elizabeth had perked up at the sight of the year, 1714, as it was the same as the date of the codicil to the will she'd found. Clearly there was a connection between the writer's changes to the will and the other woman's decision to return to her diary of the witch trials. If only Elizabeth could decipher the handwriting in that part of the diary. It was particularly faint and blurry, as though written by an uncertain hand.

Try as she might, though, she couldn't figure it out that day. She photographed it and sent it to her friend Andy, a paleography specialist who'd also helped her with documents for her dissertation—and for her father's pet genealogy project. Hopefully, she could help decipher the fainter scrawls; she sent the email with attachments and called it a day. After grabbing a quick snack at a convenience store, she'd headed to the shop, never expecting that it would be quite so packed that late in the evening.

Rita, the harried assistant, recognized her. Her usually immaculate black lipstick was smudged and her black braids were falling apart. She'd evidently been tugging on them out of the stress of handling the overflow of customers. Her usual detached Goth composure was nowhere to be found.

"Thank goodness you're here," said Rita with a smile of relief. "I need a cigarette so bad. Can you watch the register for a bit? Most of these people are just browsing."

"Where's Hazel?" said Elizabeth to Rita's retreating figure.

"Tarot readings," came the reply, and then Rita disappeared through the curtains at the back.

Moments after Rita stalked off, some teen girls, also dressed all in black with heavy eye makeup and thick platforms on their steel-toed boots, came up carrying black candles, incense sticks, and packs of tarot cards. They reminded Elizabeth of some of the girls she'd gone to high school with. She could never understand the point. Surely these young women were smart enough to know that none of this stuff was real. And if dressing in all black and pretending to do witchcraft was supposed to be a way of bucking the trends of society, then surely dressing identically defeated the point of being different?

Still, she supposed shops like Hazel's provided a small sanctuary for people who were different or didn't fit in. And maybe, just maybe, they would one day stop in and buy a good, solid history book along with their incense.

Elizabeth rang them up and even managed to locate some paper sacks for the items. The girls paid in cash, which threw her momentarily for a loop, as she was still having trouble with American currency, especially the nickels and dimes. But she figured it out quite quickly and sent them all off on their way, satisfied with their purchases, she hoped.

The teens were quite impressed with her British accent, which pleased her. Regardless of what the shop sold, she found herself enjoying interacting with so many different kinds of people while in Salem—and she got the satisfaction of helping Hazel some more, too.

She rang up a mum buying her son a kids' book about the witch trials, and then an older gentleman came in to buy postcards. From some of the conversation she overheard between the boy, his mum, and the older man, it sounded like they were locals. They spoke very highly of the shop, and it was clear that the kid's book was for a school project on the witch trials. Their conversation made Elizabeth rethink the purpose of the shop. It was a nexus of community interaction that provided locals as well as out-of-towners with many options for learning and fun.

Finally, there was a lull, and Rita reappeared.

"Everything okay?"

"Yes. It's all gone swimmingly. This is kind of fun, isn't it?"

Rita rolled her eyes. "Yeah, when you only have to do it for five minutes, sure, it's fun."

The young shop assistant made to come around the counter to relieve Elizabeth, and up close Elizabeth could see she was quite tired. She'd been working extra hours, and while apparently this was normal, maybe Rita had been working a tad *too* much.

"Wait," said Elizabeth before Rita could come around the counter. "Why don't I finish up the rest of the stuff here, and you can start closing up? I don't mind at all." She smiled reassuringly, and Rita reluctantly flashed her a smile, too. There were suddenly several more people in line waiting to make purchases now that the shop was closing.

"Wow, yeah that'd be great. If I don't change the sign to 'closed,' we'll never get out of here."

There were still about six or seven customers milling about the shop, and one by one they also got in line to purchase their wares while Rita locked the door, changed the sign, and straightened up the products that had become disarrayed over the course of the day.

By half past seven, the shop was empty of customers except two young women in their twenties waiting for their palm readings.

"I'm off," said Rita after retrieving her backpack from the back room. "Need anything else?"

"No, cheers. Have a nice night, Rita."

As Rita left, Hazel emerged from the alcove where she did readings along with a young man who had apparently had a very difficult tarot reading, if the tears in his eyes were any indication. Elizabeth fought the urge to roll her eyes. Honestly, who could believe this bunk?

Hazel rubbed his back encouraging. "Remember, the cards only tell you what you need to hear."

The young man nodded and smiled, and, although she found the whole idea of tarot cards bizarre, Elizabeth had to admire how well Hazel connected with her customers. It reminded her in a nice way of her grandparents and their shop, and how they knew their regular customers' names and had relationships with them. Even if running a business wasn't her passion, she admired those who did it well.

Hazel locked up after the young man left so no more errant customers could slip in. She turned back to the counter and finally noticed Elizabeth standing at the register.

"What are you doing here?" she said. "You know I've got another reading…"

Elizabeth held up her hands. "I am at your disposal, madam. I was helping Rita close up, and now I'm waiting for you to be done so I can whisk you away to dinner."

"Oh. That's so nice," said Hazel. "Let me finish up with these customers." She ushered the women waiting for her into the alcove and disappeared behind the curtain.

Elizabeth looked around herself for a moment, realizing how stupid she'd been. Instead of going to the archives today, banging her head against a wall of indecipherable old handwriting, she should have come to the shop to help Hazel. How silly of her. After all, those historical artifacts would still be there next week, and meanwhile it was obvious that Hazel and Rita were swamped.

There was no time like the present, however, to make good on that idea. After all, the more she helped Hazel, the sooner Hazel would be ready to go home.

When Hazel emerged a half hour later, Elizabeth barely noticed. She was delighted with the progress she'd made in the shop.

"What's going on?"

"Oh! You startled me," said Elizabeth.

Hazel raised her eyebrows in curiosity, and Elizabeth let out a hoot of laughter.

"Uh-oh. Should I be worried?"

"No. Not at all. I'm just laughing at your expression. You look so worried. And now I get to tell you that there's no need to be. I'm simply chuffed at myself for thinking up some ways to help you here at the shop."

"Oh?" Hazel surveyed the counter area where Elizabeth had rearranged some of the items. Several items that had been relegated to other shelves were now neatly arranged on a display tray that Elizabeth had found on one of the shelves under the counter, hidden behind some packing paper.

"I changed your display so you can sell more of those, what do you call them? Impulse buys."

Hazel grinned and Elizabeth could feel herself beaming.

"Anything else I should know?"

"I counted up the money in the register, and you're all square for today. And don't worry—I know what I'm doing. I think I mentioned the first time I came here that I worked in my grandparents' shop for ages back home."

Hazel looked impressed. She checked everything and verified that it was all in order. Elizabeth showed her how she'd organized the receipts, made notes of stock that was low in the shop, and inventoried the items that had been selling the most that evening.

"My goodness, you're a small business genius. Really, I'm in awe."

Elizabeth flushed with pleasure. She'd forgotten how good it felt to do something unexpected and useful for someone else—especially someone as busy as Hazel. If Rita, the assistant, was tired, then it was to be supposed that Hazel was, too.

"Gosh, you look beat," said Elizabeth. "I thought maybe I could convince you to come out for supper with me—something romantic and delicious. But now I see that might be a bit much."

Hazel smiled thinly. "That's sweet of you, but I really should go home, take a shower, and hit the sack. I have to do this all over again tomorrow and, really, the whole rest of the week." She yawned. "I feel tired just thinking about it."

"I brought you some chocolate," said Elizabeth, proffering Hazel some chocolate truffles wrapped up individually in gold-colored foil.

"Life saver," said Hazel. Her lips closed over the delicious, rich flavors of hazelnut and dark chocolate. "There's something about chocolate that makes everything better."

"Agree."

Elizabeth helped Hazel carry her bags and purse out to the car and gave her a chaste kiss good-bye. Hazel looked awfully tired, and although it felt like she was cutting off a limb when she did it, Elizabeth told her to go home and get some rest. She could use a long walk to clear her head, and the rain from earlier had cleared up. She needed some time to think up the perfect plan to make time for her research but also help Hazel with the shop. Unless Hazel got help, she'd never have the time or energy for all the things Elizabeth wanted to do with her. And to her.

She smiled a little bit to herself with that last thought. It wasn't like her to make naughty pillow talk, but something about Hazel was bringing out all sorts of parts of her personality that she didn't even know she had, and she liked it very much indeed.

CHAPTER EIGHTEEN

Two days later, after spending a chaste but very cuddly night together at Hazel's house, and thankfully no sign whatsoever from the ghost of the house, Elizabeth had declared her intention to help at the shop that weekend and the following week leading up to Halloween. She was at a pausing place in her own research and needed to step away from it all for a couple of days.

"A couple of days away won't do any harm," she said at the breakfast table before giving Hazel a peck on the cheek.

It was hard to believe this was the same Elizabeth who'd started her time in Salem with a sixty-hour work week after a grueling international flight. Hazel knew it was one of the effects of the love potion. Even three days later, it still held Elizabeth in a strong grasp.

When she'd finally had a chance to go to the office and do a proper inventory of all the vials, she found the evidence she'd been suspecting all along. The small pink vial of the old potion was still safely in the medicine cabinet, which could only mean that Camille had stolen two vials of the new batch—the one that didn't rely on visual confirmation at all.

Which meant that Elizabeth did, in fact, have feelings for Hazel before she took the potion—quite strong ones in fact. It made her heart flutter thinking about it. The potion had worked almost too well because Elizabeth was already crushing on Hazel. What would happen when Hazel gave her the antidote? Elizabeth would remember everything that'd happened while under the spell of the potion, and there was no way of knowing how she'd feel afterward. This was all new territory for Hazel. After all, the antidote was so seldom necessary. She had no idea if it would remove all the feelings Elizabeth had for her, or if the sudden loss of the super strong emotions and the return to mild crush or infatuation would be too little to interest her any longer.

There was just no way to know, and it was tying Hazel in knots. The longer Elizabeth was under the spell of the potion, the more Hazel got used to their new relationship. It was kind of nice to skip all the awkward dating, the trust issues, the getting-to-know you talk. Instead, they'd zoomed through all of that to a later part of the relationship— something closer to the third or fourth month of dating someone successfully. They were comfortable with one another, there was trust between them, but it was all still new and exciting.

Of course, Elizabeth's enthusiasm for getting physical was… problematic. Hazel wasn't interested in doing anything with Elizabeth that she wouldn't have done on a first or second date since that was essentially where they were in the dating stage before becoming enchanted. Brief kissing and hugs, some cuddling, that was it. It was getting harder and harder to stave off Elizabeth's advances, though, as she was obviously interested in going further.

Hazel was seriously considering exiting the love potion business. It was a dwindling business anyway as she rarely had repeat customers. If the potion worked, then that was the goal: no more need for it. She would make the antidote, give it to Elizabeth, and then use the rest to neutralize the new batch of love potion and destroy it. Messing with emotions was far too dangerous.

Her regular business was booming, and the side business wasn't really necessary. With Halloween just ten days away, the shop was hopping.

She hadn't heard from Roxy except for a terse text message saying she was going out of town, and her heart hurt that her best friend was gone. Lucky for Camille that she hadn't shown her face, or Hazel might have tried to turn her into a frog.

Thank goodness for Elizabeth's help. Hazel felt a little guilty taking advantage of it, but she'd offered to pay her and she'd refused. She would offer again after the antidote took effect. Elizabeth constantly found ways to help around the shop, including ingratiating herself with Rita. The sullen young woman rarely smiled and could usually be heard making ironic comments about anyone over the age of twenty-one, but she idolized Elizabeth; either that, or she was just grateful to have help at the shop during this busy time. Hazel had never seen Rita smile so much at the cash register until that week.

Whenever it wasn't necessary to have all three of them on the floor at once, Elizabeth would go into the office and work on paperwork—all the stuff Hazel loathed and always put off doing. Elizabeth's archival skills and attention to detail very easily transferred to a business setting.

Soon enough, Elizabeth was researching new books to order for the shop in addition to preparing some small business grant applications in Hazel's name. This was on top of doing inventory work and putting in a rush order for crystals that had sold out the week before. Hazel had meant to do it herself but was overwhelmed by all the work at the shop and the preparations for the Halloween festival.

To celebrate Elizabeth's amazing abilities, they decided to go out to dinner to none other than Luigi's on Monday, Hazel's only day off the following week.

The small, homey restaurant was quieter on a weeknight, and they enjoyed the attention of the owner, including champagne and an amuse-bouche on the house.

"You know, I was a little nervous about coming back here," said Elizabeth, her cheeks red from wine, her eyes glowing with happiness. "After what happened with Roxy."

"I hope you're having a good time tonight."

"Oh, yes." Elizabeth gazed contentedly at Hazel. "I've had a great time this weekend. I never thought I'd find satisfaction working at a shop rather than at my research, but oddly enough, it's been very satisfying. And fun."

"I'm glad. I wouldn't want to take you away from your research."

"After Halloween I'll have to get back to it. I suppose I'll have to think about starting the Boston portion of my research fairly soon, as well."

Hazel could feel her face fall with that news. Elizabeth, she noted, didn't look very happy about it herself.

"Boston isn't that far, though. Plenty of people commute." Hazel tried not to sound too pushy. After all, it was likely that after Halloween, Elizabeth would be happy to put as much space between her and Salem as possible.

"True, though I've never been a fan of that. But then again, I really have fallen in love…with Salem."

She added the last part somewhat quickly, and Hazel wondered if she had been about to tell her that she loved her. She had already been feeling warm from the wine; now she felt positively feverish. She knew for Elizabeth it was the love potion talking, but she didn't care. She loved Elizabeth, too, and she wished she could tell her. Even though they'd only known each other for a brief time, she felt it was true. *You're such a lesbian.* "I'm glad to hear that," she said after getting a grip on her emotions. "I'm glad all our magical mumbo jumbo didn't turn you off."

"No, no," said Elizabeth, shaking her head. "I've come to enjoy the kitschy aspects of it, just like you said. Roxy helped me appreciate that, even if her ghost tours are a bit awful." She laughed. "I know she hams it up for the tourists. I don't know why she doesn't stick to the real historical facts. Those are mad enough to make your head spin."

"Yes, but people always want the untold stories, right?" said Hazel, finishing off the last bite of her pumpkin ravioli with vodka sauce— her favorite. "They want the stuff that's not in the history books—the legends and myths and scary stories."

Elizabeth sighed. "I suppose you're right. Still, it's such nonsense."

A sudden sadness came over her. Elizabeth's words reminded her that while she'd come to enjoy Salem, she didn't really understand its true meaning as a haven for all things magical. Even if the original witch trials had been misguided and wrong, the town was, due to its history, a magnet for many magical creatures and the Otherworldly. It had a culture that Elizabeth would never, could never, be a part of, not because she was a mortal—but because she refused to believe in it. What kind of future could they have, even without the meddling love potion, if Elizabeth could never know Hazel's true nature?

Hazel mulled this over, trying to keep her thoughts from painting themselves all over her face. Luckily, Elizabeth was keeping up the conversation on her own, talking about a recent phone call with her family. When the server came over for dessert orders, they ordered the cannoli tray. The mini cannoli arrived not too much later, and they savored the sweet flavors of the Italian cookies.

"I told my parents about you," said Elizabeth, licking the powdered sugar remnants off her lips and looking mischievously at Hazel. "I hope that's all right."

Hazel's heart about stopped. Yet another complication. At least she had the consolation that Elizabeth's family were an ocean away and not likely to confront Hazel any time soon.

"Oh, really?" The chocolate dipped cookie went down her throat hard, its sweet cheese filling suddenly tasteless in her mouth.

Elizabeth nodded with satisfaction. "Oh, yes. They were very curious to hear about the woman I'd met. You know, I've never had a girlfriend serious enough to mention to them before. They can't wait to meet you when they fly over to visit for Christmas."

Hazel started to cough on her cookie crumbs.

"Oh dear, are you all right? Keep breathing." Elizabeth reached over and patted Hazel on the back before handing her a glass of water. Finally, Hazel stopped coughing.

"Your family is coming over here in December? I thought you were going to go there for the holidays."

"We changed our plans. I invited them here. They love America, but they've never been to New England. My mum wants to do Christmas in New York, and then they'll come up to Boston for New Year's—and of course they want to see Salem, too."

Elizabeth continued to chat merrily about her family and what they hoped to see on their visit. She alluded several times to the fact that she hoped Hazel could meet them during their stay. Hazel was having a hard time not letting the tears that were building up inside her spill out. Instead, she tried to focus on Elizabeth's lovely, animated expression of adoration. She wanted to remember that expression forever. She had forgotten what it was like to be admired like this. It was intoxicating.

The rest of the week was a bit of a blur at the shop, but having Elizabeth there to help out was a godsend. She'd told Hazel she'd decided to do research through lunch, and then she'd come to the shop just after lunch each day and help put out product, tidy up, and ring up customers. By Friday, it all felt like old hat.

It was a beautiful day and Hazel needed to go to the bank to make a deposit. It was a little slow at the shop, so after Rita came back from lunch, she and Elizabeth walked over to the bank together.

They enjoyed the brisk fall weather, the bright blue sky and sunshine that warmed their faces even as the wind kicked up the ends of their scarves.

They walked hand in hand down the street, handled their business, and then returned via a different route, so that they walked right by the *Bewitched* statue, which had recently been cleaned and purged of all signs of vandalism.

"Let's take a photo," said Elizabeth with more enthusiasm than Hazel would've expected from her. "My parents'll get a kick out of it."

Elizabeth stood next to the smiling form of Elizabeth Montgomery, the actress who played the witchy homemaker on the 1960s television show, and Hazel snapped a pic. They looked at it together.

"Cute," said Hazel.

"Thanks," said Elizabeth, turning to consider the statue again. "It's fun that they put this here. Is the show set in Salem?"

"No, but four episodes were filmed here. Some people think the show resurrected interest in the town's history back in the sixties."

"Fascinating. I've never watched it."

"Oh really?"

"No. I'm afraid I grew up on British telly—*Are You Being Served?* Things like that."

"I love that show. But I love old American TV shows, too. I never much liked *Bewitched*, though." She looked around as if making sure that no one could hear her. "Shhh, don't tell anyone."

Elizabeth laughed. "Don't worry, I won't." They started walking back slowly to the shop. "Why didn't you like it?"

"In the show, the husband Darrin doesn't know his wife Samantha is a witch until after they're married. When he finds out, he tells her he doesn't want her using her powers. Of course, sometimes she does, mostly because her mother meddles in her life and Samantha has to undo the problems she causes."

"Sounds like a very silly sitcom."

"Oh yes, it was. But what I never liked about it is the idea that the husband wants his wife to be someone she's not—and she's okay with that. She's always getting mad at her mom for using magic. She wants to be the perfect wife by denying a part of who she is."

"But didn't she lie to her husband before marrying him? That's not exactly perfect wife material."

"I don't like that part either." Hazel sighed. "A good relationship shouldn't be built on lies. But I guess without lies, there wouldn't be any sitcoms."

"True," said Elizabeth. She paused. "I hope you feel like you can tell me anything."

They were nearing the shop now, and Hazel wished she had the courage to tell Elizabeth the truth about herself. Maybe under the spell of the potion, Elizabeth's prejudice against magic wouldn't be quite so strong.

It was on the tip of Hazel's tongue to tell her the truth when she was distracted by the sight of a petite raven-haired woman in a long, red wool cloak...Camille.

She was sitting on a small wooden bench outside the shop, looking as though butter wouldn't melt in her mouth as she chatted up some tourists loaded down with bags from the Witch Is In.

"The nerve of her," muttered Hazel. "Excuse me, Elizabeth. I have to deal with a...situation. I'll meet you in the shop."

Elizabeth gave her a peck on the cheek and rubbed her arm encouragingly. "Don't let her get to you," she said before going into the shop.

Hazel took a deep breath to steady herself before striding over to Camille. The tourists she'd been talking to had just gone on their way, and Camille was busy organizing a stack of what looked like postcards in her lap. Hazel cleared her throat to get her attention.

"You've got a lot of nerve coming here after what went down last week," said Hazel with quiet intensity.

Camille looked up, her expression carefully neutral. What Hazel wouldn't give to be able to read her thoughts.

"Hazel, I've been waiting for you."

"To apologize? To make things right?"

Camille's expression was pained. "Can we talk privately?"

"You don't deserve that courtesy, but since I don't want to scare my customers away, *fine*. We can go into the break room. Don't steal any potions." Camille stepped toward the entrance to the shop. "Not the front door. Let's go through the back."

They trudged in silence around the block to the back parking lot where just a week earlier, Camille had been attacked by Beezle—in retrospect, a clear warning that she hadn't picked up on. Poor Beezle! Hazel's cheeks burned as she thought about what Camille had done.

But now she was also angry at herself. She'd been messing around with love potions for far too long, thinking her business was immune to abuses and scandals. And she'd been far too preoccupied with Elizabeth to notice that Camille had set her up perfectly: she'd convinced her to turn off her vampire alarms and to invite her into the shop at the start of October. Her beautiful familiar had tried to warn her, repeatedly, and she'd ignored him.

She was so dumb. How could she have let Camille bring down her defenses like that? Of course, Camille had preyed on Hazel's good nature and her desire to be a people pleaser. It was a great personality trait in the world of customer service, but it was easy to go too far in that direction. She'd been working on being less of a doormat, and now was her chance to set things straight.

In the break room, Hazel pulled out a chair at the table for Camille to sit in, but Hazel remained standing.

"Well? What do you have to say for yourself?"

Camille toyed with one of her many silver rings before speaking. She was beautiful, as usual, with her raven-colored hair spilling down over her red satin cloak. And yet, she didn't quite seem herself now that Hazel studied her closely.

"Hazel, I…I'm so, so sorry," she said, after a moment. She spoke so quietly, Hazel had to strain to hear what she was saying.

"What?"

"I never meant this to happen. I don't even know who I am anymore."

"Oh, please. You're however-hundreds of years old, and you don't know who you are? You expect me to believe that?" It felt good, really good, to lay into Camille. All the stress of the last week, the pain from the fight with Roxy, her worries about how Elizabeth would react once she drank the antidote, the mountain of things to do before Halloween… it fueled her anger and resentment. Camille was the perfect target to absorb it all and, after all, she deserved it. She'd meddled in things no one had a right to.

"I'm not *that* old, Hazel. But actually, that's beside the point. I know I behaved very badly. I crossed a line—"

"Yes, you did. How could you glamour my best friend? That's unforgivable. And to try and get me to drink a potion as well…honestly, the whole situation is reprehensible, and completely your fault."

"Oh, Hazel." Camille's voice broke, and the second word ended in a sob.

Hazel couldn't believe it. Her vampire ex-girlfriend was crying in her shop. No, actually in her arms, because Camille threw herself onto Hazel, wrapping her cool arms around her and holding her close.

"I'm so sorry. I never meant for this to happen. This is the *opposite* of what I wanted. I can't believe I ever cheated on you or left you for Natasha. I thought I could only be happy with another vampire, but I knew it was a mistake as soon as I left Salem. All I could think about was you."

The words came out in a jittery rush, punctuated by sobs. Hazel hardly knew what to do with herself, and after a moment, she patted Camille on the back. She'd never seen Camille lose control like this before. She was always controlled and cool. It had been one of the major problems in their relationship that Hazel hadn't realized until long after they'd broken up. And yet, here she was, utterly broken down and sobbing in her arms in the middle of the day—as if Hazel didn't have enough going on that week without her ex having regrets about their breakup.

Finally, the sobbing subsided, and Hazel pulled away gingerly. Camille found a chair and lowered herself into it, pulling a beautiful lace-edged black hanky from her leather pocketbook and delicately dabbing her face.

"I'm so sorry, Hazel," she said, her voice still thick with tears.

Hazel poured herself a cup of her magic brew from the coffee pot and sat down opposite Camille. She looked so miserable that Hazel already felt a little vindicated.

She sipped on her dark roast and waited for Camille to find the right words, even as she was dying to know what reason Camille was going to offer for doing what she'd done.

"I love you, Hazel. I'm in love with you. Breaking up with you, cheating on you, was the stupidest thing I've ever done. And I've done a lot of stupid things." Camille breathed deeply and sighed. She sat back in the chair and looked at Hazel calmly. "There, I said it. I should have said it weeks ago, but I guess I wasn't confident enough. I wanted to observe you and see what you were up to. But I shouldn't have waited. I shouldn't have lied. And I shouldn't have meddled with Elizabeth. I see that now."

It appeared that Camille was telling the truth. Hazel hadn't wanted to believe it when she'd essentially said the same thing at Faye's. But the streaks of tears on Camille's face vouched for the truth of her confession. And even though none of it excused what Camille had done, Hazel couldn't help feeling the tiniest shred of pity for her.

"I'm sorry, Camille. I already told you: it's too late. I'm not in love with you anymore. I'm in love with someone else. And because of your meddling, I may have lost my chance with her forever." Hazel had wanted to be truthful without being unnecessarily cruel, but she couldn't help adding that last part. She felt the pricking of tears in her throat and her eyes. As she said it out loud, she realized it must be true. Elizabeth would hate her once she was un-enchanted. She would drink the antidote and realize what a fool she'd been acting like for the last two weeks, and she would blame Hazel and probably leave Salem forever. And then, if Hazel told her the truth about who she was…

Just the thought made Hazel want to cry and puke at the same time. She was really falling in love with Elizabeth. It hit her all over again like a freight train and she felt dizzy with it—the hope, the fear, the desire, and the knowledge that it was all for naught made her light-headed. Thank goodness she was sitting, she thought.

Camille stared at her, shock painted across her face. She evidently hadn't believed Hazel at the bar when she'd admitted to being interested in Elizabeth. She hadn't realized how serious Hazel was—and how strongly she felt for Elizabeth. This was no passing fancy, no silly crush. And now it was Camille's turn to be crushed all over.

She stood up, still crying, and made to leave.

"Camille, stay. We have to talk this out."

"No, I can't. I have to go, Hazel. I have to—"

But Hazel never found out what Camille had to do, because at that moment Rita showed up, looking utterly frazzled, to tell Hazel that they had a line at the cash register and customers who wanted to make appointments for tarot readings, and she and Elizabeth were barely holding down the fort.

Camille took the opportunity to breeze out of the shop through the back door, and Hazel followed Rita up front. With less than a week left until Halloween, it was sure to be nothing but madness from here on out, for which Hazel was extremely grateful. She needed a distraction.

CHAPTER NINETEEN

Roxy watched the sun reflecting off the lake and listened to geese honking in the distance. She wished, for a moment, that she too could migrate south for the winter and get away from all the complications in Salem. Her heart ached with a sense of profound loss that felt real but she knew was manufactured.

She didn't want to think about Elizabeth. It only caused her pain. And because the potion heightened whatever feelings she'd had for Elizabeth, no matter how small, her feelings for Alicia were inaccessible. They'd been kind of weak in the first place, so there was no point in trying to spend time with her either.

Instead, she'd gone up to her grandparents' cabin in Maine. It was her favorite place in the world, on the edge of a small lake, in the middle of the woods. Her grandparents weren't in great health anymore and they rarely came there, but the place was filled with memories of time spent with them.

This had been a refuge growing up: the only place where she felt free of the pressure to show who she loved more—her mother or her father—free from the noise of their arguments, away from the second families they'd started after the divorce. Her grandfather had it in his will that the cabin would be Roxy's after he passed, and she was still in awe of his generosity.

She had a key to the property, in the meantime, and she'd promised to look after it once he moved into a nursing home. She really should visit him down in Boston, but first she'd been busy all summer with the kayak tours, and then in the fall with her ghost tours and historical tours. None of it made a lot of money, so she didn't want to cancel any.

She was already taking a hit by canceling her tours the week before Halloween.

It was a necessary evil, though. She had to get away and press the reset button, so to speak. In the days after drinking the potion, she'd tried to keep doing her tours, but she could barely concentrate on them. She'd finally decided to cancel this week's tours and drive up to Maine to cool off. She'd recharge her battery and then go back to Salem for the last few days leading up to Halloween.

The week away had helped—a little bit. The effects of the love potion had dimmed somewhat but were still palpable. She distracted herself with time spent in nature.

She reeled in her line, added fresh bait, and cast her fishing line yet again. She didn't expect to catch anything, but the motions were familiar and soothing. It was her grandfather who'd taught her how to fish, how to whittle, how to start a fire. He'd always been such a calming presence for her, so when she did any of the things he taught her, it was like channeling his spirit a little. She wondered if he knew she was thinking of him. She liked to think that they shared a connection, like old souls that had wandered the world together over the course of many lifetimes.

A shadow came between her and the lake, and when she looked up, she was surprised and horrified.

"Camille? What the hell are you doing here?" She dropped the fishing pole and stood up, grabbing the crucifix around her neck from under her shirt and brandishing it in front of her. "Don't come any closer."

She wasn't sure if a crucifix would actually stop Camille, but ever since she'd put a glamour on her, she'd decided it would be prudent to try any and all deterrents she knew of. She had a garlic wreath around the door of the cabin, and she'd put holy water from a church in Salem into the vial left over from the love potion. Beyond that, she supposed she could break the fishing reel and use it as a stake…

Camille lifted up both hands in the universal sign of *I mean you no harm*. "I'm not going to hurt you. Or glamour you. I came to apologize."

"You scared the crap out of me. Did you really have to apologize to me when I'm alone in the woods?"

"I…didn't think how creepy that would be. I'm sorry."

Roxy had never heard or seen Camille so contrite before.

"You don't look so great." Roxy noticed that Camille looked a little lackluster. She wasn't wearing makeup and she looked...tired. Roxy hadn't thought it was possible for vampires to be tired.

"I...I've actually been feeling...guilty. I haven't felt that since I was human." Camille's expression was one of confusion and exhaustion as she sat down on a nearby stump.

When Roxy was a teenager, she'd get permission to bring Hazel along to the cabin, and that stump had always been Hazel's stump. It made Roxy inexplicably angry to see Camille sitting on Hazel's stump. She was Hazel's best friend and was allowed to be angry at her on occasion, but her loyalty kicked into high gear when she saw the woman who'd meddled in both their lives sitting there, invading their space.

"Look at you. Sitting there looking sorry for yourself. You ought to be back in Salem fixing everything you messed up."

Camille sighed. "You're right. But until Hazel brews the antidote, what can I do?"

Roxy groaned. "Have you even apologized to Hazel?"

"Yes, I have," said Camille, sounding mildly offended. "Have *you*?"

"Me? For what?"

"For getting into an argument with her? For hiding here in the woods when she could use a friend? She certainly doesn't want me around." Camille gave her a stern look.

"Hazel needs to apologize to *me*. She let me stay glamoured while she went off to find Elizabeth. It kind of feels like she *wanted* Elizabeth to fall in love with her. To keep her for herself." All her feelings of betrayal came back to her. It had been unspeakably awful learning she'd been under the power of someone else—the person staring at her right then. "And how dare you come here and talk to me about mending faces when you put me under your spell!"

Camille looked confused for a moment. "You mean 'mending fences'?"

"Whatever. Good gravy, is now the time to be correcting my grammar?"

"I wasn't—Look, I did something wrong. Awful. I've promised myself never to use my power to do that again. Ever." Camille looked upset. "I'm in love with Hazel, and I know it was a mistake to do what I did, but when I saw her with Elizabeth, when I saw she'd moved on, it shocked me. I wasn't thinking. But now, all I want is her to be happy again."

Unless she was an extremely good actress, Camille was completely sincere. And Roxy could understand wanting someone so bad, you'd do just about anything to have them—like giving them a love potion. Maybe Camille wasn't so inhuman after all. She opened her mouth to speak, but Camille spoke first.

"I've been watching Hazel a lot lately, maybe more than I should. I suppose you could call it spying, or eavesdropping, and I know, I know, it's not right. But I think you need to know that she went to find Elizabeth that night because she didn't want her to drink the potion. She thought she could find her *before* she drank it."

"So why didn't she come and find me once she saw it was too late?"

"That I don't know…but if there's one thing I've learned lately, it's that you should give someone as good and kind as Hazel the benefit of the doubt. I think we've both taken advantage of her kindness in the past."

Camille's words struck home. Roxy knew in her heart of hearts that Hazel had always been there for her. Even when she was upset after the breakup with Camille, Hazel still made the time and effort to take care of Roxy. To have her over for dinner, to listen to her love woes, to give her a tiny bit of love potion now and again. And when her mother had gotten yet another divorce and had started calling up Roxy for a loan—money Roxy didn't have—it was Hazel who listened to her vent for hours on end. She'd always been there for Roxy. Even her trips to the cabin when they were teenagers were more for Roxy's benefit than her own. Who would want to spend a weekend in a cabin with a friend whose mother and stepfather were constantly bickering in the background? Only Hazel.

Roxy felt a profound sense of gratitude for having such a wonderful friend, followed by a deep sense of shame. Here she was, wallowing in her own feelings of torment, when Hazel was dealing with the fallout of Camille's meddling on her own. Of course, she had Elizabeth fawning over her, but Camille's words made sense. Hazel wasn't the kind of person to take advantage of the situation. It struck Roxy right then that it must be a very specific kind of torture to have the attention of someone you're into—but knowing it's not real.

"I can't believe I'm about to say this," said Roxy, "but you're right." She started gathering up her fishing pole and tackle. "I'm going to clean this up and head back to Salem. I've got to figure out how to make it up to Hazel. You should do the same." She glared at her. "Without meddling."

She left Camille sitting on the stump, deep in thought, staring out at the lake, which now glimmered with the last few rays of sunlight. When she looked back out the window of the cabin from inside, the vampire was gone.

Roxy spent the rest of the evening mulling things over and cleaning up the cabin. She would hit the road bright and early the next day. Hopefully by the time she was back in Salem, she'd have the perfect idea for how to make things up with Hazel and survive the next week until the antidote was ready.

CHAPTER TWENTY

Elizabeth looked over at Hazel from across the table. She was absorbed in what she was doing—carving jack-o-lanterns for the shop—and didn't notice Elizabeth had stopped working on her own pumpkin. She took a moment to reflect on how much things had changed in her life in the last month.

She'd arrived in Salem feeling a little out of her depth—not because she'd never traveled to do research before, but because this time, she was getting paid to do it. The research fellowship she was using was extremely competitive; people from all over Europe applied for it and she'd been one of the lucky few recipients. Between that and the fact she'd landed a university teaching gig at a time when such jobs were extremely scarce, she'd felt she had to be extremely productive in her research—as if she still needed to prove herself.

Part of that need and her ferocious imposter syndrome were undoubtedly driven by her terrible experiences in graduate school, where she'd been made to feel like she was never good enough. Her dissertation topic had been ridiculed. She'd been told that there was nothing new to say about the Salem witch trials. The topic was passé. When she added to that her parents' disappointment in having an academic for a daughter, it had felt all too much, like she'd made a mountain of wrong decisions.

Coming to Salem and actually finding something new—new and fascinating and potentially field-changing—gave her an enormous sense of validation. She'd been right, and the naysayers were wrong.

And yet, that discovery was so much sweeter because she could share in it with Hazel. She found herself mentally composing the acknowledgments section of her book sometimes, thinking about how she'd like to frame her very big thank you to the woman who helped her find archival gold—and an equally priceless feeling of satisfaction and contentment in her personal life.

Of course, there was still the question of bedroom compatibility… Hazel had been very adamant that they wait until they knew each other better before hopping into bed together, but surely that moment was very near. Or so she hoped.

She felt like she'd learned so much about Hazel just in the last week. How she ate chocolate truffles when she was stressed. How she always sneezed three times in a row. How she rubbed her chin with her middle finger when she was lost in thought, so it looked like she was making a rude gesture. Elizabeth couldn't help chuckling at the memory.

"What?" said Hazel, looking up. She brushed some curls off her face and set down the tiny filing tool she'd been using to carve out the ears of a cat on her current pumpkin. She looked over to where Elizabeth was still sawing at the mouth of her jack-o-lantern.

"I was just thinking about how much things have changed since I got here. I feel so refreshed. Being away from my job and the university. Meeting you." Her voice trembled unexpectedly over the last two words.

"Are you all right?"

"I am," said Elizabeth, sniffling a little and smiling again. "I've just never felt so…satisfied, before. It's as though I was carrying a very heavy box, and I've finally been able to set it down. I feel light as a feather."

Hazel rubbed Elizabeth's arm. "I'm sorry things have been so hard for you."

"That makes it sound as though I was dealing with some horrible tragedy. I'm making too much of it. I only meant that I'm happy. Here with you."

"Everyone's problems are different, but that doesn't make them any less difficult to deal with."

"Very true," said Elizabeth, admiring how Hazel, although a few years younger than her, was very mature for her age. She always felt like they saw eye to eye. "I suppose I should get back to my pumpkin."

Hazel nodded with mock solemnity. "Come on, minion. Back to the salt mines."

They worked in companionable silence for a while. It was a rainy Monday afternoon, the shop was closed, and Beezle was curled up on his little bed in the break room, purring through his sleep.

After a while, the jack-o-lanterns were carved, and Hazel announced she would go looking for the electric tea lights later, as she needed a break from pumpkins.

"We should work on costumes," she said. "I have an idea for yours."

"Oh?" said Elizabeth. She wasn't keen on costumes, never had been, but for Hazel, she was willing to give it a shot.

When she saw what Hazel had prepared for her, she changed her mind. She'd feared Hazel would want her to wear a stifling mask or something ridiculous looking, but none of that was in the plan. Instead, she found herself excited for the concept.

"Now that I know you're on board," said Hazel, "let's go to the thrift store and find the last few items for your costume."

❖

Several hours later, they were back at Hazel's house. The costume shopping was done, and they would spend the evening at Hazel's sewing machine, putting it all together. Every year, Hazel vowed she'd make her costume ahead of time, and every year she ended up throwing it together at the last minute. The fact that Roxy wasn't right there beside her made her heart ache again. Their yearly tradition had been broken, and although it was fun doing it with Elizabeth, part of Hazel's soul was missing with her best friend gone.

As Hazel worked at the sewing machine, Elizabeth busied herself with cooking a simple stir fry with things she found in Hazel's well-stocked pantry. Before long, Hazel's stomach was growling, and they sat down to eat.

"Mmm, this is delicious," she said, finishing the last bite of sweet potato and eggplant. "I would never have thought to combine those flavors."

"It's something I came up with while at uni. I had a vegetarian housemate, so I taught myself how to make several fast and easy meals we could both enjoy."

"That sounds nice."

"It was. I sort of miss living with someone, but after uni it felt a bit silly to still have housemates. It's so much cheaper up north than in London, so I rented my own place, but it is a bit lonely." Elizabeth looked thoughtful as she sipped some of the red wine they'd bought on the way home. "What about you? Do you ever get lonely in this big old house?"

"No, not really," said Hazel truthfully. "Between the cat and the gho—the go-go-go of running my own business, it doesn't feel so empty." She'd almost said *between the cat and the ghost.* She glanced around surreptitiously, suddenly afraid Colin would come floating through a window.

Just as she breathed a sigh of relief, she noticed some telltale plumes of apparitional pipe smoke emanating from the butler's pantry and the echo-y and ethereal cough of her own private spirit. She coughed to cover the noise.

"Are you all right?"

"Fine," said Hazel, pushing away from the table and walking as fast as she could to the butler's pantry while still faking a cough. "I'll be right back."

In the butler's pantry, Hazel found Colin floating next to the wine rack and Beezle growling at him.

"Naughty kitty," said Colin, blowing another plume of ghastly smoke out his nose.

"Colin, get out of here," said Hazel as quietly as she could. "I've got company."

"I like your lady friend. Been here an awful lot lately. Setting up for a Boston marriage, are we? Playing house?"

"I know you think you're awfully droll, but seriously, beat it. No one wants to hear your polo jokes."

Colin affected mock heartbreak. "Hazel, you wound me." He put a hand on his forehead as though he felt a fainting spell coming on. Beezle's growl turned into a high-pitched whistle, like a kettle brought to a boil.

"Knock it off, Beez, she'll hear you. Both of you, go outside before I shoo you out of here with a broom."

She watched while the two of them skulked off, though not before Beezle gave her a look that said, "Are you kidding me?" He wasn't happy to be classified along with the ghost, but honestly, she couldn't deal with either of them acting funny around Elizabeth.

Hazel sighed and returned to the kitchen, where she found an empty table. Elizabeth had wandered into the hallway with her glass of wine and was studying the pictures of Hazel's family and ancestors that hung on the wall. Every single member of Hazel's immediate ancestry were magical folk, and seeing Elizabeth there among them, even in pictorial form, drove home to her how little chance there was of everything working out.

Or did it? Why couldn't she be the first?

"Is this all your family?" Elizabeth gestured expansively at the wall.

Hazel nodded. "Yep. Most of our ancestors all the way back to the end of the eighteenth century. My dad was a genealogy nut and my mom's family was always wealthy, so they had portraits done back in the day."

"That's nice," said Elizabeth. "I guess our fathers have that in common."

"True. No lapsed earldoms in our family, though. Some interesting characters nonetheless."

"I can see that," said Elizabeth, gesturing to Hazel's great-grandparents on her mother's side. "Some really wonderful fashions here too. Judging by the photograph, I'd say this was the 1920s, but the clothing looks…well, I don't know. Medieval, maybe?"

"Ah, yes, that would be Great-granny Brunhilda and Grandad Aloysius. They were…eccentric. A lot of my family was." Why couldn't she just come out and tell Elizabeth the truth? What was holding her back? "I think the family story is that they wanted to be photographed as medieval alchemists. It was a project on the history of magic."

"Ah, that makes sense," said Elizabeth with a smile. "They lived in Salem, too?"

"Yes. Great-granny did a whole series of costumed photographs. I think there's an album somewhere…"

"You know, I've never been much of a fan of costumes, but I can see now how they might be a really interesting way of preserving history."

Hazel knew that of course to her great-grandparents, those outfits weren't costumes at all. They were their magician's robes, worn at festivals and holidays. But how to explain that to someone who saw costumes as something either historical or educational? Still, that wasn't fair to Elizabeth. Hazel hadn't given her a chance to know the truth. This was the perfect opportunity, after all.

"Actually, they aren't really costumes—"

Elizabeth wasn't listening, though. She was checking the time on her watch.

"Hazel, it's after nine."

"Shoot."

"Do you still want to do the costumes tonight? It's so late. We could pick it up tomorrow?"

Hazel knew that was no good; she had to work on the costumes that night, as every other evening was packed with other activities. It was now or never. The conversation with Elizabeth would have to wait.

They worked on the costumes nonstop until eleven, and then Hazel called it a night. She was so bleary-eyed, she could barely see. Elizabeth had been so helpful, though, ironing and pinning material so Hazel could run it through the machine, making them extra cups of tea, and keeping up a cheerful banter that helped Hazel stay awake. These sixty-hour weeks were a bit much, and she was thankful that she'd already planned to take three days off the following week to recuperate.

She tried to send Elizabeth home that evening to her own bed, but she refused, insisting that Hazel go to sleep and get some rest, and she'd tidy up the costume mess. Hazel was so tired, however, she found it difficult to fall asleep. Instead, her mind kept dwelling on how easy and comfortable it was to be with Elizabeth about ninety percent of the time…but how even their best moments felt incomplete. And it wasn't just because Elizabeth was still under the power of the love potion. It had everything to do with the fact that Hazel hadn't shown Elizabeth her complete self.

She tossed and turned, trying to decide when and where to tell Elizabeth the truth about herself. When Elizabeth finally joined her in bed and kissed her gently on the forehead, she feigned sleep. She could hear Elizabeth drifting off to sleep herself, her breath getting deeper, and her heart ached to tell her the truth, but just as she was about to fall asleep, all her thoughts crystallized.

There was no point in telling Elizabeth the truth until after she took the antidote. If she still wanted Hazel even after all that, *then* she would tell her the truth. Looking at that wall of ancestors had made her realize she couldn't share her entire family's secret with an outsider unless they had something solid—something that wasn't founded on a love potion.

Halloween was only three days away. She could wait another three days.

CHAPTER TWENTY-ONE

Elizabeth awoke before Hazel. She looked so peaceful asleep; Elizabeth hated that Hazel couldn't take a break until the following Monday. It was clear she was over-taxing herself.

She surreptitiously turned off Hazel's alarm and walked quietly downstairs. She made herself some tea and checked her phone messages. She'd sent Roxy a text the night before and was delighted to see that there was a response already.

Sounds good. I'll stop by the house at eight. I'll make sure Vampira gets the message, too. PS Sorry I was a jerk the other day!

Roxy's message made Elizabeth smile. Camille did, in fact, always look like a tawdry TV movie vampire. Still, as long as she helped out with her plan, she didn't care how much velvet and lace she wore.

She was enjoying having a secret plan; it was fun sneaking around if the objective was to help the most adorable, beautiful, curly-haired but utterly exhausted shopkeeper in Salem.

She dashed off a quick note to Hazel in case she woke up, but she had a feeling that without an alarm to wake her up, Hazel would just keep sleeping. In fact, she was counting on it.

Promptly at eight, Roxy rolled up in her beat-up green truck.

"Thanks for being my partner in crime," said Elizabeth as she stowed several bags of decorations for the festival booth in the flatbed before hopping into the passenger seat.

"Sure thing," said Roxy with a smile. "Listen, I'm really sorry about the other morning. And about disappearing. I know this's been a busy time for Hazel." She sighed and gave Elizabeth a pained look. "But I'm glad I can help her out now."

Elizabeth nodded. "That's lovely."

Soon they arrived at the shop, and the two of them carried the bags into the storage room before grabbing some mops and buckets. The floor was getting filthy and there was hardly a moment to mop it. The windows needed a cleaning, too, as well as the counters.

"I know it's not very glamourous work," said Elizabeth, "but I know it'll mean the world to Hazel."

Roxy groaned. "Don't use that word."

"What?"

"Glamourous." She shuddered unexpectedly. "But I know what you mean. And it's okay. I have to clean the kayaks in the summer and that's pretty grimy work, too. This is easy by comparison. Plus, I really owe Hazel a lot."

"It sounds like you've been friends a long time."

Roxy nodded enthusiastically while mopping under some display tables. "We have. Ever since elementary school. We were both sort of outcasts, and we ended up becoming friends and standing up for each other."

"Were you bullied for being gay?"

"Sometimes in middle school, yes. I got more shit for it because I've always been a tomboy. I shaved my head with my dad's clippers when I was thirteen. I thought it was so badass, and then I went to school and everyone called me a dyke."

"That's awful," said Elizabeth, squeegeeing the front windows and checking for streaks. "I thought things were bad when boys in high school called me a lesbian because I was a girl with opinions. They used 'lesbian' as an insult."

"I'm sorry. That sucks." Roxy moved into the other part of the shop to continue mopping, and their conversation paused until she returned. "Whew! I think I got all the mess back there."

"That's great," said Elizabeth. "She was just saying yesterday afternoon that she never lets it get this dirty."

"Oh, yeah. I think normally she just uses her…uh…her cleaning service."

"That sounds nice. You should let me know which one it is later, and I can see if I can book them for after Halloween."

"Um, I think they're busy all next month. That's why…that's why she couldn't book them."

"Good thing she's got us then."

"True."

Just then they heard Rita entering through the back door.

"Hazel? Are you here? I didn't see your car in the lot, but the door is open." Rita walked into the main shop and was surprised to see Roxy and Elizabeth hard at work.

"We decided to do some sprucing up," said Elizabeth. She turned to Roxy. "I'll be off, then. Thanks so much for your help." She turned to Rita. "Roxy will be helping out at the shop this morning. Camille should be in shortly as well. Hazel is taking the morning off. She'll be in after lunch."

"Why don't you take my truck and drive home?" said Roxy, throwing the keys to her before she could respond.

Elizabeth knew it would be much faster if she drove, but she'd been putting it off. Driving on the right side of the road? She wasn't so sure about that. She checked her watch. It was nearly nine. She preferred to be back at the house when Hazel woke up, and it was a half-hour trudge in the cold if she walked.

Fortunately, driving on the right wasn't nearly as terrifying as she'd feared. Salem was easy to get around, and before she knew it, she was in front of the beautiful Victorian mansion yet again. Beezle was sitting in the window watching her. He appeared content, and as she entered the house, he settled back to cleaning himself.

The house was quiet. Elizabeth assumed Hazel was still asleep and set about making them some coffee and breakfast. When everything was ready, she walked quietly upstairs and opened the door to the bedroom. At the slight sound of the door opening, Hazel opened her eyes.

"What time is it?"

Elizabeth sat on the bed next to her and pushed away some stray hairs from Hazel's face before bending over and kissing her gently on the lips.

"I called in some favors so you could have a lie-in and get some rest."

"What?" Hazel was confused. She sat up in bed and grabbed her wristwatch off the nightstand. "Oh my God, it's nearly ten. I've got to—"

"You've got to rest. You've been working so hard. And Halloween isn't here yet. You need your strength."

Hazel lay back down on the pillows and studied her carefully. "You look very satisfied with yourself."

"I am. Roxy and Camille are both on duty this morning at the shop, helping Rita out. And Roxy and I went in early to mop and wipe the windows. I know it's been bothering you how untidy things are at the shop."

"Oh, Elizabeth, you shouldn't have," said Hazel, her face flushing with pleasure. "That was really sweet of you." She paused. "How did Roxy seem?"

"Very apologetic. I think she feels bad about your row the other day."

"I feel bad about it, too. Not everything she said was wrong; I was partly to blame."

"None of that talk, now, young lady. We have until one in the afternoon to make the most of the morning."

After breakfast, Hazel showered, and they drove out to the beach. It was blustery and cold, and they had the small beach in Salem to themselves. Elizabeth brought her thermos again, and they sat in a sheltered spot in the sun, sipping tea and enjoying the view.

"Thanks for this gift of a morning," said Hazel. "I feel rested again for the first time in weeks."

"I'm glad to hear it." Elizabeth sipped her Earl Grey. "As a girl, I never thought twice about the work that went into running my grandparents' shop, but now, seeing how it works as an adult, I just can't imagine doing it full-time."

"It's not always this crazy. In fact, it's pretty quiet in winter. That's when I catch my breath."

"Was it always your dream to run a paranormal shop in Salem?"

"Actually no. It was always my dream to have a bookstore, but it's a hard business these days. The Witch Is In allows me to live my dream but also make a living."

"That makes sense."

"So you don't mind that you're dating a witch?"

"What? Oh, yes, the name of the shop." Elizabeth smiled. "Very clever. It's true you've got a magic touch when it comes to small business."

"But seriously…when you first arrived, you didn't seem to much like any of the campy side of Salem. And here we are, dating and...I do tarot card readings."

"True," said Elizabeth, feeling a little embarrassed. "To be honest, it was a little off-putting at first. But after working in the shop off and on and helping out, and being here longer, I realized I was judging Salem and the shop, and you, on a first impression."

"Really?"

Elizabeth nodded. "Absolutely. This past week I've sold a lot of postcards and crystals, but also a lot of books. And I've seen how people love the shop, and they love you. The shop is a community space where people come in to learn, to connect. You've created a really lovely space. I admire that."

"Thank you," said Hazel, her voice sounding a little emotional.

She smiled, and Elizabeth felt a surge of warmth. She put her arm around her and kissed her. They had the beach to themselves. She held Hazel close and deepened the kiss. It felt like a rare luxury to grab this moment by themselves amidst the madness of the shop and the festival, and Elizabeth didn't want it to stop. Hazel's lips were warm and soft, and she felt a fire ignite inside her. She wanted more, but Hazel was already pulling away.

"I'm getting pretty cold just sitting here. Let's go for a walk and then head back for lunch." She smiled warmly at Elizabeth, and somewhat reluctantly, she got up to walk along the beach. The wind was fierce, and they didn't last long, but still, Elizabeth was glad she could spirit Hazel away from the shop and her work responsibilities, even if only for a little while.

As they drove back to the shop, Elizabeth let her mind drift a bit. She had been looking forward to the end of October so much lately that she hadn't stopped much to think that the end of October meant her research trip to Salem was already one-third over. Two more months and it would be Christmas and New Year's. Of course, she had time planned for travel, and she could certainly extend her return flight. England in winter was miserable, and at least here she could enjoy some snow and more downtime with Hazel. But what about after that? Originally, she'd planned to spend the spring semester of her fellowship back in England working from home, but now she was wondering if there was a way to extend her stay in the US.

She'd been trying to ignore the question of what would happen in the New Year, reasoning logically that it was too soon in the relationship to worry about that. But now, she felt so close to Hazel, and yet, they'd only just begun. She wanted to see where things would go.

Don't get ahead of yourself. There was still plenty of time to develop their relationship, she reminded herself, and she'd have plenty more time with Hazel once the Halloween festival was wrapped up.

CHAPTER TWENTY-TWO

They returned to the shop in the afternoon, as promised. Hazel was pleasantly surprised to find everything working smoothly. Camille and Rita were running the registers while Roxy straightened shelves, ran price checks for customers, and swept up messes as needed.

Roxy looked a little shy of her when she came over to see how she was rearranging the display of books on the history of Halloween.

"Hey."

"Hey yourself," said Hazel. "Elizabeth told me how you helped her engineer this whole morning off for me."

"It's the least I could do, milady," said Roxy, bowing low and doffing an imaginary hat.

When she stood up again, Hazel threw her arms around her in a bear hug. She'd missed Roxy so much since their fight. "I'm so sorry for not coming to find you as soon as Camille told me what'd happened. You were right. I was being selfish."

Roxy shook her head vehemently. "Nuh-uh. You're not going to take the blame on this one. The only person, er, *being* to blame for all this is Camille."

"You're absolutely right. I guess it turns out you've always been right about her."

Roxy shrugged. "Someone's gotta be the brains of this operation." She glanced at Camille. "But we had a little chat, and I talked some sense into her. I mean, I still wouldn't trust her to water my plants, but she knows she messed up big time. When I told her what we were doing today, she was in."

They chuckled, and already Hazel felt better. "Forgive me? Friends again?"

"Absolutely," said Roxy. She lowered her voice. "Just so you know, though, I am still counting on you to come through with that antidote. That potion is still making me low-key *obsessed* with you-know-who and it's not a good look on me. I'm managing, but it makes me feel all kinds of crazy."

Hazel looked more carefully and saw that indeed, Roxy was looking pale and drawn under the facade of cheerfulness. "Oh, Roxy, I'm so sorry. Yes, it'll be ready on Halloween. Stop by in the morning, and I'll give you some then and there."

"What about her?"

"Yes, I'll give it to her, too. I just have to decide when will be the best time to do it." She paused, feeling completely transparent. "Don't judge me."

"Who? Me? Never," said Roxy with a smile. "I know you'll do the right thing. Anyhoo, I've gotta dash. Got some errands to run. By the way, is your costume ready?"

"Yes, though just barely," said Hazel. "I procrastinated as usual."

"Ha! I got you beat, then. Mine's been ready for ages."

Hazel was intrigued.

"Okay then. Let's keep it a little secret and we can do our big reveal on Halloween."

"Sounds good to me," said Roxy.

Hazel walked Roxy out of the shop and then checked the look of the window displays from the outside, as well as the positioning of the twinkle lights around the windows. She had to admit, everything looked pretty amazing now that the windows were crystal clear and clean. Between the festival preparation, love potion fiascos, and the stress of not knowing where she stood with her best friend and her romantic interest, all her cleanliness charms had faded away, leaving the shop looking the worse for wear.

She'd studiously avoided looking back at the register earlier; she wasn't ready to talk to Camille yet. She took a deep breath and sighed. She supposed they would have to interact again at some point.

When she returned to the shop, though, Camille was gone. It was just as well. She needed to focus on preparing for the festival. Now that things were a little more settled with Roxy, some of the emotional drama was finally dying down, and she felt like she could breathe a sigh of relief.

That evening, Hazel and Elizabeth went out for pizza at another pizza by the slice place. Hazel had a slice of mushroom and olive, and Elizabeth went for a classic slice of pepperoni.

"Mmm, this is to die for," she said, closing her eyes. "I don't think I'll be able to have pizza again when I return to England. Everything there pales in comparison."

"Just wait until you get to New York. The pizza there is even better."

"I can't imagine anything better."

"Thank you, again, for everything. For helping at the shop, for giving me a morning off…I feel like a new person."

"My pleasure. It looked like you and Roxy patched things up."

"Yes, thank goodness," said Hazel. "And I have you to thank for that, too."

"I like doing nice things for you, Hazel. Sometimes I feel like it's been a while since anyone did anything nice for you. Roxy included."

Hazel sighed with pleasure as she finished off the last bite of pizza. "She can be a little selfish, it's true. But I think she's realizing it more and more."

"She mentioned the two of you have been friends for ages. That's really amazing. I don't think there's anyone from primary school that I'm still friends with."

"We are pretty lucky. Friends ever since the second grade. I brought Beezle to school for show-and-tell, but when I told kids that Beezle was my best friend and I could talk to him and he understood me, the other children laughed. Only the skinny, funny-looking new kid at the back of the class, the one that nobody could figure out if they were a boy or a girl, wasn't laughing."

"Roxy, I take it?"

Hazel nodded.

"The teacher told everyone to settle down, but it was still very upsetting to be laughed at by the entire class at the tender age of seven. At recess, it was Roxy who came and found me, alone, under a tree, trying not to cry. She told me she believed me that I could talk to my cat and helped me plan a prank to get back at the biggest class bully." Just a for a moment, it felt like that day in second grade was just yesterday.

In spite of everything, she knew she and Roxy would always be close; they had a history that bound them together. "Ever since, we've been thick as thieves. We grew apart some while I was away at college, but when my dad died, she was absolutely there for me."

"And you've always been there for her, too."

Hazel nodded. She wished she could tell Elizabeth the rest of the story from the second grade. She remembered that blustery October day like it was yesterday, and she allowed herself to drift into the memory.

She'd been sitting on the playground, and the girl with short, dark hair, dressed in boy's clothes came over to say, "Hey, I liked your cat."

"Thanks."

"I believed you, you know. That you can talk to your cat. Those other kids are jerks."

"Thanks."

"Wanna go put bugs in their lunch?"

Hazel giggled. "That sounds awful. Won't we get in trouble?"

"Probably, but that's never stopped me. I'm Roxy, by the way."

"I'm Hazel." She looked at the tomboy next to her and decided to trust her. "I have a secret. I'm a witch, and I can do magic."

"Cool!"

"Forget the bugs, I have a better idea."

Roxy had accepted Hazel's difference without so much as a blink of an eye that sunny, blustery day on the playground. She watched with excitement and approval as Beezle liberated himself from the classroom, where he'd been forced back into his carrier, and made his way over to the class bully, Jimmy Johnson. As a young witch, Hazel couldn't do much magic, but she could communicate with her familiar easily.

Gleefully, Hazel and Roxy had watched as Beezle went over to Jimmy on the playground and wound his way around Jimmy's legs, as though affectionately caressing him. Suddenly, though, they saw Jimmy go stiff, his eyes big with fright as he looked at the cat and then over at Hazel and Roxy, who were dying with laughter.

He ran over to them, his eyes flashing with anger and fear.

"What did you do to that cat? How did you? How?" He could barely get the words out.

"What on earth do you mean, Jimmy?" asked Hazel between giggles. "All I saw was that Beezle seems to like you." She scooped up the black cat that was now rubbing itself on her own legs. "Aren't you a friendly kitty, Beezle."

Jimmy pointed an accusatory finger at Hazel and the cat.

"That cat…it…it said something! It called me a dingbat!"

A crowd of kids had gathered to watch the confrontation, many of them the same ones who had laughed at Hazel at show-and-tell. Now, though, they were laughing at Jimmy.

"Don't be silly, Jimmy. You said it yourself in class. Cats can't talk."

Roxy's voice cut through the noise of the laughter, and Jimmy stalked off in anger.

Later, once everyone had dispersed, Roxy asked Hazel what Beezle had actually said to Jimmy.

"Beezle told him he's a dingbat and a meanie."

"So he actually talked in a human voice?" Roxy was impressed rather than disbelieving.

"Something like it. He doesn't like to talk to humans other than me, but he told me he'd make an exception for the school bully, especially one who insulted his intelligence."

"Cool," said Roxy, and that was the end of it. They spent the rest of recess talking about their favorite games and toys, and Hazel knew instinctively, in her little seven-year-old heart, that she had met her best friend.

Now, of course, she knew how lucky she'd been that Jimmy hadn't tattled about her little trick to his parents, because she certainly would have gotten punished for using her magic in such an irresponsible and potentially dangerous way. Mortals weren't supposed to know about magic due to their inherent suspicion and abuse of it, as Hazel's mother had told her more than once. It had been a lesson that had taken Hazel many years to learn.

Her parents had never minded, though, that she shared her abilities with Roxy. Somehow, they'd known from the start that Roxy would always be a loyal friend, even if they couldn't have predicted her addiction to love potions.

She was startled out of the old memory when Elizabeth squeezed her hand.

"Roxy mentioned that the two of you always stood up for one another," said Elizabeth. "I wish I'd had a friend like that in school. The closest I ever had to that was a girl in high school, Jasmine. She was West Indian, and at my school, she stuck out, too. We were never quite as close as you and Roxy, but I suppose we helped each other survive."

"Yes, I know I'm lucky in that respect. It's probably why I've let Roxy get away with murder sometimes. She was always the leader in our twosome—always bolder and braver. But she's a softie underneath all that swagger."

Elizabeth smiled. "I'm glad you've made up, in that case," she said, suddenly looking thoughtful. "You mentioned your cat, Beezle, in that story at school. But that's not the same as the current Beezle, is it? Was that Beezle the First and this is the Second?"

Hazel's eyes got wide. She'd forgotten to edit that part in the retelling. "Oh yes...of course. He'd be a pretty old geezer of a cat otherwise."

"Very true."

The smell of dirt and wood smoke hung heavy in the night air as Hazel gently stirred the antidote simmering in her cauldron. She was working, as she often did, in her own backyard, which was shaded from prying eyes by thick boxwoods on every side. The old Victorian house sat on a large lot, which offered additional privacy.

The clear, somewhat shimmery liquid was nearly ready. It was October 30 and a full moon, and the antidote now needed a night of moonlight exposure to be fully mature. The top of the cauldron was already enchanted so that no leaves or dust specks or pollen or anything else could accidentally fall in overnight. Tomorrow morning, Halloween, the potion would be ready to be administered and—

Hazel hated to think what would happen after Elizabeth drank the antidote. They'd spent nearly every moment together since Elizabeth had drunk the potion two weeks earlier. And Hazel was starting to get used to it.

She hadn't fully given in to her desires—though she had engaged in a lot of kissing with Elizabeth. She supposed that there was relatively little harm in that.

Hazel heard a rustling in her hydrangeas and was momentarily distracted by the flicker of a black tail. Beezle. So he *was* still around;

he'd been boycotting her ever since she'd kicked him out of the house with Colin.

Just as she was about to pet him hello and scratch him under the chin, they both heard a distant, "Hello?" It was Elizabeth. She'd insisted on coming around that evening ostensibly to pick up her costume but also because the love potion appeared to be working as strong as ever.

This gave Hazel hope that they could still work things out even after she drank the antidote the next day. Elizabeth's feelings for Hazel, even before she drank the love potion, were already quite warm.

She'd gotten used to their friendly banter, their deep conversation about family and history, their flaming hot kisses that left her wanting more every time…She wanted that life so badly, and yet here she was, brewing the antidote that would end it all.

Was she crazy for giving Elizabeth the antidote? After all, she'd already started to have feelings for Hazel even before drinking it. Maybe the potion simply speeded things up?

On the other hand, she couldn't just keep lying to Elizabeth. Someday the truth would come out and it would bite her in the ass. Plus, her feelings of guilt were eating her up; she couldn't admonish Roxy for abusing the potions and then ignore those rules because they were inconvenient for her own personal life. She hoped whatever feelings Elizabeth had had before the potion were strong enough to get them through this.

Lately, she'd been daydreaming about how they could accommodate both of their lives as a couple, should things work out.

In one daydream, Elizabeth decided to move to the States— maybe there was some way she could find a job at a university in New England? After all, they were brimming with universities and colleges in this part of the world, and she'd said herself how stressful her job in England was. Maybe she'd be interested in changing universities.

Or maybe she could write her history books and work part-time at the shop? The shop was doing well, and Hazel had no mortgage payments to speak of, so they could certainly live off the profits of the shop. With Elizabeth's brains for business, they might eventually be able to even open a little online operation and expand their reach and their profits.

In another daydream, she sold the shop and moved with Elizabeth to England; she imagined them living in an adorable cottage surrounded by a thriving garden, just a short walk to a cute pub and tea shop. Perhaps she could set up the Witch Is In in a touristy town over there? It wasn't impossible. And with Elizabeth's family in business themselves, they could probably help her with all the paperwork and bureaucracy. Anything was possible.

But then Hazel thought again about what Elizabeth had said that night at Luigi's—that she didn't understand how people could believe in magic. And more importantly, she was hostile to the whole idea of magic in general. It was one thing to admire Hazel's business acumen—it was another to truly accept the reality of the supernatural. What if she didn't accept Hazel once she knew the truth? Could Hazel simply hide who she was?

It was all a moot point. In her heart of hearts, Hazel knew she couldn't be with someone who loved her only because she was enchanted or who loved her without knowing her in full. She longed for true love—not fabricated infatuation. She had to give Elizabeth the antidote to find out what would happen.

CHAPTER TWENTY-THREE

Halloween was a beautiful, bright sunny day, and Hazel awoke with a sense of calm. Today, everything would be revealed.

As she often did when facing a momentous occasion, she pulled a card from her favorite tarot deck to see what the day boded. She was alone in the kitchen, up earlier than Elizabeth, who had recently been sleeping later than her usual routine. Being in love agreed with her, thought Hazel ruefully.

The sun was filtering in through the kitchen curtains, filling the space with bright, positive light. The smell of coffee wafted through the air, and with a preternatural calm, Hazel pulled a card from the deck and turned it over.

The Lovers.

Hazel's heartbeat sped up.

Was this a sign? Was she not supposed to give Elizabeth the antidote? The little vial was burning a figurative hole in the pocket of her bathrobe. She still hadn't decided when to slip it into her drink.

Part of her was urging her to dump the whole thing in the coffee pot to ensure that Elizabeth drank some. Another part of her was more wary. Maybe she should wait until there were more people around? She didn't know if she wanted to be alone with her when Elizabeth realized she wasn't *actually* in love with Hazel.

But maybe this was a sign that she shouldn't give Elizabeth the antidote. The cards were inscrutable.

Hazel pulled another one.

The Magician.

She sighed. This was hopeless. Of course a magician was involved. Combined with the Lovers, maybe this simply reflected the situation—that Hazel had enchanted herself a lover? She needed more information. She pulled another card.

The Three of Swords.

Hazel gasped aloud.

The Three of Swords depicted a large red heart pierced by three swords, and it was hardly a good omen. Quickly, not wanting to even think about what she'd seen, she shuffled the cards again, putting back all three that she'd pulled out.

She shuffled and shuffled and, her curiosity getting the better of her, she flipped the top card over. One more card, she told herself.

The Lovers.

Hazel sighed and put the cards away. She was too worked up to think about them logically, and now she could hear Elizabeth stirring upstairs. Soon she'd be down in the kitchen with her, and Hazel needed to make a decision about the antidote.

There was a knock at the side door, and moments later, Roxy breezed into the kitchen.

"Good morning," said Hazel, holding out one of the two small vials of antidote she'd prepared.

"Oh, thank goodness," said Roxy, visibly relieved. Without another word, she popped the small cork and downed the whole dose. Hazel watched her, on pins and needles, waiting for Roxy's reaction.

Roxy shook her head like a dog coming in from the rain. "Oh. My. God," she said, emphasizing each word. "Hallelujah! I feel like a new woman." She put her arms around Hazel in a big bear hug and lifted her off her feet for a second.

"Roxy, put me down."

"Okay, okay."

"Feeling better?" Hazel was grateful to have both feet back on the ground again. The day was making her jittery, and she needed to stay grounded.

"You have no idea." Roxy heaved a giant sigh and flopped into one of the kitchen chairs. "I feel like myself again. Whew!"

"I'm glad to hear it." She handed Roxy a mug of coffee. "It's nice to see you in my kitchen again. I missed you these past two weeks."

"Me, too. This has got to be the weirdest Halloween ever. Between the poltergeist at the archives and Camille actually apologizing for being a dick, honestly, the love potion mix-up is hardly the weirdest part of it."

"Excuse me? Camille apologized for something?"

Roxy nodded. "She actually came to the cabin last weekend when I was up there. Talked some sense into me. Weird, right?"

"Super weird."

Hazel was still trying to process the fact that her ex was now trying to interfere in her life for the better, when Elizabeth entered the kitchen. Warm hands reached around Hazel from behind her, pulling her into a soft embrace, punctuated by a warm kiss on the neck.

"Good morning, my darling," Elizabeth murmured into Hazel's ear in her sexy English accent. Hazel loved Elizabeth's voice so much, she could listen to Elizabeth read the phone book—if phone books still existed. "Hello, Roxy. I thought I heard your voice."

"Good morning," said Hazel, double-checking that the remaining vial of antidote was still in her bathrobe pocket. She'd find a way to slip it to her that morning. They would be working together at her booth for the Halloween festival most of the day, and surely Elizabeth would get coffee at some point. And if the disenchantment happened in the middle of the day, maybe that was better. Hazel would have other things to keep her busy.

Roxy chugged the rest of the coffee and stood up. "That's my cue. I've gotta bounce. I promised I'd take the first time slot running the booth for the tour company. I'll see you broads after lunch." With her trademark wink, she was off. Hazel was delighted to see Roxy back to her usual, positive self.

After a quick breakfast, she and Elizabeth drove to the shop to pick up the booth materials and headed to the festival. Hazel tried to savor the final moments of easy companionship and warm touches between her and Elizabeth. Who knew what things would be like later that day?

❖

Around noon, Elizabeth went off to get coffee and sandwiches at a nearby deli, the Magic Bean being far too busy that day to even bother.

As she walked back to the booth with their lunch, Elizabeth tried to ignore the itchy feeling caused by the makeup on her face. Since

Hazel and Roxy had decided on a Red Riding Hood theme, Elizabeth had agreed to be the Forester who saved Red from the Wolf.

In spite of her dislike of costume makeup, Elizabeth had agreed to a small mustache. It tickled like crazy when Hazel drew it on, but the effect was excellent, if a little bizarre. Elizabeth could hardly believe how much the mustache made her look like her father when he was twenty years younger. She could hardly look at herself in the mirror—it was uncanny.

Soon she could see Hazel in her Wolf costume. She had used craft materials and spirit gum to stick furry tufts of costume fur to her face, hands, and neck, and then painted on the wolfish features on her face. She had sewn more tufts of fur onto a tight gray sweater dress she had found at the thrift store and paired it with tight gray jeans, out the back of which stuck out a jaunty wolf's tail made of a fluffy dust wand stiffened with wire. The effect was both terrifying and sexy at the same time. Hazel was truly a costuming genius, thought Elizabeth, admiring how the sweater and jeans hugged Hazel's curves in all the right places.

She kissed Hazel on the top of her head and dropped into the chair next to her at the booth, setting their lunches and the coffee carrier onto the table.

"I got us both coffee and sandwiches. Tuna, and ham and cheese. You can choose which one you want, or we can share both."

"Ooooh, let's share both," said Hazel, turning to smile at her gratefully. "That sounds great. Which coffee is mine?"

"That one," said Elizabeth, indicating the one with milk. Elizabeth preferred her coffee dark unless it was late in the day.

"Great. And are there any napkins?"

"I completely forgot." Elizabeth got to her feet. "I'll go get us some."

It took a couple of minutes, but Elizabeth managed to get some napkins from a food truck that was much closer than the deli. She handed Hazel a stack when she got back.

"Here you go, hon."

"Thanks, hon."

The Halloween festival was so much more fun than Elizabeth had initially anticipated. It was like the festivals she'd gone to in the village with her parents as a child. Everyone was in costume, and some of them were truly epic. People had taken a lot of care to re-create costumes from movies, TV shows, videogames, literature, and history. It was hard not to take photos of everything she saw.

At their booth, Hazel was doing quick tarot and palm readings and also selling some of the smaller items from the shop—a small selection of the bestselling aromatherapy oils, candles, jewelry, some books about the witch trials, and tarot cards, of course. Sales were slow but steady, but the bigger draw was the game Hazel had invented that customers could play to win a small prize.

Festival goers could spin a Wheel-of-Fortune type wheel and try to answer a question about Salem history off the cards she and Hazel had worked on earlier that week. If they were right, they could choose a small prize: a semi-precious stone of their choosing, a coupon to the shop, or a five-minute palm reading, depending on the difficulty of the question.

Elizabeth ran the game while Hazel rang up sales and did tarot and palm readings, but around lunchtime, things had slowed down a little, as many other people at the festival had the same idea about getting something to eat.

The two of them sat in their lawn chairs munching their sandwiches, and Elizabeth couldn't stop thinking about how perfectly content she was. The day was beautiful, sunny, and dry. She was helping a gorgeous, clever woman she admired run her small business, and even the sandwiches tasted delicious.

Finally, Elizabeth took a long sip of her now cold coffee, which still tasted wonderfully perfect: an ideal balance of bitter and sweet, with deep flavors of mocha and cinnamon.

A moment later, Elizabeth jerked her head up. Had she fallen asleep for a few seconds? Or for longer? Hazel was still next to her, talking to a customer, but Elizabeth had an odd feeling, as though she didn't quite know how she'd ended up here, at the festival, in this chair, next to Hazel, holding the unfinished half of a tuna sandwich.

She felt disoriented and wondered if she'd developed vertigo. She stood up and stretched, but she didn't feel dizzy, which was reassuring—and yet she still felt somehow off.

There was no reason to feel that way, though. Here she was, sitting next to Hazel, who was her friend. Girlfriend? Her thoughts were muddled as she reconstructed the last two weeks in her mind. She'd been spending so much time with Hazel...snuggling Hazel, kissing her, sleeping in the same bed together, spooning…her heart gave a little jolt when she thought about it, though not unpleasantly so. She was confused, however, about how she had gone from being too busy to leave the archives, to helping Hazel in her shop every day.

"Hey, Hazel, do you mind if I walk around a bit? I'm feeling a little…headachy or something. I don't feel like myself."

The customer finally left, and Hazel turned to Elizabeth, studying her carefully. There was something in her expression Elizabeth couldn't quite read, almost as though she sensed that she wasn't feeling well.

"Sure, of course. I'll be okay here. I had a bathroom break a little while ago so I'm good. Go ahead."

Elizabeth nodded mutely before walking off into the crowd.

She didn't know how she found herself there, but somehow Elizabeth's feet propelled her to the Scarlet Letter. The bar was open all day for the festival, and Elizabeth ordered a beer and sat down at an empty booth.

She was trying to puzzle together the last few days. She'd been spending a lot of time with Hazel, and things were going well, though she couldn't quite figure out how they started dating. There was a kiss in the woods…that was coming back to her now, but that didn't explain her boldness in pursuing Hazel the last few days. Or was it weeks?

"Well, hello there," said a cool voice behind her.

Elizabeth turned around and found herself face-to-face with a petite, raven-haired beauty with paper white skin and violet eyes. Camille. Hazel's cheating ex. She'd never seen her this close before and something about her gave Elizabeth the chills.

"Mind if I join you?" Camille sat down opposite her along with a violet-colored beverage in a martini glass.

"Sure." She was a little annoyed at this other person who was disturbing her as she tried to piece together the last few days. She remembered everything that'd happened, but she didn't understand it. Something was missing from her memory.

"You look a little shaken, Doctor."

Elizabeth judiciously chose not to reply.

"I know I have little to recommend me." She paused and gave Elizabeth a penetrating stare. "The truth is, I messed things up with Hazel. She's really wonderful. And I didn't see that until it was too late."

Elizabeth felt oddly protective of Hazel at that moment. Her concerns about the last few weeks receded as she considered the offending woman in front of her. She'd broken Hazel's heart and just recently she'd been the cause of a major argument between Hazel and Roxy. Elizabeth was glad she was trying to make amends, but everything about her was repellent, and she really wished she'd just leave her alone.

"Yes, Hazel *is* wonderful," said Elizabeth finally, when the silence between them stretched too long.

"I agree," said Camille with a smirk. "That's why I intend to try to get her back as soon as possible."

Elizabeth felt her heart start pounding. The thought of Hazel with Camille made her feel heavy and awful and slightly nauseous. "What makes you think you have a chance?" she asked, trying to appear nonchalant and failing miserably.

"Hazel's so fragile these days. Once you leave town, she'll need a shoulder to cry on. I may have screwed up, but there's nothing better than makeup sex, am I right?" She shrugged her shoulder casually, fixing Elizabeth with her violet gaze, challenging her to respond.

Elizabeth couldn't stand to hear another word from this foul creature. She finished her beer in a big gulp and set the glass down hard.

"I think I've heard enough. You had your chance with Hazel, and I'm certainly not going to miss *my* chance." She stormed out of the bar, her shoulders set, her head held high. The mere thought that this woman would win back Hazel after all she'd put her through, after cheating on her no less, was disgusting.

Hazel deserved someone so much better. She was kind and smart, funny and adorable. Elizabeth didn't know quite how she'd gotten the courage to kiss Hazel, much less cuddle her in bed the last several days, but it didn't matter now. She couldn't ruin things because she was a little confused about how they'd gotten to be so close so fast. The important thing was that they *had* happened. And the last couple of weeks had been the happiest of Elizabeth's life, she realized. With Hazel, she had no one to impress and she could be herself. Hazel was the kindest person she'd ever met—and she was sexy as hell.

The realization of her feelings for Hazel fueled her every step back toward the Halloween festival.

CHAPTER TWENTY-FOUR

The afternoon crowd was beginning to thin out as the temperatures dipped lower. Roxy had gotten roped into helping out at the adventure store booth the rest of the day, but Hazel was handling the table just fine on her own.

She took advantage of the lull to rearrange some stock on the table and add extra tape to the sign advertising her booth. The wind was getting stronger, and she was starting to think she wasn't going to last much more than another hour.

She had just spoken on the phone to Rita, who was staffing the shop along with a temp, and she said things were picking up over there. As it got colder outside, more people preferred to do their shopping indoors.

The festival was in full swing, though, and the fifth band of the day was taking the stage. Hundreds of people of all different ages were still milling about the booths, getting fake tattoos, shopping for various Halloween-themed paraphernalia, buying food from the food trucks, and children were playing various games organized by different local organizations.

In another hour or so, though, the sun would disappear over the square and people would head home. In the evening, the party would shift to the carnival. Hazel wasn't sure she'd still be up for that if Elizabeth dumped her that afternoon.

She was trying not to think about Elizabeth, and instead distracted herself with some chocolate she'd put on the table to entice customers. As she was popping the truffle into her mouth, she spotted Elizabeth in the distance, striding purposefully toward her.

Hazel braced for the worst. Was Elizabeth the yelling-angry type? Or was she the quiet-angry type? Hazel wasn't sure which was worse. But as Elizabeth got closer, Hazel could see a giant smile on her face, and her heart leapt in her throat. She thought of the tarot card she kept pulling that morning: The Lovers. Maybe it'd been a good omen?

Hazel stood up to greet her, and Elizabeth walked right up to her, drawing her into her strong arms and planting a hot kiss on Hazel's lips. Hazel closed her eyes and moaned. Their bodies were flush with each other, and despite the many layers of their costumes, Hazel could feel the warmth of Elizabeth's entire body against her own. Her soft lips caressed hers before deepening the kiss, pushing lips on lips, tongue on tongue, so that finally Hazel felt like she was completely melted into Elizabeth—right there in the middle of the Halloween festival for everyone to see.

Finally, Elizabeth pulled away and looked deeply into Hazel's eyes.

"I think I love you, Hazel," said Elizabeth, her voice breathless, low and intense.

"I think I love you, too, Elizabeth," said Hazel, enjoying saying her name even as she marveled at her own daring to say the words out loud.

Her heart was soaring, knowing that this was the real Elizabeth saying these words to her, not an enchanted Elizabeth. These words meant something; this kiss meant something. And maybe they'd gotten a little help getting to this moment faster than they would have otherwise due to Camille's scheming, but none of it mattered now.

Hazel hugged Elizabeth close and rested her head on Elizabeth's shoulder. She liked the height difference. It was sexy. Elizabeth's arms closed around her tight, and as they stood like that, Hazel felt more joy and contentment wash over her than she'd ever felt before.

They were drawn apart again, though, when a large gust of wind overturned several displays of tarot cards on the table and some flyers went airborne.

"Oh no!" Hazel jumped as the papers on their table took flight.

The two of them began grabbing what they could, but the wind wasn't giving up. Hazel indicated to Elizabeth that they should start packing up everything. It was after three, and the crowds were getting sparse.

They made short work of it all, packing the plastic boxes full of inventory into Hazel's car before driving over to the shop. Their hair was crazy and windblown, and they were laughing with the excitement of rushing around. Hazel marveled at how different she felt now than she had that morning, when she didn't know how things would end. Now it felt like the most obvious thing in the world that they would spend the rest of the evening together.

❖

The carnival was going strong by the time Hazel and Elizabeth got there later that evening. Everywhere they went, there were bright colors and lights, the smell of popcorn and funnel cake, and the sounds of friends and families enjoying the rides. Here there were even more people dressed in costumes than earlier. There were witches and vampires, clowns and superheroes, princesses and knights, and on and on. There were children dressed as their favorite cartoon characters, teens in "sexy" costumes, Goths of all ages in their most Goth-ish of outfits, as well as plenty of people who were simply dressed for the cold night air.

The carnival had dozens of rides, games, and booths, like any other carnival, but it was bigger than most of them. The carnival boasted no less than five haunted house rides in honor of Salem's favorite holiday, as well as a witch history display.

They took a loop around the carnival before deciding what to do first, and many of Hazel's neighbors, fellow business-owners, friends, and steady clients were among the crowd. Several of them recognized her and waved or even stopped to say hello, complimenting her on her costume. After all the work of the last month, it felt like a wonderful reassurance to know that people recognized her and her business. Hazel could tell that Elizabeth was impressed by her popularity in town, and she felt the glow of pride in her success, and she was glad she could share that evening with Elizabeth.

They even saw Rita with a group of her sable-clothed Goth friends, all of whom stopped to chat briefly with Hazel and praise the shop or express how nice it was to meet the person who was helping Rita finally get her studio space. Hazel beamed with joy; there was nothing like getting praise from notoriously critical teenagers.

Finally, they decided to stop wandering and check out some

classic carnival snacks and activities. After introducing Elizabeth to funnel cakes, Hazel got in line to buy tickets for the rides. She felt like a kid again and couldn't wait to feel the thrill of the roller coaster while holding Elizabeth's hand.

She bought her tickets and rejoined Elizabeth just as Roxy showed up.

She looked amazing.

Her Little Red Riding Hood costume had turned out better than Hazel could have imagined. She was wearing a bright red leather motorcycle jacket and a beautiful red fedora along with black jeans and black motorcycle boots that accentuated her sexy butch swagger. This Little Red Riding Hood could take down any old wolf.

"Hey, you look incredible," said Hazel.

"Your wolf is pretty cool, too." said Roxy modestly. She looked over at Elizabeth. "I see you're the Forester."

Her expression was unreadable, just for a moment, and Hazel worried that maybe she should have done a different costume for Elizabeth. After all, in the story, the Forester saves Red Riding Hood from the evil wolf. Maybe it wasn't the right message...

After a moment, Roxy's face lit up with a smile.

"So in this retelling, Red, the Wolf, and the Forester team up to fight the forces of evil; I like it."

"That's exactly what I was thinking," said Hazel.

"I tried to convince her I ought to be the poor granny eaten by the wolf, but Hazel said she'd rather see me in drag," said Elizabeth.

"Makes sense to me," said Roxy. "Nice 'stache."

Elizabeth laughed. "I've had a hard time not rubbing it off. Hazel had to redraw it twice today."

"Let's take a photo now that Roxy's here," said Hazel, fishing out her phone and looking around to see if there were any carnival-goers who looked keen to snap a picture of the three of them.

Just then, a perky blonde in a cheerleader outfit showed up next to Roxy.

"I thought I'd lost you."

"Oh, sorry, Linda," said Roxy, turning to Hazel and Elizabeth. "This is Linda. I met her at the adventure booth. She's a rock-climbing instructor. If all goes well, she's gonna get me a deal on belay certification."

Roxy looked like she'd like to get more than just a coupon from Linda. Hazel had to smile. She certainly didn't waste time wallowing.

Linda snapped a photo of the three of them, one simply smiling, and one in character. Elizabeth brandished her cardboard axe, Hazel pretended to growl, and Roxy mimed trying to punch the wolf.

They spent the rest of the evening enjoying the carnival. The four of them made the rounds on the roller coaster, the Tilt-A-Whirl, two haunted houses, and the caterpillar. The last one nearly made Hazel revisit her funnel cake, so she called it quits afterward.

She finally managed to find time to take Roxy aside at one point to talk one-on-one as they stood in line to buy some drinks for their respective partners.

"Are we cool? I really want us to be cool."

"Of course," said Roxy, giving Hazel a big bear hug. "We're cool. I'm sorry I was such an idiot. You're my best friend and way more important than some chick. And I know you'll always be there for me."

"That means a lot."

Roxy smiled sheepishly. "I guess I've been a little girl crazy lately. I don't know what got into me, hounding you for those potions. I must have sounded like an addict."

"Don't beat yourself up. It's tough being single." Hazel put her arm around Roxy and gave her a squeeze. "I want you to be happy."

"Thanks, Hazel. I think I thought if I could just lock down someone as smart and beautiful and sophisticated as Elizabeth, then happiness would follow." She shrugged a little awkwardly. This was just about as introspective as Roxy ever got. "Then when she was obviously interested in you, I got glamoured and took the love potion, and it all sort of snowballed," she added, almost under her breath.

"You're going to meet someone *amazing*. And she's going to be perfect for you. I just know it."

Roxy looked a little heartened by Hazel's confidence. "Looks like things are working out for you two." She cocked her eyebrow.

"I gave her the antidote this afternoon. I swear. But she decided to come back for me anyway."

"And you're happy?"

"So happy."

Roxy coughed awkwardly. "What about the witch stuff?"

"Which stuff?"

"W-i-t-c-h stuff. Have you told her?"

Hazel made a face and sighed. "I know I have to. I was thinking maybe tomorrow? When we're both rested?"

"Judging by the look on her face," said Roxy, "I don't think you'll be doing much resting tonight."

"Fair point." Hazel groaned.

"Hey, if she's as into you as she seems, she's gotta come around, right?"

"I hope you're right."

"When have I ever been wrong?" said Roxy with self-mockery. She put her arm around Hazel and squeezed her tight. "Feels good not to be fighting anymore and marry the hatchet."

Hazel shot her a look of confusion. "You mean, *bury* the hatchet, right?"

"Bury the hatchet? That doesn't make any sense. Why would you bury a perfectly good tool like a hatchet?" Roxy sounded indignant, even as a giggle escaped her. "I've been saying that wrong, too?"

"I'm afraid so."

They burst into laughter just as they approached the concession stand, both feeling a sense of relief that their friendship had weathered their biggest fight yet—and that Roxy's proverbial malapropisms were still intact.

They purchased drinks and rejoined their ladies. Before long, though, they were saying their good nights, the noise and crowds of the carnival getting to be a little too much, to say nothing of the chill night air penetrating the thin fabric of their costumes.

Hazel and Elizabeth walked hand in hand toward Cara Mia.

"So," said Elizabeth, "your place or mine?"

Chapter Twenty-Five

They were finally going to do it, thought Hazel. Finally for real. She could hardly believe it. The enchantment was gone, they were actually dating, they'd even said, "I love you," and she couldn't wait to go the next level with this beautiful woman sitting next to her in the car. Her body thrummed with desire and anticipation.

Hazel had to stop herself from getting distracted by thoughts of Elizabeth's beautiful body—a body she'd gotten glimpses of when Elizabeth was still enchanted. She could feel herself getting warm and jittery all over, despite the pervasive cold in the car while the heat struggled to come to life.

Elizabeth put her warm hand on Hazel's thigh, and she felt an electric shock go through her.

"Careful where you put that," said Hazel flirtatiously. "We don't want to cause an accident."

Elizabeth gave her thigh a squeeze.

"I can hardly keep my hands off you," she said, her voice already low and gravelly with desire, and Hazel avoided looking at her, knowing that wouldn't be conducive to driving them home safely.

"Tonight really feels magical," added Elizabeth.

Her choice of words, however, jolted Hazel out of her fantasies as she turned into her neighborhood. It was an unfortunate choice of words because Hazel, being Hazel, now couldn't stop thinking about the one thing that could ruin everything: magic.

Elizabeth was a skeptic, a non-believer. How could the two of them ever have a real relationship? Suddenly, she thought of every time they had talked about or argued over magic. As Hazel turned it all over in her mind, she realized with a sinking feeling, that she couldn't sleep with Elizabeth, much less have a relationship with her, if it was all based on a lie. She'd known that all along, but she'd been trying to find a work-around that didn't involve telling Elizabeth.

But Roxy, as well as her conscience, was right.

She couldn't hide who she really was from Elizabeth and, what's worse, if she slept with her tonight and then told her the truth later, or even the following morning, she would be no better than Samantha from *Bewitched*. And while the show played it all up for laughs, Hazel could imagine a very different outcome with Elizabeth. She wanted a future with Elizabeth—but not at the cost of hiding who she was. The awful realization settled over her uncomfortably as they arrived at her home.

She pulled into the driveway and cut the engine. Slowly, Elizabeth slid her hand off Hazel's leg, and they both got out of the car. The cool night air enveloped them and clarified Hazel's resolve.

While a part of her was pleading for her not to say anything, to enjoy the evening and all the pleasures it promised, the irrepressible, rational part of her knew that she would never be able to enjoy a night in Elizabeth's arms, knowing that she had lied to her: a lie of omission was still a lie.

"Earth to Hazel. It's freezing out here, let's go inside."

Elizabeth was already on the porch, waiting for Hazel to join her and unlock the house.

"Sorry about that," said Hazel, letting them both inside.

As soon as they were inside, Elizabeth wrapped her arms around Hazel and planted a big kiss on her lips. For a moment, Hazel forgot her resolve and let herself melt into the kiss. Their tongues slid together, and a deep, heavy desire for Elizabeth filled Hazel's soul.

Still, she forced herself to pull away.

"Boy, I could use a glass of water after all that funnel cake. How about you? Or maybe some tea?"

Elizabeth raised her eyebrows but followed Hazel into the kitchen.

Hazel was a flurry of activity, putting water on for tea, pouring glasses of water, preparing some mugs and loose-leaf tea.

"I'll get this all, Elizabeth. Why don't you go into the back parlor?

It's got a gas fireplace. Maybe you can turn it on for us? Wouldn't that be cozy?"

Hazel could feel herself talking at twice her normal speed. Her nerves were starting to fail her. She hated the thought of telling Elizabeth she was a witch. Maybe she wouldn't take it too badly? There was always hope.

Hazel made up a tray with the teacups, teapot, glasses of water, as well as a small tray of almond cookies that she had infused with a calming potion—a small amount meant to relax and calm whoever ate it. Perhaps she could get Elizabeth to try one before springing the news on her? She popped one in her own mouth, hoping that for once, maybe, magic would have an effect on her. She could use some calming right then.

She carried the tray carefully to the back parlor, the coziest place in the house, and found Elizabeth lounging on the sofa nearer the fireplace with Beezle next to her, purring contentedly. A merry little fire lit up the grate, and the house was feeling warmer than some minutes ago.

Hazel set down the tray and sat next to Elizabeth.

"My goodness, I thought we were done with sweets," said Elizabeth, seeing the cookies.

"These are my favorites," said Hazel, improvising a little. "I baked them the other day and thought they'd go nicely with our tea."

"Tea? I thought we were going to drink some water and take full advantage of the fireplace…" Elizabeth's voice trailed off as she gave Hazel a look full of desire. She ran her hand over Hazel's arm, which was still covered in tufts of fur, as they were both still in their costumes.

Beezle took this as his cue to hightail it out of the parlor, and Hazel didn't blame him.

"Oh. Yes, um, yeah, I mean, sure, I thought…we should have some tea first. I'm a little cold." Hazel stumbled over her words, trying to buy time. Her self-will was already pretty low, and Elizabeth's hands on her body were making it no small task to concentrate and stay the course.

"I know of plenty ways we can warm you up."

She cupped Hazel's cheeks. The electric shock that passed between them had nothing to do with static and everything to do with their magnetic attraction.

Hazel jumped up and stood closer to the fire, trying to avoid

Elizabeth's gaze while screwing up her courage to tell her the truth. But how exactly to phrase it?

Elizabeth watched Hazel pacing back and forth, concern visible in the creases that now appeared between her eyebrows.

Elizabeth opened her mouth to speak, when there came a loud creaking, like a door opening somewhere, followed by some strange laughter. It was high-pitched, but somehow not feminine either.

"What was that?"

Hazel knew exactly what that was. It was Colin. He was obviously in a mood, and she needed to speed up the pace of her revelation—otherwise Colin would do it for her.

"I'm a witch."

The words tumbled out of Hazel's mouth, unplanned. She had wanted to ease Elizabeth into this knowledge, but she didn't know how.

Elizabeth looked at her, uncomprehending. "I thought you were supposed to be the Big Bad Wolf?"

"That's my costume. But what I meant to say was…I *am* a witch. For real," she added, somewhat lamely. She didn't know what else to say.

"I don't understand." Elizabeth's brows were furrowed, and she crossed her arms after putting down her teacup. She leaned back on the settee and sat in silence. She was waiting for Hazel to explain what she meant.

Hazel cleared her throat, which had suddenly gone quite dry. She picked up her own teacup from the table and sipped at it, her hand shaking. She set it down again to keep from spilling before taking a deep breath and trying again.

"I love you, Elizabeth. I really do. I don't think I've ever felt this way about someone before. Never. Definitely not with Camille." She smiled at Elizabeth and flushed a little.

Elizabeth smiled too and leaned forward. "I love you, too. I don't even care I've only known you for six weeks. I could shout it in the streets. You've made me so happy, Hazel."

"That's why this is so hard," murmured Hazel. "But it's also why I have to do this. I can't start a relationship with a lie."

"Sit down, at least," said Elizabeth, gesturing to the armchair next to the settee. "You look like you've seen a ghost."

Again, Hazel inwardly cursed Elizabeth's choice of metaphors. *Colin, please stay away.* She did sit down, however. She could feel her legs getting weak as she pondered how to go on.

Best to get it over with, she decided. Like ripping off a Band-Aid.

"I have never enjoyed time with anyone more than you. It's been so wonderful. And I really want to make this work. But for us to be together, you have to know something about me and who I am. I am a witch. Magic is real. And I know you don't want to hear that or accept it," she hurried on before Elizabeth could respond, "but it's all true. The reason things moved so fast between us the last two weeks was because Camille, who is a vampire, glamoured Roxy into slipping you one of my love potions, but it didn't work. Or it didn't work correctly. Anyway, it made you fall in love with *me*—or more in love, I guess. But I gave you the antidote today. In your coffee. That's why you didn't feel so great this afternoon. And you decided you still wanted to come back to me. So, while it's true that the love potion jump-started our relationship, there's no reason not to think it won't work out…"

Hazel's voice finally trailed off as she ran out of steam. She had been avoiding Elizabeth's gaze, too scared to look at her, but she ventured a small peek at her now.

Elizabeth's face was pale and expressionless, as if she couldn't comprehend what Hazel was saying.

"I'm so sorry," said Hazel finally, to break the silence. "I never intended—"

"Is this a Halloween joke? You know I'm not much for practical jokes." Elizabeth's voice was even and calm, with a touch of confusion.

"No. It's the truth. It's who I am. Earlier this week you told me you didn't want us to have any lies between us, so that's it. I'm done lying."

Elizabeth was silent for a moment, mulling things over.

"You're right," she said slowly. "No lies. I'm sorry you didn't feel you could tell me earlier that you're Wiccan. It's not my religion but I'd hate for you to think I wouldn't accept that about you." She smiled. "I suppose I should have realized it. The shop, the tarot cards, the sage burning kits."

Hazel sighed. "That's not what I meant. I'm not Wiccan at all.

Wicca is a specific belief system. I'm a witch. My whole family are witches, wizards, warlocks. I don't know how to else to explain it. Spells, potions, the supernatural. It's all real."

Silence filled the room, and only the merry sound of the fire crackling occasionally interrupted. After waiting a couple of beats, Elizabeth finally made a movement as though she was going to leave.

"Maybe I should go. We're both tired. Let's finish this conversation in the morning."

"Wait. Please wait," said Hazel, pleading. She had to do something, she thought wildly. She should *prove* to Elizabeth she wasn't a liar or a jerk.

She could see Elizabeth was tired and frustrated, and her mind was suddenly empty of all ideas. Frantically, she looked around the room. The fire.

With a wave of her hand, Hazel turned the fire green, then blue, then purple. She pointed at it.

"See? Look. I'm making it different colors."

Elizabeth looked at her as though she had lobsters crawling out of her ears. Before she could speak, Hazel waved a hand over her hair, face, and arms, changing her hair from chestnut to bright blonde and magicking away her wolf costume to replace it with a ball gown.

Elizabeth stumbled back, her eyes wide.

"Hazel, what are you doing? Am I high? Did you slip me something?"

A note of hysteria had entered Elizabeth's voice. Quickly, Hazel snapped her fingers, and everything returned to normal. "No, I'm trying to *prove* to you that magic *is* real. This is my life. Magic. I'm a witch." She was having a hard time keeping the hysteria out of her own voice. "I used magic in the archive to help you find that diary."

Elizabeth was shaking all over. "I think I need to leave. Right now."

"No, please. Elizabeth. I love you. Please don't leave. I just don't want to lie to you about who I am."

"I think I've seen enough for one evening."

Elizabeth turned to leave and came face-to-face with Colin.

Hazel saw it all happening as though in slow motion, and she was powerless to stop it. She was rooted to the spot in horror.

Elizabeth, too, was speechless, stunned in place. The silvery outline of a man stood before her in his dandified nineteenth-century evening wear, and yet he was transparent. They could see the hallway beyond Colin, the stained-glass window above the door, and the beautiful woven rug on the floor of the corridor leading back to the kitchen and front door.

Colin was smiling deviously, obviously aware that there was someone in the house who hadn't known of his existence. He looked over Elizabeth before floating through an armchair over toward Hazel and winking.

"Really, Hazel, isn't she a tad too pretty for you?"

At the sound of his odd, ethereal voice, Elizabeth was jolted out of her horrorstruck motionlessness. She whirled around to Hazel, her eyes full of horror and fear. "What is happening?"

Without waiting for Hazel to respond, Elizabeth ran out of the room. Hazel watched her go, desperate to run after her, but at the same time knowing it was futile.

"Bit skittish that one, my dear," said Colin cattily.

"Oh, leave me alone, you old queen," shouted Hazel, throwing herself violently onto the settee that had only recently been occupied by Elizabeth.

Colin tsked at Hazel, shaking his head and muttering something about her temper, but eventually, he obligingly disappeared through the wall above the fireplace, and soon all was quiet and calm again in the parlor.

The fire continued to crackle merrily in the fireplace as though nothing had happened. Hazel could feel her face getting hot—but not from the fire. No, they were hot tears of frustration and heartache streaming down her face, and she let herself sprawl out on the length of the settee to have a good cry.

They had been so close—so close—to finally being together and being happy. And what had she done? She'd ruined it. Why had she bothered to try to tell Elizabeth the truth? What did it matter?

She chastised herself over and over again. She barely used magic in her day-to-day life. She could give up her side businesses. She could even get rid of Colin—there were ways, after all.

As her tears subsided, though, Hazel knew in her heart of hearts that she could never truly give up magic. It was who she was. It was her family, too. How could she ever introduce Elizabeth to her mother and sister if Elizabeth didn't know that side of them? You can't change who you are, Hazel's voice of reason reminded her. She'd done the right thing.

If that was the case, though, then why did this hurt so much?

CHAPTER TWENTY-SIX

The cold night air was refreshing and calming. Elizabeth never thought she'd be so happy to leave Hazel's house. In fact, earlier that day, she'd hoped she wouldn't be leaving until the next morning. She tried not to ponder that fact, knowing how close she was to crying right there on the sidewalk.

She tried to steel herself and not let her mind replay everything that'd happened over and over again. Their closeness and intimacy, the car ride over, their sexy kisses…all suddenly replaced by Hazel's strange behavior and then…that weird lie. Or confession. Or whatever it was. And that floating man…

Elizabeth paused in front of the house, wondering if Hazel would run after her and apologize and hug her and kiss her and they could forget this one last Halloween trick.

But Hazel wasn't coming.

Elizabeth started walking home, dragging her feet, a part of her still hoping they could mend things.

Could Hazel be telling the truth? Elizabeth's mind was crowded with too many thoughts and she couldn't make sense of them all. She had thought for sure Hazel felt the same way about her as she did about Hazel. So why would Hazel insist on ruining their night talking about magic and then playing all those tricks on her? *Were* they tricks?

A small part of Elizabeth felt like what she'd seen had really been the supernatural at work. Those weren't regular magician's tricks. Maybe she hadn't known Hazel for very long, but she felt that she knew her well enough to know that she wasn't the type to play practical jokes. It was so strange. She couldn't understand it. Nothing made sense anymore.

And then there was all that talk about love potions. She couldn't deny that she'd felt strange earlier that day after lunch. Like the entire last two weeks were nothing but a dream. But honestly—love potions? That sounded like something her loony aunt Laura would believe in. Snake oil was what it was.

But again, it didn't make sense with what Elizabeth knew about Hazel. She wasn't impulsive or rash, and she'd been very hurt the day at the archive when Elizabeth had accused her of playing a trick on her.

But then the rational, logical part of her mind couldn't accept what Hazel had said. And who could? Only a Believer like Roxy. Love potions, glamours, vampires, ghosts... As a historian, she knew that people often saw what they believed; she'd studied the people in the witch trials who actually believed in the idea of witches because they'd been taught it was real. But many people in the witch trials had capitalized on the situation to get their neighbor's land or other material goods. It was easy to get land cheaply if the owner was hanged as a witch.

She tried to clear her mind. She pulled her coat on and started walking a bit more quickly down the sidewalk in the direction of her rented bungalow. She tried to focus on one idea: magic was not real. The supernatural was not real. Because if it were, then it would challenge everything she knew about the world—and maybe quite a bit about her research.

Elizabeth turned a corner, and all of a sudden, she was flooded with memories of all their time spent together. Just that day, they'd cuddled and laughed, kissed and hugged, sat on the Ferris wheel together, hand in hand...the day had been absolutely perfect. And Hazel was so wonderful: beautiful and smart, kind and fierce. Elizabeth could feel the tears rising as she reached the end of the next block.

She paused at the corner and wiped her eyes with the back of her jacket sleeve before checking the name of the street. The street was empty; the houses were quiet. Everyone was either at the festival or already in bed; after all, it was getting late. The street was eerily dark, and Elizabeth started to doubt she was heading in the direction of her bungalow at all. Nothing was familiar.

She'd been so lost in her own thoughts, that she must've taken a wrong turn, and now she was definitely on a street she didn't recognize.

Fuck. As if this night couldn't get any worse.

Clouds moved over the small sliver of moon in the sky, and the street was drenched in a darkness that the few streetlamps could hardly penetrate. Elizabeth had ice in her veins. All the fear and dread from earlier poured over her yet again. Her heart started thumping in her chest and her palms were sweaty all over again. It was just like when the guys had played tricks on her in grad school, making her jumpy and scared. She hated the feeling with an intensity she had for little else.

She looked around and then riffled through her bag to pull out her phone and check the map directions, when a rustling sound, like wind through the leaves of the trees, caught her attention behind her.

Elizabeth whirled around and nearly dropped her phone in shock.

Before her was none other than Hazel's ex-girlfriend, Camille. "You. What are *you* doing here?" Elizabeth tried to keep the fear out of her voice.

"Me? I could ask you the same question."

The beautiful, luminous woman stood a couple of paces in front of Elizabeth, her violet eyes glittering with starlight, and Elizabeth was momentarily struck by Camille's beauty. She wore a crushed velvet gown in a shade of eggplant slightly deeper than that of her eyes, and a plunging neckline revealed an ample bosom that was about to pop out of its trappings. Her raven black hair was arrayed in large, bouncing curls that framed her face, and her mouth was a perfect cherry red. Elizabeth could see why Hazel had once fancied Camille. There was quite a lot to fancy. She found herself reeling from the force of Camille's beauty, speechless.

"I thought you were spending the night with Hazel." Camille's voice was quiet and soft, but with an underlying edge to it. She cocked an eyebrow at Elizabeth, who finally found her voice and cleared her throat before responding.

"That's none of your business."

"Isn't it, though? You told me at the Scarlet Letter that you and she were a hot item."

"Again, I don't see how this is any—" Elizabeth felt a chill go down her spine as Camille took a step forward toward her.

"Don't you, though? I made it perfectly clear to you before that if you didn't want Hazel, *I* certainly did. And since you've given her up, as I can see, I have no scruples in going after her myself."

Camille's eyes were hard and unreadable. Every part of Elizabeth—except perhaps her rational, logical, academic brain—was urging her to put Camille in her place and run back to Hazel…that is, if she could figure out which direction that was.

But her brain, her rational, historian's brain couldn't let it go. How could she and Hazel have a real relationship if Hazel kept bringing up the supernatural and insisting she could do magic? No. It wasn't possible. Magic *wasn't* real. Being Wiccan or pagan was one thing, and even though Elizabeth wasn't a fan of that way of thinking, she could certainly try to accept it. But Hazel had denied she was Wiccan. She'd said magic was real and Elizabeth just didn't know what to think of that.

"Excuse me?" Camille's voice broke into Elizabeth's hurried thoughts. "Magic isn't real? And here I thought you were supposed to be such a smart professor. So well read. Even researching the Witch Trials. And you don't believe in magic? It's almost too ironic." With that, Camille started laughing. It was a kind of hard, raucous laughter that dripped with condescension.

Elizabeth barely noticed it, however. She was still reeling from the fact that somehow Camille had read her thoughts. No. That was impossible. Someone must have told Camille that she didn't believe in magic, and she had made a lucky guess.

"Oh, *please.* Stop. Stop deluding yourself. Yes, of course I'm reading your mind, you silly mortal. I'm a vampire. It's one of our best tricks."

Suddenly, all of Elizabeth's fear turned to anger. Was the entire town out to dupe her? Was everyone in on it? "For fuck's sake. Stop with the magic talk. That crap doesn't work on me. Just because I research it doesn't mean—"

Camille rolled her eyes grandly skyward before taking another step closer to Elizabeth, grabbing hold of her slim wrists, looking her straight in the face, and opening her mouth to reveal a pair of fine, white, sharp fangs emerging from her gums.

Elizabeth could barely believe what she was seeing. Was it another trick? The fangs looked very real, and she couldn't imagine how they could possibly be fake, slithering out of Camille's gums right before her very eyes. Goose bumps covered her entire body and she started to shake.

"How? What? How is this…?" She sputtered, the words unable to take shape in her mouth. She felt breathless and dizzy, like she was about to faint. She took a deep breath to steady herself, and the hot, dizzy feeling receded a bit.

"Don't get your knickers in a twist," said Camille coolly. "Isn't that what you Brits like to say? I picked up some of that lingo while partying in London after the Great War."

Elizabeth simply continued to gaze at Camille, half in wonder and half in fear. Was Camille really immortal? It made her shiver just thinking about it.

Before Elizabeth could think more about the implications of what she'd said, Camille let go of her wrists and made a subtle movement with her right hand. Suddenly, Camille was nowhere to be seen, and instead, Hazel stood in front of her. Hazel. Here, out on the street, luminous and beautiful, her light brown hair framing her heart-shaped face, and her hazel eyes gleaming with moonlight.

Elizabeth felt herself melting with warmth at the sight of her beloved, the pain in her heart stabbing yet again. Why had she ever left the house? Surely, they could talk things out. After all, she was a researcher always searching for a new angle. If there was something in the universe that she hadn't heard of yet, then all the more reason to learn more about it. She knew Hazel would never lie about something important—she'd given her no reason to think she would.

"That's right," said the Hazel in front of her. "How could you accuse Hazel of lying when you know how much she loves you?"

Elizabeth's eyes widened as she began to understand. This wasn't Hazel at all—no matter how much it looked and sounded like her. In a flash, Hazel was gone and in her place stood Camille again.

"Like that, did you? Sorry, it was a glamour. Another one of my vampire tricks. Or should I say—vampire magic?"

Elizabeth was in such shock, she hardly knew what to say. She merely stood there with her mouth wide open, gaping at her. Camille took hold of her wrists again and, with a whooshing of wind in her ears, and a dizzying sense of movement, Elizabeth found herself transported along with Camille to the statue of Samantha from *Bewitched*.

After Hazel told her about the show, she'd found clips of it online.

It was a fairly par-for-the-course midcentury American sitcom, and she'd put it out of her mind for the most part. More tourist schlock, though the statue, in the middle of the park, was fun. Her parents loved the picture she'd sent them with it, and now they were dying to see it for themselves.

Now, in the moonlight, it had an eerie glow, and Samantha's smile appeared more menacing than inviting.

"Why are we here?" Elizabeth managed to string an entire sentence together.

"You know, for a professor, I'm starting to think you're not very smart," said Camille. "Does that PhD stand for Ph-Dumb?" She laughed at her own joke far longer than it warranted.

Now it was Elizabeth's turn to roll her eyes. She was suddenly less fearful and more curious. She wanted to know what exactly Camille had up her sleeve because apparently sucking her blood and leaving her for dead so she could go pursue Hazel for herself wasn't what she had in mind.

"So? Explain it to me. And hurry up. It's freezing."

"Ah yes, of course. I forget. Some of us have warm red blood pumping through our veins," said Camille, tracing a cold finger across Elizabeth's cheek. Elizabeth flinched. Of course, she'd read Elizabeth's thoughts again.

Camille hopped up on the broomstick behind Samantha, her voluminous skirts draping around her like a Victorian lady riding sidesaddle.

"Are you prepared to be Darrin, and make Hazel give up who she is to be with you? Make her promise not to do magic ever again? Personally, I always thought this was the most unbelievable part of the story. If you had access to magic, wouldn't you want to use it all the time? Silly me, I thought the writers had come up with an incongruous setup for a show. And yet, it turns out, there are silly mortals like Darrin right here in Salem."

Elizabeth felt a flash of outrage. "That's hardly fair."

"Isn't it, though?" Camille looked very satisfied with herself.

"I love Hazel. I just don't believe in magic. And honestly, who over the age of ten believes in magic? It's not real." Faced with what she'd seen tonight, her position didn't seem nearly as solid as it had just that morning.

Camille rolled her violet eyes again. "Oh, please. People believe in all sorts of magic every day: angels, devils, possession, miracles… You, my dear, are quite in the minority."

She had a point, Elizabeth thought. She sighed. "I'm a history professor. I don't believe in any of that. I believe in research and what can be found in the archive, and even that has to be analyzed carefully because people lie all the time. Even in official documents."

"Magic is all over archival documents. What you're saying is that you won't believe something until you see it with your own eyes, except now you're *actually* face-to-face with magic. Real magic. And the woman you love is telling you her most secret of secrets…and you reject her. You don't believe her. What kind of love is it that rejects someone for who they are? Would you rather never know the truth? Or force Hazel to give up magic and be someone she isn't? Would you truly rather be ignorant of the reality of the world than choose to believe in something you previously didn't?"

"Just…how could it be real? It goes against everything I know…"

Camille rolled her eyes and heaved a frustrated sigh. "I can't believe I'm wasting my time like this. You have all the proof you need right in front of you and still you hesitate."

Elizabeth felt a flash of anger. How could Camille expect her to change who she was and her entire understanding of the world in one evening? She needed time to think things through. Even if she accepted that Hazel was a witch, she wasn't sure what that meant for their future together. She was tired and confused and completely over being berated by Camille. "I wouldn't expect you to understand. You're apparently incapable of thinking of anyone other than yourself."

"I could say the same of you."

"Just leave me alone. I want to go home." Elizabeth felt tears of frustration springing to her eyes. She wanted to be alone, in bed, away from Camille. She needed time to think.

"Fine. I'll get you home," said Camille. She came down off the statue and approached Elizabeth. "But know this: I'm hoping you'll be stupid enough to go home, pack your bags, and never come back. I wasn't lying before. I made a mistake with Hazel; I lost the best thing I ever had. I'm going to give you twenty-four hours. Make things up with Hazel or else *I will*."

With a whoosh of wind in her hair, Elizabeth found herself in front of her bungalow, alone. Everything appeared to be quite mundane and normal. She felt exhausted just then. She let herself inside and went straight to bed, hoping that when she woke up the next morning, she would know exactly what to do.

❖

The next morning, Elizabeth went to the archive.

After a night of sleeping like utter crap, she'd given up around five in the morning and started scrolling through email instead. She hadn't checked it at all the last forty-eight hours and she'd missed the message from her friend and colleague Andy, the paleography whiz. Andy'd helped her father with genealogical research as well as helping her decipher archival texts she'd used in her dissertation. She'd sent snaps of the sections of the diary, and Andy'd finally responded—she'd deciphered quite a bit.

Elizabeth opened the email and started reading. Andy, as usual, cut right to the chase.

You won't believe this, Liz, but I think this diary actually belonged to someone in your family! I remember the name from the genealogical research. Mary Amelia Waters, née Cowley. She was already a widow at the time of the trials, and she left all her worldly goods to her niece, Elizabeth Cowley. The niece and her husband eventually came back to England and changed their name to Cowrie to avoid being connected to the family members who participated in the trials. I can't believe you found her diary. Amazing work!

Her breath caught in her throat as she lay in bed, staring at those words. She'd already known much of that part of the story from the earlier research, but somehow, hadn't put two and two together. To know now that she'd found the diary of this person, with her own thoughts and ideas written in her own hand, was stunning in the best of all possible ways.

Of course, *she* hadn't found it. Hazel had found it. Her heart squeezed just thinking about Hazel.

She focused instead on the email and what it meant. There was a document attached with the transcription of each photo. She decided she'd read the transcriptions with the physical diary in her hands at the archive. Quickly, she got up, showered, dressed, and had breakfast before leaving for the archives.

The town was quiet. The cleanup after the festival was still going on in the center of town, people were off to work and children to school, but everything felt a little quieter than usual. She walked quickly, pulling her wool coat closer to her throat. It was windy, cold, and cloudy, as though the weather were mirroring her state of mind: disordered and foggy.

Still, if there was one thing that was sure to clear the cobwebs from her mind, it was her research. And she hadn't been giving it her fullest attention lately; she'd been consumed with the preparations for the festival just like everyone else. This was the perfect moment to get back to it, now that she had this new, exciting information.

Part of her desperately wanted to go to Hazel's house instead, but she knew it was useless. She hardly knew what to say to her. She needed more time to think, in a quiet space dedicated to the preservation and pursuit of knowledge.

She flashed her reader card at Scott quickly, making sure to slow down only just enough that she could hand him the slip of paper with the item she needed to look at. She had no wish to chat with him that morning; small talk was the last thing on her mind.

She took her time in the locker room and bathroom, hoping that by the time she got to the reading room, everything would be waiting for her and Scott would be gone. She got her wish. The reading room was deserted when she entered, the diary lying on a couple of green foam supports that ensured the book's old spine wouldn't break while lying open.

Elizabeth sat down in front of it with the attachment open from the email and started reading. At first, she felt she'd never be able to concentrate enough on what she was reading to make sense of it, but soon she found herself engrossed. The voice of the woman writing the diary was strong and engaging, despite the differences in word choice and usage over time. She was reflecting on the witch trials, which had happened soon after the death of her husband. She knew the girls who'd been pointing fingers—and she knew many of the people accused. It was a small community. Her words were filled with pain and regret for not speaking up for the people unjustly sentenced to death, even though, as a widow, it would have been much too dangerous for her to speak up just then.

"Every one believed them that pointed the fingers, and none believed them that said they also spake truth. We all thought there was but one truth to believe, not knowing there was more than one truth."

Those words took Elizabeth aback. They spoke directly to her and her situation. Could there be more than one truth? Clearly there were truths that existed regardless of whether people believed in them or not: gravity, viruses, black holes. Humans couldn't see them and yet they existed. We can choose not to believe in them, and they still exist, thought Elizabeth.

There would always be those who insisted that things they couldn't see or understand didn't exist, and Elizabeth had always judged those people for their ignorance. Was it possible she was doing something similar?

Some of Camille's words came back to her. People smarter than Elizabeth believed in things like destiny, miracles, fate. And what about magic? Hadn't Elizabeth used that word to describe her evening with Hazel just the day before?

What was magic but a word to describe a power she couldn't understand?

"Thank you," muttered Elizabeth to the author of the diary, wishing she really could travel back in time and meet the women who'd realized their mistakes of the past and sought to rectify them. In Amelia Waters's will, Elizabeth realized, she'd named benefactors who were the children and grandchildren of those condemned for witchcraft. She'd sought to make reparations for those whose deaths she hadn't been able to prevent. She'd made a mistake, and she'd tried to fix it, setting an example for her niece, Elizabeth.

The situations were not entirely parallel, but Elizabeth felt she'd found her own way to accepting Hazel's truth—whatever it really was.

She gathered her notes and picked up her bag and coat in the locker room before setting off to one of the many witch museums in town. In fact, she did all of them that day. They didn't take long, after all. They were silly, campy places, and she still cringed that they were called "museums," but she tried to see them from a new perspective.

What would it be like to grow up in such a place as Salem? To be surrounded by histories of magic and witchcraft, and to know that there was some truth to them? She remembered Camille's fangs glinting in the moonlight and shuddered a little. To know that true evil existed in the world, and powers beyond our comprehension—that could be very frightening. But Hazel and her family had found ways to use whatever powers they had for good, to try to help one another. Her beautiful home, the shop, her friendship with Roxy were all a testament to the good-natured person Hazel was. If even her vampire ex-girlfriend was willing to step aside for Elizabeth to try to make Hazel happy, then didn't that also speak to how important a person Hazel was to all these people?

Elizabeth mulled these things over as she left the Witch Trial Museum. It was now after three, and her stomach was grumbling. She decided to get lunch for two to go and walk over to the shop and try to make up with Hazel.

Loaded down with a large bag filled with bagel sandwiches and hot soup, Elizabeth soon found herself in front of the Witch Is In. There, she was informed by Rita that Hazel had never shown up for work. She'd texted instructions to Rita and promised to pay her overtime to work a short shift that day. There were still tourists in town, after all, who would stay into the weekend for the celebrations.

As Elizabeth left the shop and turned to walk toward Hazel's home, her stomach squeezed uncomfortably. She wasn't hungry anymore. She felt sick. What had she done? Was Hazel at home, too upset to come to work? Would she be so upset she wouldn't want to make up with Elizabeth?

The thought was too awful to bear, and she walked as fast as she could without dropping her bags of food. No matter what Hazel believed, no matter what the truth was, Elizabeth couldn't deny that her life was magical with Hazel in it.

CHAPTER TWENTY-SEVEN

Since Elizabeth left the night before, Hazel couldn't find the will to do anything. Her entire body felt leaden, heavy with disappointment and a profound sense of emptiness that consumed her. She hardly slept. Her mind kept replaying the entire conversation at her house in her head, over and over again.

Had she made a mistake telling Elizabeth? She shouldn't have done it. She was an idiot for telling her the truth. No one should know. Her mother had warned her so many times about giving herself to a mortal. *They'll never understand us*, she told Hazel time after time. *They are utterly different.*

She'd tried many times to set Hazel up with the daughters of fellow witches, but Hazel hated a setup. It was too awkward. But now, in the deafening silence of the empty house, she couldn't help feeling that her mother was one hundred percent right. Elizabeth had definitively broken her heart.

She'd been so upset after Elizabeth left the night before that she hadn't the will to do anything, much less remove her costume. She'd been too tired and upset to take it all off or even shower. She'd lain on the settee for a while, crying into a decorative pillow until she had no more tears to cry. Then she'd gone upstairs in a daze, flopped on the bed, and simply lain there, obsessing over everything she'd ever said to Elizabeth, and everything Elizabeth had ever said to her, occasionally dozing off, but never for long.

The following day, in the dim light of the cloudy morning, she'd stretched and felt the spirit gum on her forehead pucker and flake off uncomfortably. She'd forced herself to take off the costume, remove the tufts of fur, and wash the makeup off her face and arms. She could have done it all with magic, of course, but there was something comforting about the ritual of doing it all by hand. Next, she'd hopped into the shower and turned it up as hot as she could stand in hopes of washing away some of the despair and tension. Sometimes the simplest comforts were the best, after all.

She'd peeled off her clothes and stepped under the hot stream of water and, for a moment, relaxed completely. She'd been outdoors all the previous day, and her hair was tangled from the wind, her body tired from sleeping in that silly costume all night long. Well, except for the tail. She'd remembered to remove that before flopping into bed.

But just as she was starting to feel a little better, Elizabeth's horrified, angry expression appeared in her mind, and she felt the tears start flowing again, mingling with the water from the shower. There was really nothing worse than crying in the shower, she'd thought through the tears. A sob had escaped her, much louder than she'd intended.

A moment later, she'd heard a voice from inside the house.

"Hazel?"

She shut off the shower and wrapped herself up in a towel, with another towel for her hair to avoid drips.

"Yes?" she called out the door, hoping against hope it was Elizabeth.

"Whew, glad I found you." There'd been no mistaking Roxy's voice. She bounded up the stairs until she was face-to-face with Hazel. "Everyone thought you'd run away to join the circus with Elizabeth."

"Everyone?"

"Well, maybe just me and Rita. I texted you like a zillion times and you never responded, so I stopped by the shop, and Rita had no idea where you were."

Hazel walked over to the bed and sat down. She just felt so tired. How was she supposed to go to work?

"What time is it?"

Roxy checked her wristwatch. "Ten thirty."

"Oh God," she'd said, rubbing her eyes. They felt cottony and dry from crying, and her head was heavy.

"You look a little rough, Haze," said Roxy, giving her an appraising glance. "Did Elizabeth wear you out last night?" She looked around. "Where is she, anyway?"

"Nothing happened, Roxy," she'd said, letting her body sort of flop onto the bed. The towel on her head slid down to cover her eyes, and she appreciated the momentary darkness. She wanted to ignore the rest of the world until the feelings of massive disappointment disappeared.

"Crap. I'm sorry." Roxy sat next to her on the bed. "Did you…"

"Yup. I told her I was a witch. And not a Wicca-witch. A witchy-witch."

"How did she take it?" Roxy's hesitation suggested she already knew the answer to that question.

"Not great." Hazel sighed. "And then Colin showed up."

"Double crap."

"Uh-huh."

They sat there in silence for a long moment.

"At least you were honest with her," said Roxy finally. "You told her before you, uh, did the funky monkey dance?"

Hazel groaned. "I can't believe you still call it that."

"Made you laugh, though, didn't I? At least on the inside. I can tell."

That made Hazel laugh for real. "Yes, it was before we did anything. I didn't want to lie. So I told her. It didn't go well. She left. We're over, I guess."

Roxy let out a low whistle.

"Exactly."

"Can I take you out to lunch? Take your mind off stuff? There's that place that serves brunch all day long every day."

As if on cue, Hazel's stomach growled.

"And I think that's a yes. I'll go downstairs and text Rita you're alive. You get dressed, missy. Let's go."

Several hours later, Hazel felt somewhat better. Her chest still ached with the feeling of emptiness like a part of her was physically missing, but now she was full of pancakes and her head felt a lot clearer after a walk in the Salem Woods. Being out in nature, even on a cold cloudy day, was great for clearing out the cobwebs. She was thankful she didn't have to go into work and that Rita was okay working the shop on her own two days in a row. She didn't think she had the mental wherewithal to deal with making change and helping customers that day.

Around three o'clock, after their hike, she'd dropped Roxy off in town as she had several tours to lead that afternoon and evening, and she'd driven home. She found Beezle waiting for her, and she petted him and gave him some treats after hanging up her coat and hat in the foyer.

Even though she'd taken a shower not long ago, she felt cold again, and she had the brilliant idea of filling her clawfoot tub in the guest bath with water and bubbles and having a nice long soak. With a glass of wine. Why not? There were no rules now.

The hot water melted away the cold of the day, and Hazel relaxed. She sipped the glass of red, set it back down, closed her eyes and leaned back against the inflatable bath pillow that made the bubble bath that much more comfortable. She had Brandi Carlile playing on her little portable speaker, and she let herself unwind completely.

While with Roxy, it'd been easier to think about things other than Elizabeth. They'd talked about Roxy's plans to teach ski and snowboard lessons that winter, and how possibly Hazel would do a snow-cation up at the same resort so they could hang out in the evenings. They'd discussed Thanksgiving plans as well, since it was their tradition to do the holiday dinner together up at Roxy's cabin every year along with her mom, who lived in Maine, too. The end of the year, with all its hectic energy, was not far off. In the woods, they'd talked about the books they were reading and shows they were watching, and Hazel was extremely grateful that Roxy had a thousand different topics to bring up that had zero to do with Elizabeth.

In the quiet of the house, though, all she could think about was Elizabeth. How warm her smile was when she looked at Hazel; how hard she'd worked at the shop the last few weeks to help make things less stressful for Hazel; how easy things had been between them in the countless minutes they'd already spent doing mundane things together like drinking coffee, making dinner, driving in the car. Now, with Brandi Carlile's song about forgiving the love that hurt you playing on the speaker, Hazel felt a rush of sadness.

She let herself slip under the surface. The hot water on her head and face felt good; it distracted from the tears that'd been about to well up in her eyes again.

She heard a voice from a distance, and she slowly emerged from the water and listened. It was silent for a moment, and then she heard it again.

"Hazel?"

It was muffled by the many walls and doors that stood between them, but she definitely heard a female voice saying her name.

"Hazel?"

The voice was louder, closer, more insistent now, and Hazel recognized it instantly.

Elizabeth.

She stood up quickly in the tub, her body covered in bubbles, and stepped out onto the bath rug. She threw on her plush white bathrobe and twisted a towel around her head. She was dripping wet underneath the robe, but she didn't care. She flung open the bathroom door and stepped into the hallway. "Elizabeth?"

The voice was coming from downstairs, but Hazel could hear footsteps on the creaky old steps and before she knew it, she saw Elizabeth coming toward her, her face streaked with tears, her hair blown askew. Her entire body was thrumming with anticipation, and yet she couldn't move. She was rooted to the spot, thrilled that Elizabeth had come back but also a tiny bit worried about what would happen next. Her mind was so confused that for a second, she wondered if Elizabeth had forgotten something at the house. Gloves? A hat? She wasn't really here, couldn't actually be there for her. Could she?

Before she knew it, Elizabeth was folding her into her arms, crying, and she was crying, too.

"I'm so sorry, Hazel. I'm an idiot. I'm sorry, I'm sorry," sobbed Elizabeth, her whole body shaking with emotion.

Hazel hugged her all the more tightly. "I can't believe you're here. You're really here."

"I was so stupid…" She cried and cried, clutching Hazel even tighter.

"It's okay. You're here now. No one is stupid. I'm so glad you're here. I can't believe you're here."

The hot tears streaming down Hazel's face were now tears of joy and relief and disbelief that this was actually happening.

After a moment, Elizabeth pulled away enough to be able to look at Hazel, her arms still firmly holding her closer, her hands now warming up against the fluffy bathrobe, and Hazel could feel desire replacing her fear and apprehensions.

Elizabeth met her gaze cautiously and hopefully. "I was so wrong.

I don't know what I was thinking. I'm sorry. I love you, Hazel, and I should never have accused you of lying or making up stories. I've known you for so short a time, but you are so, so important to me. And I know you'd never lie to me or trick me, and maybe I'll never fully understand, but I want you exactly as you are. Can you ever forgive me?"

"Yes. Yes, you are forgiven, my darling, my sweet," said Hazel, the words tumbling out of her mouth. She wanted to call Elizabeth every sweet silly name she could think of. "I love you, too. I hardly know how it happened, but I do."

The last word was hardly out of her mouth when Elizabeth's lips were hot on hers in a passionate kiss that lit up Hazel's entire body with heated desire. She moaned and Elizabeth slipped her tongue between her lips. Desperate desire filled her body, a tingling warmth igniting between her legs.

Elizabeth moved her tongue around Hazel's mouth, their warmth and wetness mingling. She tightened her hold around Hazel's torso and hugged her close, and Hazel was suddenly keenly aware that under the fluffy bathrobe, she was completely and utterly naked. Elizabeth sighed and pushed Hazel up against the wall in the hallway, moving her hands to the opening of the robe, and pulling the fabric aside to reveal Hazel's breasts.

"Oh God," she moaned, moving her mouth to Hazel's nipples, first one, then the other, nibbling and sucking until Hazel arched her back with desire, sighing and groaning with each little love bite. Encouraged by her reaction, Elizabeth began massaging Hazel's breasts with her hands while moving her lips across Hazel's chest up over her collarbone and up to her neck, pausing to suck and bite her neck harder and harder until Hazel was sure she was seeing stars.

Hazel hardly knew where she was at that point, except that she knew she was still standing up because her legs were tired and heavy with desire.

"Oh God, let's go to the bedroom," she murmured.

"Not yet," said Elizabeth, her voice low and raspy. She gave Hazel a naughty glance before kneeling down in front of her, parting the robe still farther, and placing her hands under Hazel's backside, cupping her buttocks with one hand while spreading Hazel open with her thumb and forefinger with the other.

Hazel uttered a small moan of surprise and intense, hot desire. Soon, though, she couldn't make any sound at all; she was overwhelmed as Elizabeth began softly probing her with her tongue, licking and stroking her all over.

The sensation was enough to knock her off her feet, but Elizabeth's hands stayed strong and supported her, and her entire body became one with the sensation of soft but overwhelming electricity wherever Elizabeth's tongue came in contact with Hazel's body. When she finally allowed her tongue to circle around her center, Hazel felt such a jolt of desire that she thought she might have climaxed. Her entire body shook with the feel of it. But no, it wasn't the end yet. She didn't want it to be. She wanted this to go on forever.

Elizabeth, sensing Hazel's growing eagerness, stopped immediately and stood up, gazing into Hazel's eyes and taking her by the hand.

"Let's go to the bedroom," she said.

There, they undressed Elizabeth before sliding Hazel's robe onto the floor, where the towel wrapped around her hair soon joined it.

Their bodies melted into one another, skin on skin, hands exploring all the softness between them, with Elizabeth on top of Hazel. Her mouth found Hazel's even as her fingers began sliding between Hazel's legs, gently caressing and rubbing, and yet again Hazel felt the intense heat and need building.

"God, that feels good." She sighed into Elizabeth's mouth.

"Good," said Elizabeth, her lips curling seductively before latching onto Hazel's neck, sucking there until she was sure there would be a hickey the next morning. But Hazel didn't care. All she could think about was the heat and the need building steadily between her legs, down to her toes, and up her stomach to her breasts, as Elizabeth's fingers moved dexterously over the slick wetness between her legs and then slipped inside her, over and over again until Hazel felt her entire body go stiff and explosions of pleasure and desire coursed through her.

She convulsed with erotic pleasure even as Elizabeth's fingers never stopped playing with her. She came and came again, over and over, until her entire body was covered in a fine sheen of sweat and she was bucking beneath Elizabeth and shouting and crying, "Oh God, oh God, oh God."

Finally, Hazel lay spent next to Elizabeth, their bodies wrapped up against one another, both of them sticky with sweat and hot with their lovemaking. Through her haze of pleasure, Hazel smiled up at Elizabeth and planted a soft kiss on her chin.

"Mmm…that was amazing."

"I'm glad you liked it." She ran her hand over Hazel's body, sending little fires of desire coursing through her. This was going to be a long, but very pleasurable night, thought Hazel.

"What are you smiling about?" said Elizabeth, cocking an eyebrow.

"Oh, nothing. Just how much I want to make you moan with pleasure next."

"Oh really?"

"Oh yeah."

Refreshed after cuddling, Hazel sat up and threw her leg over Elizabeth's naked body, straddling her hips low so that the warmth and wetness between her legs was pressed into Elizabeth's.

Elizabeth's expression of surprise was soon replaced with one of intense desire, and she pulled Hazel down toward her so their breasts were pressed together, as were their lips. They kissed intensely, fiery passion lighting up their bodies yet again, and Hazel ground her hips against Elizabeth's before the two of them rolled to their sides, their entire bodies pressed together.

Hazel slipped her hands around Elizabeth's firm buttocks and squeezed as she moved her lips to her lover's neck and breasts. She sucked on each nipple until it puckered, and she could hear Elizabeth moan with pleasure. She gave her ass a little slap before squeezing it again.

"I could just hold on to your ass forever," said Hazel, her voice low and full of desire.

"That's the most romantic thing anyone's ever said to me."

Hazel gave a playful laugh before planting her lips onto Elizabeth's, stifling both of their giggles and taking them back to where they'd left off: hot and heavy, naked, bodies entwined. Hazel plunged her tongue into Elizabeth's mouth, and Elizabeth moaned with pleasure. Her hand played with Hazel's breast, and Hazel could feel herself getting wetter as she brought Elizabeth closer to her apex.

She slipped her hand between Elizabeth's legs and found the soft folds of flesh there, warm and wet for the taking. She slipped one, then two fingers inside, rubbing in and out, while she slid her thumb over

Elizabeth's clit. Elizabeth's entire body shuddered with desire, and she threw her leg over Hazel's hips to make it easier for Hazel to touch her. They kissed again passionately, deeply, as Hazel slid her fingers in and out of Elizabeth's wetness. Soon Elizabeth's breath became ragged, and suddenly Hazel felt her fingers squeezed with pleasure and passion.

Elizabeth's own voice rang out with pleasure as her hips moved back and forth against Hazel's hand, squeezing as much pleasure as she could, her body out of her own control and completely given over to desire.

After a moment, Elizabeth sighed with contentment and lay back, spent and covered with the glow of desire.

"Oh God, that was good," she said, her voice still breathless. Hazel nestled her head on Elizabeth's shoulder and lay her arm across her hot, sweaty body. Slowly, Elizabeth's breath evened out, and she pulled her arm around Hazel, holding her close. "Magical, even, I dare say," added Elizabeth, giving Hazel a sly look.

Hazel tensed, feeling a little uncertain, but after a second, Elizabeth's face broke into a smile, and she began to laugh. She pulled Hazel into a full body caress, and Hazel relaxed against her, starting to giggle and guffaw after a moment of hesitation.

Yes, it had been a magical afternoon.

Later, much later, after more kissing and cuddling, they showered together, dressed, and ordered Chinese food. They were both starving after their afternoon acrobatics, and a feast of lo mein, crab Rangoon, egg rolls, and Hunan chicken was just the ticket.

Hazel could hardly believe that Elizabeth was there with her, that they'd had amazing, delicious sex, that they were bantering and ordering food together. It felt surreal but also completely normal. While she was delighted by it all, she felt she had to clear the air a bit.

They'd just finished eating and were studying their fortunes.

"Mine says, 'Good things come to those who wait,'" said Elizabeth. Her eyes glittered. "*In bed.*"

"Especially in bed," said Hazel, giggling along with her. "Mine says, 'Lower your expectations and you will always be satisfied.'"

"No," said Elizabeth, disgusted. "That can't be right."

Hazel showed her the piece of paper.

"How awful."

"They can't all be winners," said Hazel with a shrug and a chuckle.

"Just so you know, you have exceeded my expectations." Elizabeth paused and her expression changed to one more thoughtful. "I gave things a lot of thought before coming here today. I wanted us to have a shot at something special. I knew I had to find my own way of dealing with what you told me yesterday."

"That I'm a witch."

"Yes. About being a witch. And having a family that is magical."

Hazel felt a tremor of anxiety. She wasn't sure where this was leading. "Yes. My whole family."

"I was thinking, maybe you could tell me a bit more about it all? I think the more I know, the better I can understand it." She smiled shyly at Hazel. "Would you mind telling me about being a witch? What does that mean, exactly? What kinds of powers do you have?"

"Of course I can tell you more about it," said Hazel, feeling relieved. "I want to share that part of me with you, too." She paused. "I have some books I can give you to read about the history of witches from our perspective. That will give you more answers. But the short version is that it's genetic. Witches are born with the ability to tap into powers that humans can't—but they still have to be taught how to use them."

"Does that mean that witches aren't human?"

Hazel nodded. "You got it. Completely different sort of animal. We live longer, age more slowly, and are able to communicate with other magical folk."

"Like vampires and ghosts?"

"Among others. There are fairies, too, and mermaids."

"Really?" Elizabeth gave her a disbelieving look that was quickly replaced with curiosity again. "I'm sorry. I don't mean to sound incredulous. It's just all so new to me."

"Of course," said Hazel. "It'll take time. Baby steps. And we can take them together."

"That sounds like a plan," said Elizabeth. She paused again. "What about Camille? She said she could read minds. Can you read minds also?" She looked a little guilty posing the question.

"I guess I could, if I wanted to, but it takes a lot of concentration, and it doesn't last long." She put her hand over Elizabeth's. "I would never use magic on you without your knowledge. Or read your thoughts.

No one in my family would either. There is a code of ethics among the Otherworldly—magical folk, that is—about how we use our powers. What Camille did, stealing my love potions and bewitching Roxy with her powers, is against that code. There aren't a whole lot of ways to enforce the code, it's true, but if she did it enough, other magical folk would intervene."

"That's a relief," said Elizabeth with a sigh, "though I think she may already have learned her lesson."

Elizabeth recounted her meeting with Camille the night before. Hazel was stunned.

"I can't believe she did that. How terrifying for you," she said finally. She was so angry with Camille that the part about her encouraging Elizabeth to go after Hazel barely registered.

"It's okay. It was the kick in the arse I needed, apparently." Elizabeth leaned over and kissed Hazel gently on the lips. "It brought us together, and truthfully, it made me less able to explain away the idea of magic in our world."

"I'm glad to hear that part, I guess. And I can answer any questions you have about magic, any time. I know it's all incredibly new, and I want to help you understand it."

"Me too," said Elizabeth.

Hazel muttered a quiet incantation, and moments later, they were surrounded by tiny hearts made of little bubbles.

"What is this?" said Elizabeth. "It's beautiful."

"Just a little magic for us," said Hazel with a smile. It was as though an enormous weight had fallen off her shoulders. Not only did Elizabeth accept her for who she was, she wanted to learn more. She never thought she could go from so sad to so happy in one day.

"What about the love potion?" said Elizabeth as the bubble hearts all popped and disappeared.

"Gone," said Hazel.

"Gone?"

"I destroyed the rest of the love potion. Turned it into plant fertilizer."

"Really? Why?"

"It was more trouble than it was worth. And it works great as a fertilizer. I might still be able to sell it to some select customers in its new form."

"Fascinating," said Elizabeth. "I think I'll need to read up on magical alchemy as well as the history of witchcraft."

"Absolutely," said Hazel. "I know just the book. Tomorrow I can show you the garden where I've been testing the fertilizer."

"Perfect," said Elizabeth with a megawatt smile.

Looking deeply into Elizabeth's beautiful cornflower blue eyes, Hazel was filled with a deep sense of contentment. *Tomorrow.* They had plans for tomorrow. Just that small fact made her deeply, deeply happy.

❖

The next day, after a leisurely breakfast and making love again, they had lunch, showered, and found themselves enjoying an unusually warm, dry, sunny November afternoon. After absenting himself during their conspicuous lovemaking, Beezle had rejoined them and was also enjoying the good weather, sunning himself on the patio, like any other ordinary cat.

Elizabeth sat on the patio in Hazel's garden, reading one of Hazel's witch-authored history books as Hazel attended to her garden. She usually waited to winterize her garden until after Halloween because things were too busy in October to deal with it all. They were lucky that there hadn't been too many hard freezes yet, and that day's warm weather meant the ground was soft and pliable; she was able to pull up a lot of the dried-up annuals that were past their peak.

Her witch's garden was still thriving, though, and in one corner of it, she planted sweet pea seeds. It was the wrong time of year, of course, to be planting the delicate flowers—if she'd been planting them like a regular mortal. But she blessed the ground around it with sacred spring water and honey and whispered a short incantation.

Sweet pea was symbolic of gratitude, and she wanted to acknowledge her gratitude to Camille for making the sacrifice of her own desires to make Hazel's dreams come true with Elizabeth. She could already feel the powerful connection between her and her beloved; this was true love at last.

She also, oddly, felt gratitude to Roxy for giving the love potion to Elizabeth in the first place. By giving Elizabeth some of the new love potion, Roxy had accelerated Elizabeth's existing, but somewhat dormant, feelings for Hazel—not necessarily a bad thing given that she'd initially planned to go home at the end of the year. Now, though, they were already strategizing how to keep Elizabeth in Salem through the following May.

Hazel dumped the last of the love potion at the back of her garden where it would harmlessly seep into some roses.

Next to the sweet pea, she planted ivy and chrysanthemums, blessing them with incantations for friendship and constancy, hoping that the spell would help Roxy get over her heartbreak. Roxy was alone again and now Hazel was part of a couple. She didn't want that fact to get in the way of their friendship. Roxy was too important to her.

She tended the rest of her witch's garden and herbarium, finishing with an incantation over all of it and all of Salem for love. She wanted her feelings of joy and love to spread throughout the world and connect everyone, bringing them the same peace and serenity she felt when she looked at Elizabeth, sitting on the patio, draped in blankets and heavy wool sweaters against the cool breeze.

She got up from her gardening and walked toward Elizabeth, knowing that regardless of what happened, she'd be at her side. Whatever came their way, wherever they ended up living, she knew they were meant to be. No enchantment was needed to make what they had truly magical.

EPILOGUE

The Peak District, England, the following summer

Hazel's breath caught in her throat as she took in the majestic views all around her. Green and brown hills, devoid of trees, surrounded them on all sides, dotted with sheep that, at this distance, looked like nothing but tufts of wool. The sky was a deep, saturated shade of blue, and the warm sun and cool breeze combined to make it the perfect day for a hike.

Elizabeth joined her a moment later. "Quite the view, isn't it?" She stood next to Hazel at the top of the hill and put her warm arm around her shoulders.

"It's incredible," said Hazel. Her voice was full of awe; she could feel magical undercurrents in the land all around. No wonder Iron Age people had built a fort there, whose remains were still visible. It was a sacred place, and the vibrations of power refreshed her nearly as much as a walk over the hills and dales.

After enjoying the view a moment longer and snapping a selfie, they continued their hike, and Hazel reflected on how they'd gotten to this moment, here in England, together on vacation.

They'd spent just about every waking moment together when they weren't working since that fateful November first. Elizabeth had met her mother at Thanksgiving in Maine, and it hadn't been a disaster as Hazel had feared. Apparently, Elizabeth's burgeoning interest in magical history had impressed her mother enough to overlook the fact Elizabeth wasn't a witch herself.

At Christmastime, Hazel had met Elizabeth's parents, and that'd gone reasonably well, also. Her father had been easy, it turned out: he admired Hazel's entrepreneurship and was very informal. Her mother was a bit more uptight and particular, and Hazel could see where Elizabeth got those qualities. Elizabeth assured her, though, that her mother simply took some time to warm up to new people, and Hazel tried to take her at her word.

They had yet to tell her parents about Hazel's magical abilities, though; they decided to wait to see how serious things got between them.

So far, it felt pretty dang serious, in the best of all possible ways. When Elizabeth's house swap ended in January, they'd seen no reason for her to keep spending valuable fellowship money on another rental when Hazel lived alone in a giant house. They hardly ever slept apart anyway, so it made more sense for Elizabeth to move in, especially once the winter snows kept the roads and sidewalks slick and icy. They'd enjoyed playing house together, and they found that their lifestyles meshed together well. There were few disagreements and even fewer fights.

Hazel noticed they were both loosening up a little in different ways, too. She found herself less and less likely to schedule tarot readings after business hours, and she'd gotten better about locking the door ten minutes to close so no new customers could come in at the last minute. And while it pained her somewhat to do so, she'd decided to close the shop for two weeks while they vacationed together in England. Elizabeth was still the driven researcher who enjoyed a good archive, but she too had stopped working all the time, often going home before Hazel to cook them dinner.

As winter melted into spring, and spring turned into summer, neither of them could ignore the upcoming academic year. At some point, Elizabeth would have to go back to England, permanently, and go back to teaching classes, attending meetings, and working on campus. In some ways, the trip to England was an opportunity to spend time together and focus on one another before having to make a final decision about how to handle a long-distance relationship. They'd tossed around many options, and Hazel had even suggested selling her business permanently, but Elizabeth always refused to even consider that possibility.

"That shop is your baby. You love it. I love it. We'll have to figure out something else," Elizabeth had said on the plane, the most recent time they'd discussed their future together.

But was that true? She supposed she did love the shop, and giving it up would be difficult, but that thought was far preferable to spending any significant time apart from Elizabeth. Besides, what other kind of long-term solution could there be? Although Elizabeth often mentioned how much more relaxed she was in the US, away from her academic job in England, Hazel knew how much her research and teaching meant to her. She couldn't ask her to give that all up. And now that they'd been dating longer, she'd come to understand just how unlikely it was for Elizabeth to simply drop into a professorial job in the US. The market for historians was slim to none.

This was the thought at which Hazel arrived just as they found their way back to the small town of Castleton in the Peak. It was a beautiful village full of storybook stone cottages with gardens simply bursting with multicolored roses. Elizabeth guided them to a local pub that served delicious, fresh food, and after putting in their orders, they sat down at a table in the shade with a couple of cold beers.

Despite all the beauty around them, Hazel found her thoughts returning to the problem looming ahead of them. She couldn't stand the thought of being away from Elizabeth for a week, much less for months on end.

"What's the matter?" asked Elizabeth, studying her carefully. She was tan from time spent in the sun, and her skin and hair glowed in the light of summer. "Don't you like it here?"

"Oh no...I love it," said Hazel, trying to smile. "I love being here. With you. Today was perfect. But I couldn't help worrying again about what'll happen this fall." She took a sip of beer to try to drown out the feeling of her throat tightening at the thought of returning to the States in a few days without Elizabeth. Their plan was that Elizabeth would return to the US two weeks after Hazel, no longer as a researcher but rather as a tourist. She needed extra time to take care of business at her job and visit some elderly relatives. Hazel wished she'd made other arrangements for the store because she couldn't stand the thought of being without Elizabeth for two whole weeks.

"Oh, darling," said Elizabeth, her voice catching in her throat. "I know exactly what you mean. I've been giving it a lot of thought lately, too." She put her hands over Hazel's on the table between them and gazed deeply into her eyes.

"I can't bear the thought of being apart," said Hazel, her voice breaking on the last word.

Elizabeth smiled broadly, and Hazel felt her tears subsiding. Why was Elizabeth smiling? Did she have some good news? She felt her heart start pounding in her chest with anticipation.

"I didn't want to say anything until I knew for sure, but I got the good news today. I checked my email while you were in the loo earlier."

"What good news?" Hazel was on pins and needles.

"I applied for a teaching job at an academy in Boston. It's high school, but the students there are very clever, and the staff are wonderful. Today they've let me know they want to hire me."

Hazel's jaw dropped. "What? How? When?"

Elizabeth rubbed her hands soothingly. "I'm sorry for being so secretive. I didn't want to say anything until I knew for sure. I had an interview in May. Remember that day I had to go to Boston to visit a library one more time?"

Hazel nodded slowly. It'd been the same day she'd made a killing selling one of their new products: plant pots with sugar skulls painted on them. It'd been Roxy's idea, after she went on vacation to Mexico with a new girl she was dating. The pots were a hit, and Hazel wondered why she hadn't thought to order Day of the Dead themed items before. She'd been so excited with the success at the store, she hadn't really given much thought to Elizabeth's sudden need to go to Boston all dressed up in her best work clothes.

"But...won't you miss teaching at a university? I know how prestigious that is. And it was always your dream." Hazel didn't want Elizabeth to resent giving up her dream profession. Teaching at a private high school, no matter how prestigious, didn't sound nearly as good as being a university professor.

Elizabeth shook her head. "I realized this past year that I don't miss being at a university at all. What I missed was teaching. Of course, I love doing my research, too, but there's no reason I can't keep doing that as a teacher. The school has offered me a modest travel budget for conferences and travel to archives, and one less group of students each spring so I can concentrate on my own writing."

"Really? How wonderful!" Hazel paused, letting the news and knowledge sink in. "This is really happening? You're moving to the US? We don't have to be long distance?"

"We don't have to be long distance," said Elizabeth.

They toasted Elizabeth's new job just as their food arrived, and Hazel felt certain she'd never tasted anything better in more beautiful surroundings. She could hardly believe her luck.

Later, when Elizabeth left to go to the bathroom, she shot off a text to Roxy to share the good news with her.

Moments later, Roxy wrote back. *Great news! I'm so happy for you. Can't wait til you're back and we can celebrate. Miss you two around here. Salem's just not the same without you.*

Hazel wrote back. *Miss you, too. See you soon!*

She saw Elizabeth returning to their table just then, her hair windblown, a big goofy smile on her face as she met Hazel's gaze, and Hazel felt a surge of gratitude yet again that everything was working out, despite poltergeists and ghosts, scheming vampires and love potions gone wrong. The workings of Fate were mysterious, but evidently, they were on Hazel's side in the end.

About the Author

Ursula Klein is originally from Maryland, where she grew up and attended university. She taught ESL in Europe after college, then returned to the United States and pursued graduate studies in New York. She has since lived in Tennessee, Texas, and Georgia before landing in her current location, Wisconsin. Ursula loves reading fantasy, romance, science fiction, and mysteries; she also enjoys crocheting, traveling, and spending time with her wife and young son. She is a huge fan of dressing up in costumes, loves celebrating Halloween, and was probably a witch in a past life.

Books Available From Bold Strokes Books

Deadly Secrets by VK Powell. Corporate criminals want whistleblower Jana Elliott permanently silenced, but Rafe Silva will risk everything to keep the woman she loves safe. (978-1-63679-087-9)

Enchanted Autumn by Ursula Klein. When Elizabeth comes to Salem, Massachusetts, to study the witch trials, she never expects to find love—or an actual witch…and Hazel might just turn out to be both. (978-1-63679-104-3)

Escorted by Renee Roman. When fantasy meets reality, will escort Ryan Lewis be able to walk away from a chance at forever with her new client Dani? (978-1-63679-039-8)

Her Heart's Desire by Anne Shade. Two women. One choice. Will Eve and Lynette be able to overcome their doubts and fears to embrace their deepest desire? (978-1-63679-102-9)

My Secret Valentine by Julie Cannon, Erin Dutton & Anne Shade. Winning the heart of your secret Valentine? These award-winning authors agree, there is no better way to fall in love. (978-1-63679-071-8)

Perilous Obsession by Carsen Taite. When reporter Macy Moran becomes consumed with solving a cold case, will her quest for the truth bring her closer to Detective Beck Ramsey or will her obsession with finding a murderer rob her of a chance at true love? (978-1-63679-009-1)

Reading Her by Amanda Radley. Lauren and Allegra learn love and happiness are right where they least expect it. There's just one problem: Lauren has a secret she cannot tell anyone, and Allegra knows she's hiding something. (978-1-63679-075-6)

The Willing by Lyn Hemphill. Kitty Wilson doesn't know how, but she can bring people back from the dead as long as someone is willing to take their place and keep the universe in balance. (978-1-63679-083-1)

Watching Over Her by Ronica Black. As they face the snowstorm of the century, and the looming threat of a stalker, Riley and Zoey just might find love in the most unexpected of places. (978-1-63679-100-5)

Always by Kris Bryant. When a pushy American private investigator shows up demanding to meet the woman in Camila's artwork, instead of introducing her to her great-grandmother, Camila decides to lead her on a wild goose chase all over Italy. (978-1-63679-027-5)

Exes and O's by Joy Argento. Ali and Madison really only have one thing in common. The girl who broke their heart may be the only one who can put it back together. (978-1-63679-017-6)

Paris Rules by Jaime Maddox. Carly Becker has been searching for the perfect woman all her life, but no one ever seems to be just right until Paige Waterford checks all her boxes, except the most important one—she's married. (978-1-63679-077-0)

Shadow Dancers by Suzie Clarke. In this third and final book in the Moon Shadow series, Rachel must find a way to become the hunter and not the hunted, and this time she will meet Eshee Yumiko head-on. (978-1-63555-829-6)

The Kiss by C.A. Popovich. When her wife refuses their divorce and begins to stalk her, threatening her life, Kate realizes to protect her new love, Leslie, she has to let her go, even if it breaks her heart. (978-1-63679-079-4)

The Wedding Setup by Charlotte Greene. When Ryann, a big-time New York executive, goes to Colorado to help out with her best friend's wedding, she never expects to fall for the maid of honor. (978-1-63679-033-6)

Velocity by Gun Brooke. Holly and Claire work toward an uncertain future preparing for an alien space mission, and only one thing is certain—they will have to risk their lives, and their hearts, to discover the truth. (978-1-63555-983-5)

Wildflower Words by Sam Ledel. Lida Jones treks west with her father in search of a better life on the rapidly developing American frontier, but finds home when she meets Hazel Thompson. (978-1-63679-055-8)